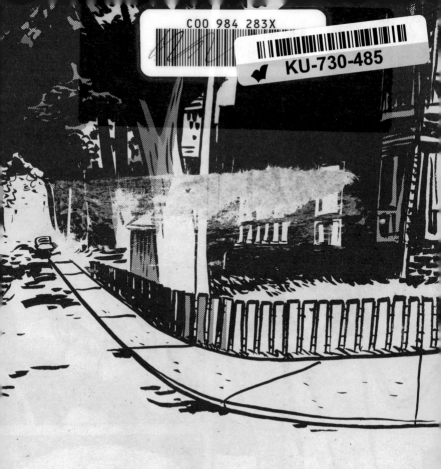

BRYAN LEE O'MALLEY'S

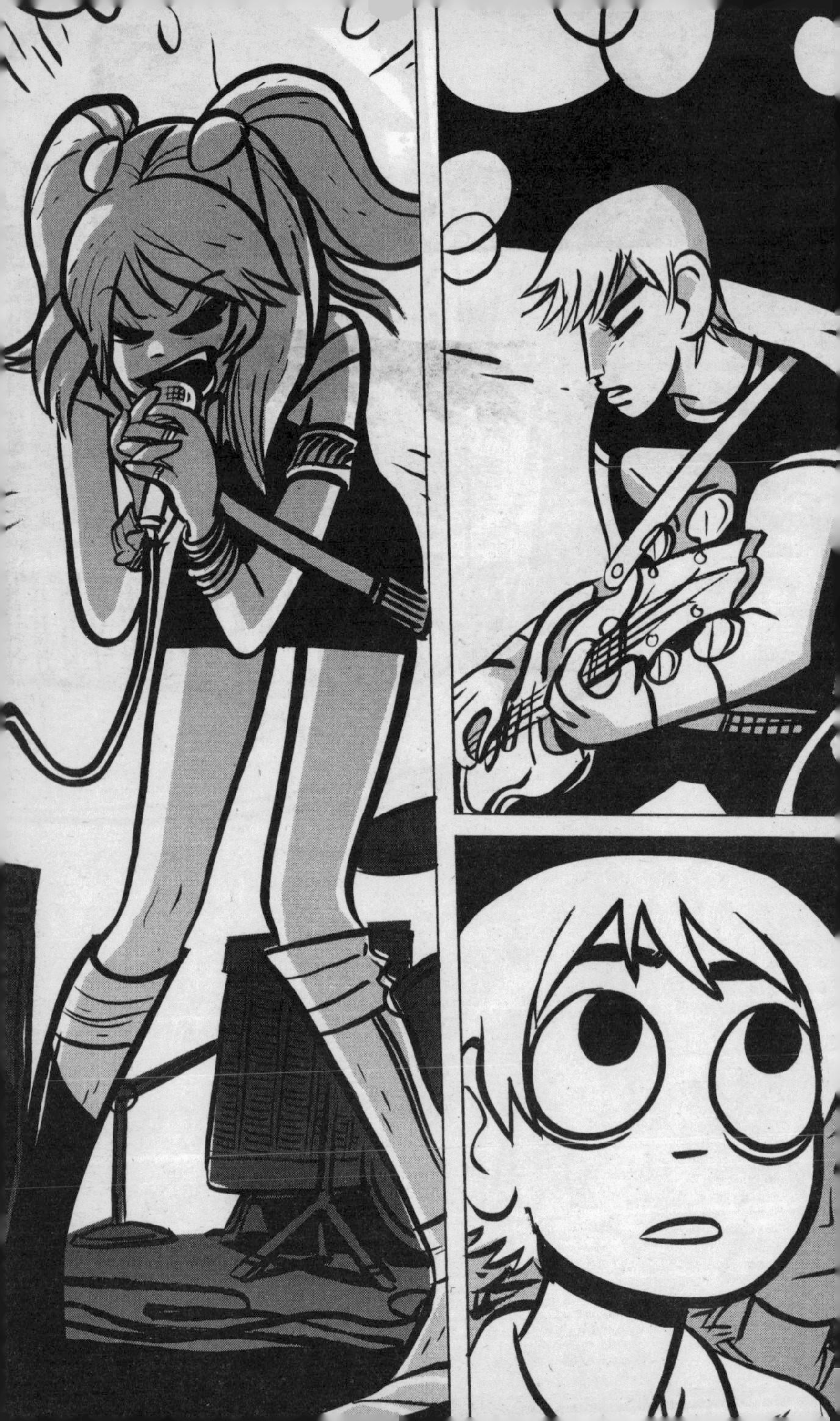

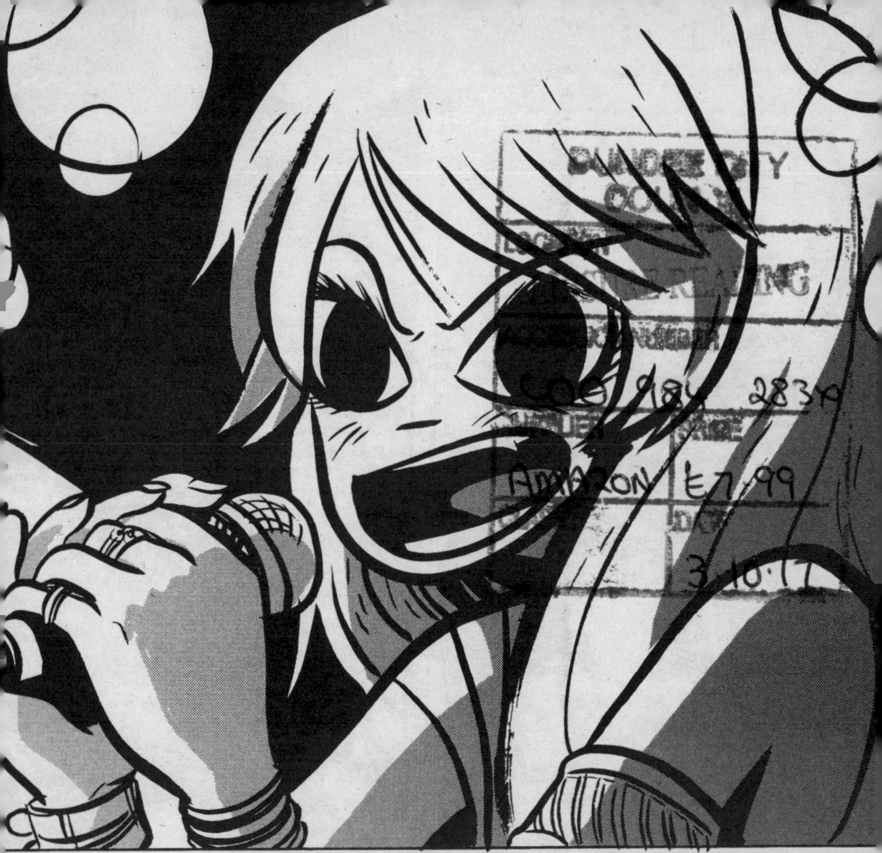

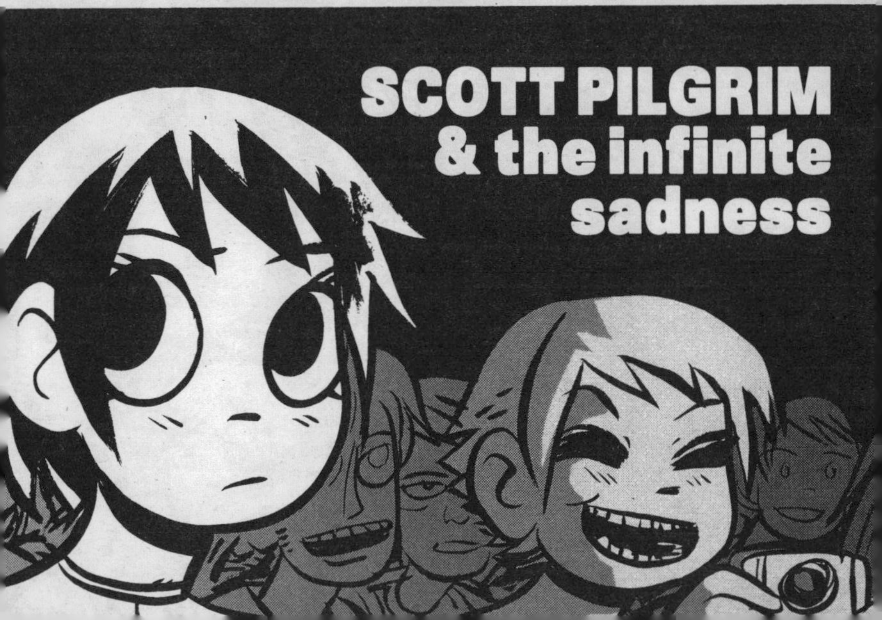
SCOTT PILGRIM
& the infinite
sadness

[redacted]

Published by Fourth Estate

Originally published in 2006 in the United States by Oni Press

First published in Great Britain in 2010 by
Fourth Estate
An imprint of HarperCollins*Publishers*
77–85 Fulham Palace Road
London W6 8JB
www.4thestate.co.uk

14

ISBN 978 0 00 735146 6

Printed in Great Britain by Clays Ltd, St Ives plc

www.4thestate.com

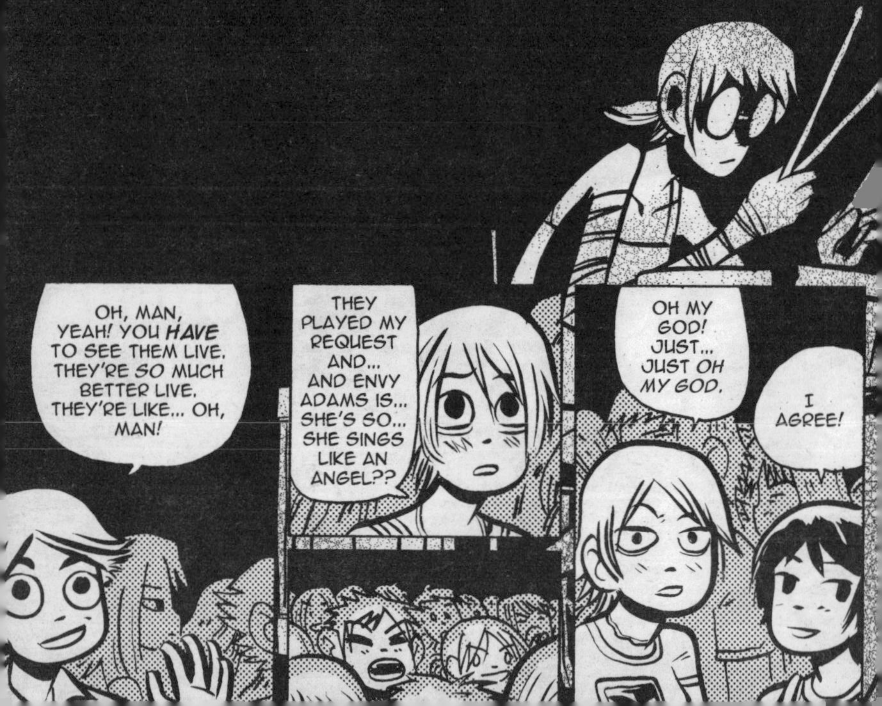
OH, MAN, YEAH! YOU *HAVE* TO SEE THEM LIVE. THEY'RE *SO* MUCH BETTER LIVE. THEY'RE LIKE... OH, MAN!
THEY PLAYED MY REQUEST AND... AND ENVY ADAMS IS... SHE'S SO... SHE SINGS LIKE AN ANGEL??
OH MY GOD! JUST... JUST *OH MY GOD.*
I AGREE!

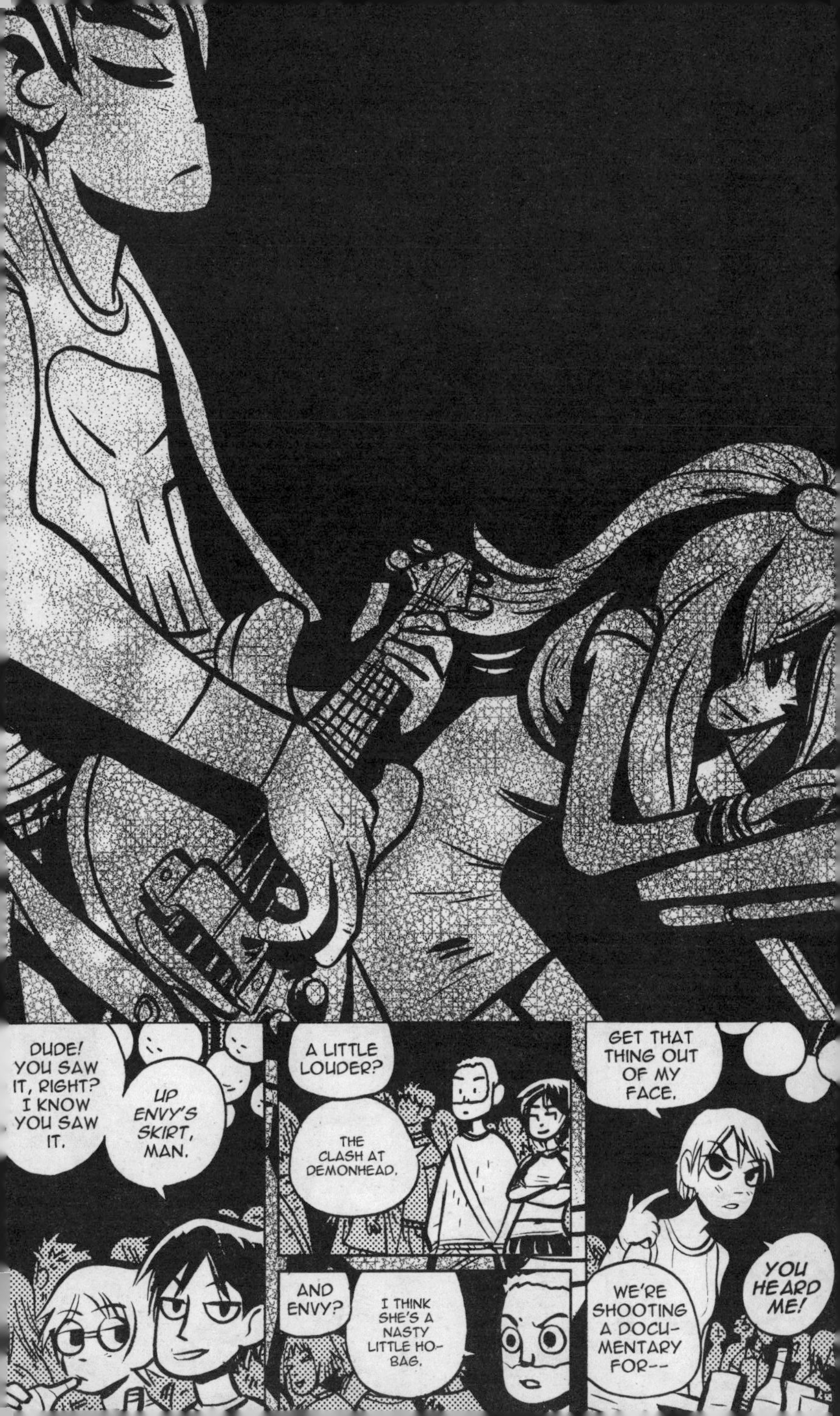
DUDE! YOU SAW IT, RIGHT? I KNOW YOU SAW IT.
UP ENVY'S SKIRT, MAN.
A LITTLE LOUDER?
THE CLASH AT DEMONHEAD.
AND ENVY?
I THINK SHE'S A NASTY LITTLE HO-BAG.
GET THAT THING OUT OF MY FACE.
WE'RE SHOOTING A DOCU-MENTARY FOR--
YOU HEARD ME!

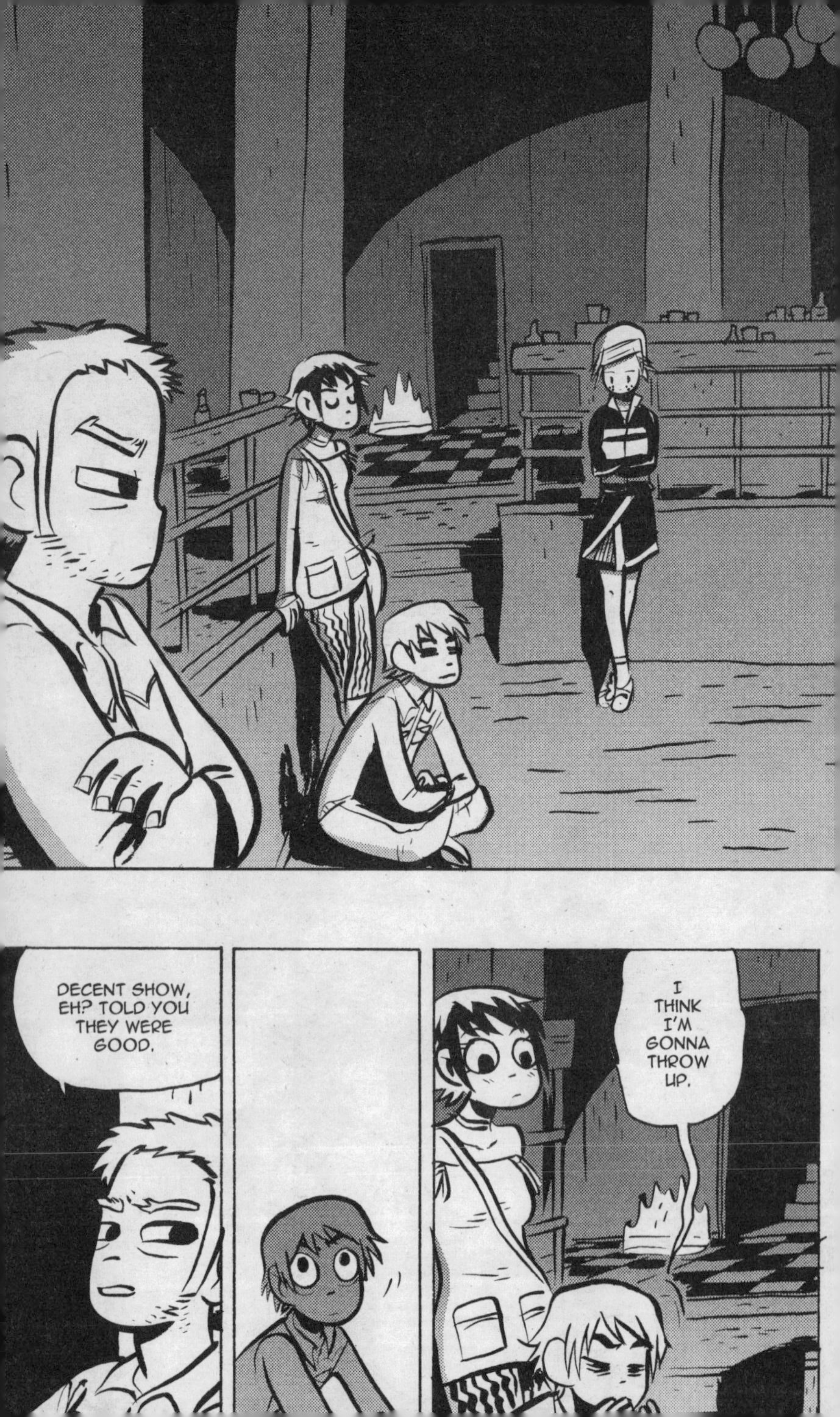
DECENT SHOW, EH? TOLD YOU THEY WERE GOOD.
I THINK I'M GONNA THROW UP.

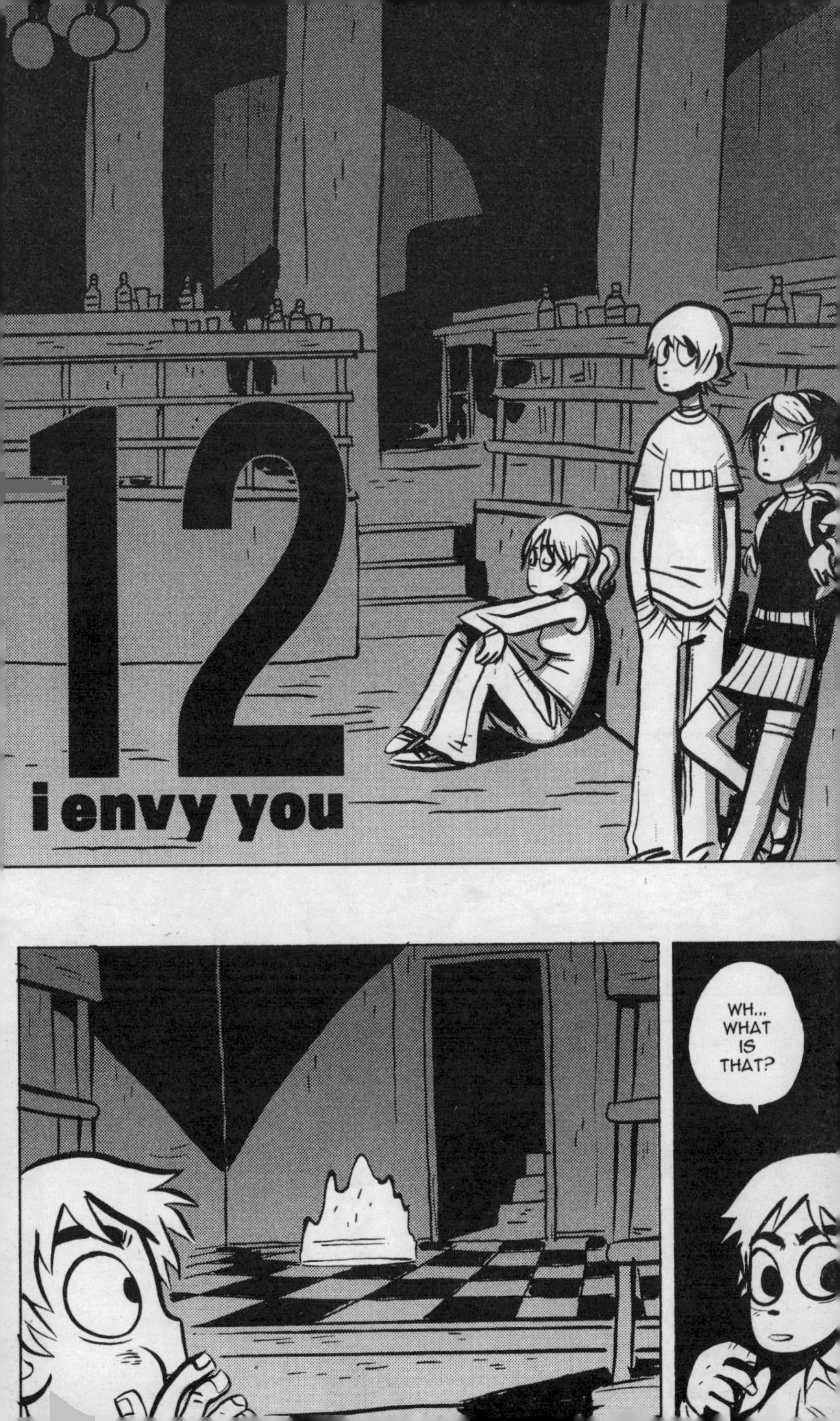
12
i envy you
WH... WHAT IS THAT?

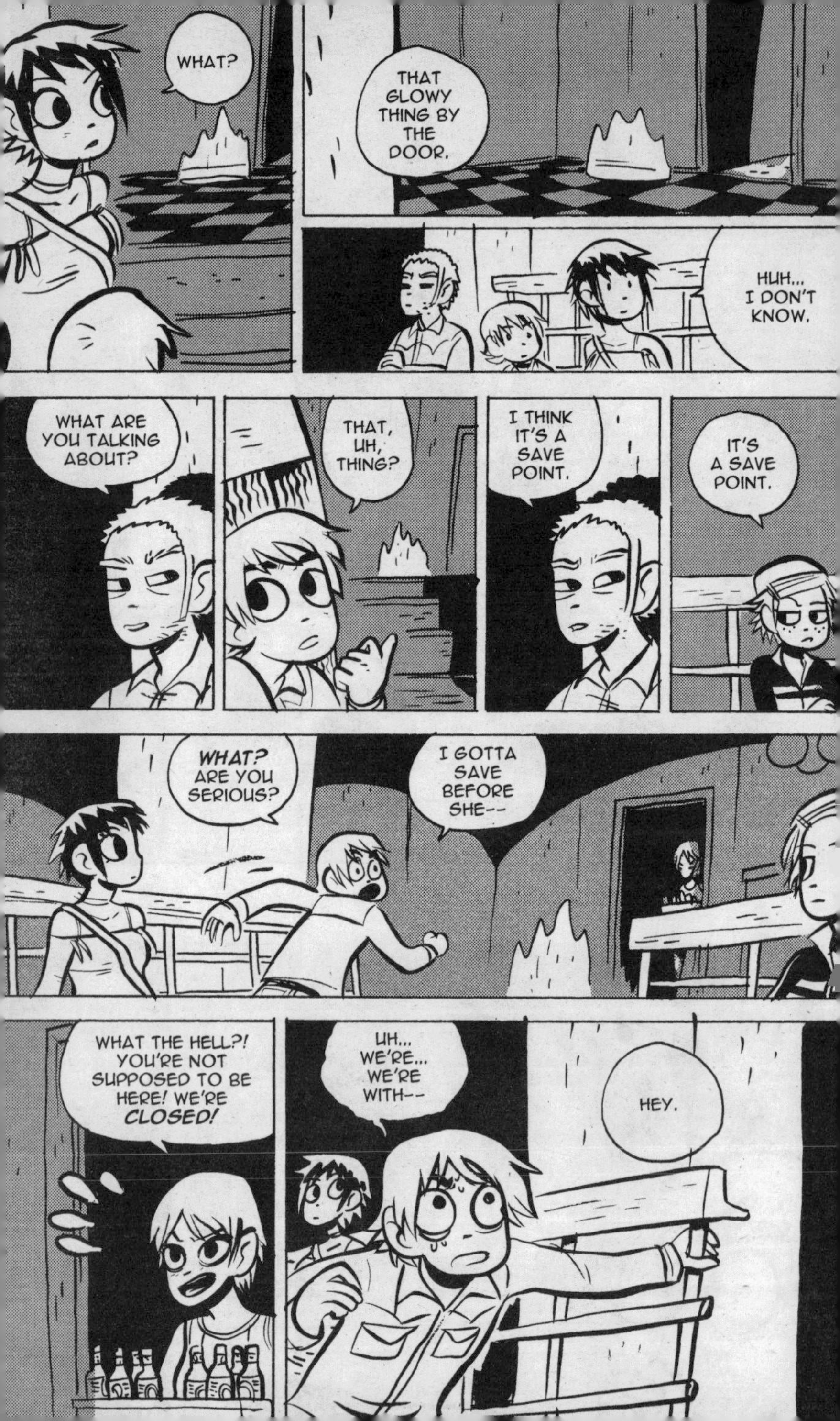

WHAT?
THAT GLOWY THING BY THE DOOR.
HUH... I DON'T KNOW.
WHAT ARE YOU TALKING ABOUT?
THAT, UH, THING?
I THINK IT'S A SAVE POINT.
IT'S A SAVE POINT.
WHAT? ARE YOU SERIOUS?
I GOTTA SAVE BEFORE SHE--
WHAT THE HELL?! YOU'RE NOT SUPPOSED TO BE HERE! WE'RE CLOSED!
UH... WE'RE... WE'RE WITH--
HEY.

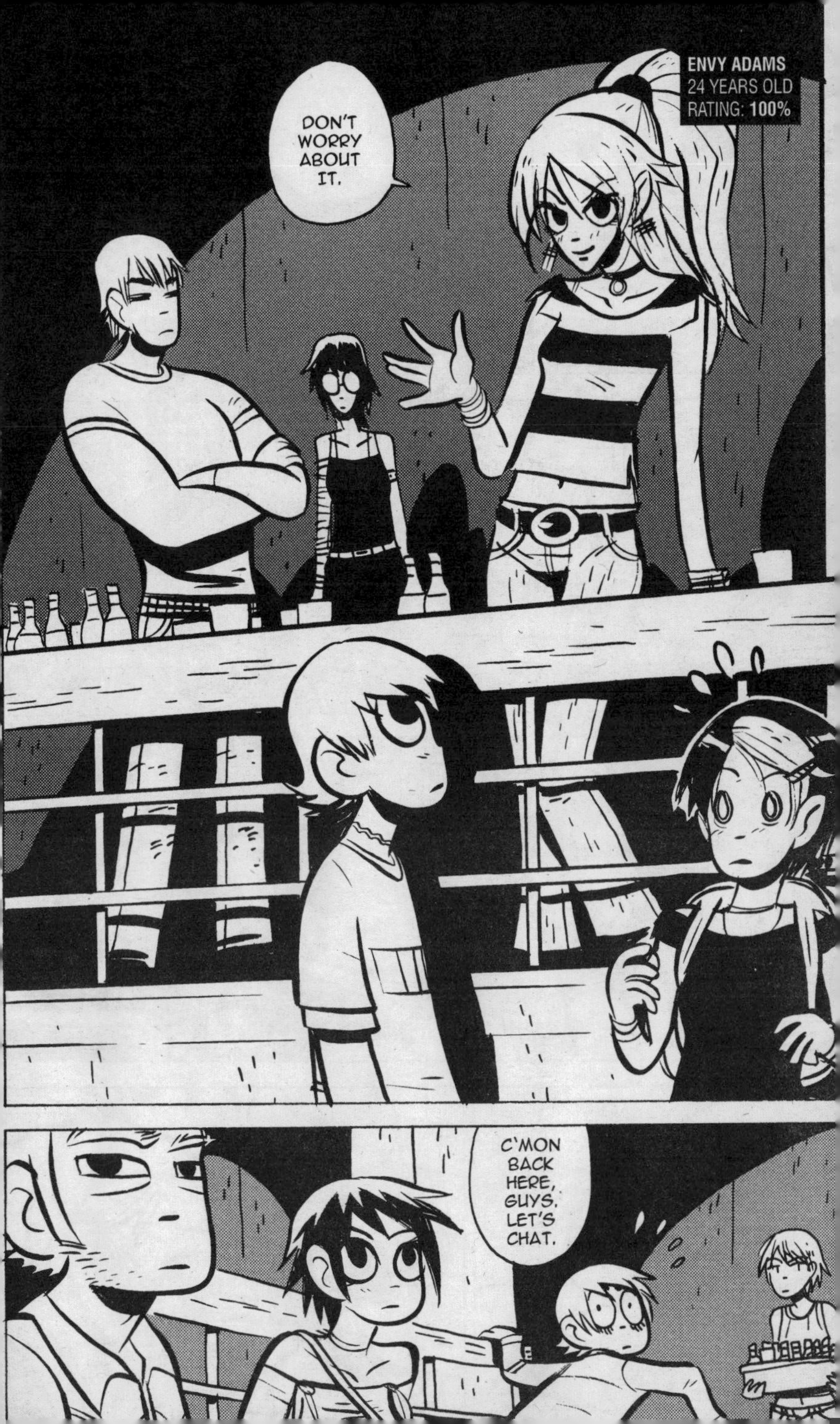
ENVY ADAMS
24 YEARS OLD
RATING: 100%
DON'T WORRY ABOUT IT.
C'MON BACK HERE, GUYS. LET'S CHAT.

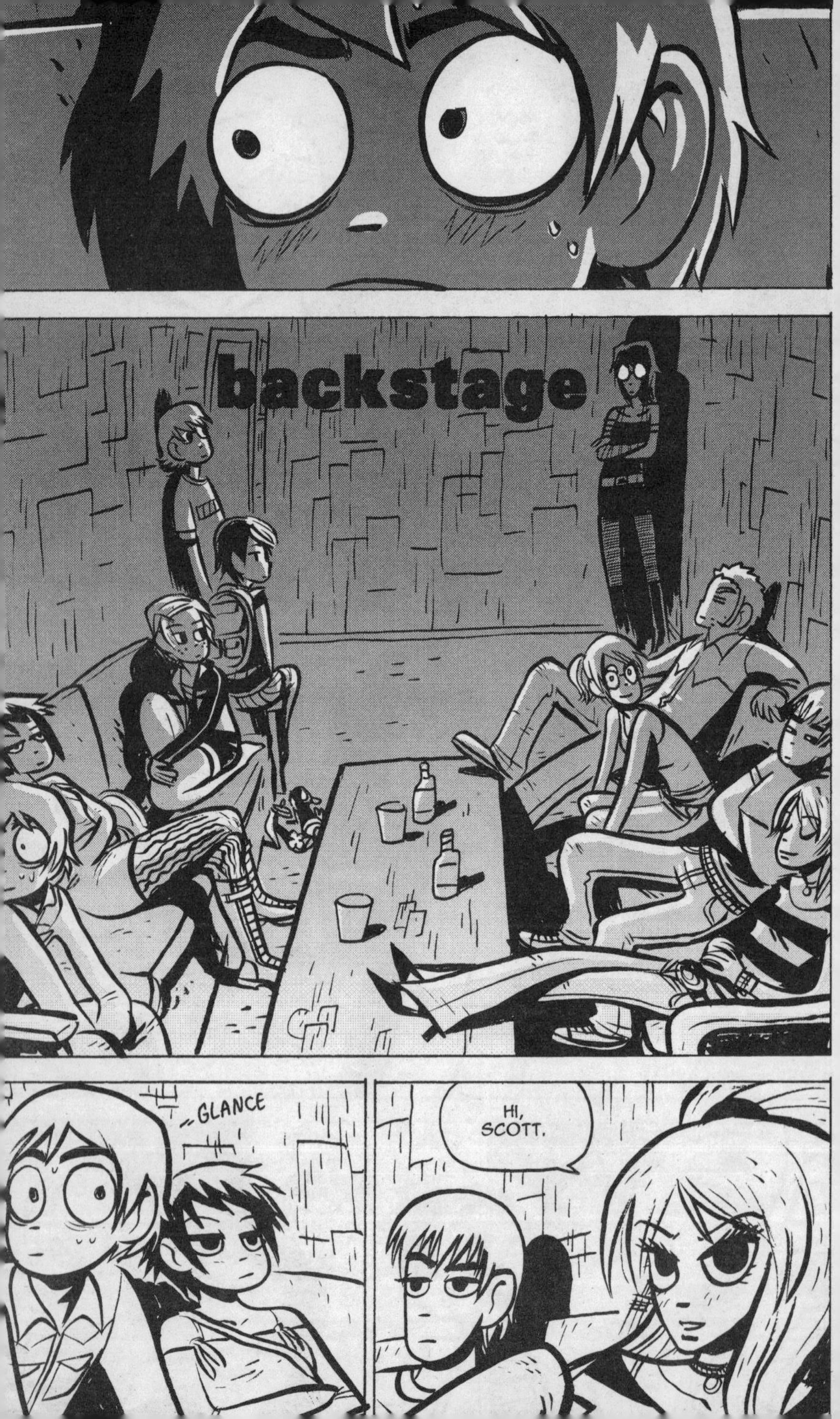
backstage
GLANCE
HI, SCOTT.

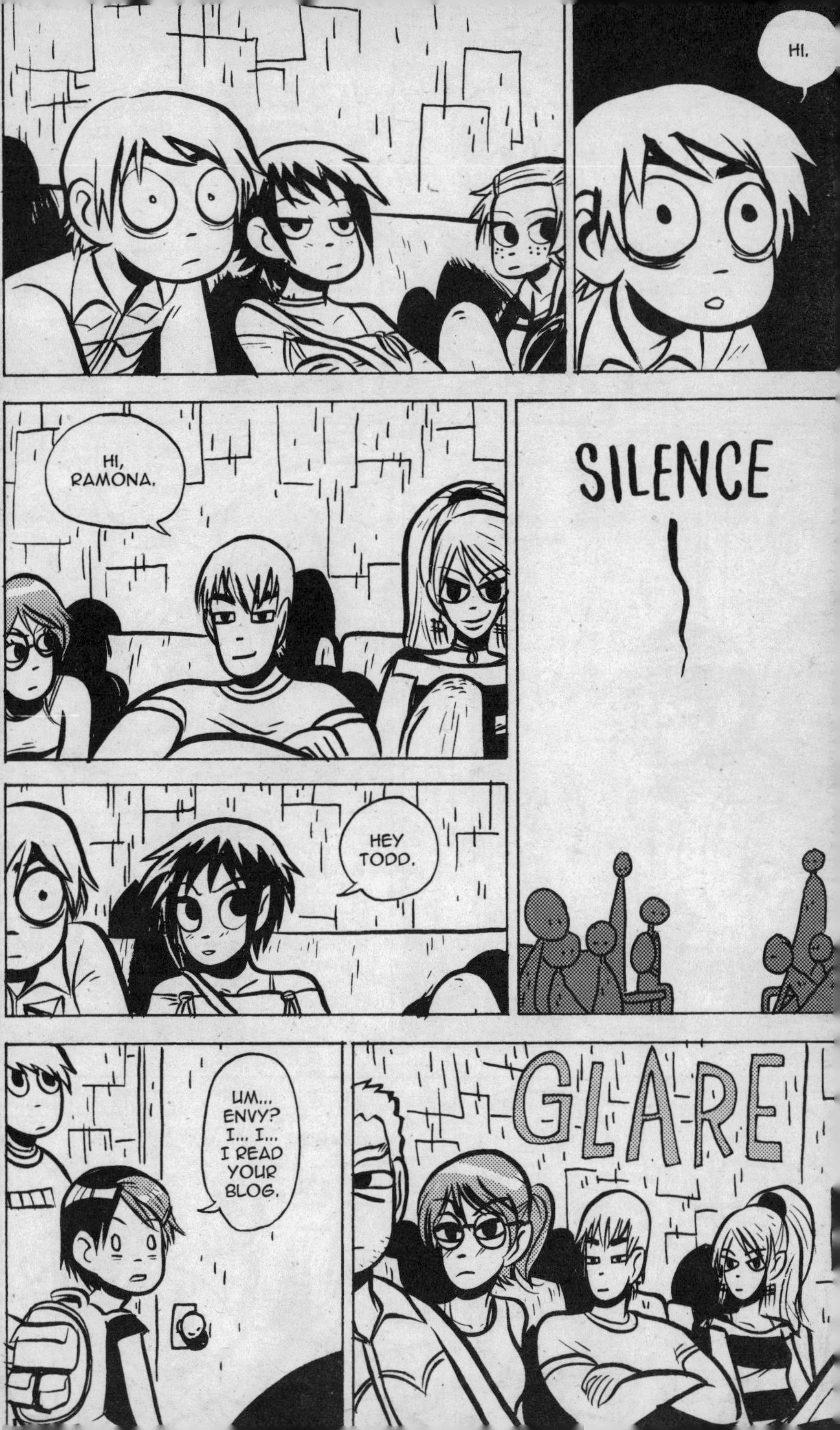
HI.
HI, RAMONA.
SILENCE
HEY TODD.
UM... ENVY? I... I... I READ YOUR BLOG.
GLARE

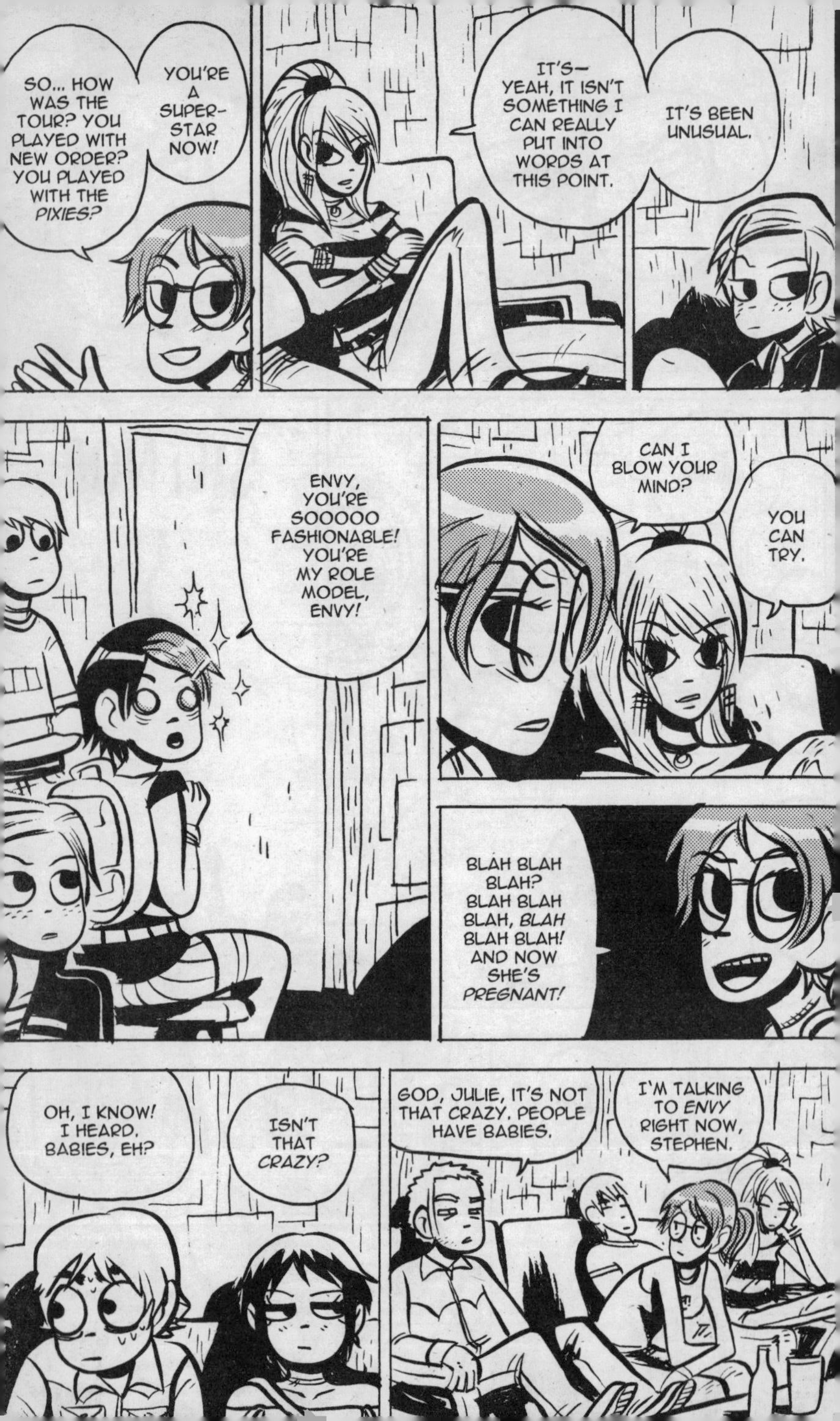
SO... HOW WAS THE TOUR? YOU PLAYED WITH NEW ORDER? YOU PLAYED WITH THE *PIXIES?*
YOU'RE A SUPER-STAR NOW!
IT'S— YEAH, IT ISN'T SOMETHING I CAN REALLY PUT INTO WORDS AT THIS POINT.
IT'S BEEN UNUSUAL.
ENVY, YOU'RE SOOOOO FASHIONABLE! YOU'RE MY ROLE MODEL, ENVY!
CAN I BLOW YOUR MIND?
YOU CAN TRY.
BLAH BLAH BLAH? BLAH BLAH BLAH, *BLAH* BLAH BLAH! AND NOW SHE'S *PREGNANT!*
OH, I KNOW! I HEARD. BABIES, EH?
ISN'T THAT *CRAZY?*
GOD, JULIE, IT'S NOT THAT CRAZY. PEOPLE HAVE BABIES.
I'M TALKING TO *ENVY* RIGHT NOW, STEPHEN.

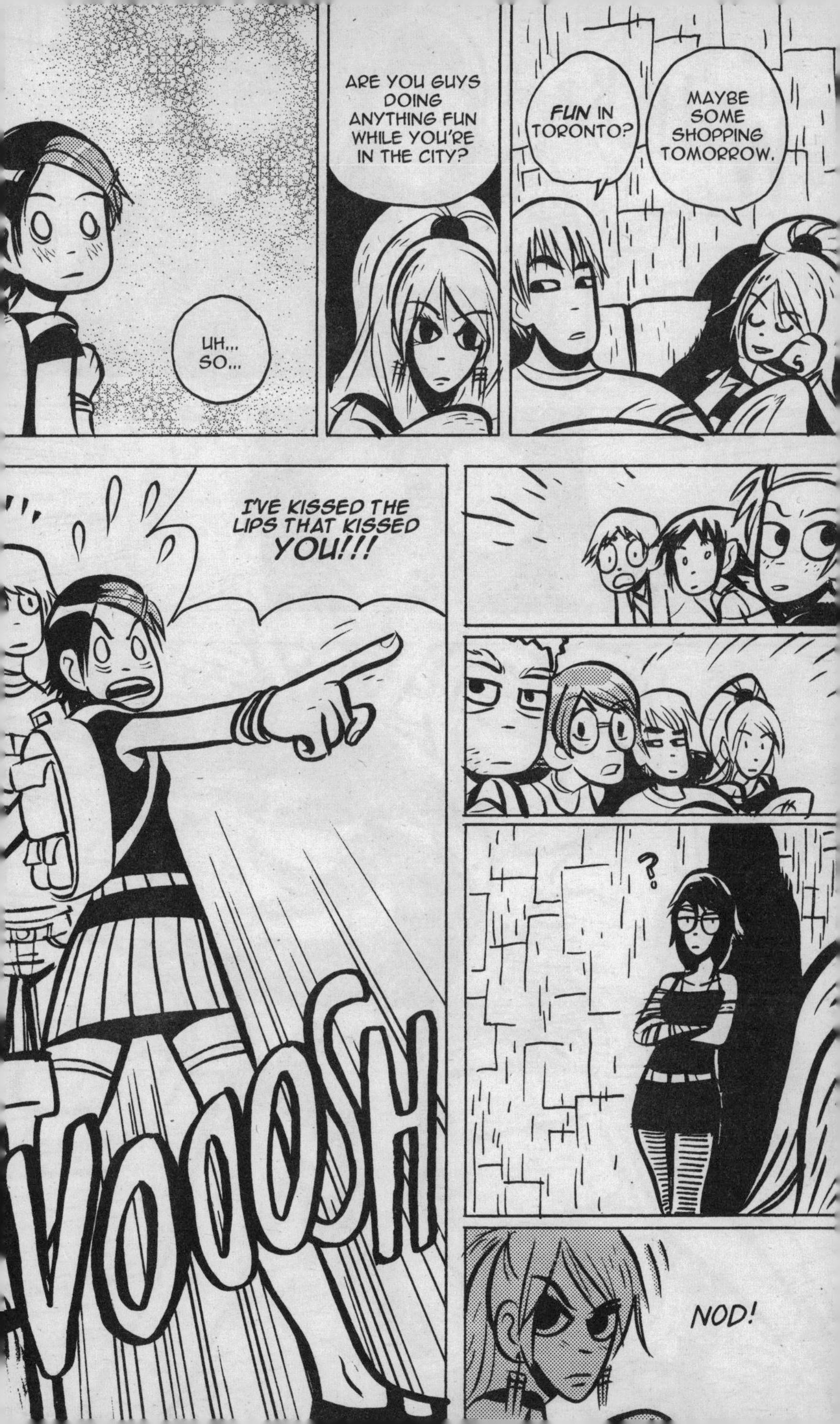
UH... SO...
ARE YOU GUYS DOING ANYTHING FUN WHILE YOU'RE IN THE CITY?
FUN IN TORONTO?
MAYBE SOME SHOPPING TOMORROW.
I'VE KISSED THE LIPS THAT KISSED YOU!!!
WOOOOSH
?
NOD!

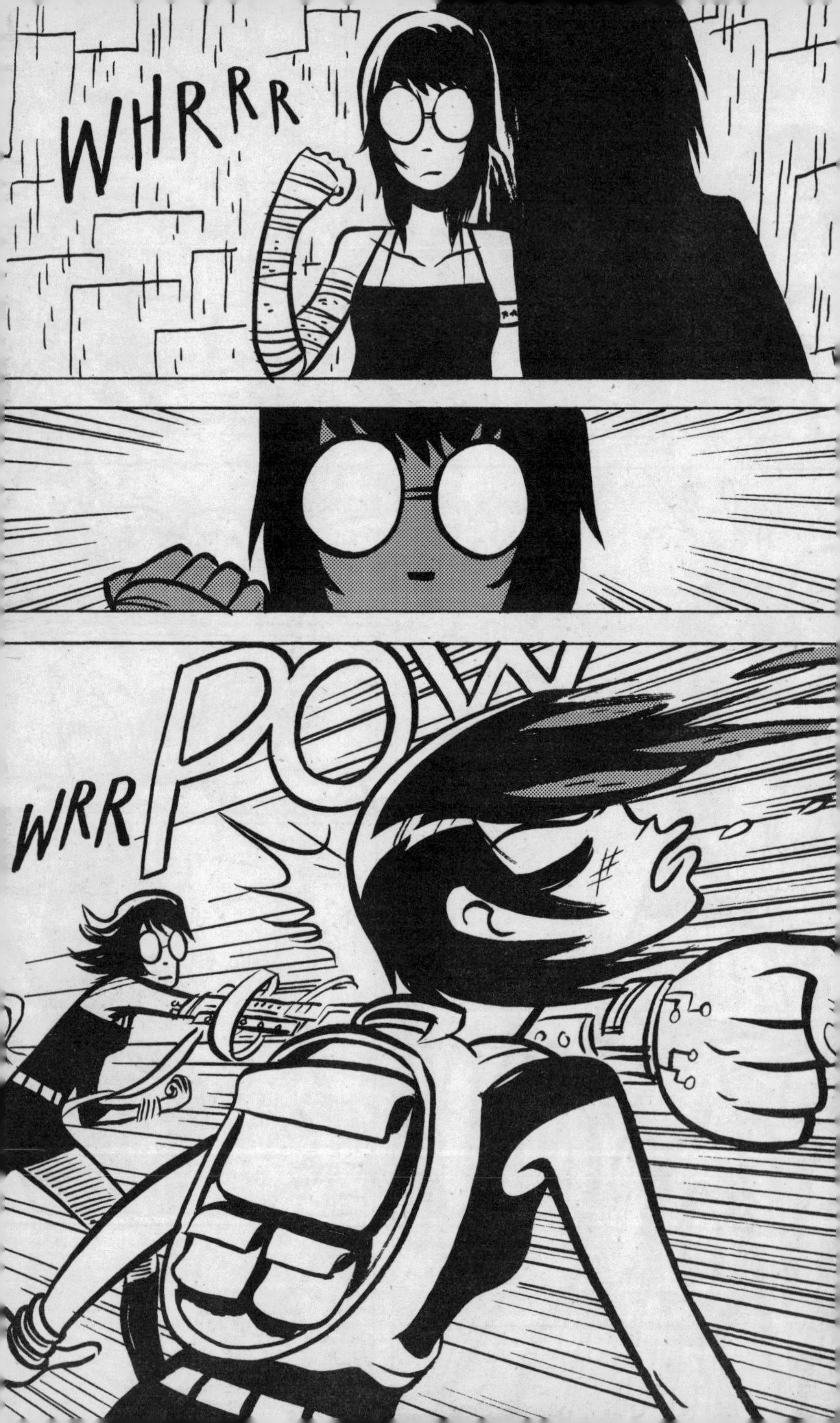
WHRRRR
WRR
POW

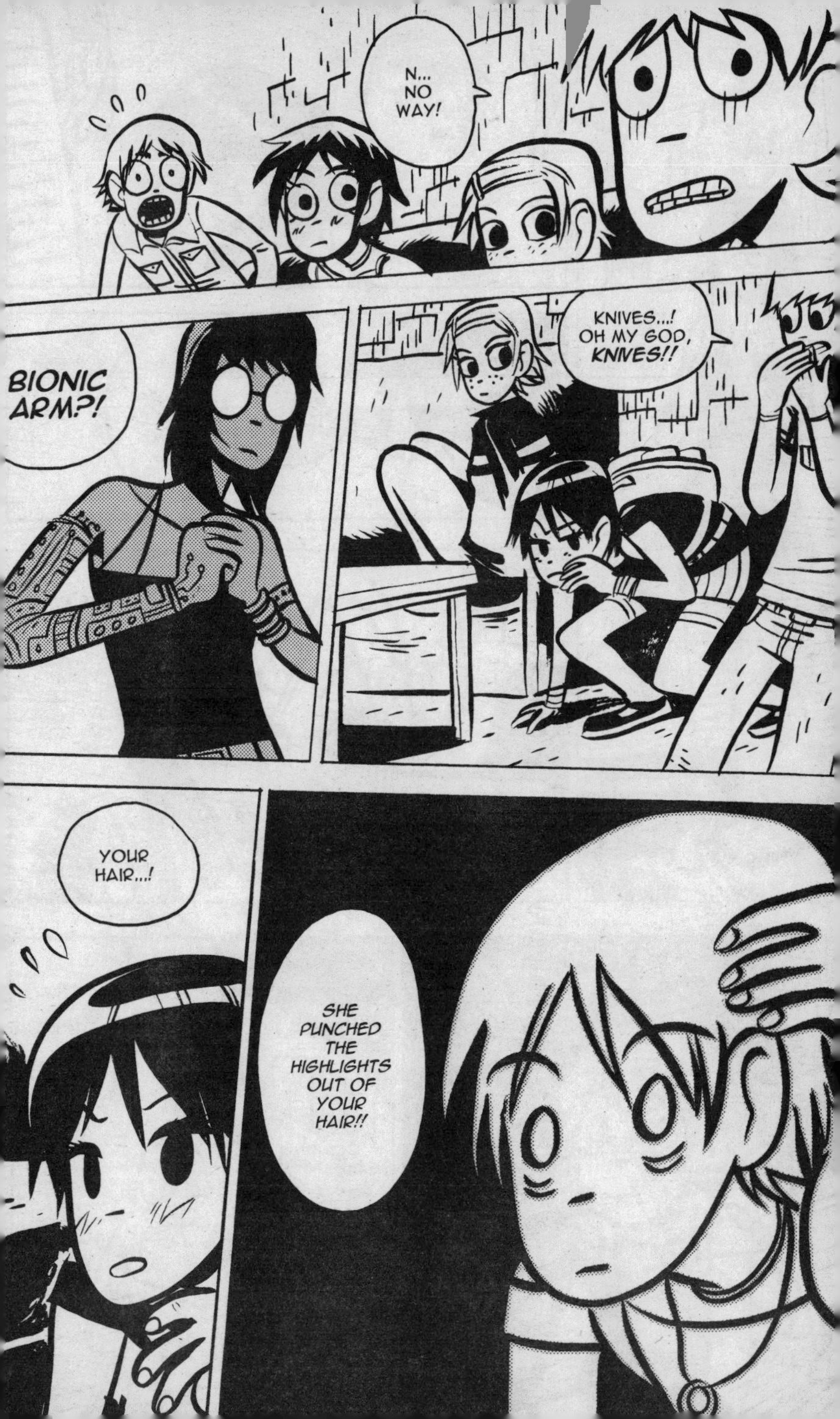
N... NO WAY!
BIONIC ARM?!
KNIVES...! OH MY GOD, KNIVES!!
YOUR HAIR...!
SHE PUNCHED THE HIGHLIGHTS OUT OF YOUR HAIR!!

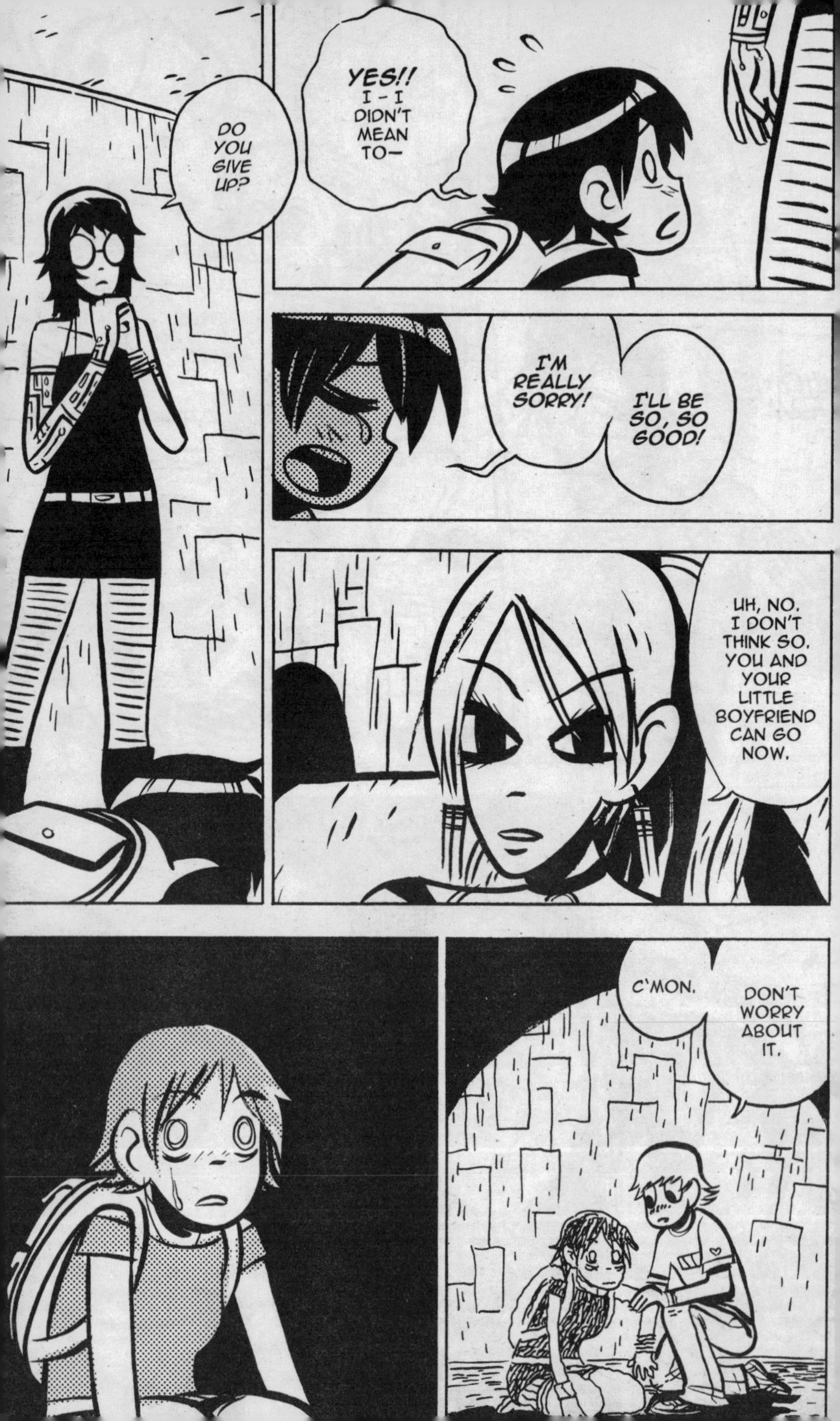

DO YOU GIVE UP?
YES!! I - I DIDN'T MEAN TO—
I'M REALLY SORRY!
I'LL BE SO, SO GOOD!
UH, NO. I DON'T THINK SO. YOU AND YOUR LITTLE BOYFRIEND CAN GO NOW.
C'MON.
DON'T WORRY ABOUT IT.

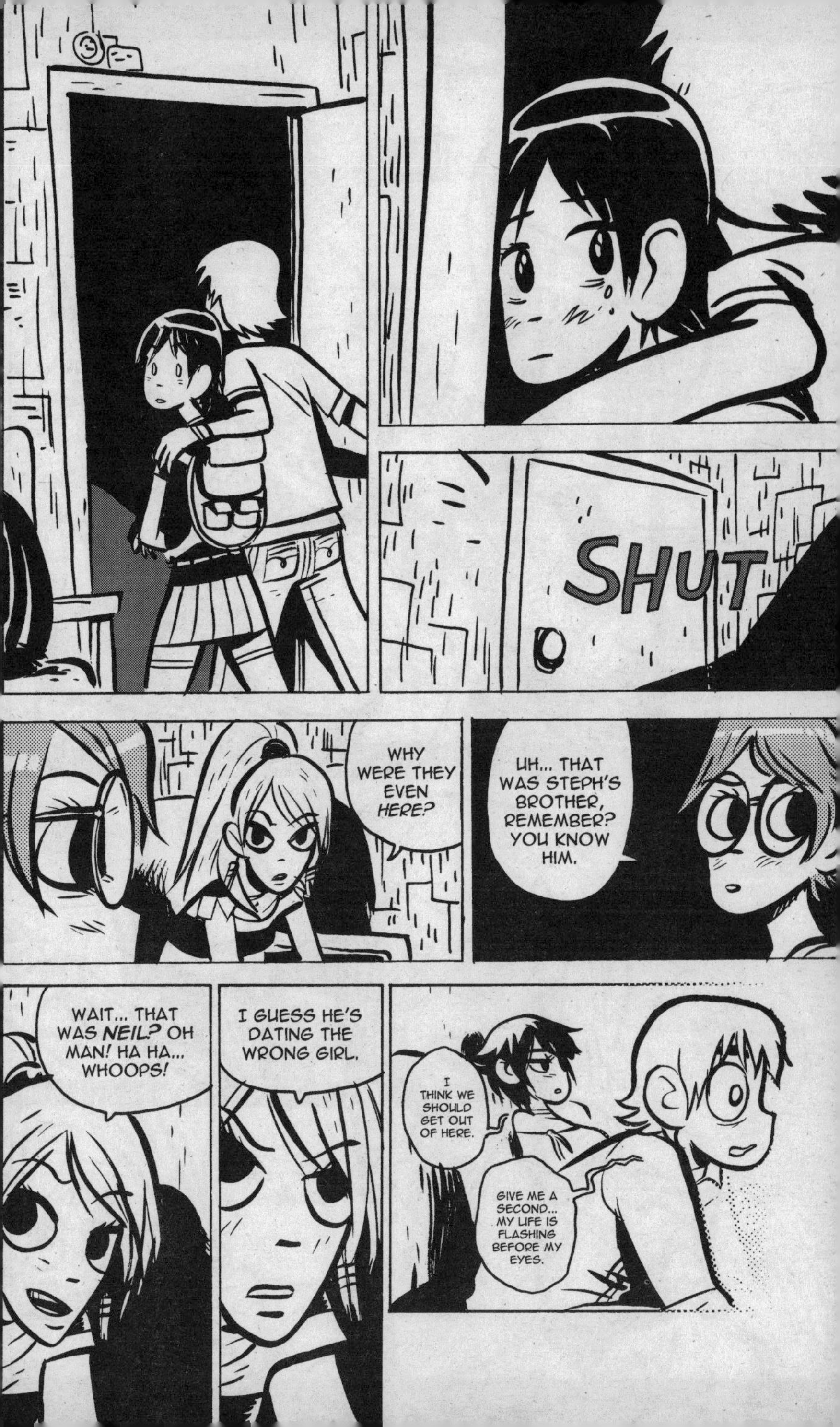
SHUT
WHY WERE THEY EVEN HERE?
UH... THAT WAS STEPH'S BROTHER, REMEMBER? YOU KNOW HIM.
WAIT... THAT WAS NEIL? OH MAN! HA HA... WHOOPS!
I GUESS HE'S DATING THE WRONG GIRL.
I THINK WE SHOULD GET OUT OF HERE.
GIVE ME A SECOND... MY LIFE IS FLASHING BEFORE MY EYES.

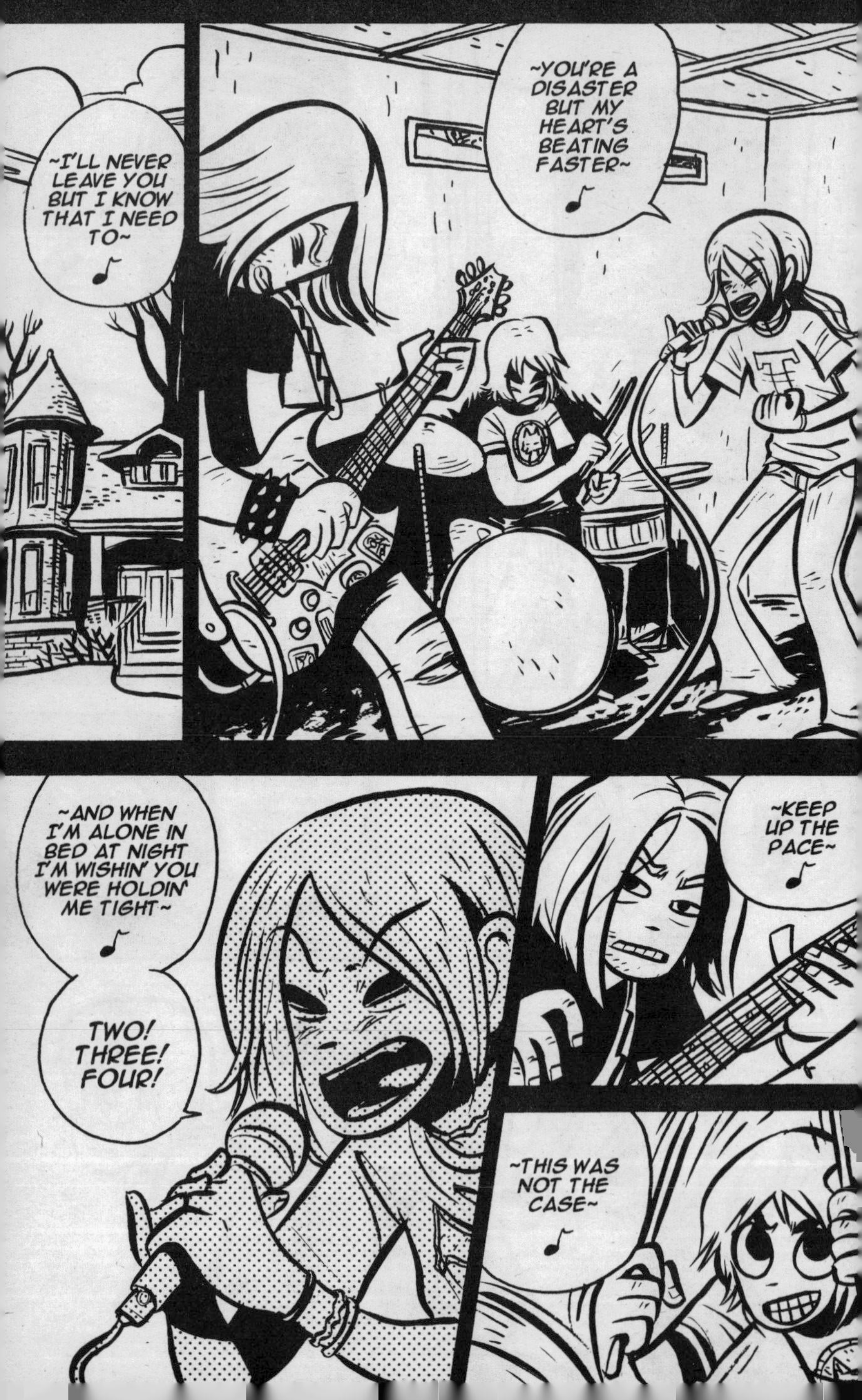
~I'LL NEVER LEAVE YOU BUT I KNOW THAT I NEED TO~ ♪
~YOU'RE A DISASTER BUT MY HEART'S BEATING FASTER~ ♪
~AND WHEN I'M ALONE IN BED AT NIGHT I'M WISHIN' YOU WERE HOLDIN' ME TIGHT~ ♪
TWO! THREE! FOUR!
~KEEP UP THE PACE~ ♪
~THIS WAS NOT THE CASE~ ♪

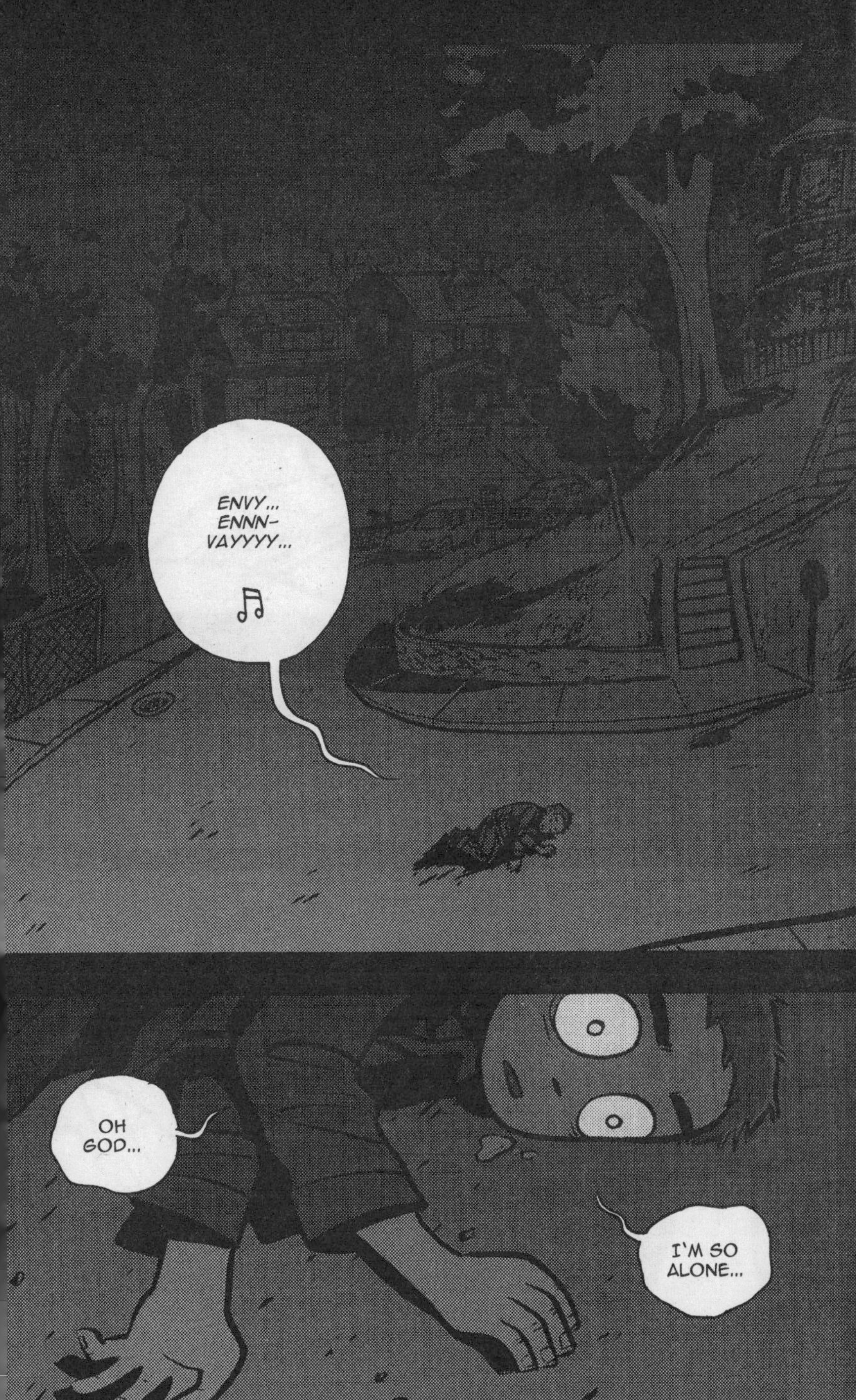
ENVY... ENNN-VAYYYY...
OH GOD...
I'M SO ALONE...

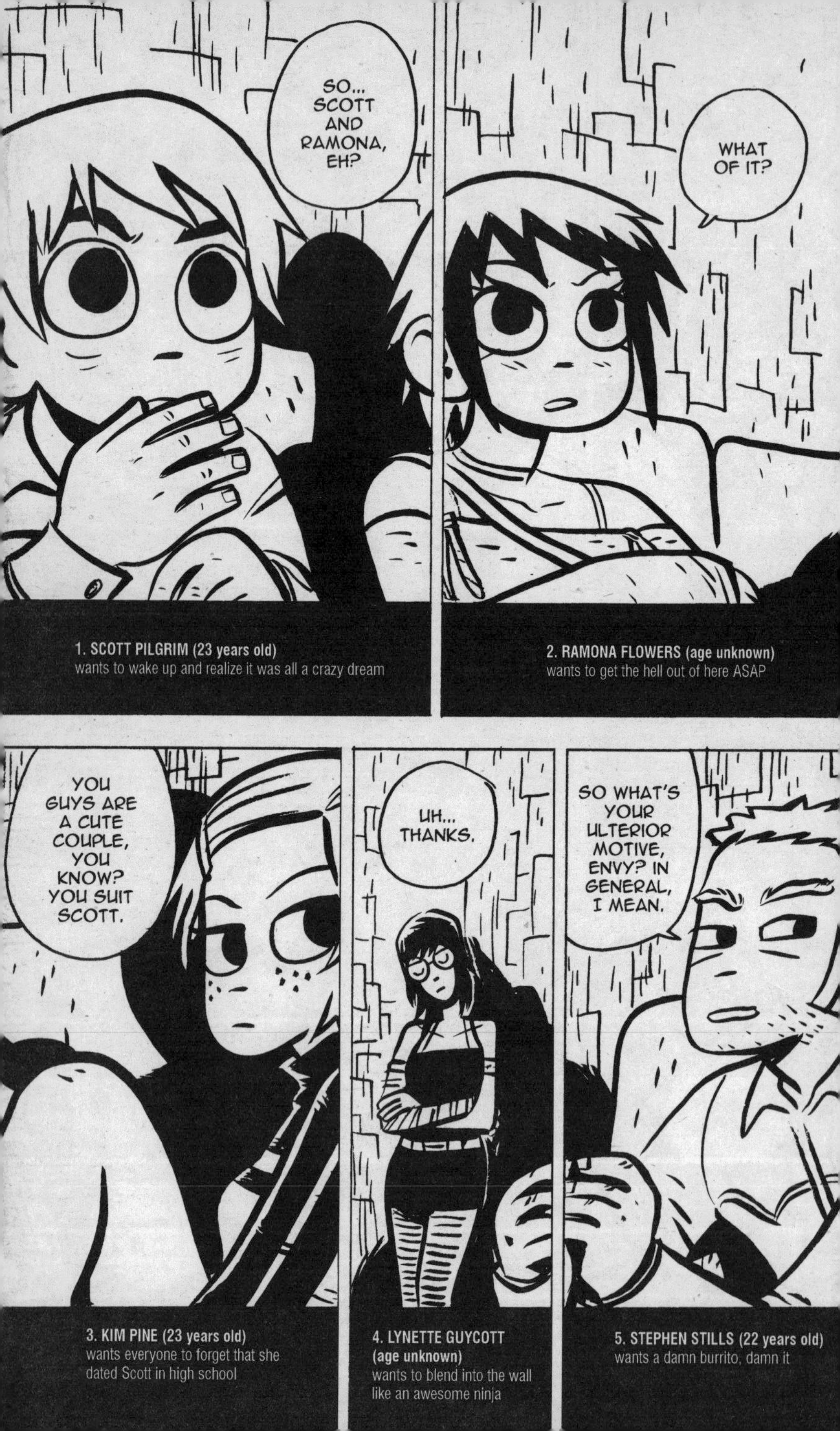
SO... SCOTT AND RAMONA, EH?
WHAT OF IT?
1. SCOTT PILGRIM (23 years old)
wants to wake up and realize it was all a crazy dream
2. RAMONA FLOWERS (age unknown)
wants to get the hell out of here ASAP
YOU GUYS ARE A CUTE COUPLE, YOU KNOW? YOU SUIT SCOTT.
UH... THANKS.
SO WHAT'S YOUR ULTERIOR MOTIVE, ENVY? IN GENERAL, I MEAN.
3. KIM PINE (23 years old)
wants everyone to forget that she dated Scott in high school
4. LYNETTE GUYCOTT (age unknown)
wants to blend into the wall like an awesome ninja
5. STEPHEN STILLS (22 years old)
wants a damn burrito, damn it

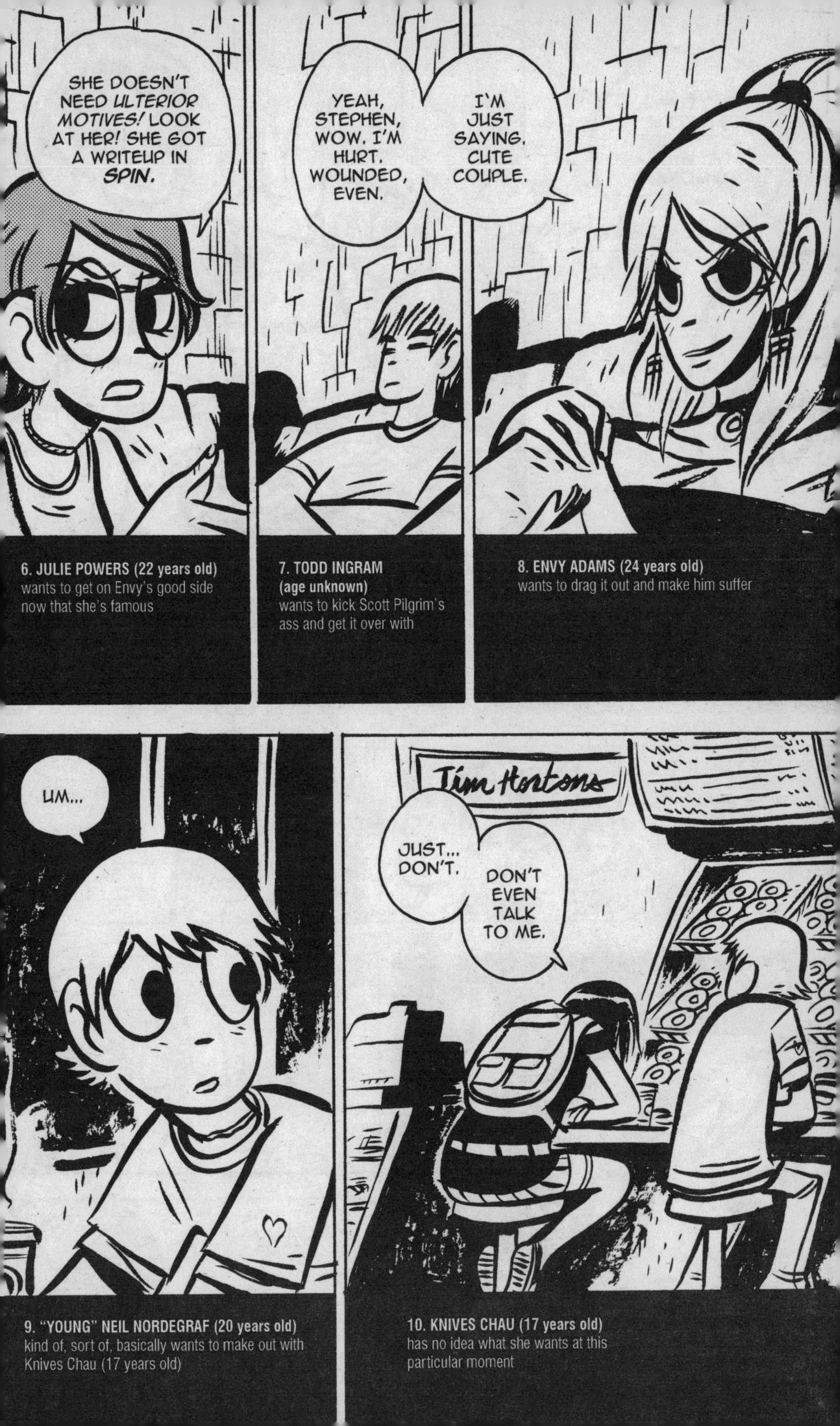
SHE DOESN'T NEED ULTERIOR MOTIVES! LOOK AT HER! SHE GOT A WRITEUP IN SPIN.
YEAH, STEPHEN, WOW. I'M HURT. WOUNDED, EVEN.
I'M JUST SAYING. CUTE COUPLE.
6. JULIE POWERS (22 years old) wants to get on Envy's good side now that she's famous
7. TODD INGRAM (age unknown) wants to kick Scott Pilgrim's ass and get it over with
8. ENVY ADAMS (24 years old) wants to drag it out and make him suffer
UM...
Tim Hortons
JUST... DON'T.
DON'T EVEN TALK TO ME.
9. "YOUNG" NEIL NORDEGRAF (20 years old) kind of, sort of, basically wants to make out with Knives Chau (17 years old)
10. KNIVES CHAU (17 years old) has no idea what she wants at this particular moment

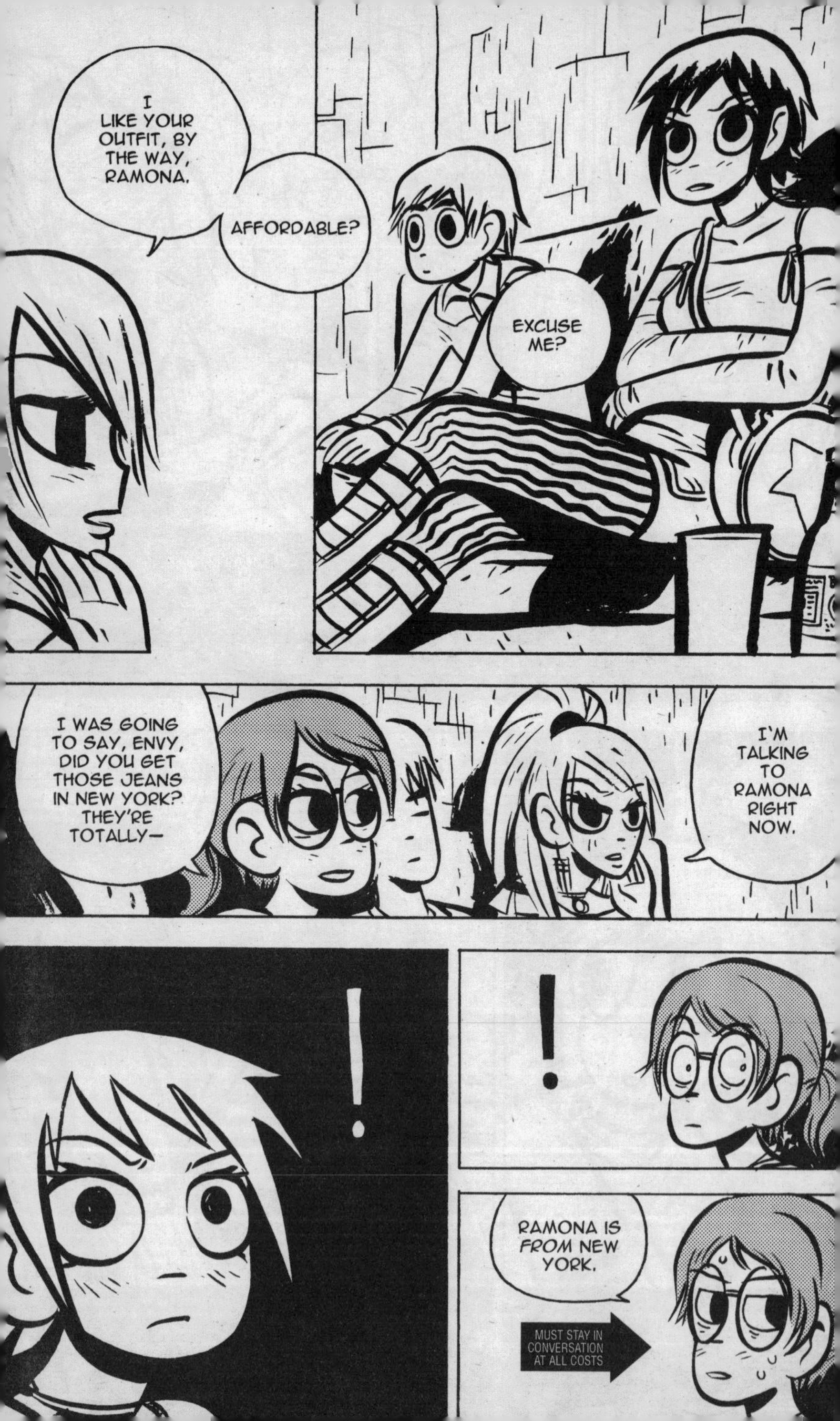
I LIKE YOUR OUTFIT, BY THE WAY, RAMONA.
AFFORDABLE?
EXCUSE ME?
I WAS GOING TO SAY, ENVY, DID YOU GET THOSE JEANS IN NEW YORK? THEY'RE TOTALLY—
I'M TALKING TO RAMONA RIGHT NOW.
!
!
RAMONA IS *FROM* NEW YORK.
MUST STAY IN CONVERSATION AT ALL COSTS

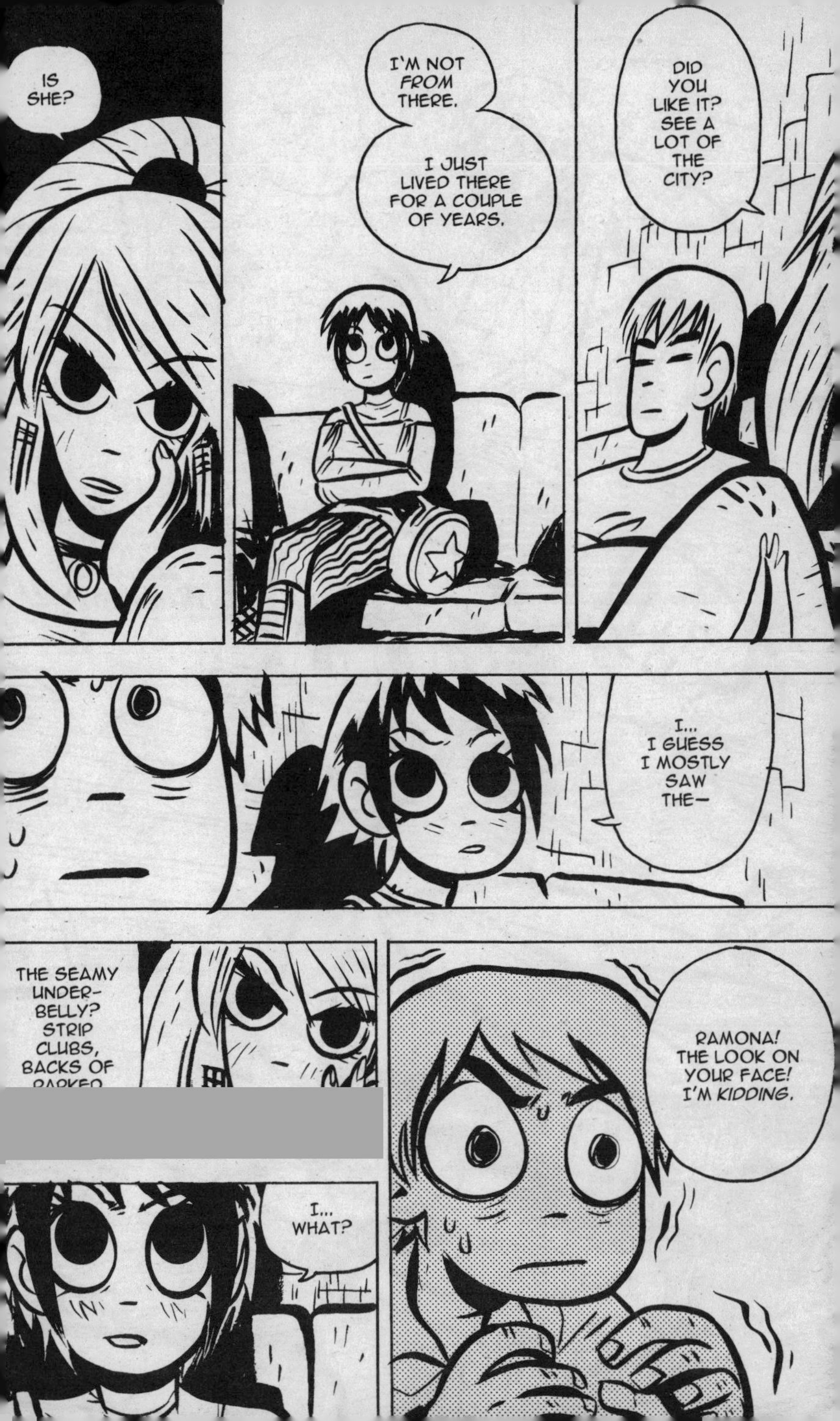
IS SHE?
I'M NOT *FROM* THERE.
I JUST LIVED THERE FOR A COUPLE OF YEARS.
DID YOU LIKE IT? SEE A LOT OF THE CITY?
I... I GUESS I MOSTLY SAW THE—
THE SEAMY UNDER-BELLY? STRIP CLUBS, BACKS OF
I... WHAT?
RAMONA! THE LOOK ON YOUR FACE! I'M *KIDDING*.

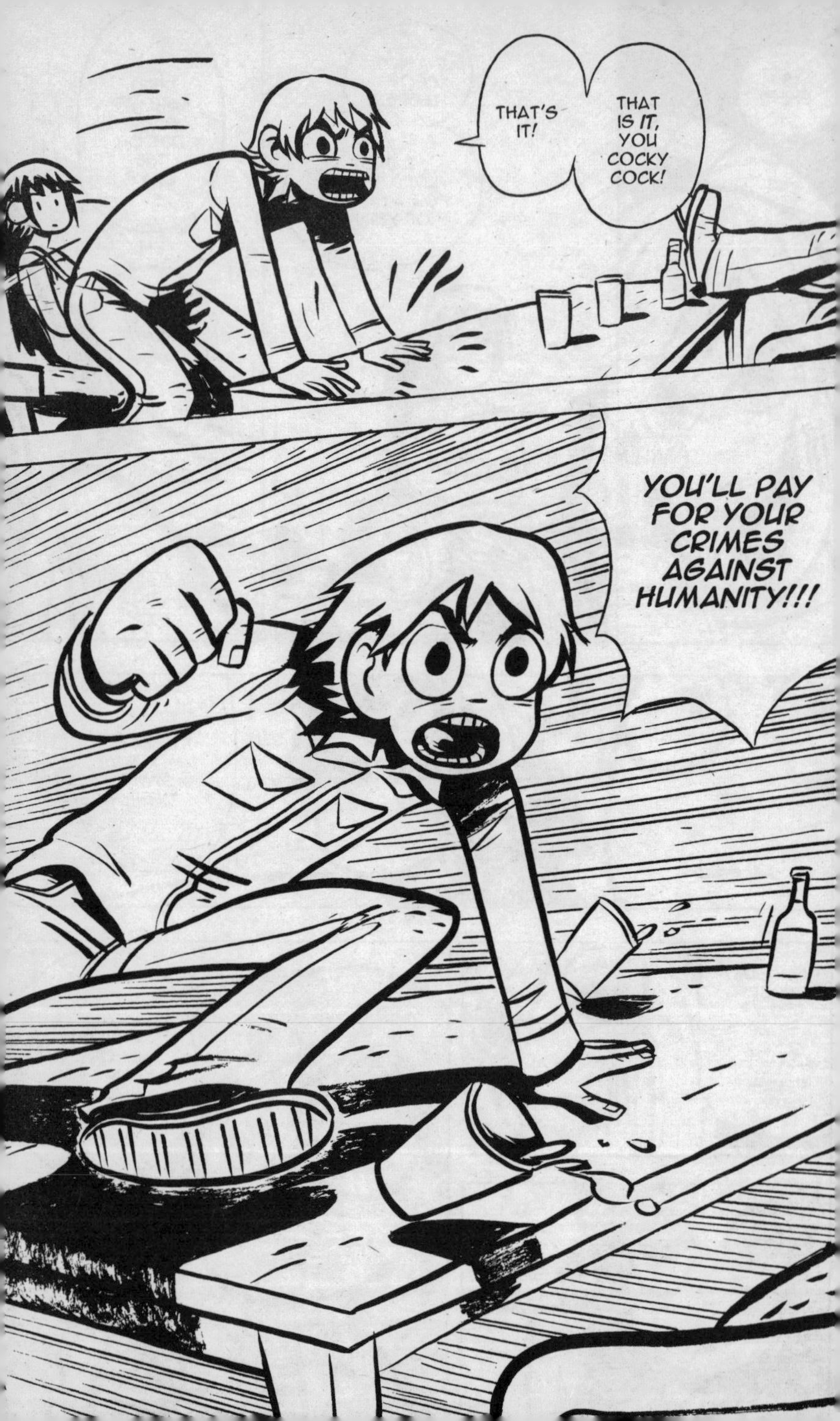
THAT'S IT!
THAT IS IT, YOU COCKY COCK!
YOU'LL PAY FOR YOUR CRIMES AGAINST HUMANITY!!!

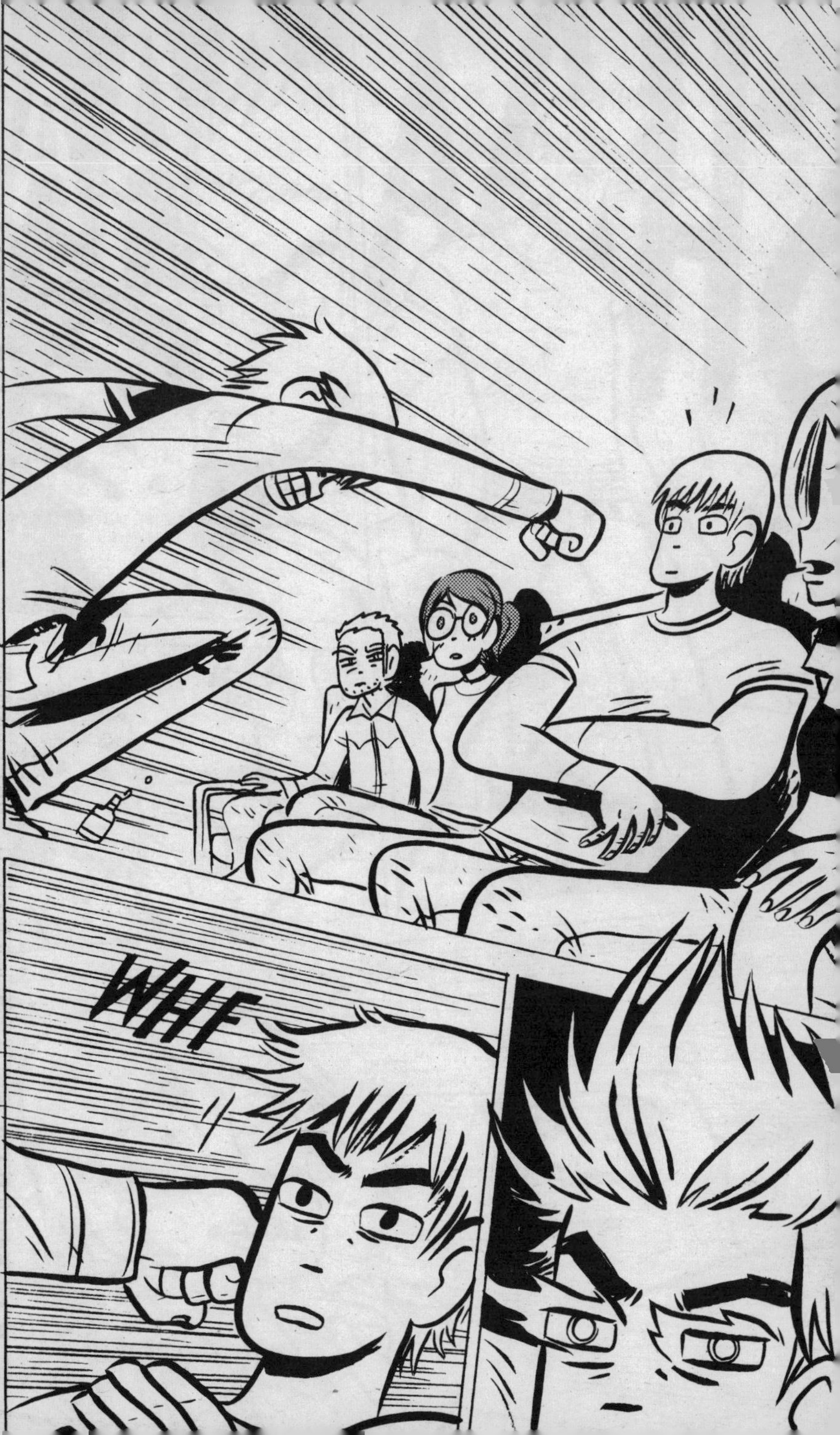
WHF

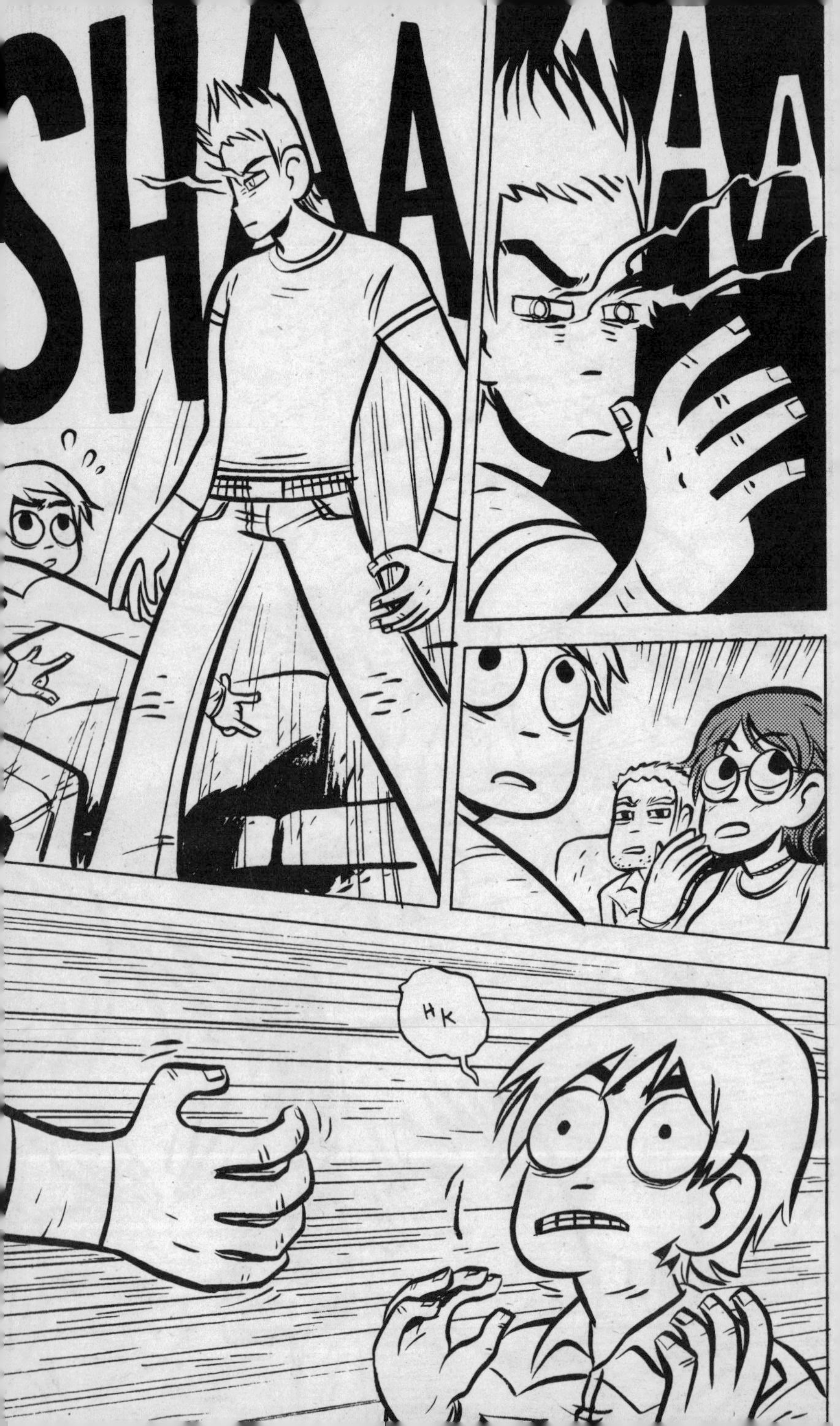
SHAAAAA
HK

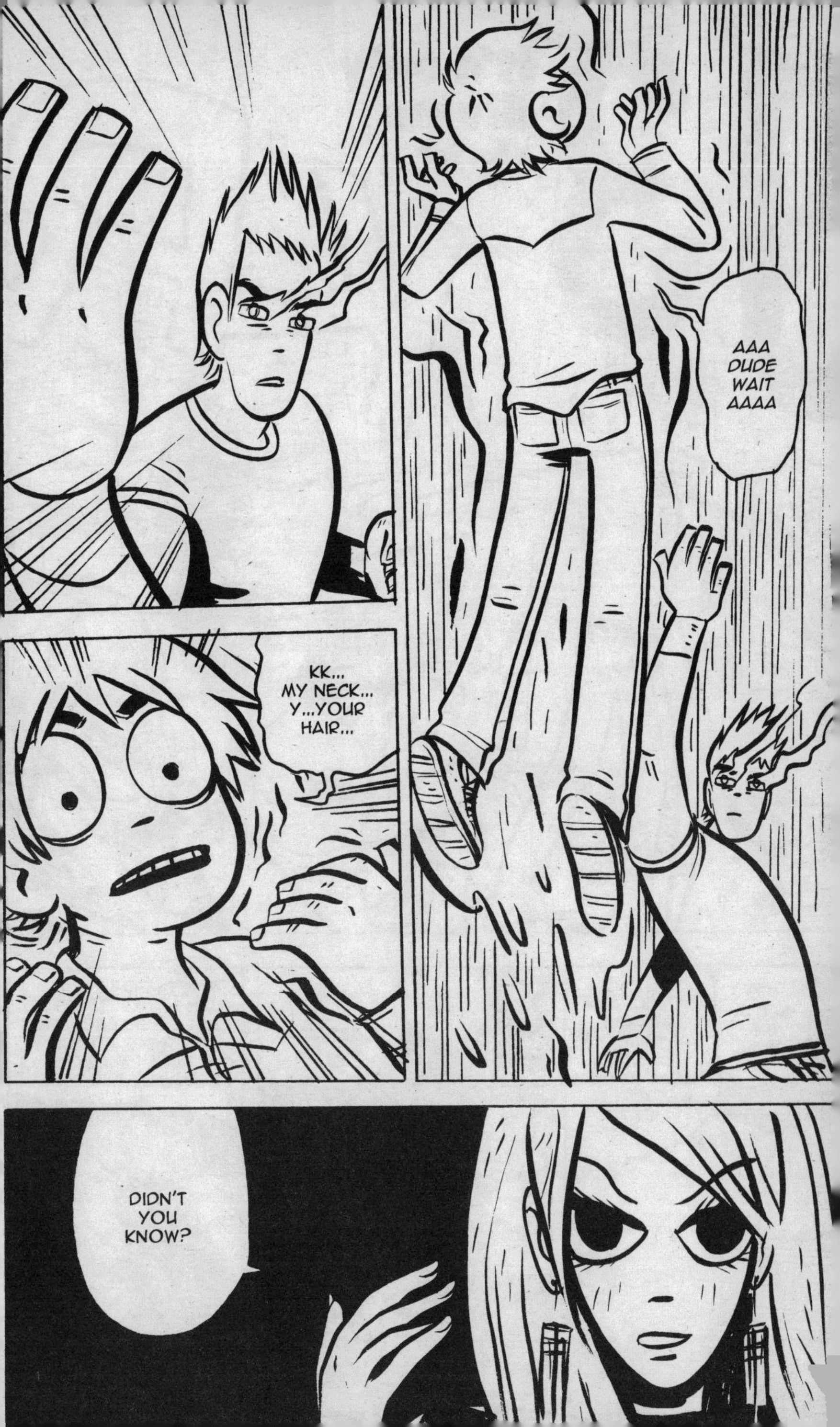
AAA
DUDE
WAIT
AAAA
KK...
MY NECK...
Y...YOUR
HAIR...
DIDN'T
YOU
KNOW?

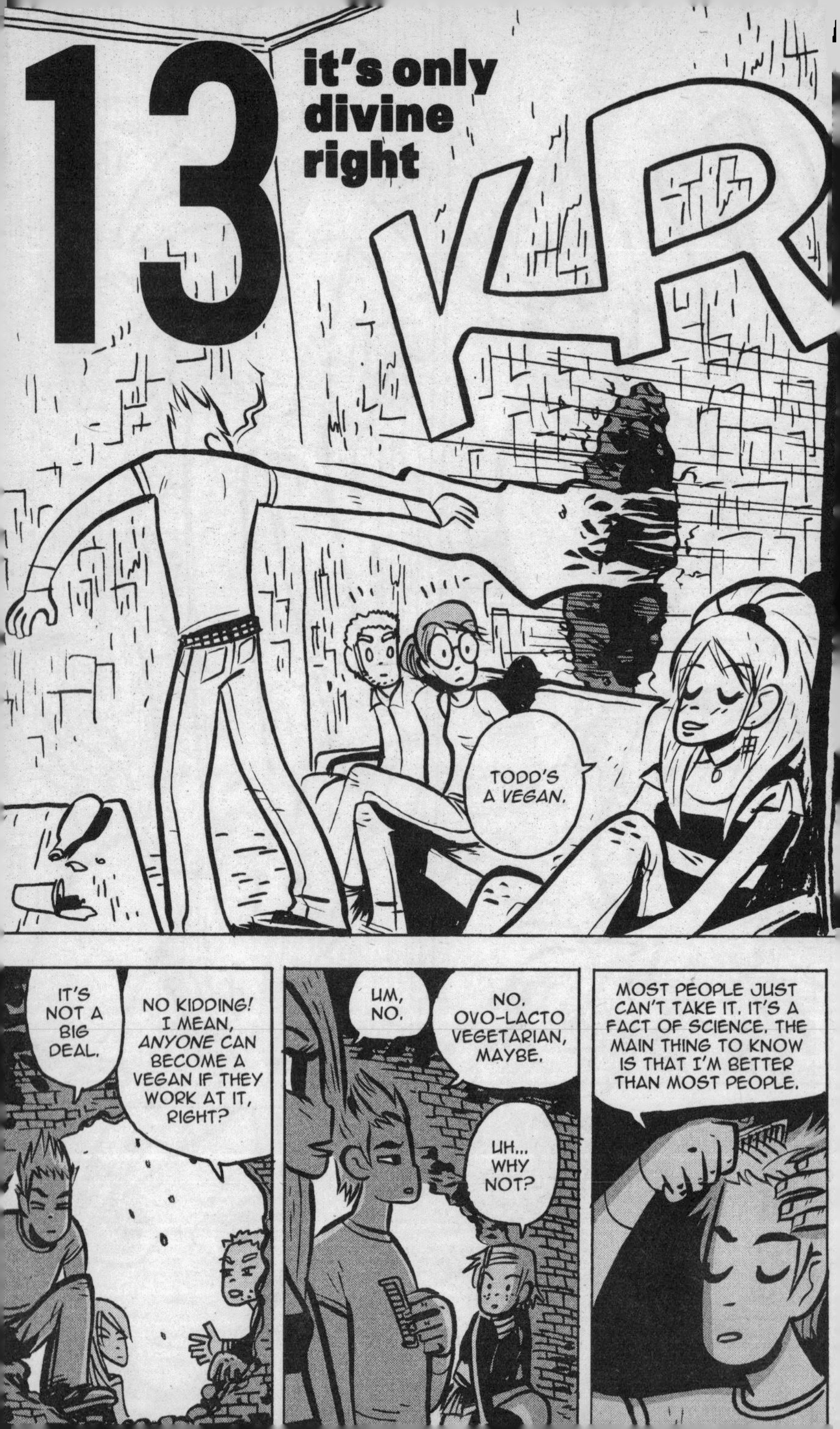
13
it's only divine right
TODD'S A VEGAN.
IT'S NOT A BIG DEAL.
NO KIDDING! I MEAN, *ANYONE* CAN BECOME A VEGAN IF THEY WORK AT IT, RIGHT?
UM, NO.
NO. OVO-LACTO VEGETARIAN, MAYBE.
UH... WHY NOT?
MOST PEOPLE JUST CAN'T TAKE IT. IT'S A FACT OF SCIENCE. THE MAIN THING TO KNOW IS THAT I'M BETTER THAN MOST PEOPLE.

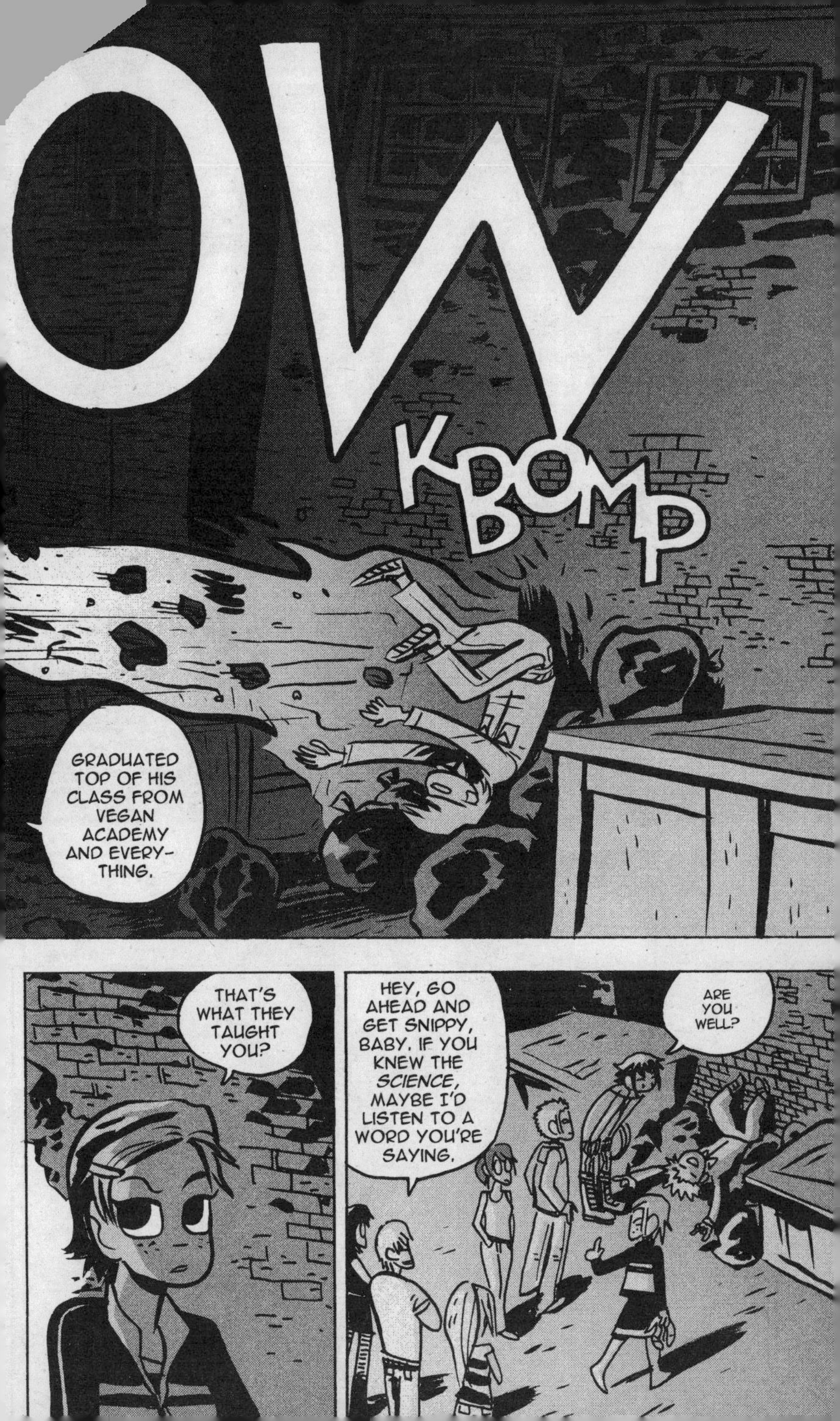
OW
KBOMP
GRADUATED TOP OF HIS CLASS FROM VEGAN ACADEMY AND EVERY-THING.
THAT'S WHAT THEY TAUGHT YOU?
HEY, GO AHEAD AND GET SNIPPY, BABY. IF YOU KNEW THE *SCIENCE*, MAYBE I'D LISTEN TO A WORD YOU'RE SAYING.
ARE YOU WELL?

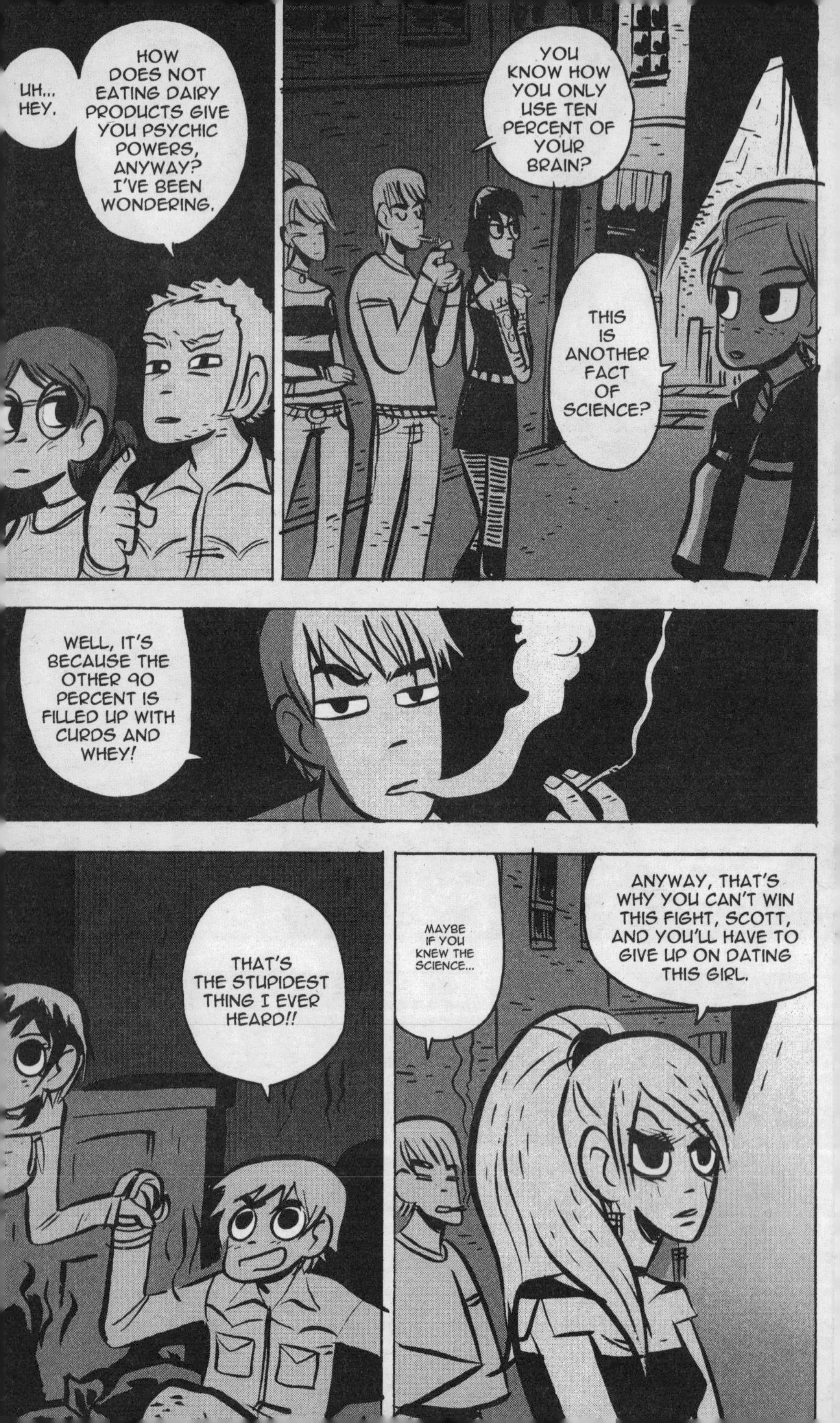
UH... HEY.
HOW DOES NOT EATING DAIRY PRODUCTS GIVE YOU PSYCHIC POWERS, ANYWAY? I'VE BEEN WONDERING.
YOU KNOW HOW YOU ONLY USE TEN PERCENT OF YOUR BRAIN?
THIS IS ANOTHER FACT OF SCIENCE?
WELL, IT'S BECAUSE THE OTHER 90 PERCENT IS FILLED UP WITH CURDS AND WHEY!
THAT'S THE STUPIDEST THING I EVER HEARD!!
MAYBE IF YOU KNEW THE SCIENCE...
ANYWAY, THAT'S WHY YOU CAN'T WIN THIS FIGHT, SCOTT, AND YOU'LL HAVE TO GIVE UP ON DATING THIS GIRL.

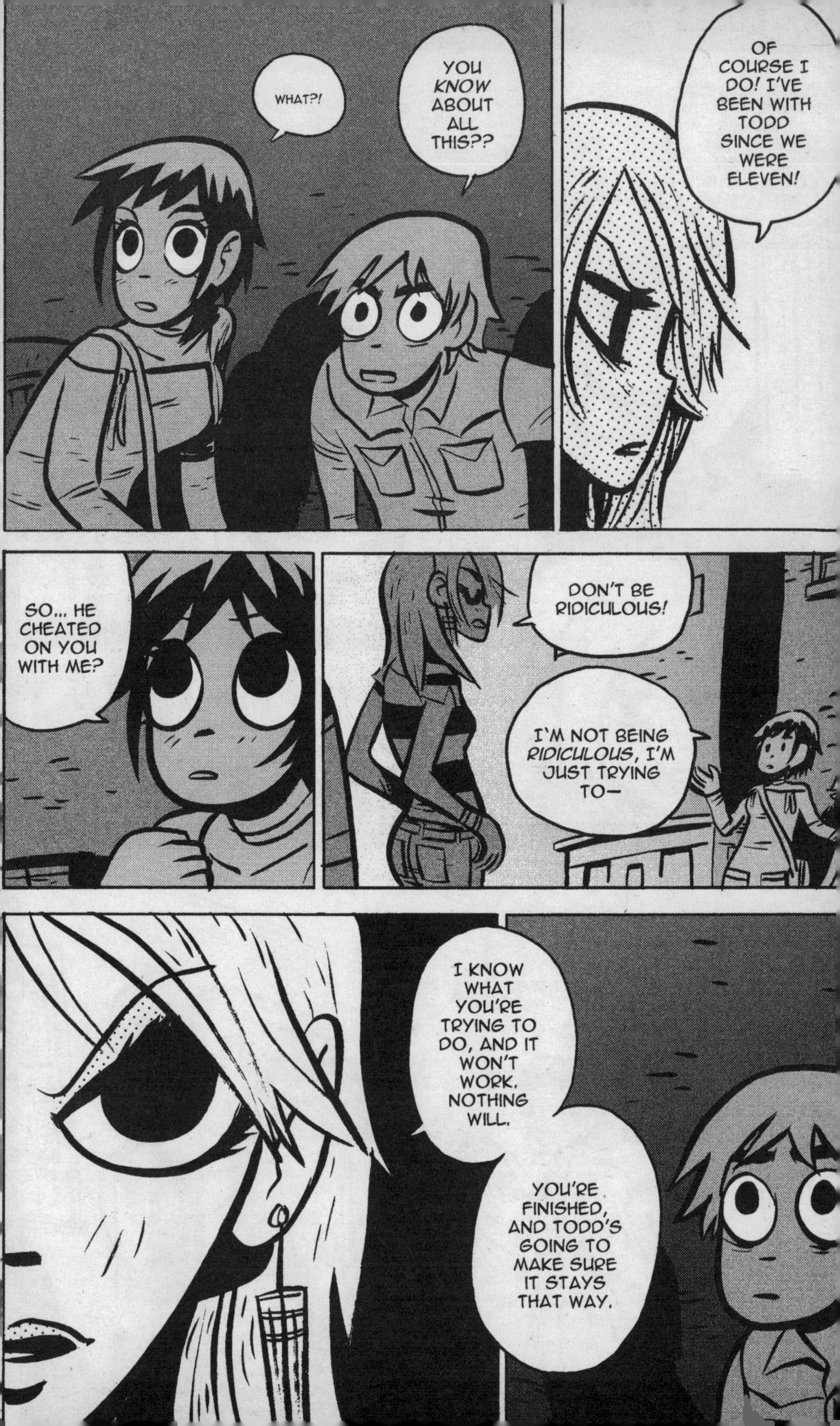
WHAT?!
YOU KNOW ABOUT ALL THIS??
OF COURSE I DO! I'VE BEEN WITH TODD SINCE WE WERE ELEVEN!
SO... HE CHEATED ON YOU WITH ME?
DON'T BE RIDICULOUS!
I'M NOT BEING RIDICULOUS, I'M JUST TRYING TO—
I KNOW WHAT YOU'RE TRYING TO DO, AND IT WON'T WORK. NOTHING WILL.
YOU'RE FINISHED, AND TODD'S GOING TO MAKE SURE IT STAYS THAT WAY.

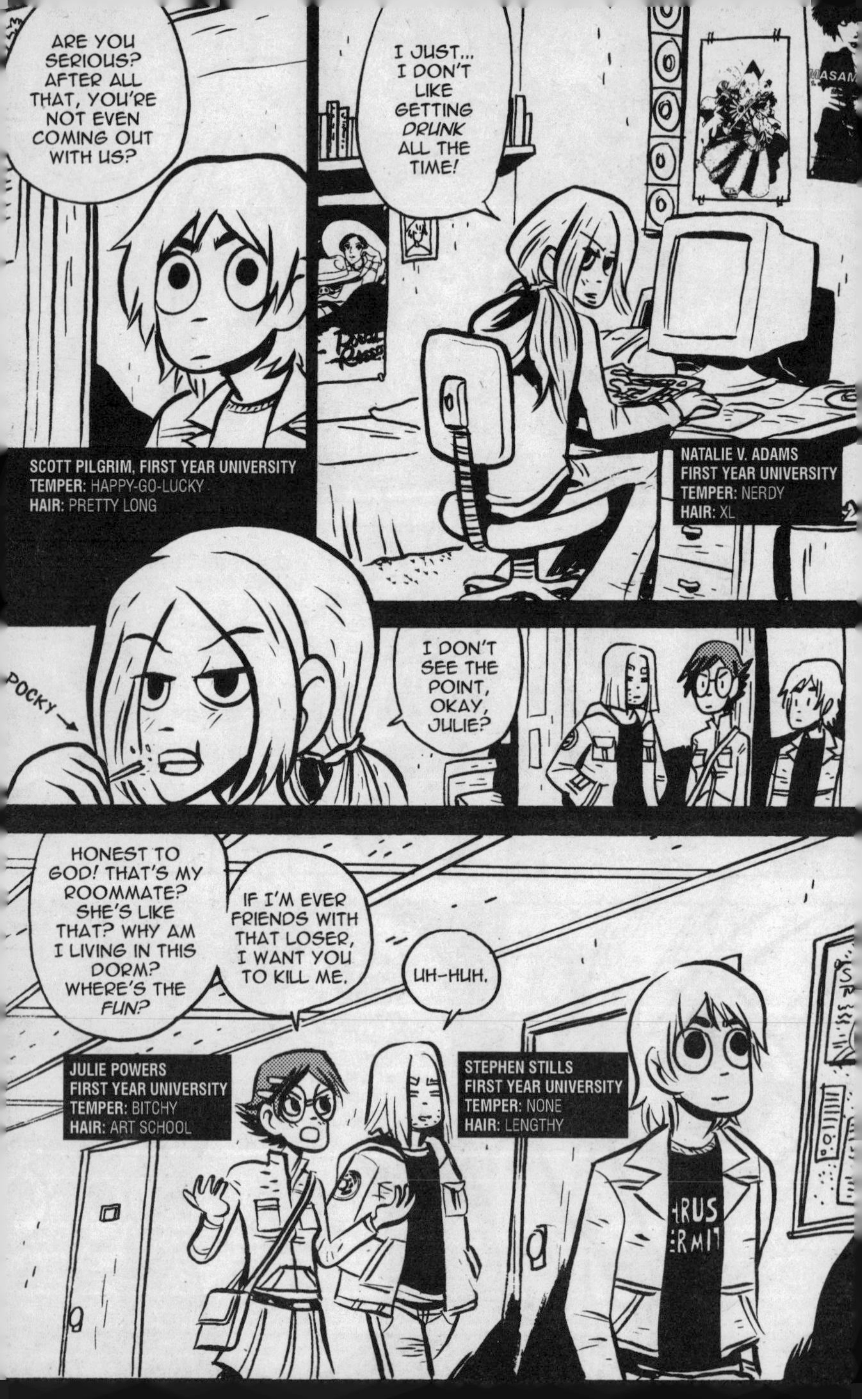
ARE YOU SERIOUS? AFTER ALL THAT, YOU'RE NOT EVEN COMING OUT WITH US?
SCOTT PILGRIM, FIRST YEAR UNIVERSITY
TEMPER: HAPPY-GO-LUCKY
HAIR: PRETTY LONG
I JUST... I DON'T LIKE GETTING DRUNK ALL THE TIME!
NATALIE V. ADAMS
FIRST YEAR UNIVERSITY
TEMPER: NERDY
HAIR: XL
POCKY
I DON'T SEE THE POINT, OKAY, JULIE?
HONEST TO GOD! THAT'S MY ROOMMATE? SHE'S LIKE THAT? WHY AM I LIVING IN THIS DORM? WHERE'S THE FUN?
IF I'M EVER FRIENDS WITH THAT LOSER, I WANT YOU TO KILL ME.
UH-HUH.
JULIE POWERS
FIRST YEAR UNIVERSITY
TEMPER: BITCHY
HAIR: ART SCHOOL
STEPHEN STILLS
FIRST YEAR UNIVERSITY
TEMPER: NONE
HAIR: LENGTHY

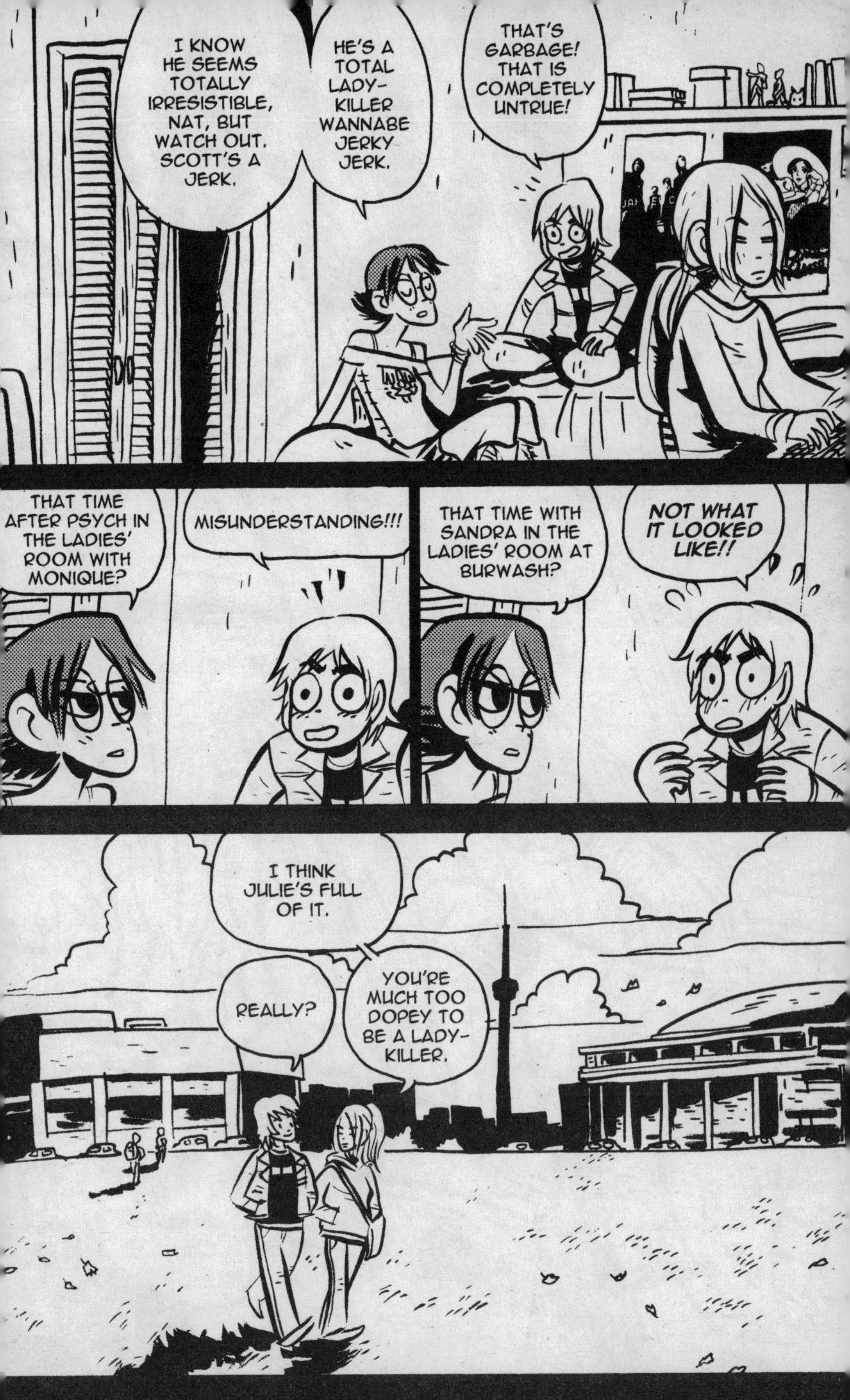
I KNOW HE SEEMS TOTALLY IRRESISTIBLE, NAT, BUT WATCH OUT. SCOTT'S A JERK.
HE'S A TOTAL LADY-KILLER WANNABE JERKY JERK.
THAT'S GARBAGE! THAT IS COMPLETELY UNTRUE!
THAT TIME AFTER PSYCH IN THE LADIES' ROOM WITH MONIQUE?
MISUNDERSTANDING!!!
THAT TIME WITH SANDRA IN THE LADIES' ROOM AT BURWASH?
NOT WHAT IT LOOKED LIKE!!
I THINK JULIE'S FULL OF IT.
REALLY?
YOU'RE MUCH TOO DOPEY TO BE A LADY-KILLER.

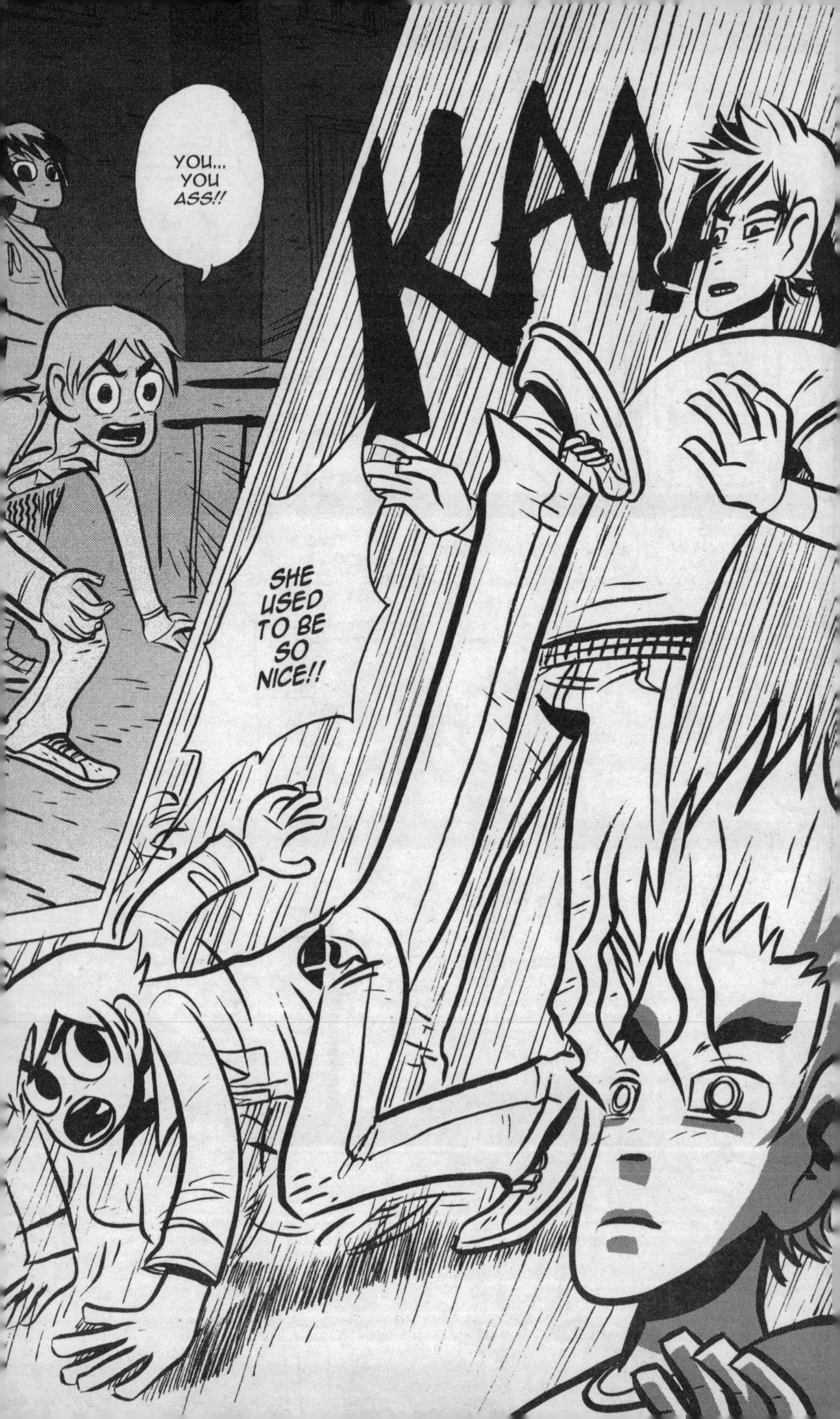
YOU... YOU ASS!!
KAA
SHE USED TO BE SO NICE!!

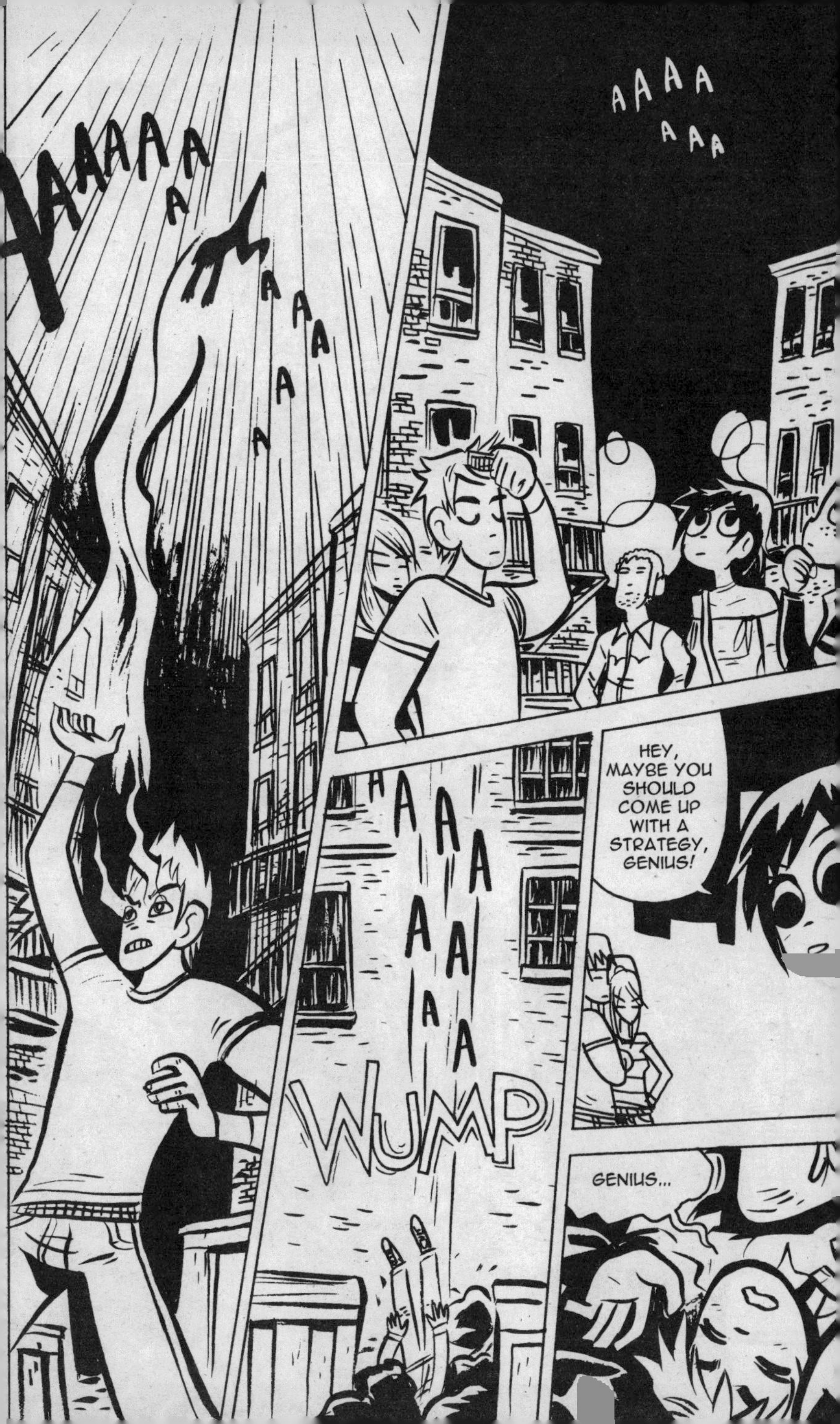
AAAAAAAAAAAAAAA
AAAA AAA
AAAAAAAAAA
WUMP
HEY, MAYBE YOU SHOULD COME UP WITH A STRATEGY, GENIUS!
GENIUS...

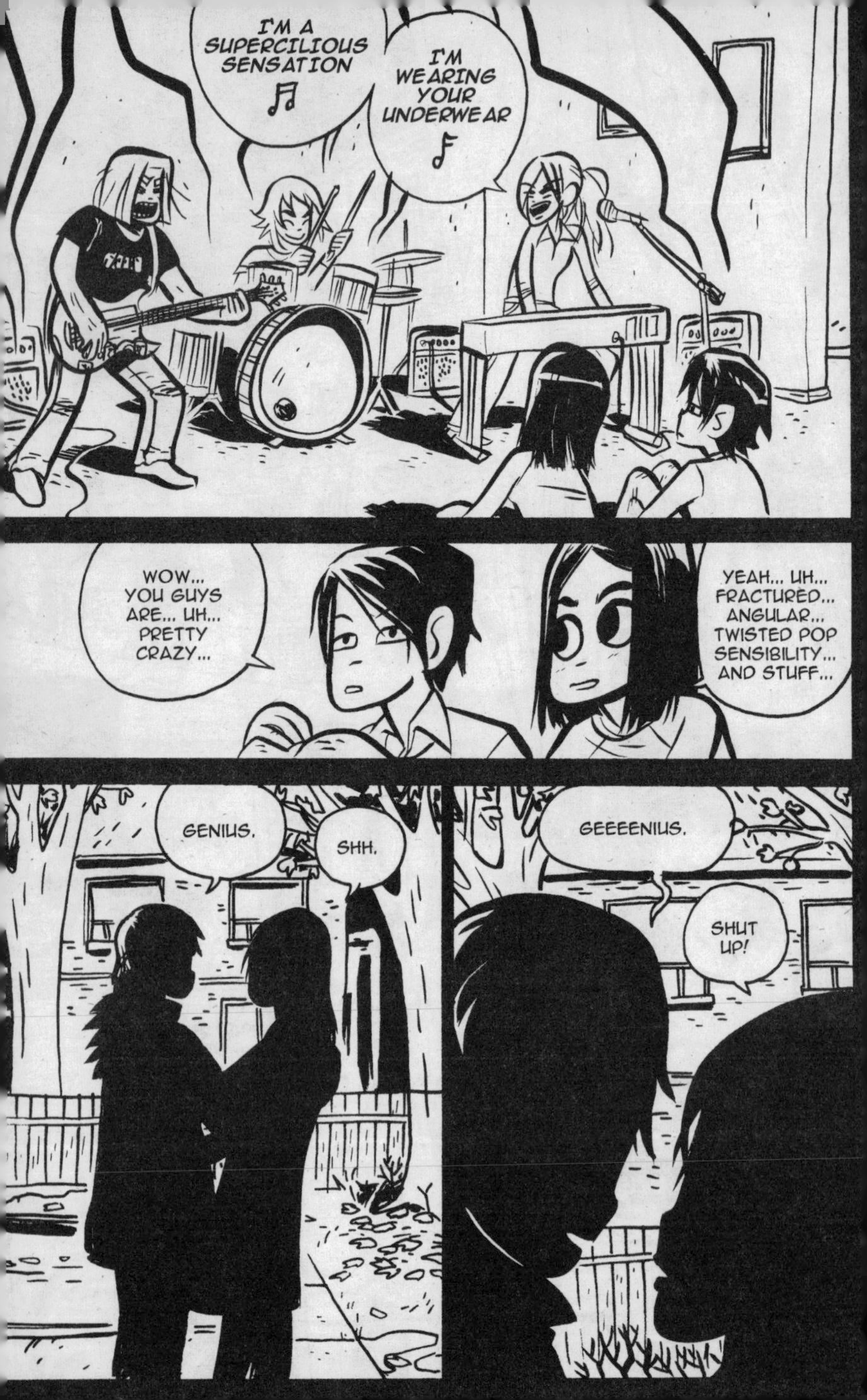
I'M A SUPERCILIOUS SENSATION
I'M WEARING YOUR UNDERWEAR
WOW... YOU GUYS ARE... UH... PRETTY CRAZY...
YEAH... UH... FRACTURED... ANGULAR... TWISTED POP SENSIBILITY... AND STUFF...
GENIUS.
SHH.
GEEEENIUS.
SHUT UP!

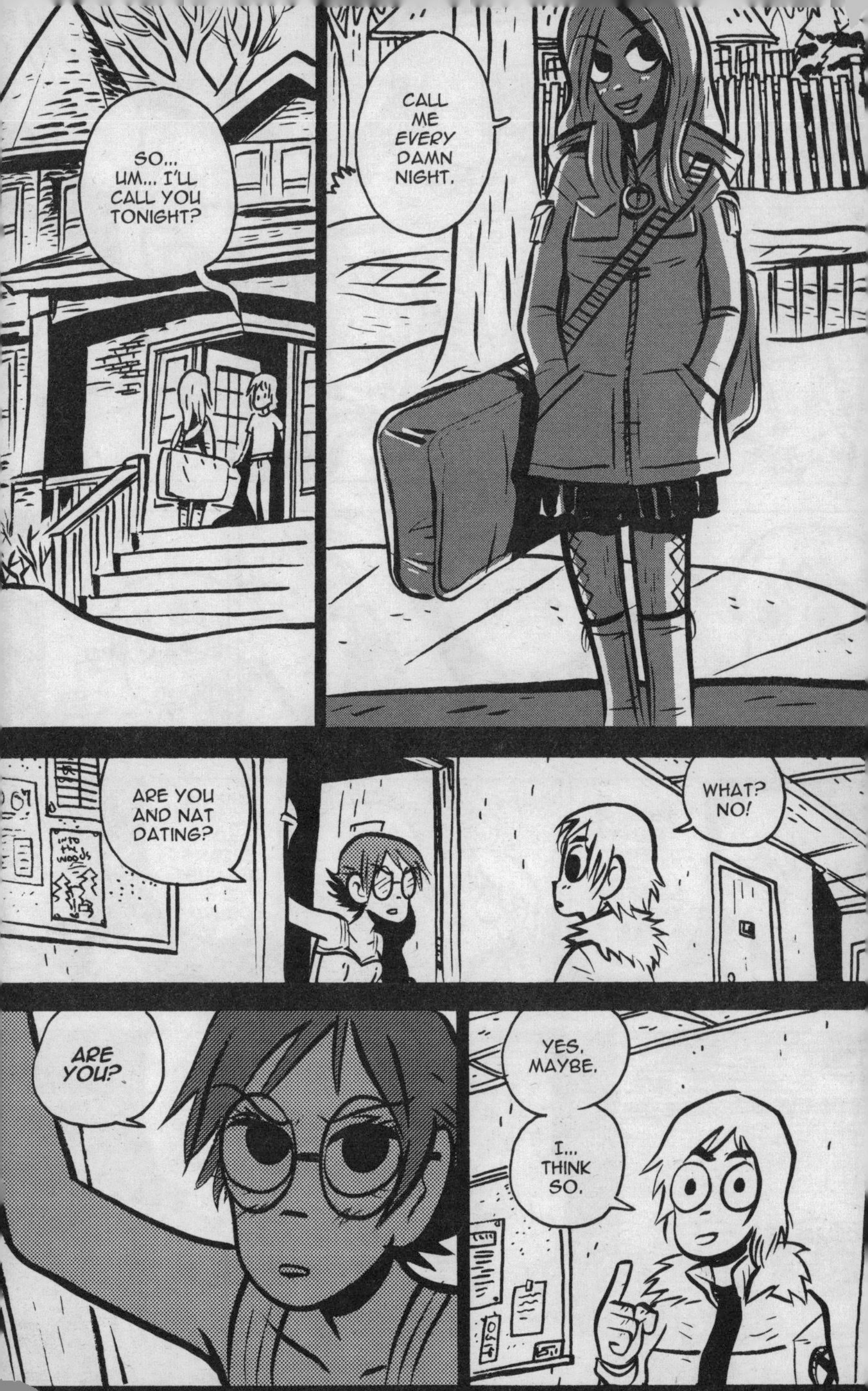
SO... UM... I'LL CALL YOU TONIGHT?
CALL ME EVERY DAMN NIGHT.
ARE YOU AND NAT DATING?
WHAT? NO!
ARE YOU?
YES. MAYBE.
I... THINK SO.

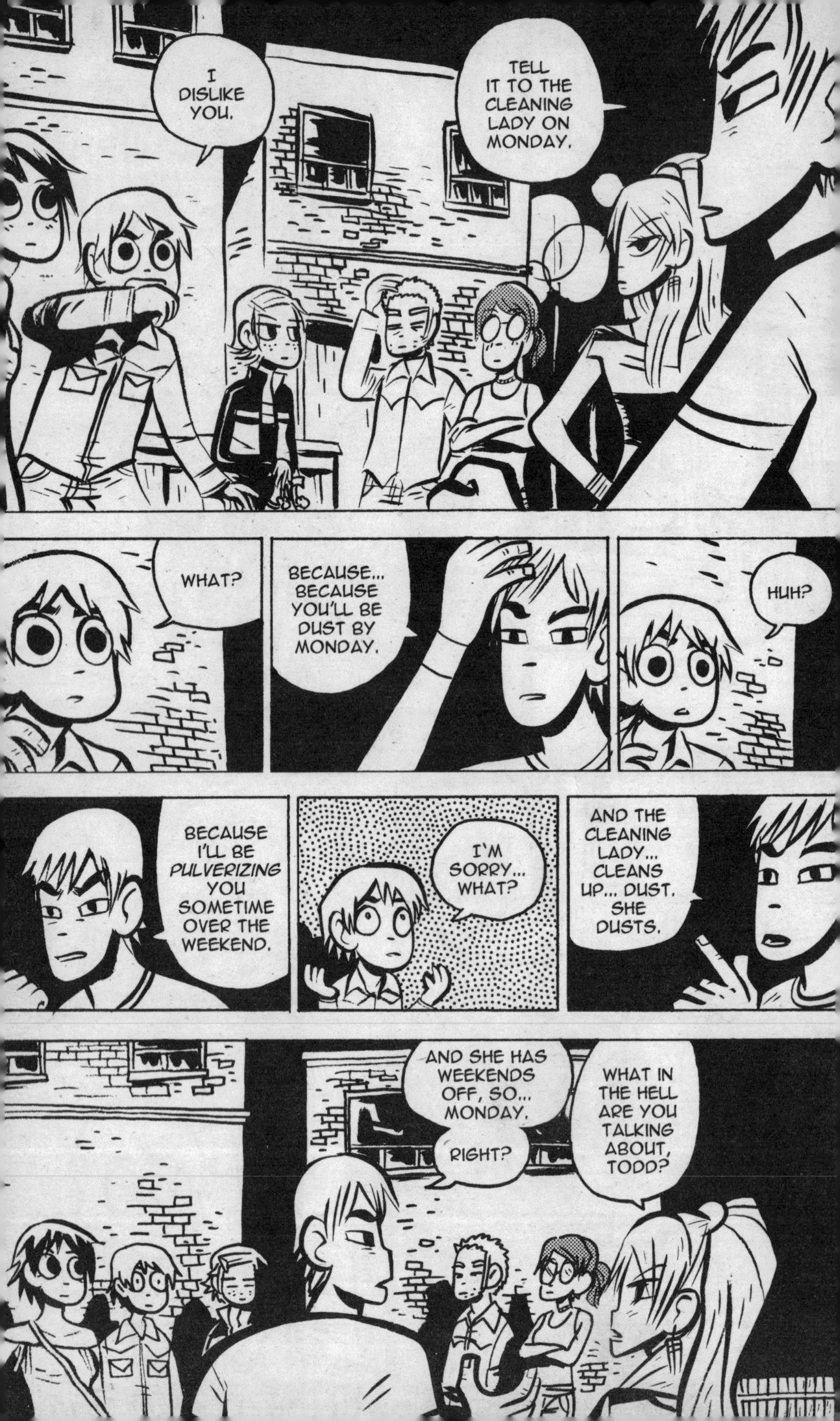
I DISLIKE YOU.
TELL IT TO THE CLEANING LADY ON MONDAY.
WHAT?
BECAUSE... BECAUSE YOU'LL BE DUST BY MONDAY.
HUH?
BECAUSE I'LL BE PULVERIZING YOU SOMETIME OVER THE WEEKEND.
I'M SORRY... WHAT?
AND THE CLEANING LADY... CLEANS UP... DUST. SHE DUSTS.
AND SHE HAS WEEKENDS OFF, SO... MONDAY.
RIGHT?
WHAT IN THE HELL ARE YOU TALKING ABOUT, TODD?

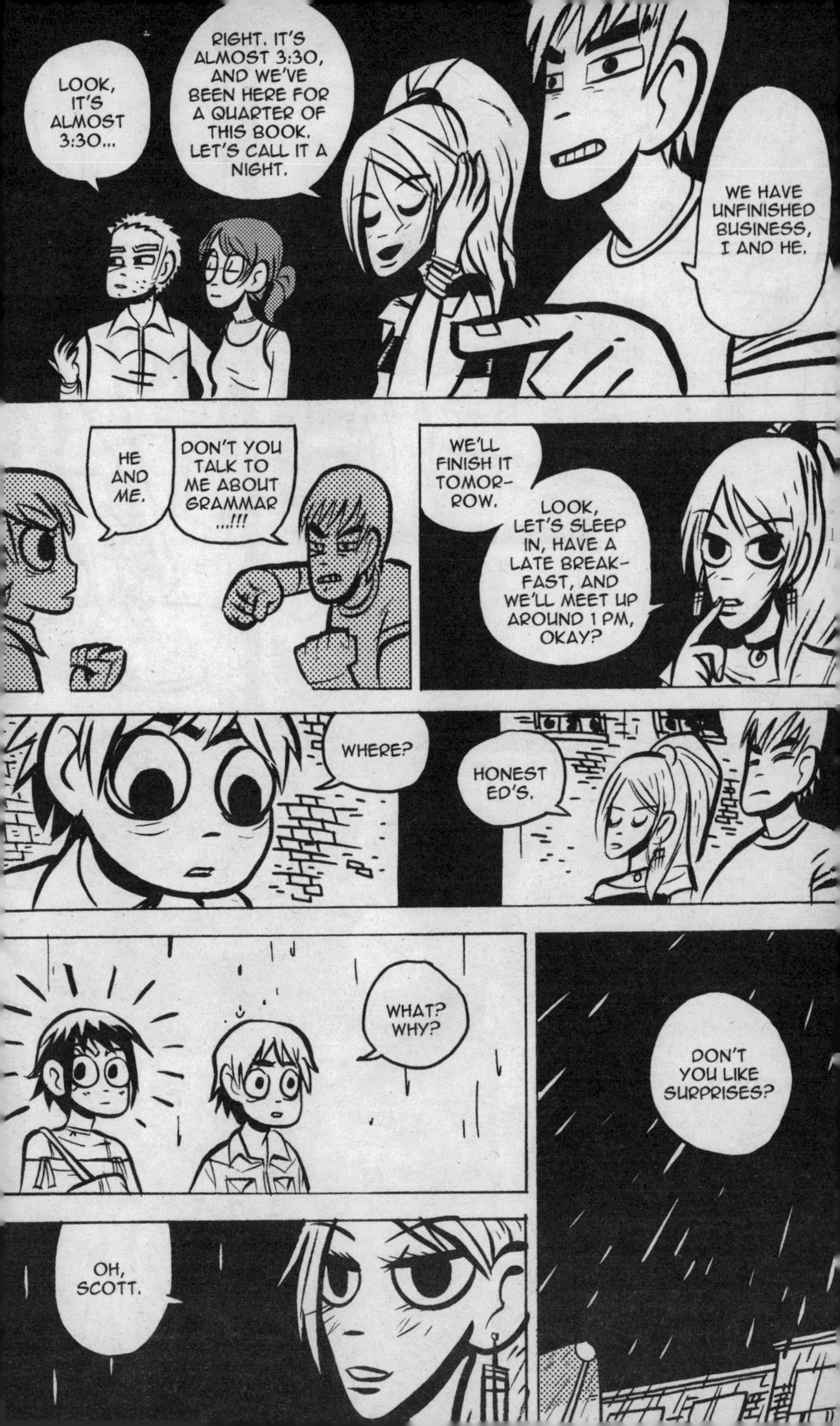
LOOK, IT'S ALMOST 3:30...
RIGHT. IT'S ALMOST 3:30, AND WE'VE BEEN HERE FOR A QUARTER OF THIS BOOK. LET'S CALL IT A NIGHT.
WE HAVE UNFINISHED BUSINESS, I AND HE.
HE AND ME.
DON'T YOU TALK TO ME ABOUT GRAMMAR ...!!!
WE'LL FINISH IT TOMORROW.
LOOK, LET'S SLEEP IN, HAVE A LATE BREAKFAST, AND WE'LL MEET UP AROUND 1 PM, OKAY?
WHERE?
HONEST ED'S.
WHAT? WHY?
DON'T YOU LIKE SURPRISES?
OH, SCOTT.

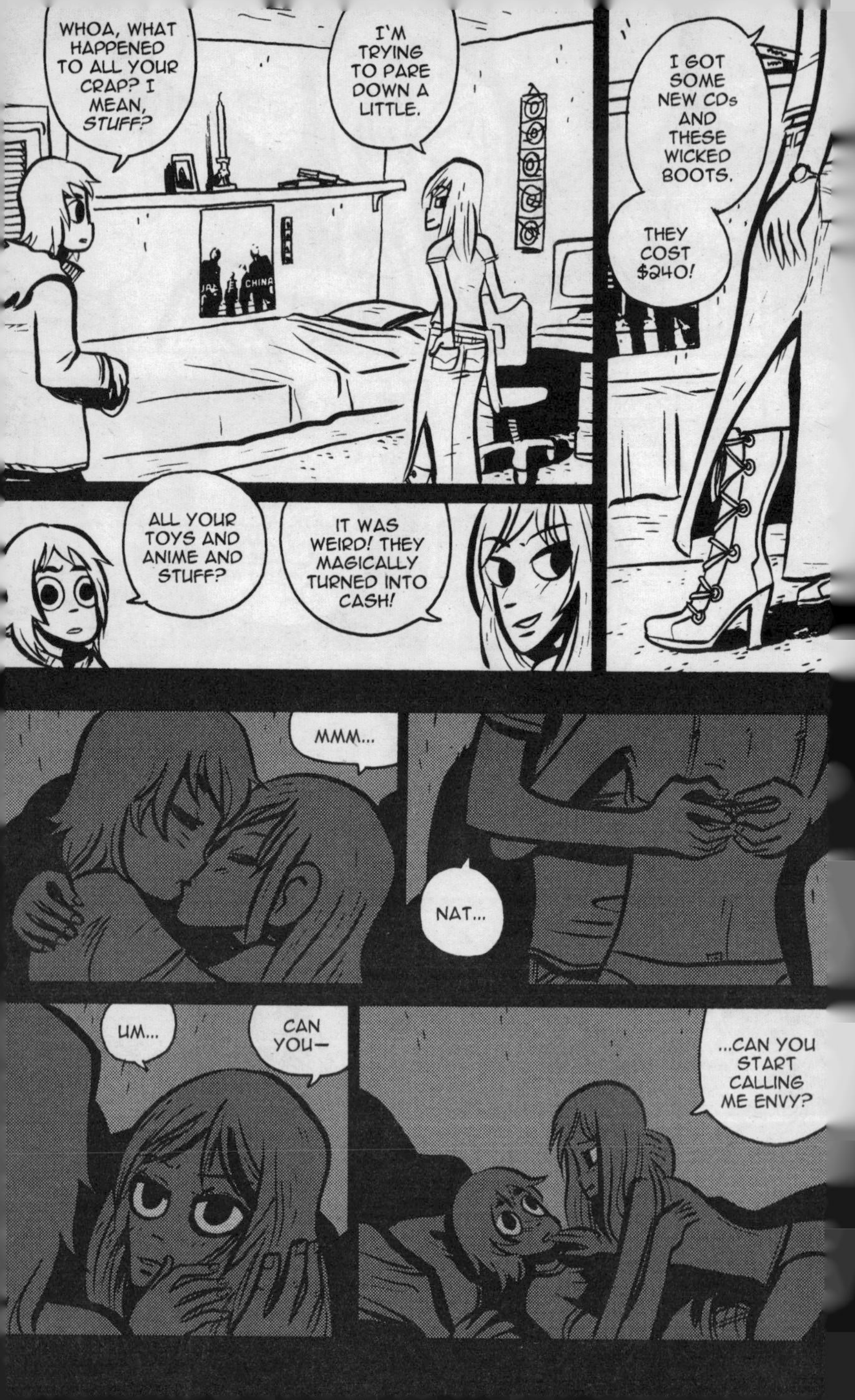
WHOA, WHAT HAPPENED TO ALL YOUR CRAP? I MEAN, STUFF?
I'M TRYING TO PARE DOWN A LITTLE.
I GOT SOME NEW CDs AND THESE WICKED BOOTS.
THEY COST $240!
ALL YOUR TOYS AND ANIME AND STUFF?
IT WAS WEIRD! THEY MAGICALLY TURNED INTO CASH!
MMM...
NAT...
UM...
CAN YOU—
...CAN YOU START CALLING ME ENVY?

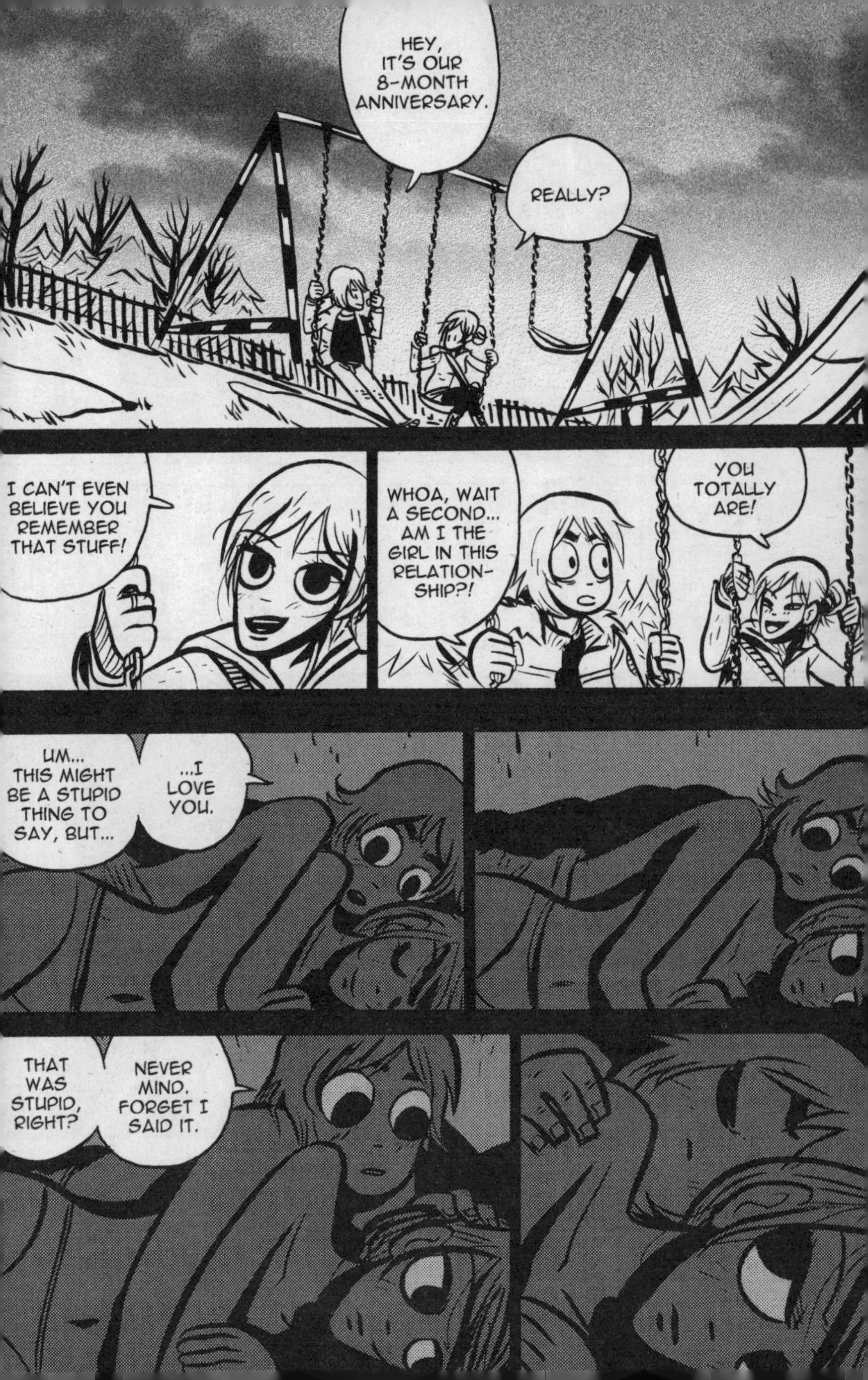
HEY, IT'S OUR 8-MONTH ANNIVERSARY.
REALLY?
I CAN'T EVEN BELIEVE YOU REMEMBER THAT STUFF!
WHOA, WAIT A SECOND... AM I THE GIRL IN THIS RELATION-SHIP?!
YOU TOTALLY ARE!
UM... THIS MIGHT BE A STUPID THING TO SAY, BUT...
...I LOVE YOU.
THAT WAS STUPID, RIGHT?
NEVER MIND. FORGET I SAID IT.

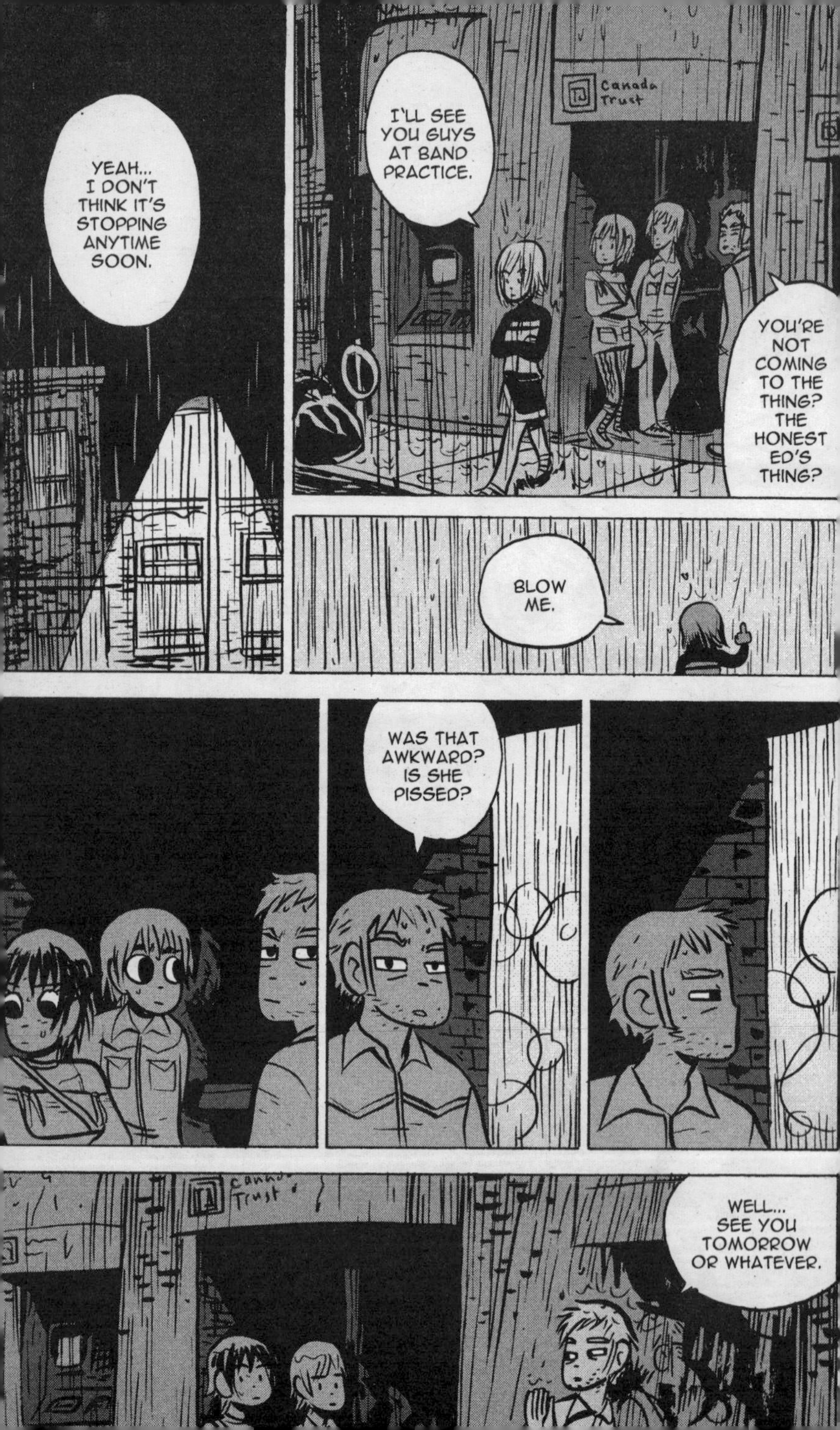
YEAH... I DON'T THINK IT'S STOPPING ANYTIME SOON.
I'LL SEE YOU GUYS AT BAND PRACTICE.
Canada Trust
YOU'RE NOT COMING TO THE THING? THE HONEST ED'S THING?
BLOW ME.
WAS THAT AWKWARD? IS SHE PISSED?
WELL... SEE YOU TOMORROW OR WHATEVER.

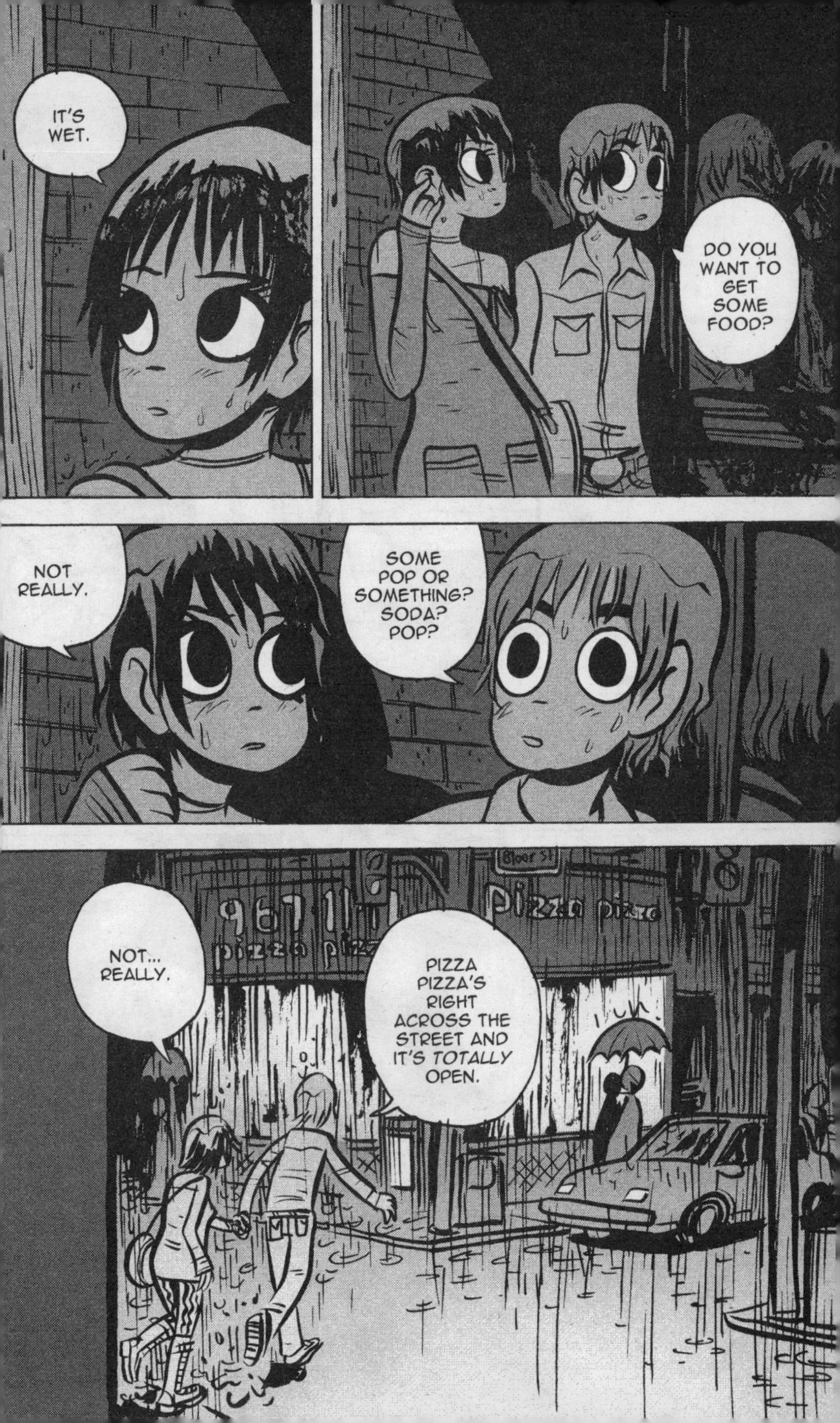
IT'S WET.
DO YOU WANT TO GET SOME FOOD?
NOT REALLY.
SOME POP OR SOMETHING? SODA? POP?
NOT... REALLY.
PIZZA PIZZA'S RIGHT ACROSS THE STREET AND IT'S *TOTALLY* OPEN.

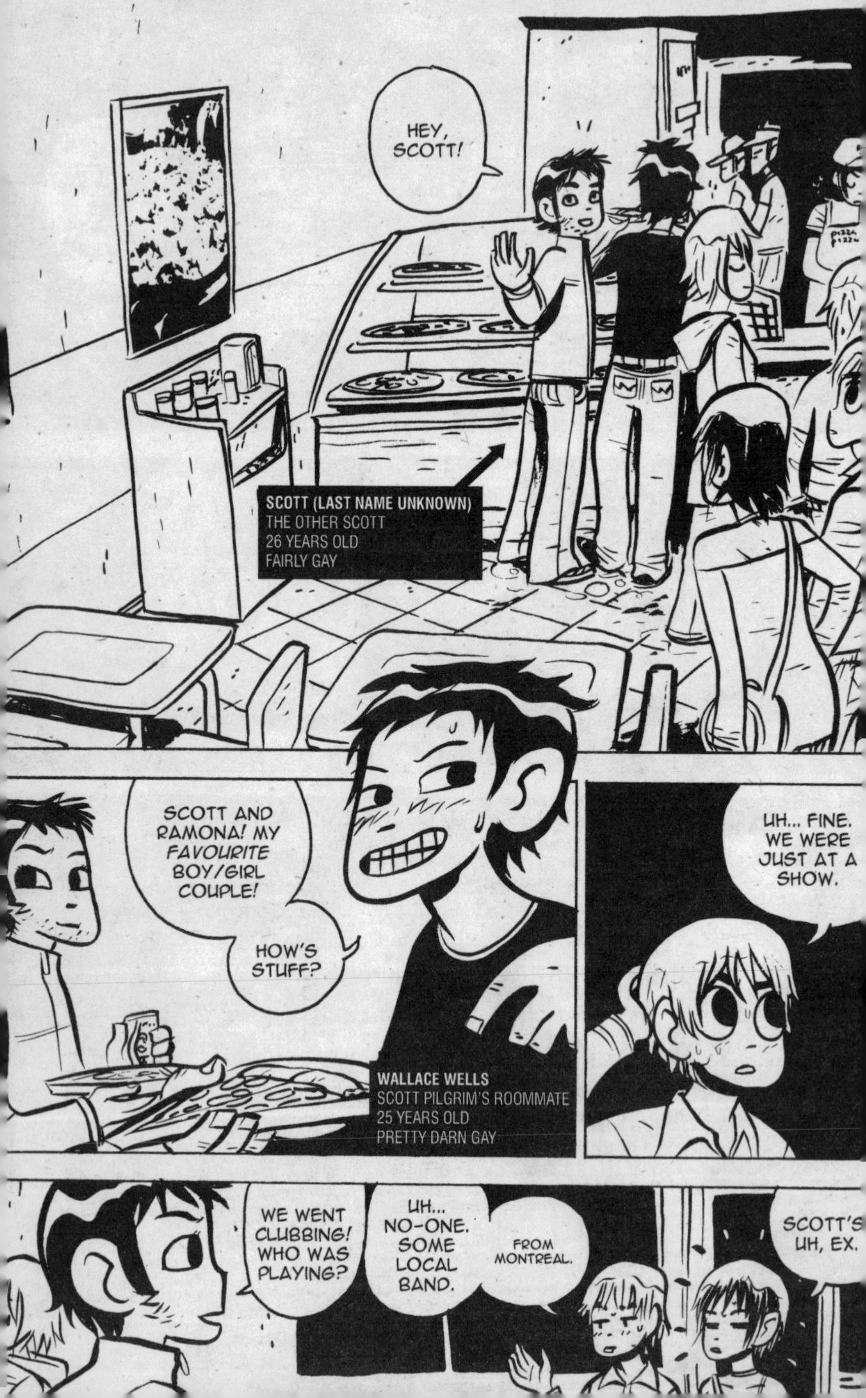
HEY, SCOTT!
SCOTT (LAST NAME UNKNOWN)
THE OTHER SCOTT
26 YEARS OLD
FAIRLY GAY
SCOTT AND RAMONA! MY FAVOURITE BOY/GIRL COUPLE!
HOW'S STUFF?
WALLACE WELLS
SCOTT PILGRIM'S ROOMMATE
25 YEARS OLD
PRETTY DARN GAY
UH... FINE. WE WERE JUST AT A SHOW.
WE WENT CLUBBING! WHO WAS PLAYING?
UH... NO-ONE. SOME LOCAL BAND.
FROM MONTREAL.
SCOTT'S UH, EX.

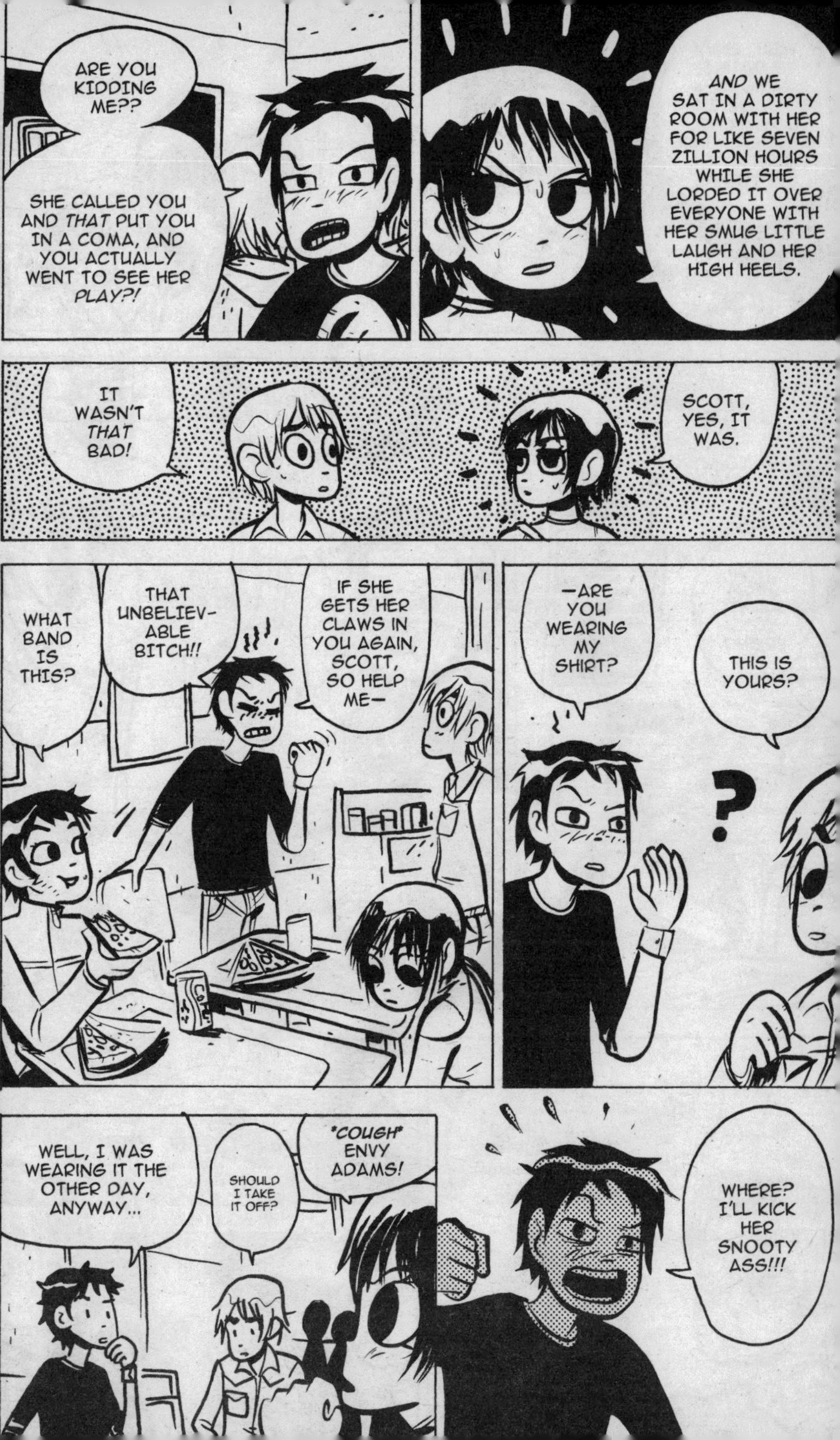
ARE YOU KIDDING ME??
SHE CALLED YOU AND *THAT* PUT YOU IN A COMA, AND YOU ACTUALLY WENT TO SEE HER *PLAY?!*
AND WE SAT IN A DIRTY ROOM WITH HER FOR LIKE SEVEN ZILLION HOURS WHILE SHE LORDED IT OVER EVERYONE WITH HER SMUG LITTLE LAUGH AND HER HIGH HEELS.
IT WASN'T *THAT* BAD!
SCOTT, YES, IT WAS.
WHAT BAND IS THIS?
THAT UNBELIEV-ABLE BITCH!!
IF SHE GETS HER CLAWS IN YOU AGAIN, SCOTT, SO HELP ME—
—ARE YOU WEARING MY SHIRT?
THIS IS YOURS?
?
WELL, I WAS WEARING IT THE OTHER DAY, ANYWAY...
SHOULD I TAKE IT OFF?
COUGH ENVY ADAMS!
WHERE? I'LL KICK HER SNOOTY ASS!!!

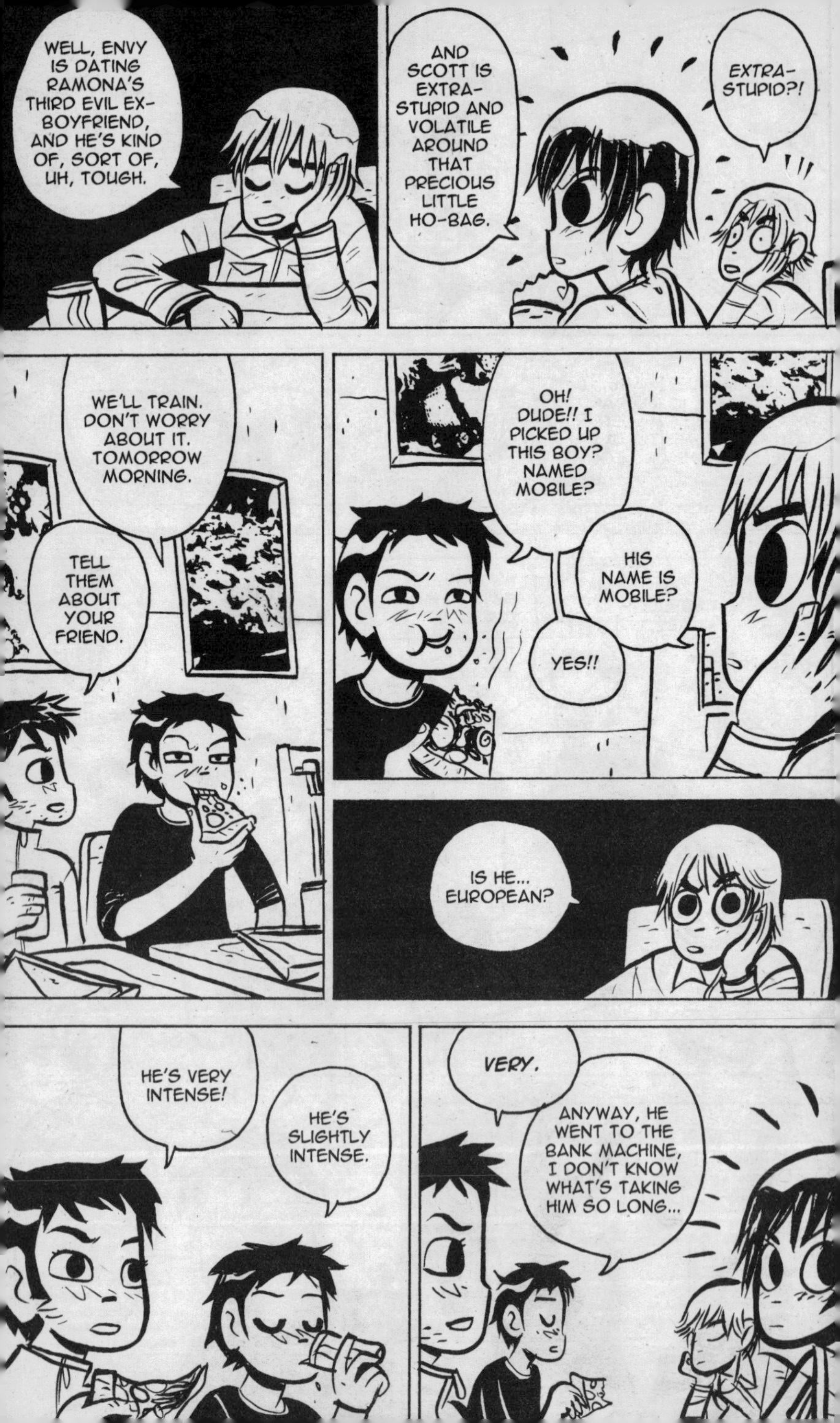
WELL, ENVY IS DATING RAMONA'S THIRD EVIL EX-BOYFRIEND, AND HE'S KIND OF, SORT OF, UH, TOUGH.
AND SCOTT IS EXTRA-STUPID AND VOLATILE AROUND THAT PRECIOUS LITTLE HO-BAG.
EXTRA-STUPID?!
WE'LL TRAIN. DON'T WORRY ABOUT IT. TOMORROW MORNING.
TELL THEM ABOUT YOUR FRIEND.
OH! DUDE!! I PICKED UP THIS BOY? NAMED MOBILE?
HIS NAME IS MOBILE?
YES!!
IS HE... EUROPEAN?
HE'S VERY INTENSE!
HE'S SLIGHTLY INTENSE.
VERY.
ANYWAY, HE WENT TO THE BANK MACHINE, I DON'T KNOW WHAT'S TAKING HIM SO LONG...

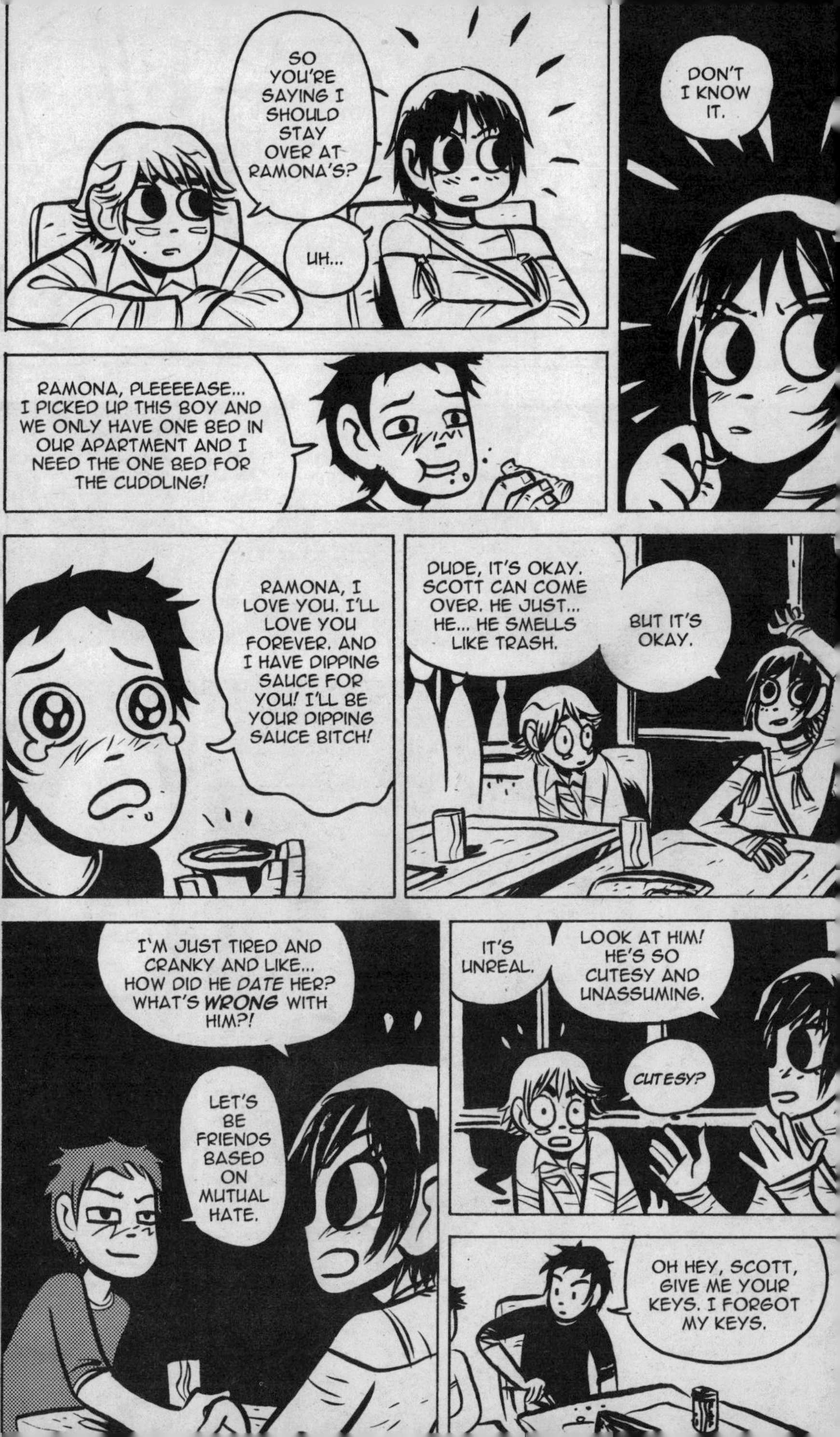
SO YOU'RE SAYING I SHOULD STAY OVER AT RAMONA'S?
UH...
DON'T I KNOW IT.
RAMONA, PLEEEEASE... I PICKED UP THIS BOY AND WE ONLY HAVE ONE BED IN OUR APARTMENT AND I NEED THE ONE BED FOR THE CUDDLING!
RAMONA, I LOVE YOU. I'LL LOVE YOU FOREVER. AND I HAVE DIPPING SAUCE FOR YOU! I'LL BE YOUR DIPPING SAUCE BITCH!
DUDE, IT'S OKAY. SCOTT CAN COME OVER. HE JUST... HE... HE SMELLS LIKE TRASH.
BUT IT'S OKAY.
I'M JUST TIRED AND CRANKY AND LIKE... HOW DID HE *DATE* HER? WHAT'S ***WRONG*** WITH HIM?!
LET'S BE FRIENDS BASED ON MUTUAL HATE.
IT'S UNREAL.
LOOK AT HIM! HE'S SO CUTESY AND UNASSUMING.
CUTESY?
OH HEY, SCOTT, GIVE ME YOUR KEYS. I FORGOT MY KEYS.

saturday morning

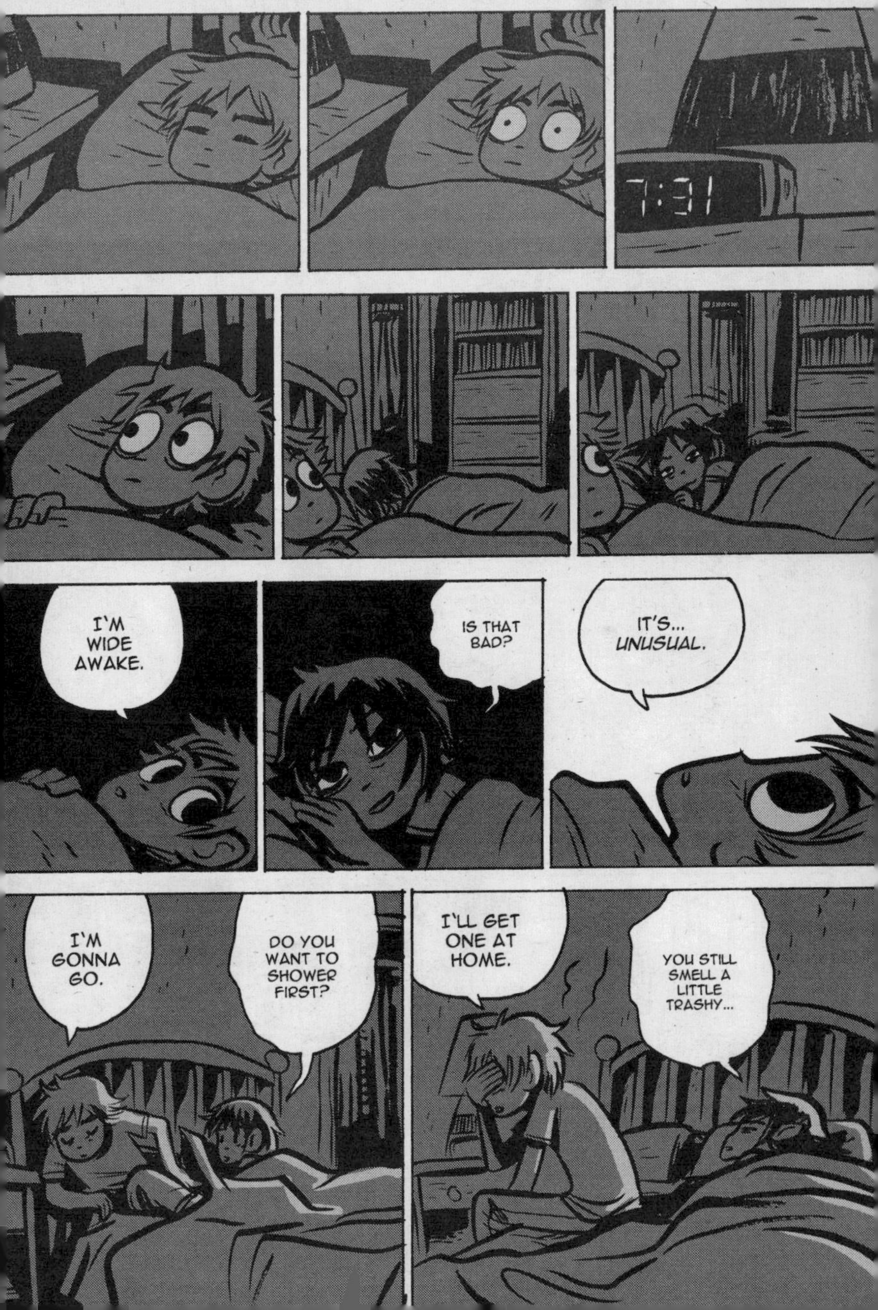

7:31
I'M WIDE AWAKE.
IS THAT BAD?
IT'S... *UNUSUAL.*
I'M GONNA GO.
DO YOU WANT TO SHOWER FIRST?
I'LL GET ONE AT HOME.
YOU STILL SMELL A LITTLE TRASHY...

14

about to e-x-p-l-o-d-e

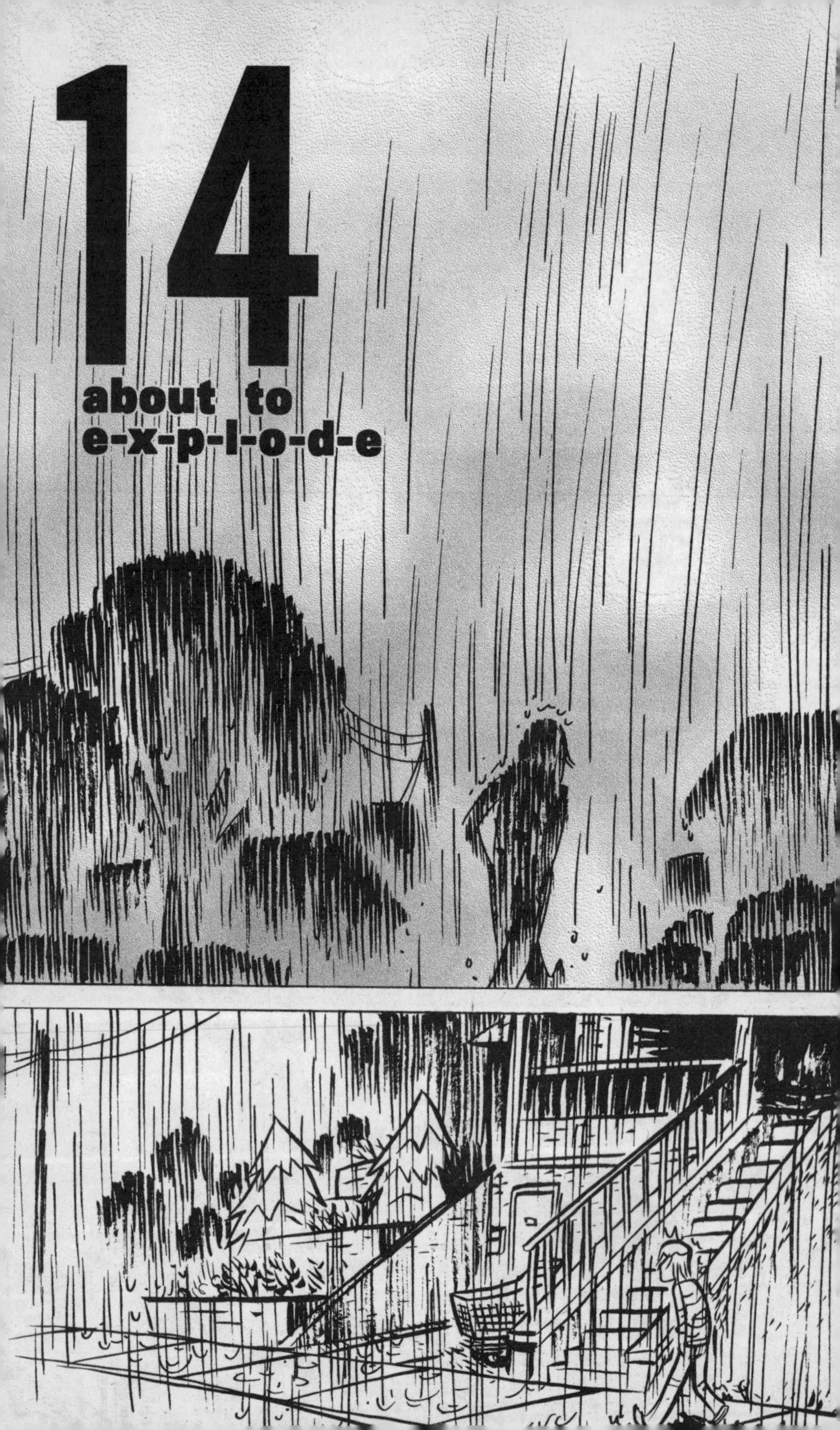

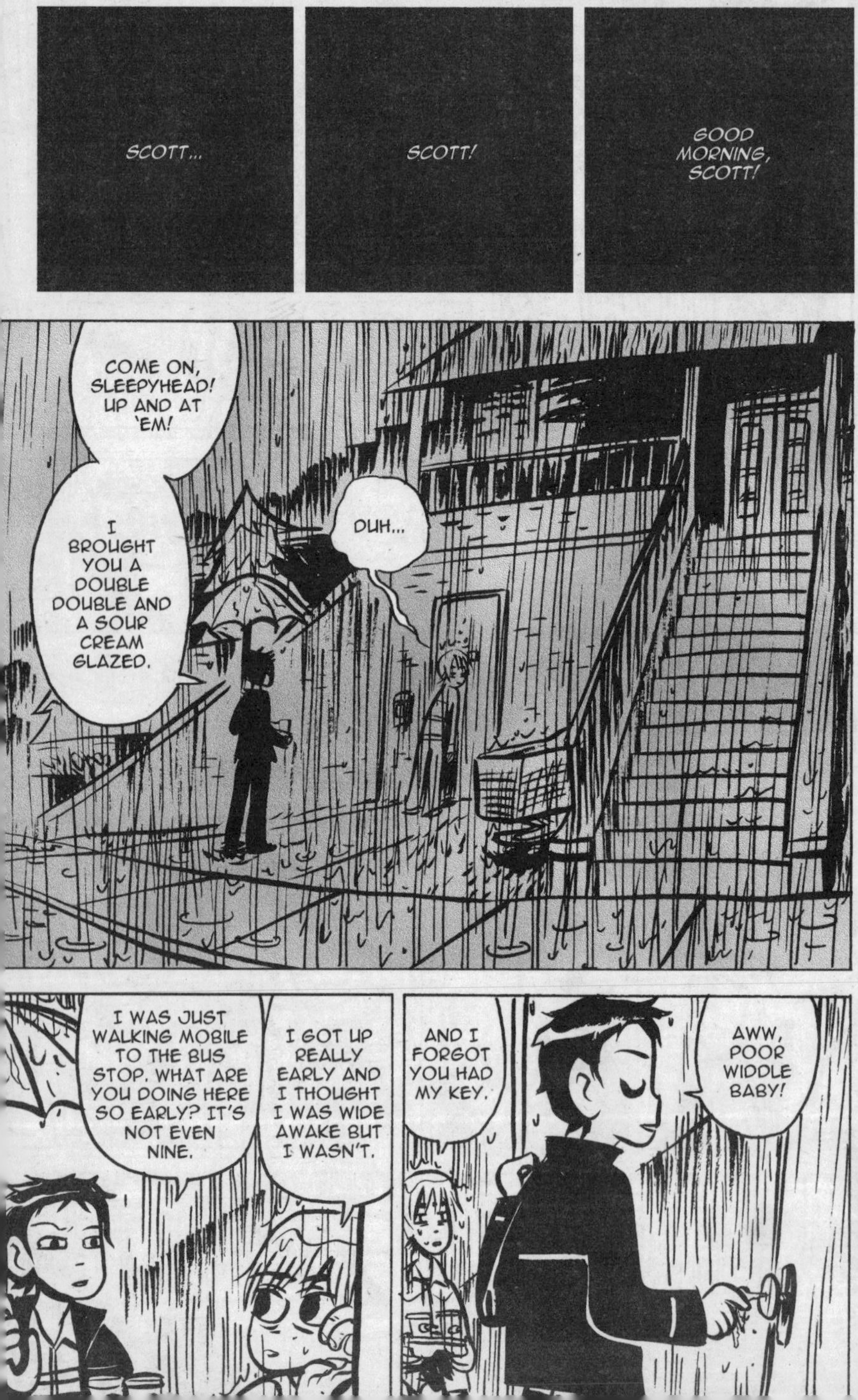
SCOTT...
SCOTT!
GOOD MORNING, SCOTT!
COME ON, SLEEPYHEAD! UP AND AT 'EM!
I BROUGHT YOU A DOUBLE DOUBLE AND A SOUR CREAM GLAZED.
DUH...
I WAS JUST WALKING MOBILE TO THE BUS STOP. WHAT ARE YOU DOING HERE SO EARLY? IT'S NOT EVEN NINE.
I GOT UP REALLY EARLY AND I THOUGHT I WAS WIDE AWAKE BUT I WASN'T.
AND I FORGOT YOU HAD MY KEY.
AWW, POOR WIDDLE BABY!

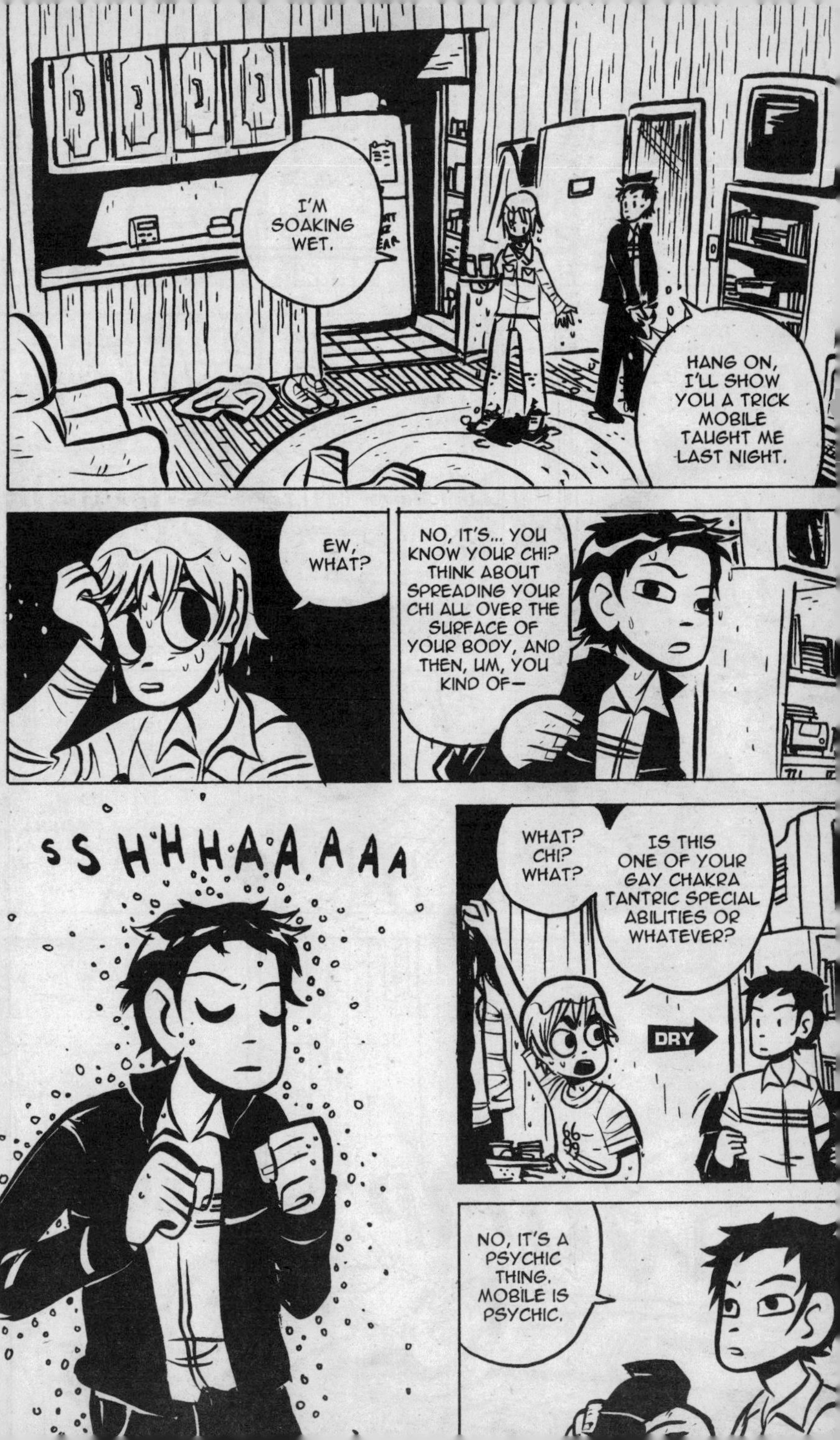
I'M SOAKING WET.
HANG ON, I'LL SHOW YOU A TRICK MOBILE TAUGHT ME LAST NIGHT.
EW, WHAT?
NO, IT'S... YOU KNOW YOUR CHI? THINK ABOUT SPREADING YOUR CHI ALL OVER THE SURFACE OF YOUR BODY, AND THEN, UM, YOU KIND OF—
SSHHHAAAAAA
WHAT? CHI? WHAT?
IS THIS ONE OF YOUR GAY CHAKRA TANTRIC SPECIAL ABILITIES OR WHATEVER?
DRY
NO, IT'S A PSYCHIC THING. MOBILE IS PSYCHIC.

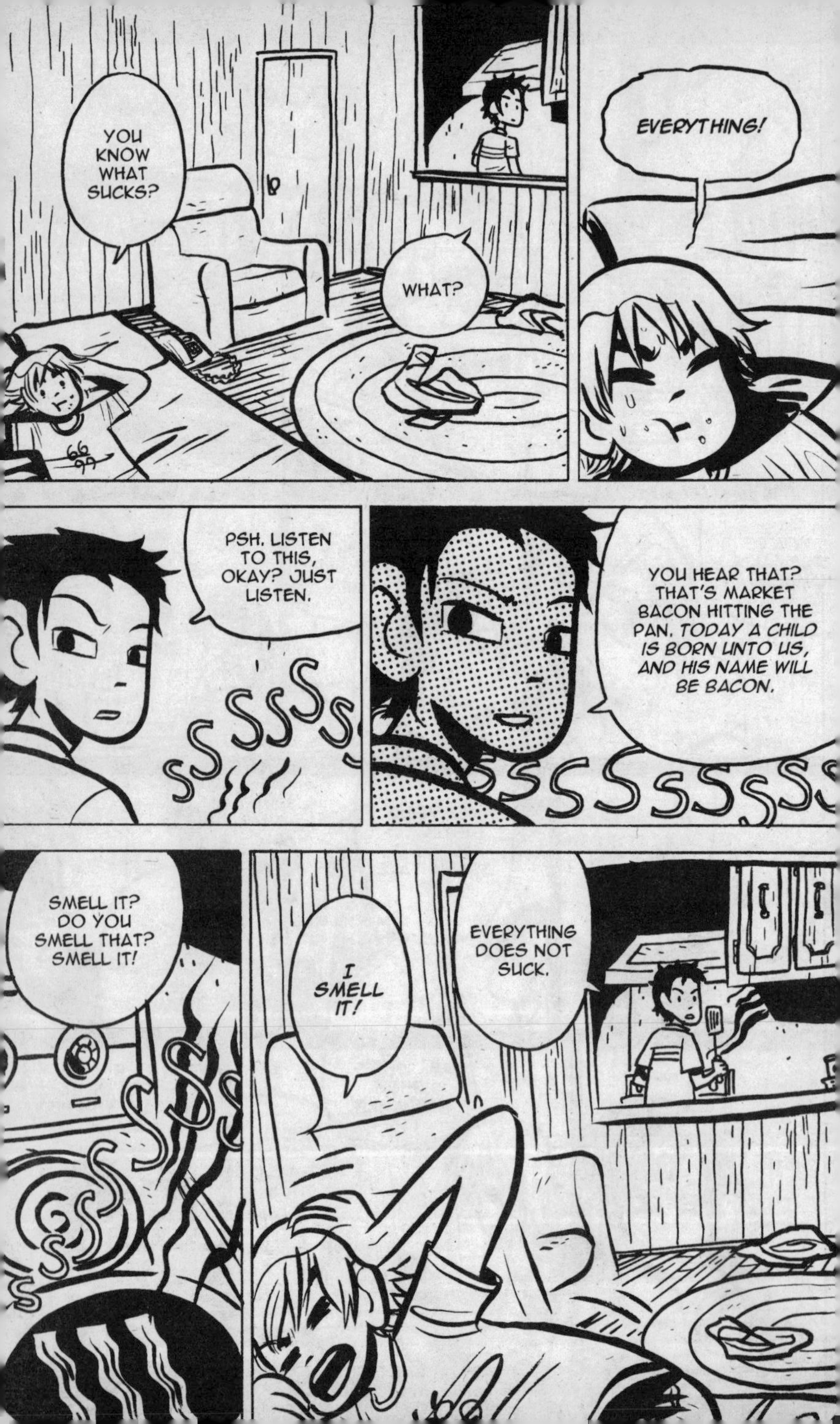

YOU KNOW WHAT SUCKS?
WHAT?
EVERYTHING!
PSH. LISTEN TO THIS, OKAY? JUST LISTEN.
SSSSS
YOU HEAR THAT? THAT'S MARKET BACON HITTING THE PAN. *TODAY A CHILD IS BORN UNTO US, AND HIS NAME WILL BE BACON.*
SSSSSSSSSS
SMELL IT? DO YOU SMELL THAT? SMELL IT!
I SMELL IT!
EVERYTHING DOES NOT SUCK.

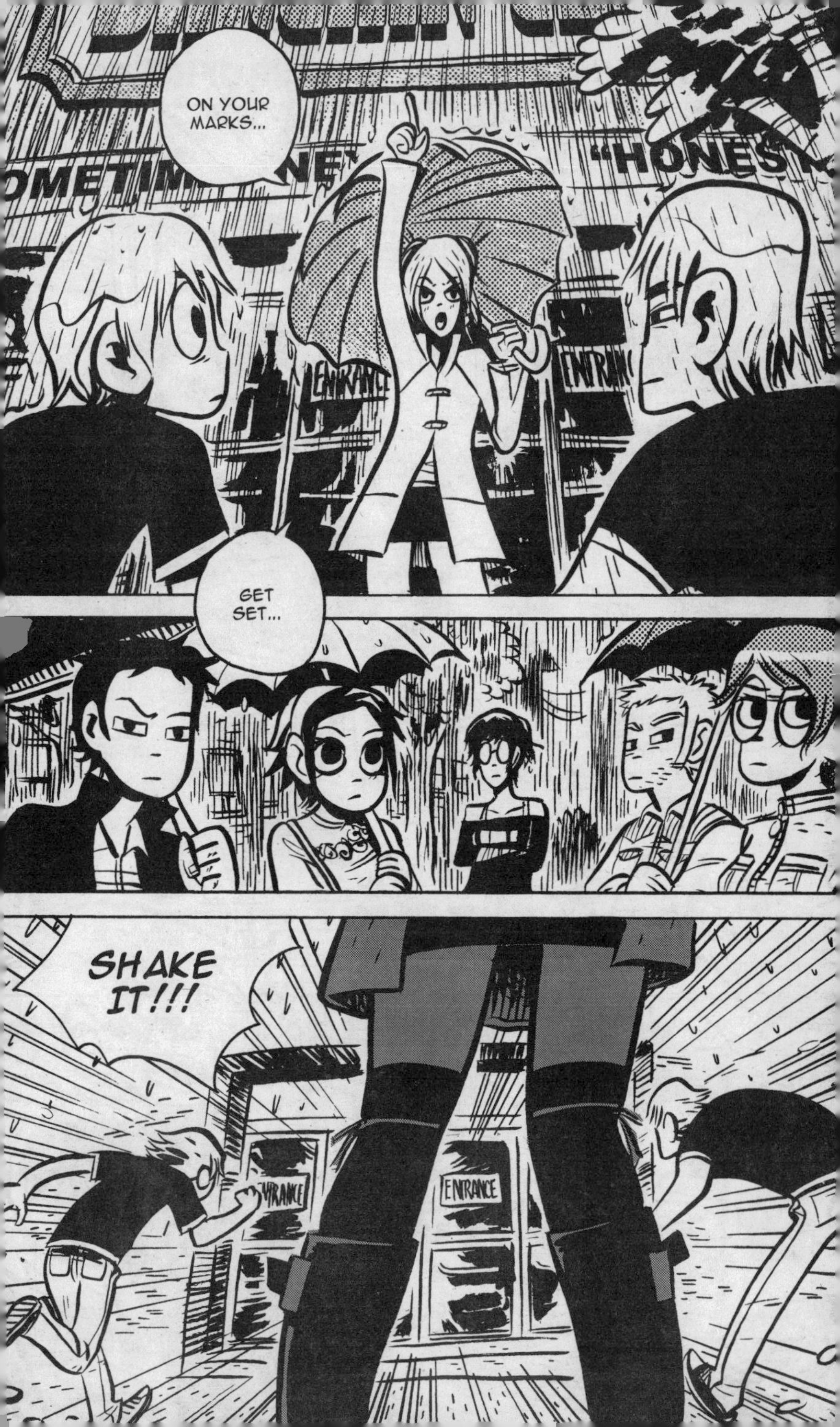
ON YOUR MARKS...
GET SET...
SHAKE IT!!!

THE STARK EXISTENTIAL HORROR OF HONEST ED'

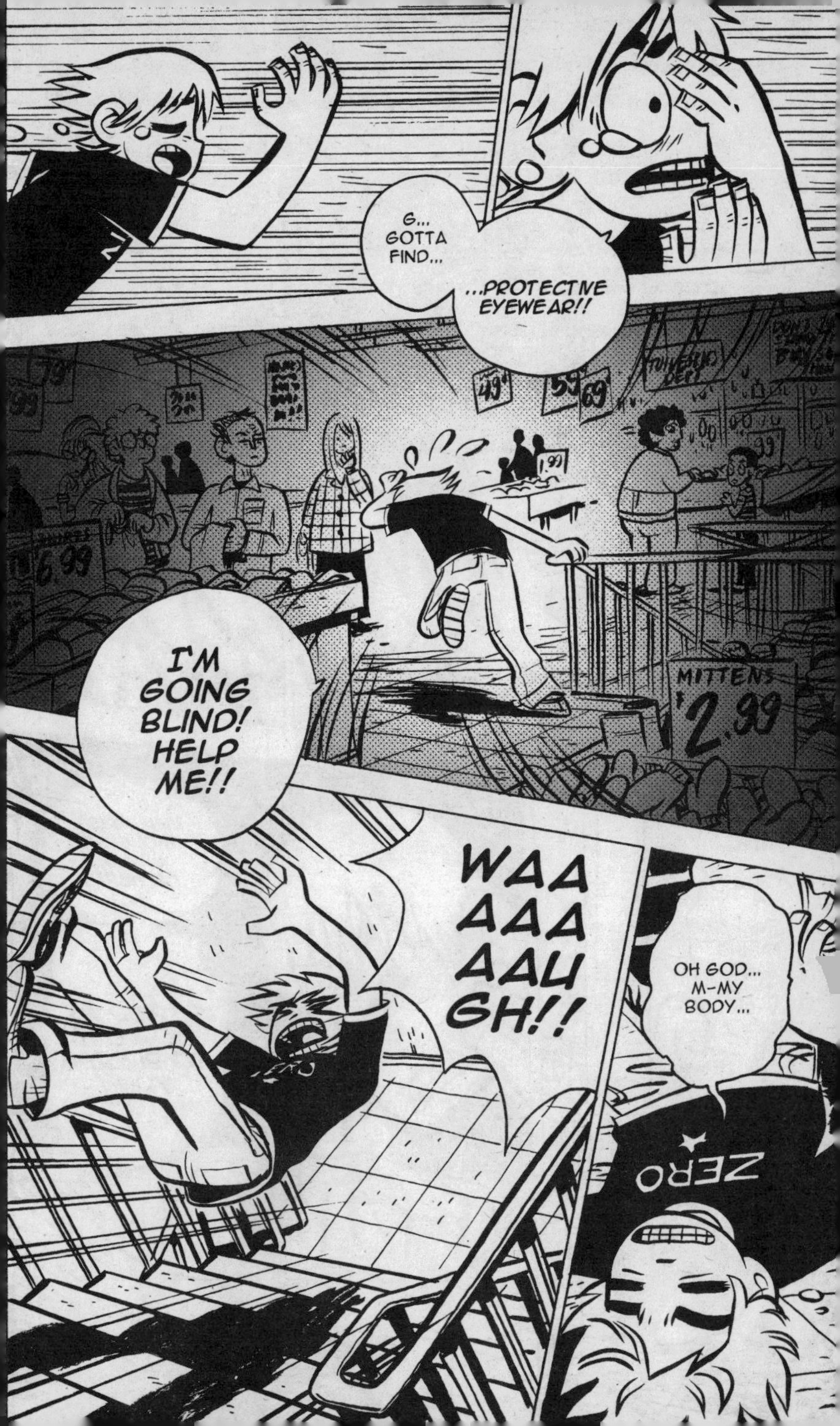
G... GOTTA FIND...
...PROTECTIVE EYEWEAR!!
MITTENS $2.99
I'M GOING BLIND! HELP ME!!
WAAAAAAAAUGH!!
OH GOD... M-MY BODY...
ZERO

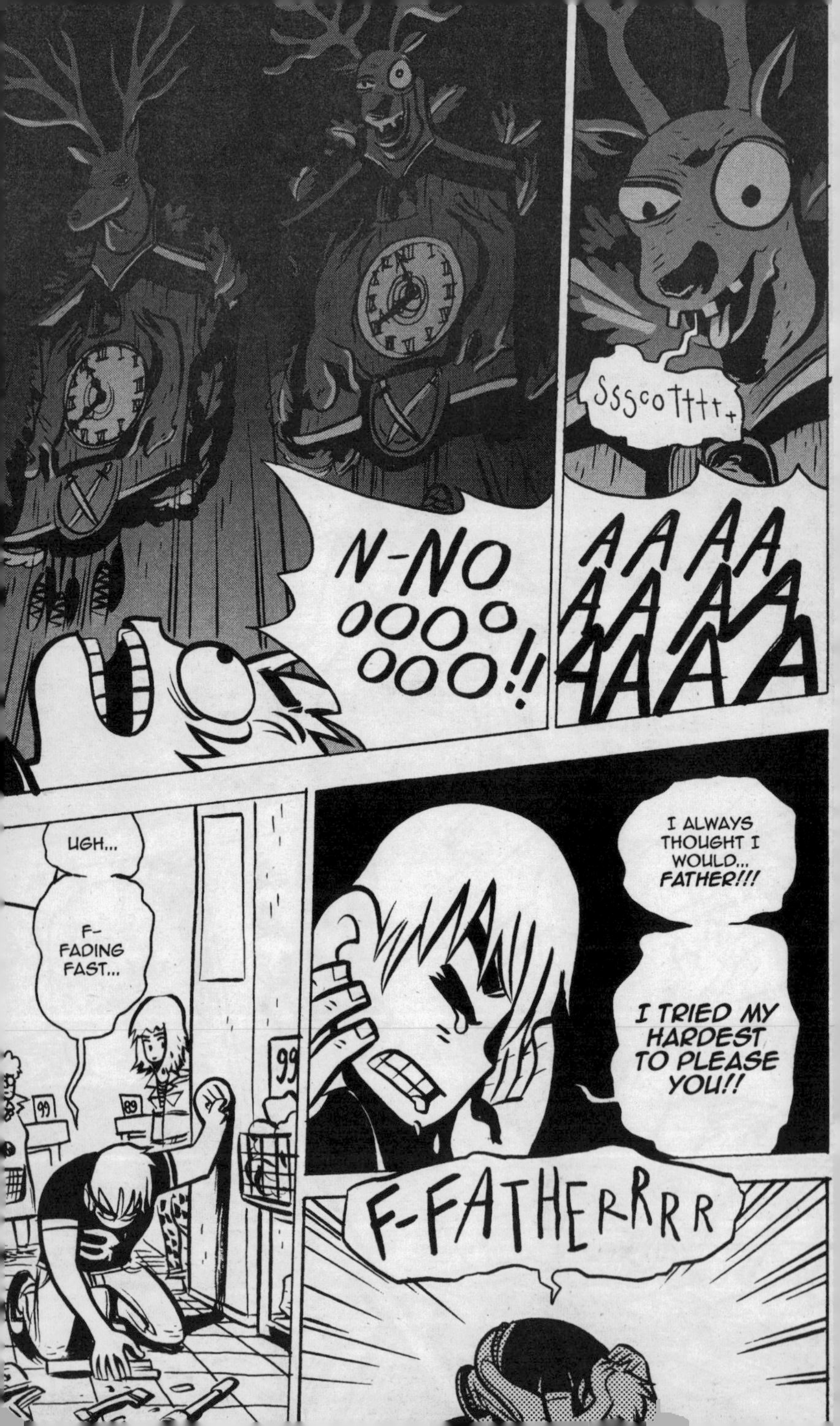
Sssco†††††
N-NO OOOO OOO!!
AAAAAAAAAAAA
UGH...
F- FADING FAST...
I ALWAYS THOUGHT I WOULD... FATHER!!!
I TRIED MY HARDEST TO PLEASE YOU!!
F-FATHERRRRR

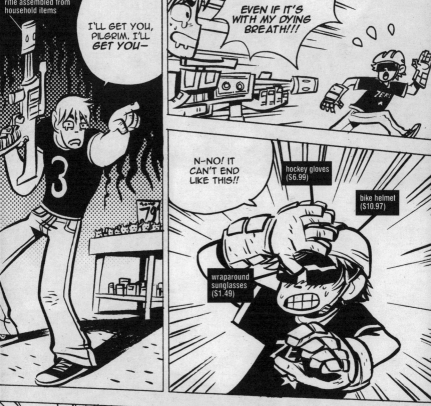

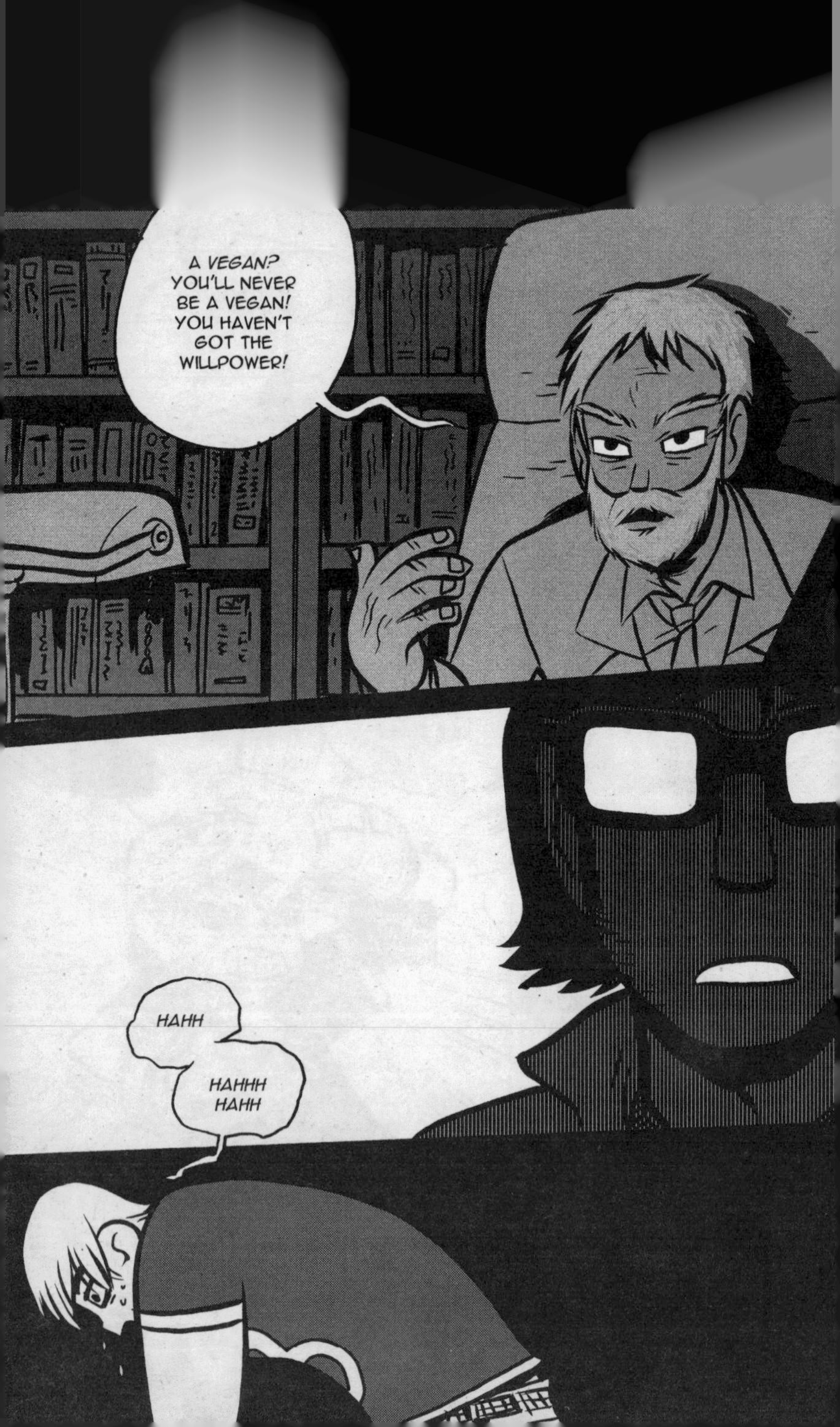
A VEGAN? YOU'LL NEVER BE A VEGAN! YOU HAVEN'T GOT THE WILLPOWER!
HAHH
HAHHH HAHH

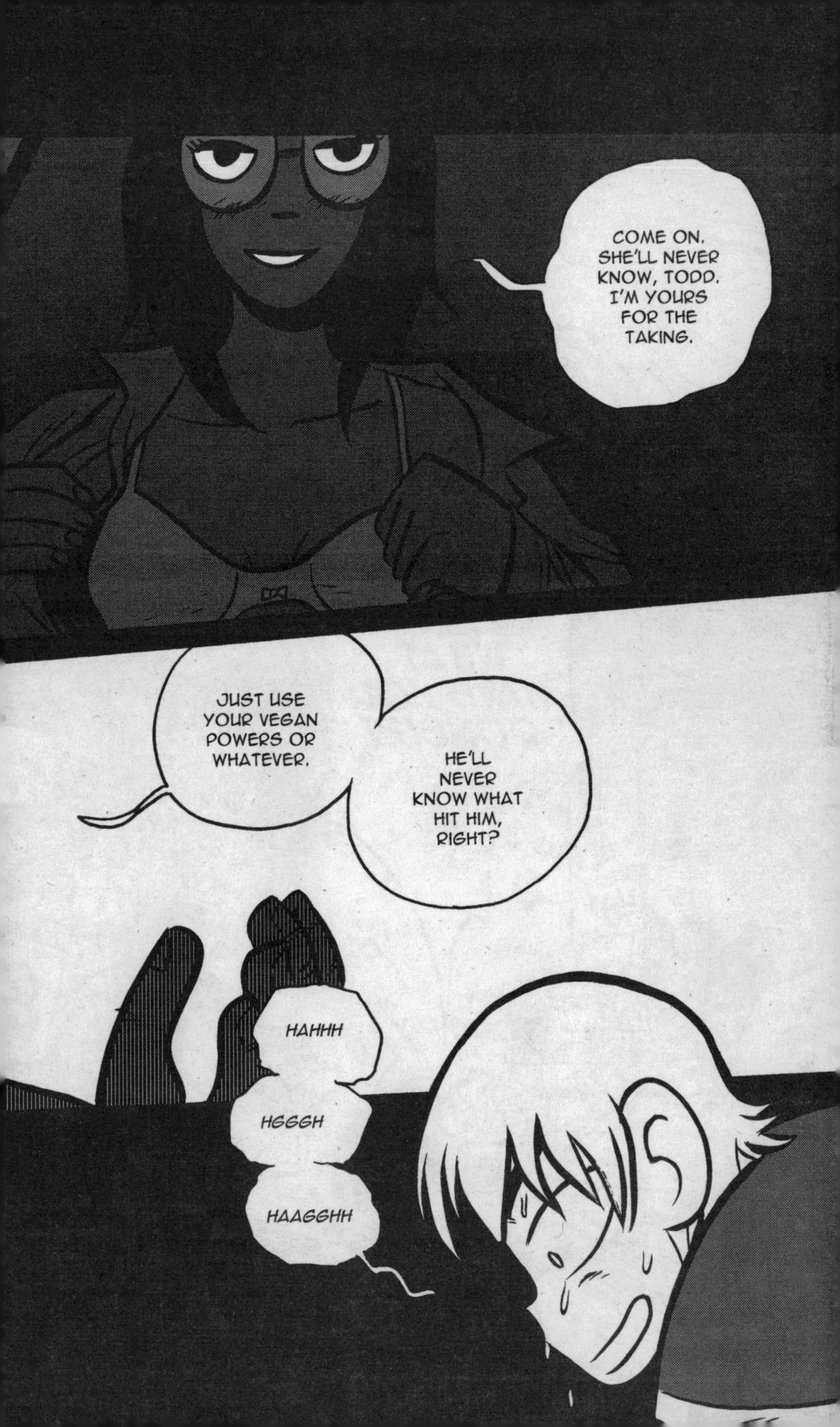
COME ON. SHE'LL NEVER KNOW, TODD. I'M YOURS FOR THE TAKING.
JUST USE YOUR VEGAN POWERS OR WHATEVER.
HE'LL NEVER KNOW WHAT HIT HIM, RIGHT?
HAHHH
HGGGH
HAAGGHH

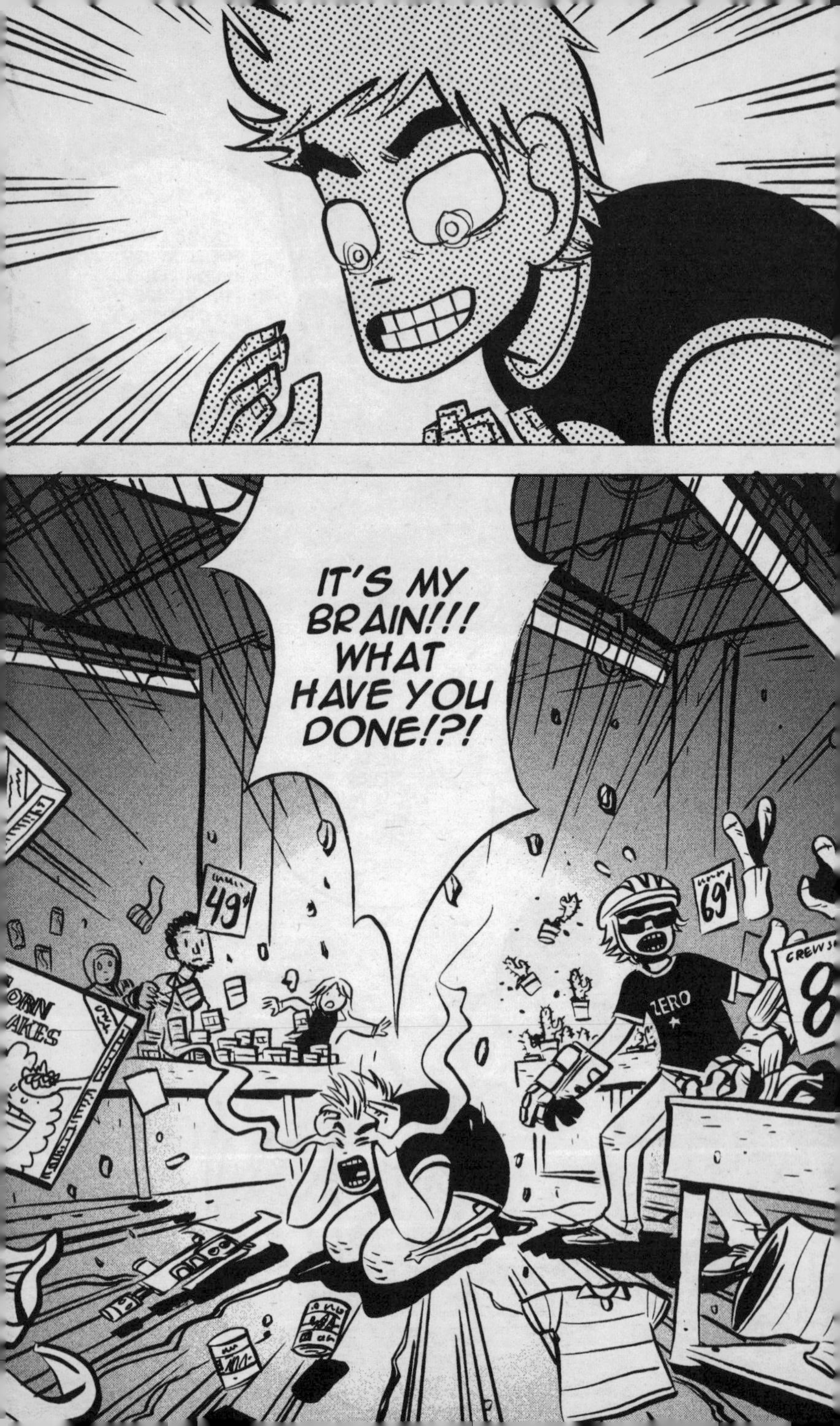
IT'S MY BRAIN!!! WHAT HAVE YOU DONE!?!
49¢
69¢
ZERO

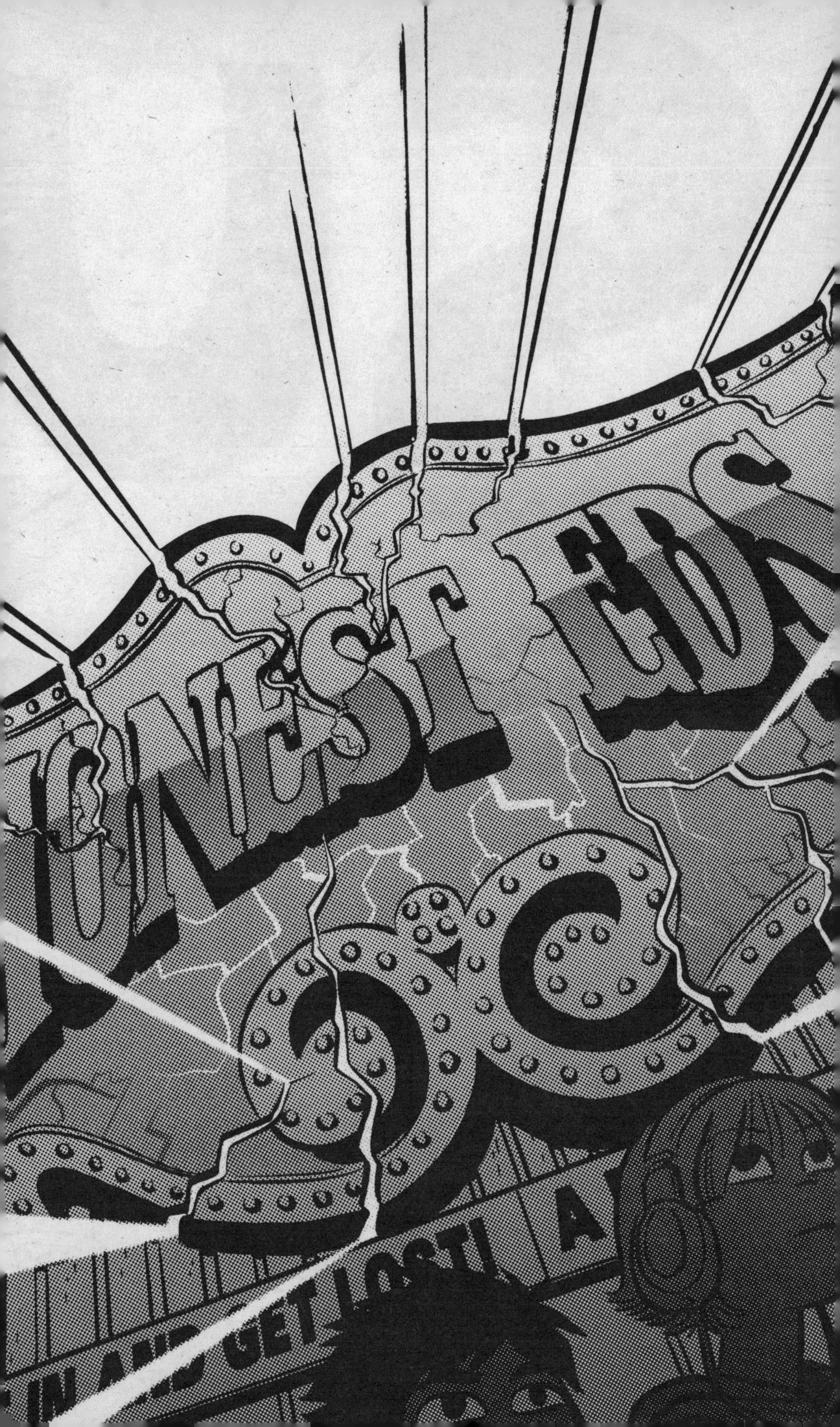
IN AND GET LOST!

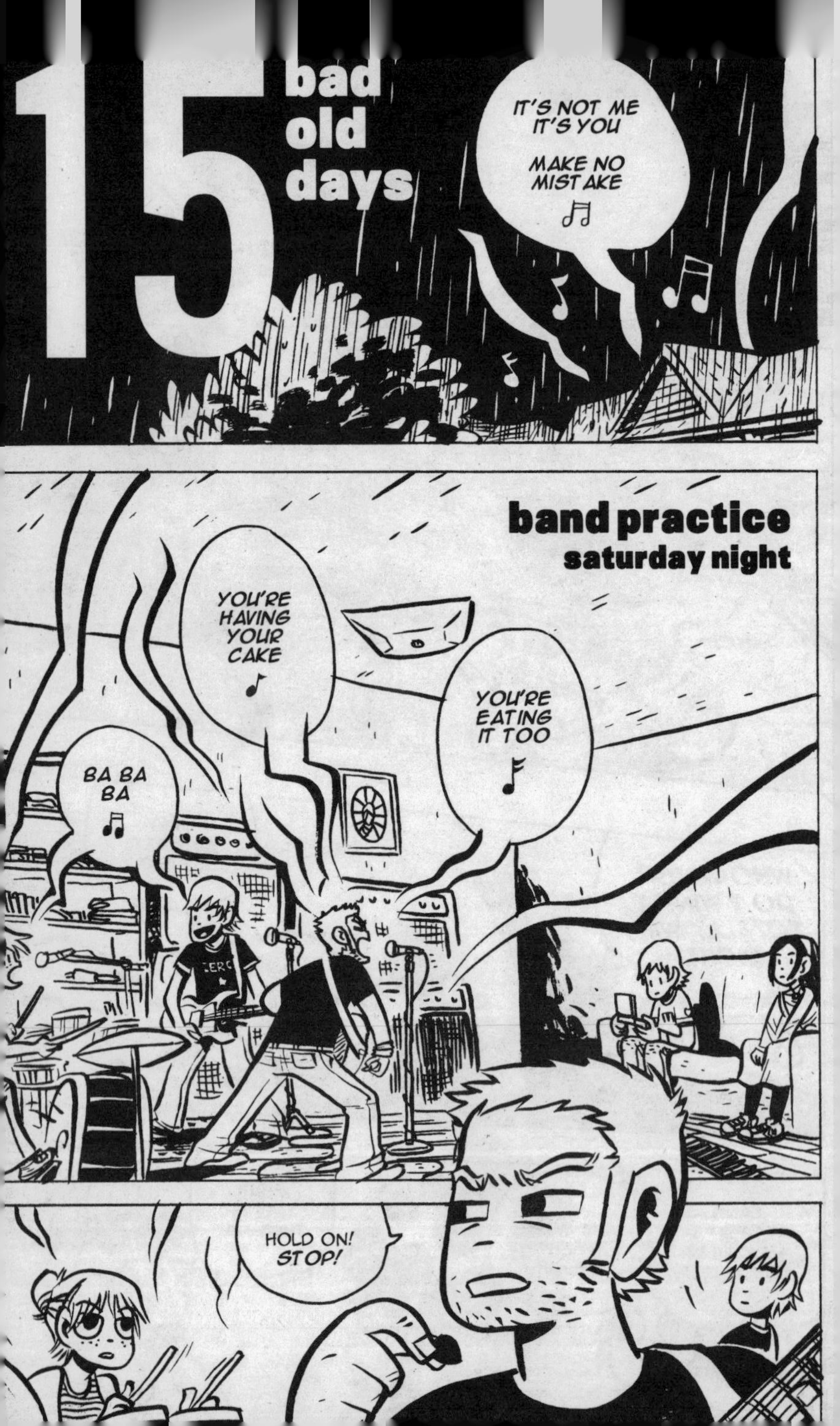
15
bad old days
IT'S NOT ME IT'S YOU
MAKE NO MISTAKE
band practice
saturday night
BA BA BA
YOU'RE HAVING YOUR CAKE
YOU'RE EATING IT TOO
ZERO
HOLD ON! STOP!

saturday night (later)

THIS IS MY FAVOURITE THING TO EAT *EVER*. OH MY GOD, I'M DROOLING. I'M SORRY.

NO I'M NOT.

WHAT IS IT?

SNAP!

IT'S LIKE A WHOLE BUNCH OF RAW SALMON ON A BED OF SUSHI RICE, AND A PILE OF THESE LITTLE EGGY THINGS!

SALMON IKURA DON

WE DON'T EAT HERE VERY OFTEN, THOUGH. WALLACE ALWAYS GETS LIKE A BAZILLION SUSHIS AND WE CAN'T REALLY AFFORD IT.

SO HOW ARE WE AFFORDING IT TODAY? AM I PAYING?

NO, IT'S COOL. I BORROWED WALLACE'S CREDIT CARD.

WHAT? YOU'RE A JERK!

I'M NOT! I'M NOT. WE HAVE AN UNDER-STANDING.

AS IN, HE UNDER-STANDS THAT YOU'RE A FREE-LOADER?

MAYBE...

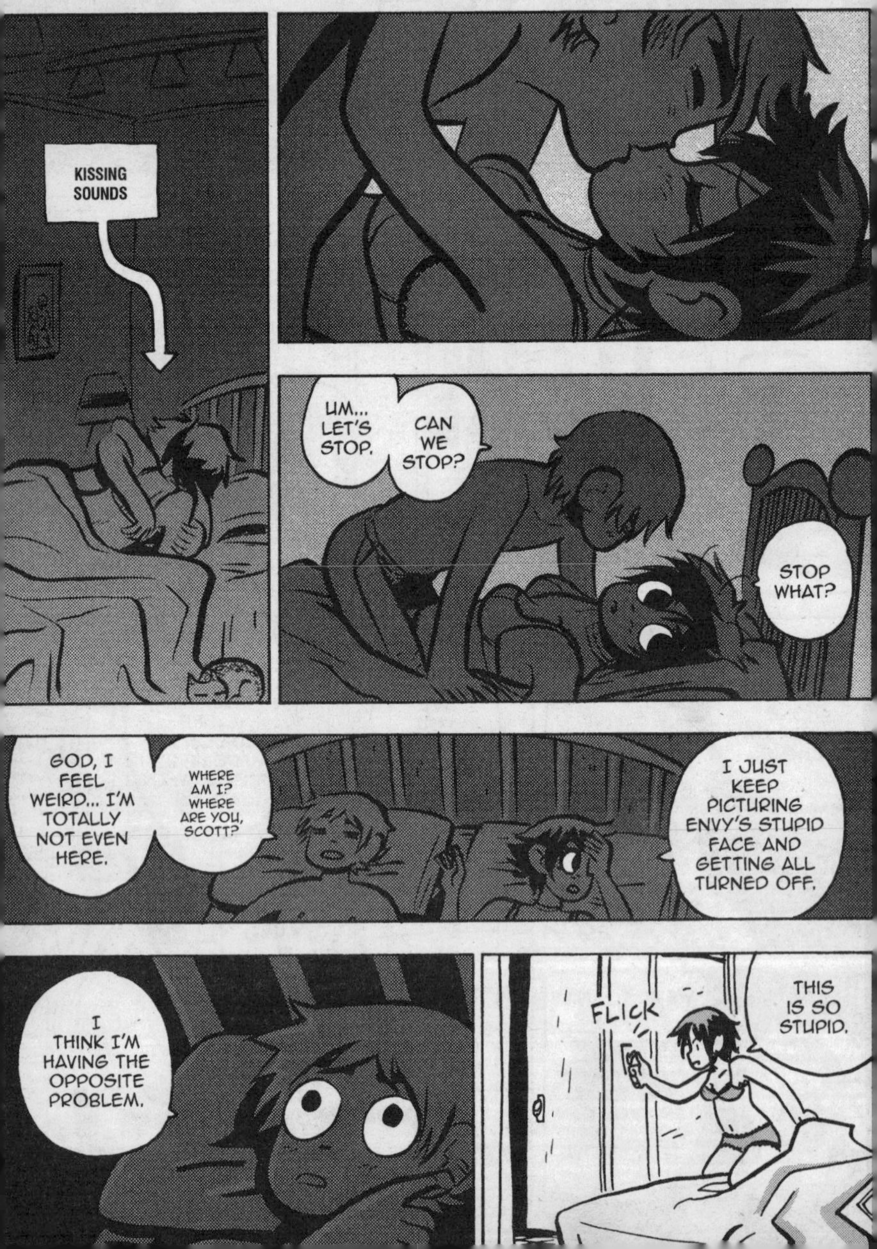
KISSING SOUNDS
UM... LET'S STOP.
CAN WE STOP?
STOP WHAT?
GOD, I FEEL WEIRD... I'M TOTALLY NOT EVEN HERE.
WHERE AM I? WHERE ARE YOU, SCOTT?
I JUST KEEP PICTURING ENVY'S STUPID FACE AND GETTING ALL TURNED OFF.
I THINK I'M HAVING THE OPPOSITE PROBLEM.
FLICK
THIS IS SO STUPID.

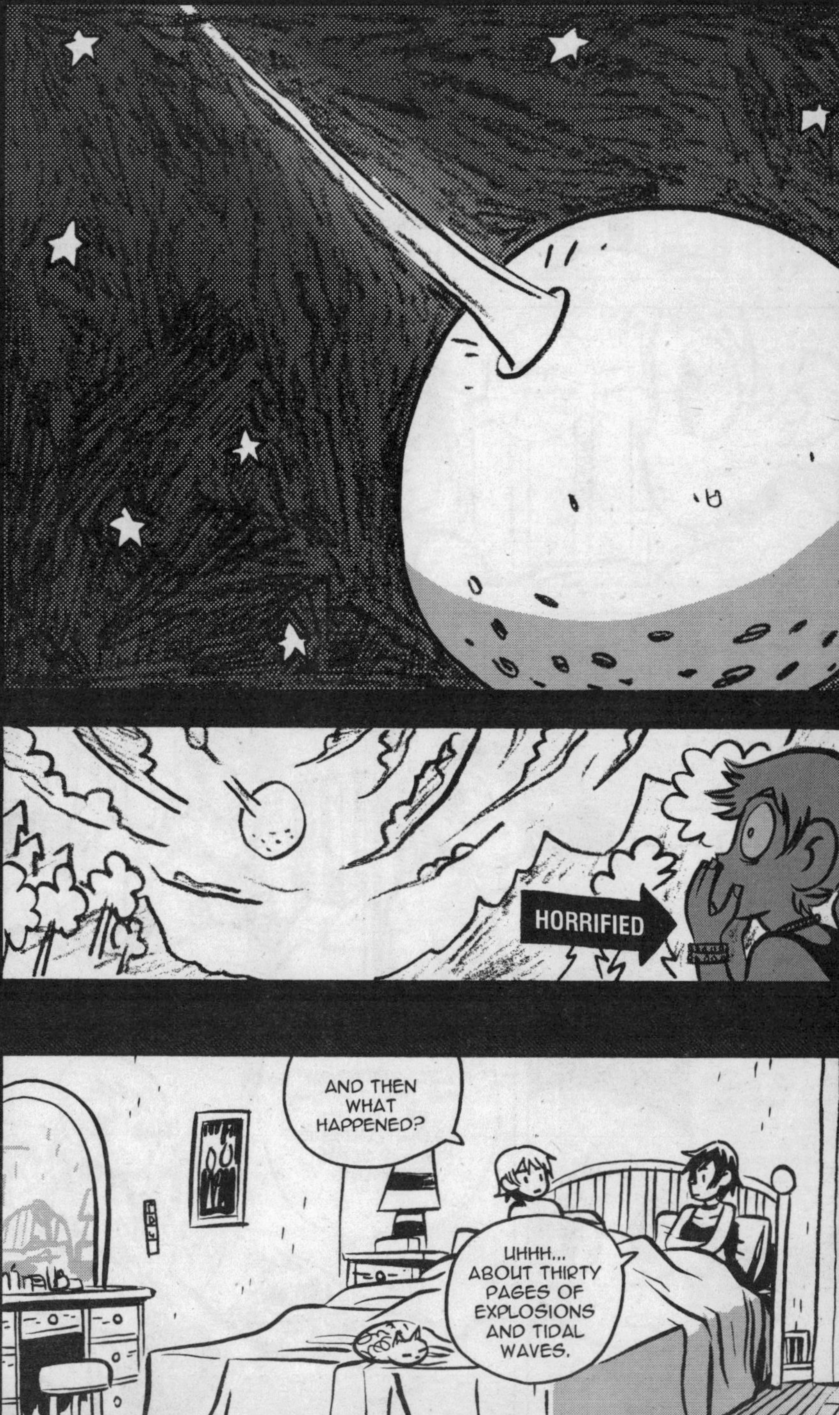
HORRIFIED
AND THEN WHAT HAPPENED?
UHHH... ABOUT THIRTY PAGES OF EXPLOSIONS AND TIDAL WAVES.

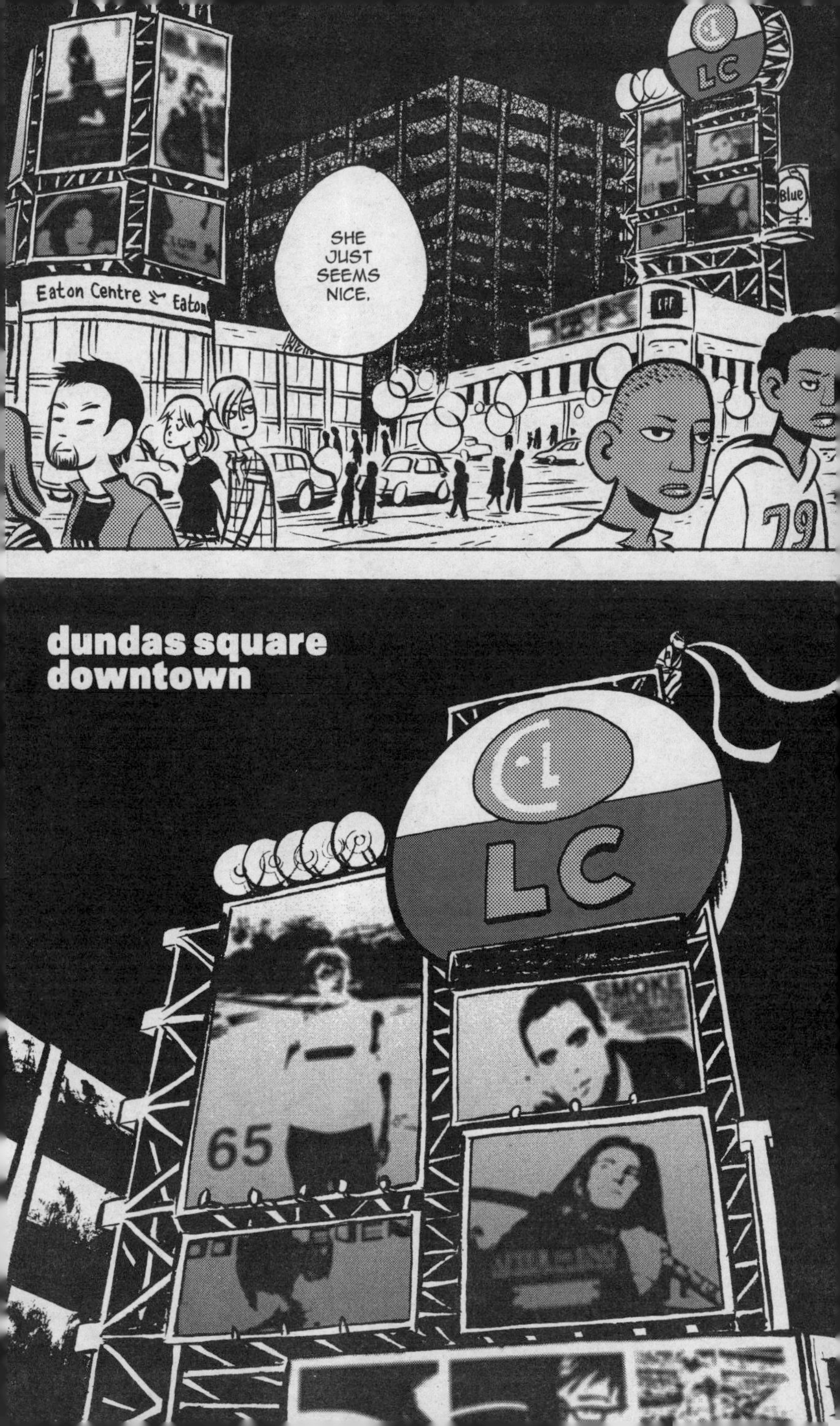
SHE JUST SEEMS NICE.
Eaton Centre
Eaton
LC
Blue
79
dundas square
downtown
LC
SMOKE
65

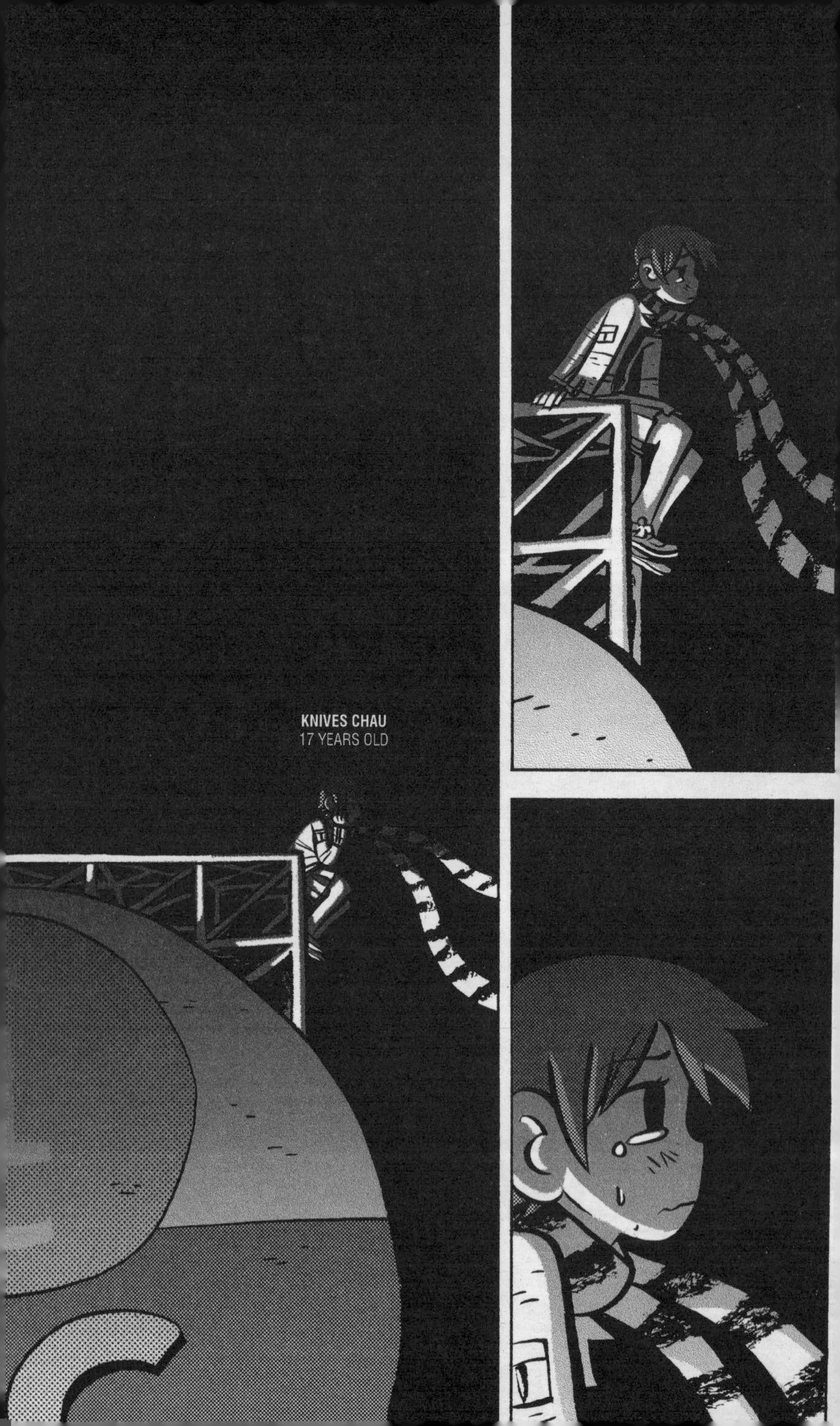
KNIVES CHAU
17 YEARS OLD

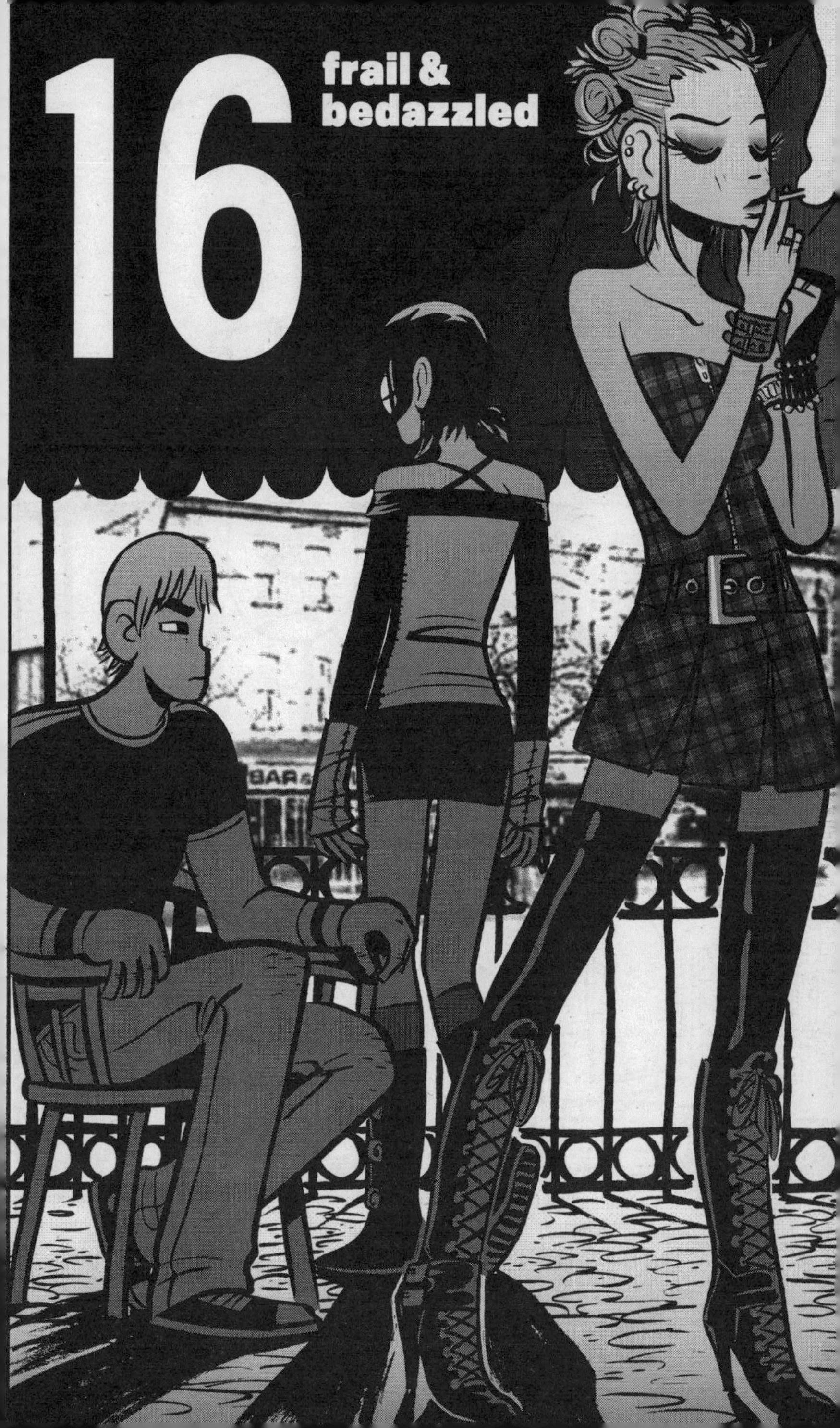
16
frail & bedazzled
BAR

sunday noonish

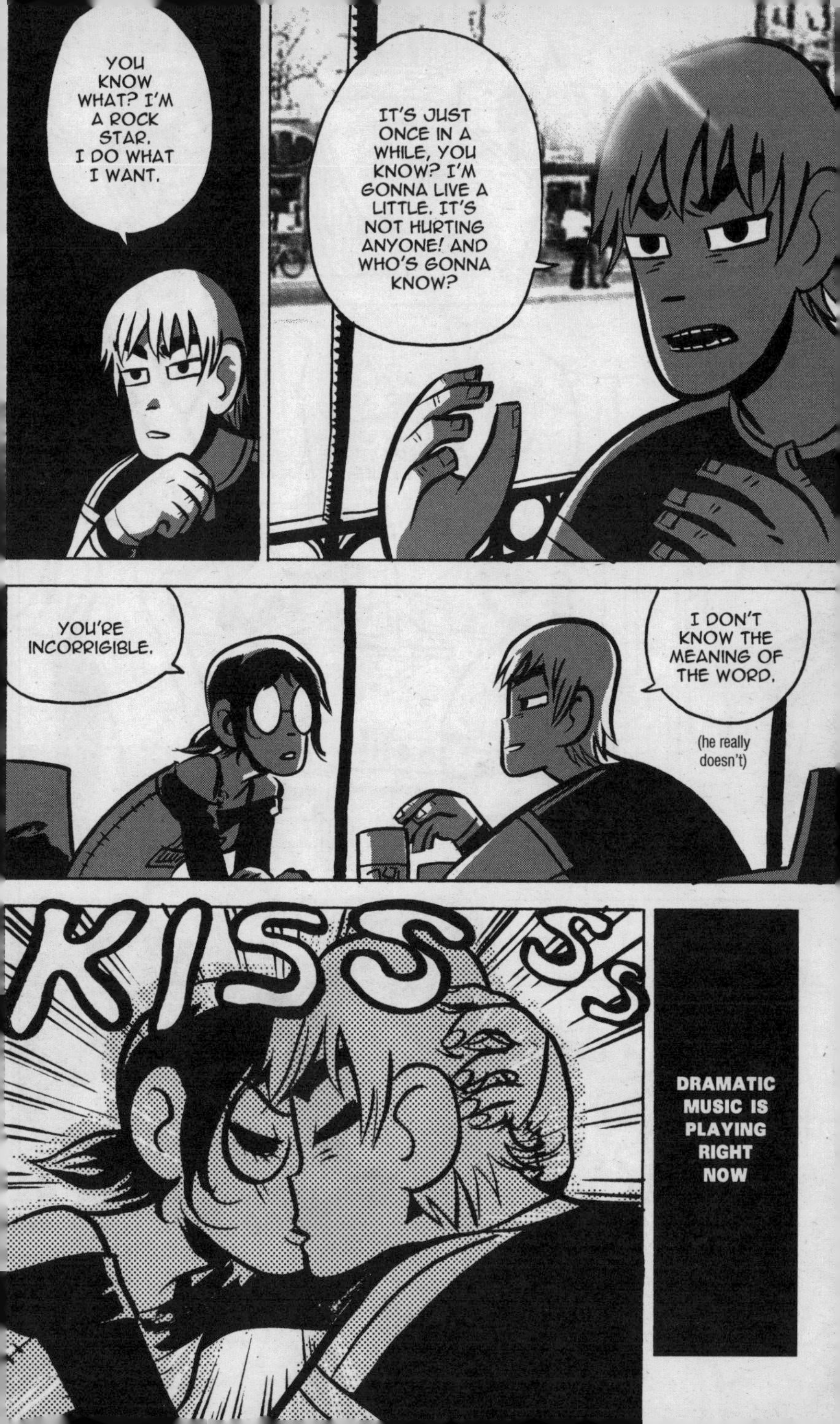
YOU KNOW WHAT? I'M A ROCK STAR. I DO WHAT I WANT.
IT'S JUST ONCE IN A WHILE, YOU KNOW? I'M GONNA LIVE A LITTLE. IT'S NOT HURTING ANYONE! AND WHO'S GONNA KNOW?
YOU'RE INCORRIGIBLE.
I DON'T KNOW THE MEANING OF THE WORD.
(he really doesn't)
KISSSS
DRAMATIC MUSIC IS PLAYING RIGHT NOW

passed

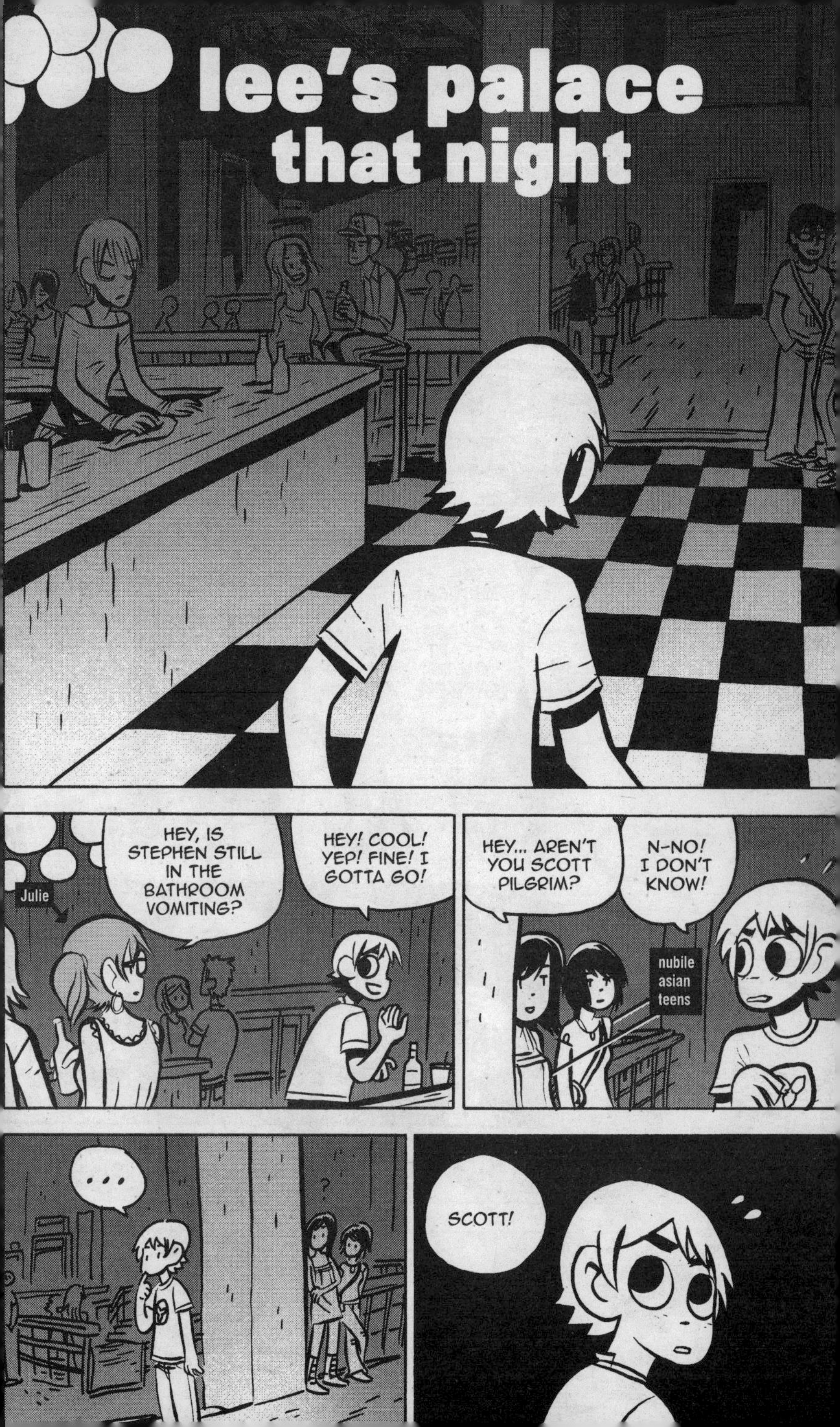
lee's palace
that night
Julie
HEY, IS STEPHEN STILL IN THE BATHROOM VOMITING?
HEY! COOL! YEP! FINE! I GOTTA GO!
HEY... AREN'T YOU SCOTT PILGRIM?
N-NO! I DON'T KNOW!
nubile asian teens
...
?
SCOTT!

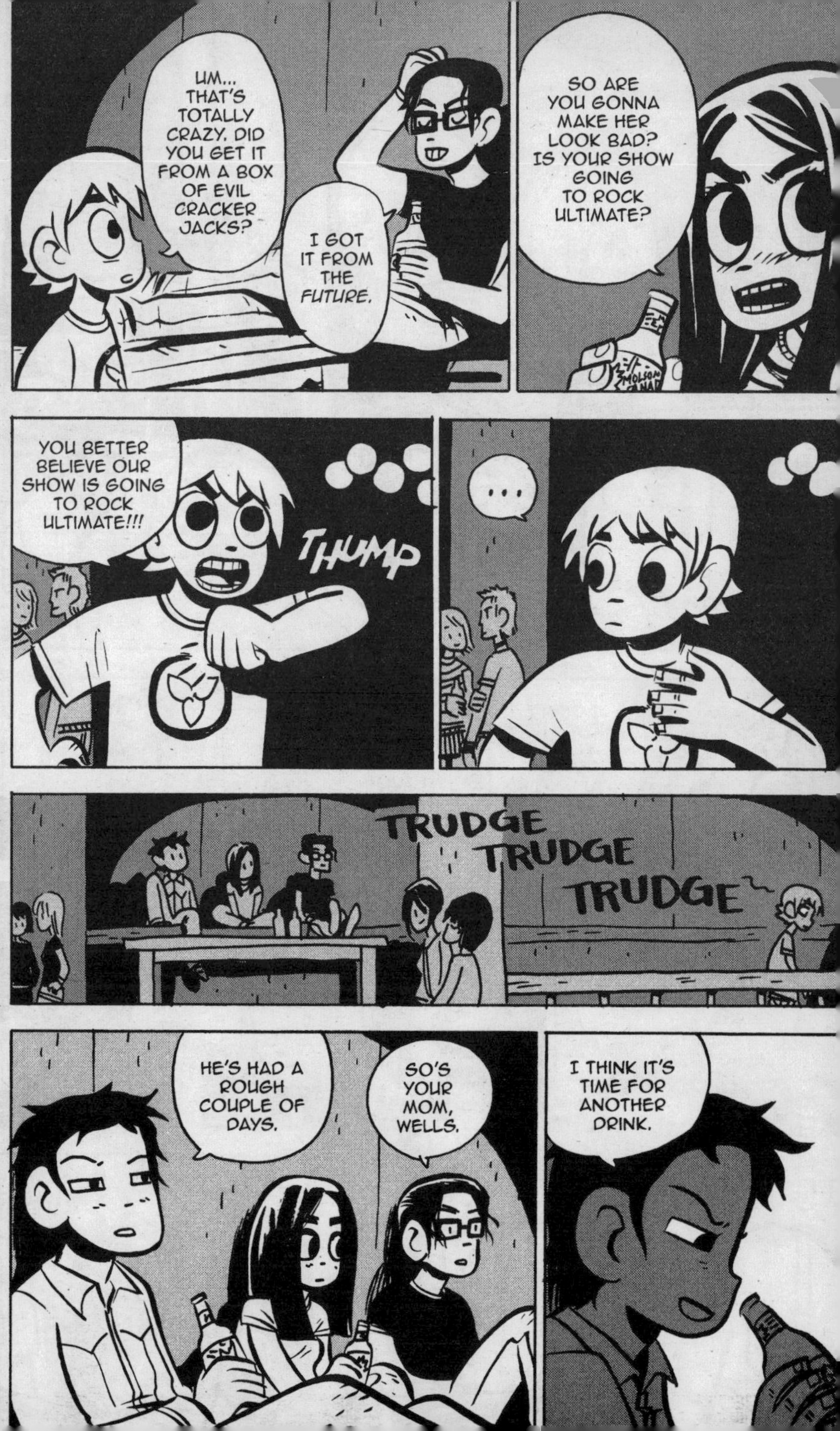
UM... THAT'S TOTALLY CRAZY. DID YOU GET IT FROM A BOX OF EVIL CRACKER JACKS?
I GOT IT FROM THE *FUTURE*.
SO ARE YOU GONNA MAKE HER LOOK BAD? IS YOUR SHOW GOING TO ROCK ULTIMATE?
YOU BETTER BELIEVE OUR SHOW IS GOING TO ROCK ULTIMATE!!!
THUMP
...
TRUDGE
TRUDGE
TRUDGE
HE'S HAD A ROUGH COUPLE OF DAYS.
SO'S YOUR MOM, WELLS.
I THINK IT'S TIME FOR ANOTHER DRINK.

Hollie works at a video store with Kim

Joseph Hollie's gay roommate

YO.

YOU GUYS CAME TO SEE THESE ASSHOLES *TWICE??*

UH... NO, WE CAME TO SEE *YOU.*

I PUT THEM ON OUR GUESTLIST, DOOF.

I CAME FOR TODD INGRAM AND TODD INGRAM ALONE.

I USED TO DATE HIM.

OKAY, TALK AMONGST YOURSELVES. I GOTTA GO CHECK ON STEPHEN STILLS.

HE'S IN THE BATHROOM THROWING UP, CAN YOU BELIEVE IT?

YES.

HEY, SCOTT.

HEY! ENVY! H-HI!

HEY, I HAD AN IDEA.

WHAT WAS THAT?

I THOUGHT MAYBE WE COULD TALK LIKE NORMAL PEOPLE.

LIKE IT USED TO BE.

HOW CAN I TALK TO YOU LIKE A NORMAL PERSON? LOOK AT YOU!

Cheese Dairy

H MY
OD,
NVY
AMS!

ENVY!

NVY,
TALK
TO ME!

YOU
IGN
CD?

ENVY
ADAMS IS
RIGHT
THERE!

O
HOT!

YO
RIGGES
AN!

NVY!
NVY!!

ELIEVE
HE'S
ERE!

GOD!
M
BY
HEART!

HT
HERE!

F I LOVE
OU

YO
ROC

NVY
AMS!

KNIVES CHAU
17 YEARS OLD

SKRTCH
SKTCH

UM...
HEY,
KNIVES.

SCOTT!

QUAY
CUR

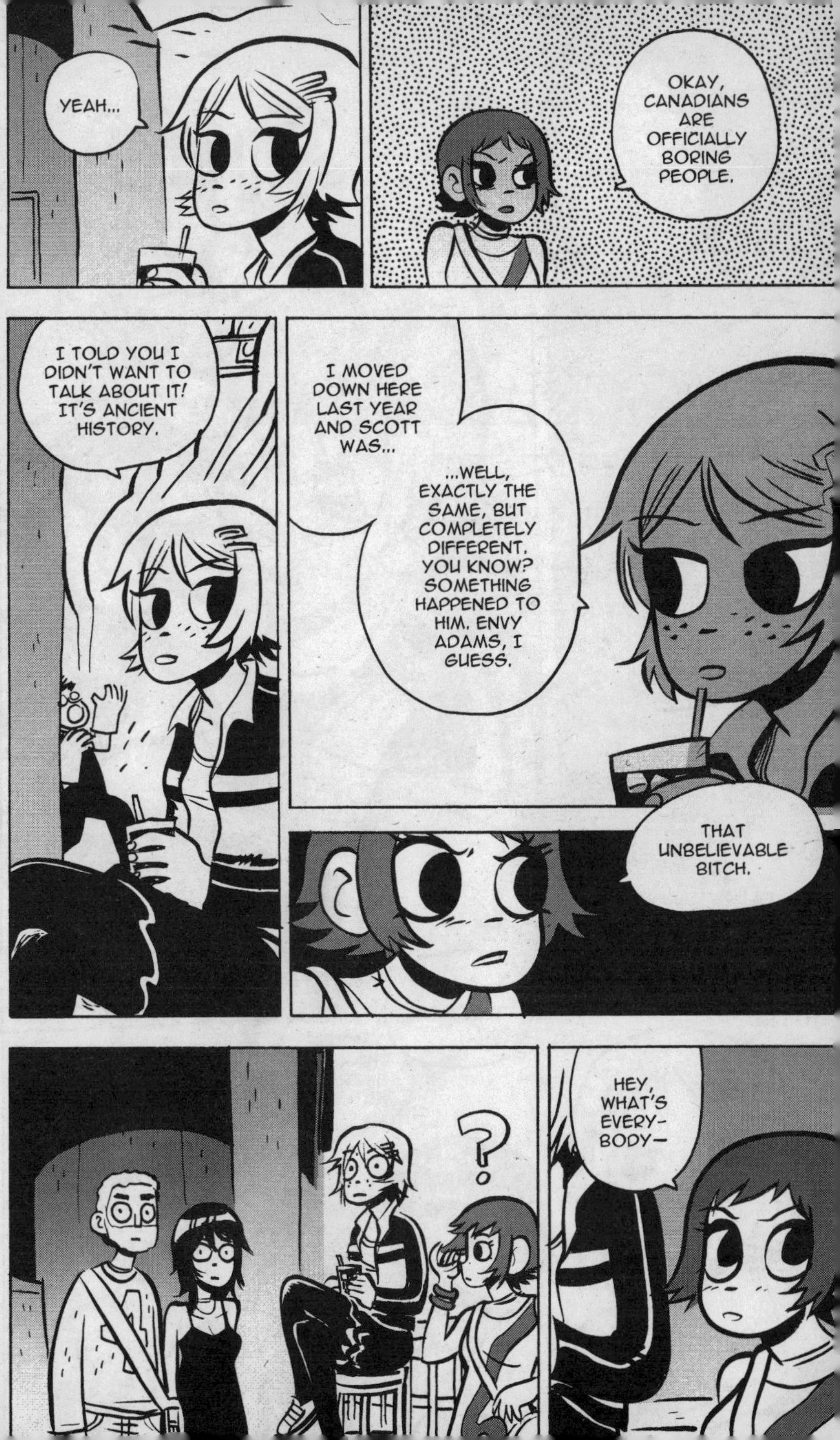
YEAH...
OKAY, CANADIANS ARE OFFICIALLY BORING PEOPLE.
I TOLD YOU I DIDN'T WANT TO TALK ABOUT IT! IT'S ANCIENT HISTORY.
I MOVED DOWN HERE LAST YEAR AND SCOTT WAS...
...WELL, EXACTLY THE SAME, BUT COMPLETELY DIFFERENT. YOU KNOW? SOMETHING HAPPENED TO HIM. ENVY ADAMS, I GUESS.
THAT UNBELIEVABLE BITCH.
?
HEY, WHAT'S EVERY-BODY—

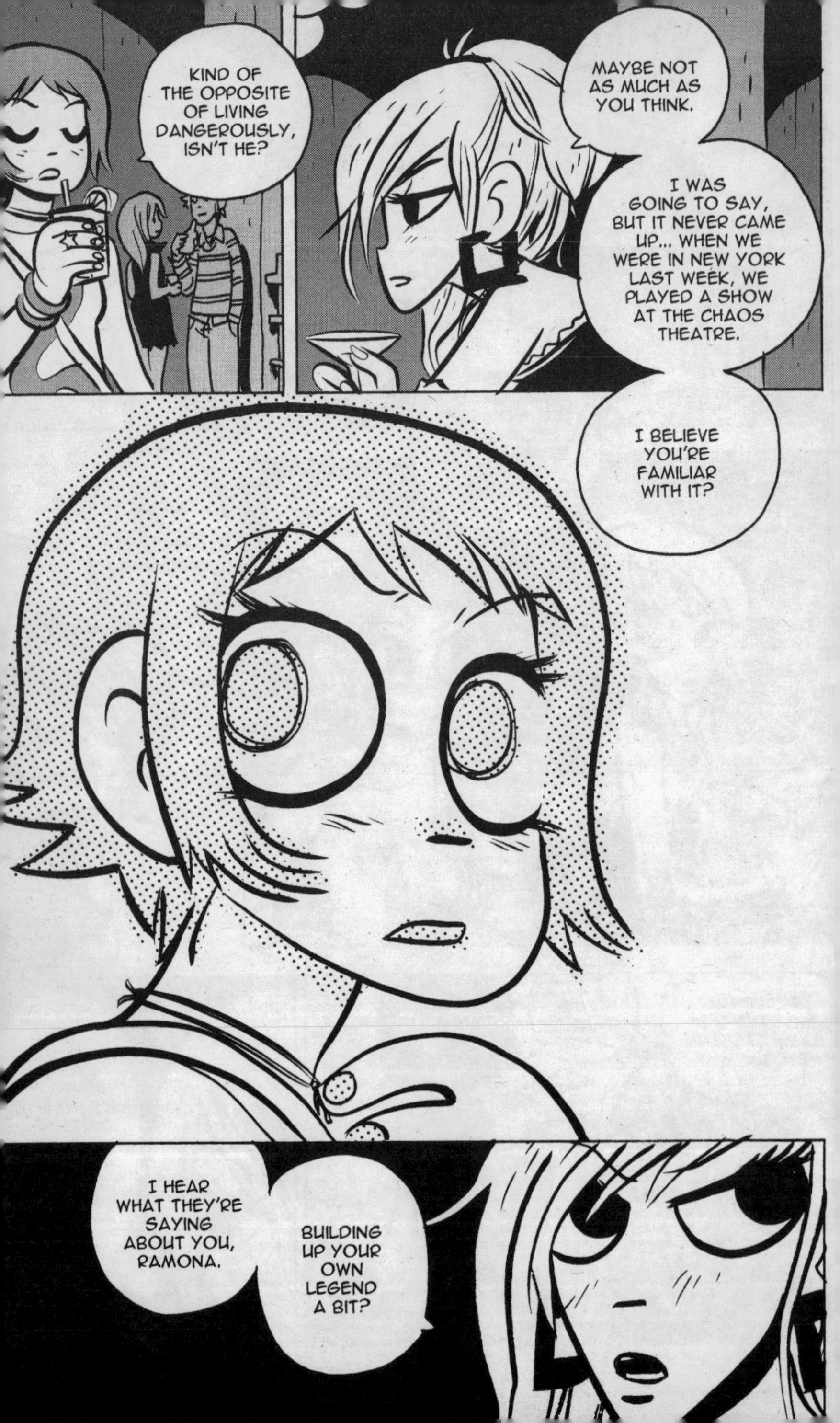
KIND OF THE OPPOSITE OF LIVING DANGEROUSLY, ISN'T HE?
MAYBE NOT AS MUCH AS YOU THINK.
I WAS GOING TO SAY, BUT IT NEVER CAME UP... WHEN WE WERE IN NEW YORK LAST WEEK, WE PLAYED A SHOW AT THE CHAOS THEATRE.
I BELIEVE YOU'RE FAMILIAR WITH IT?
I HEAR WHAT THEY'RE SAYING ABOUT YOU, RAMONA.
BUILDING UP YOUR OWN LEGEND A BIT?

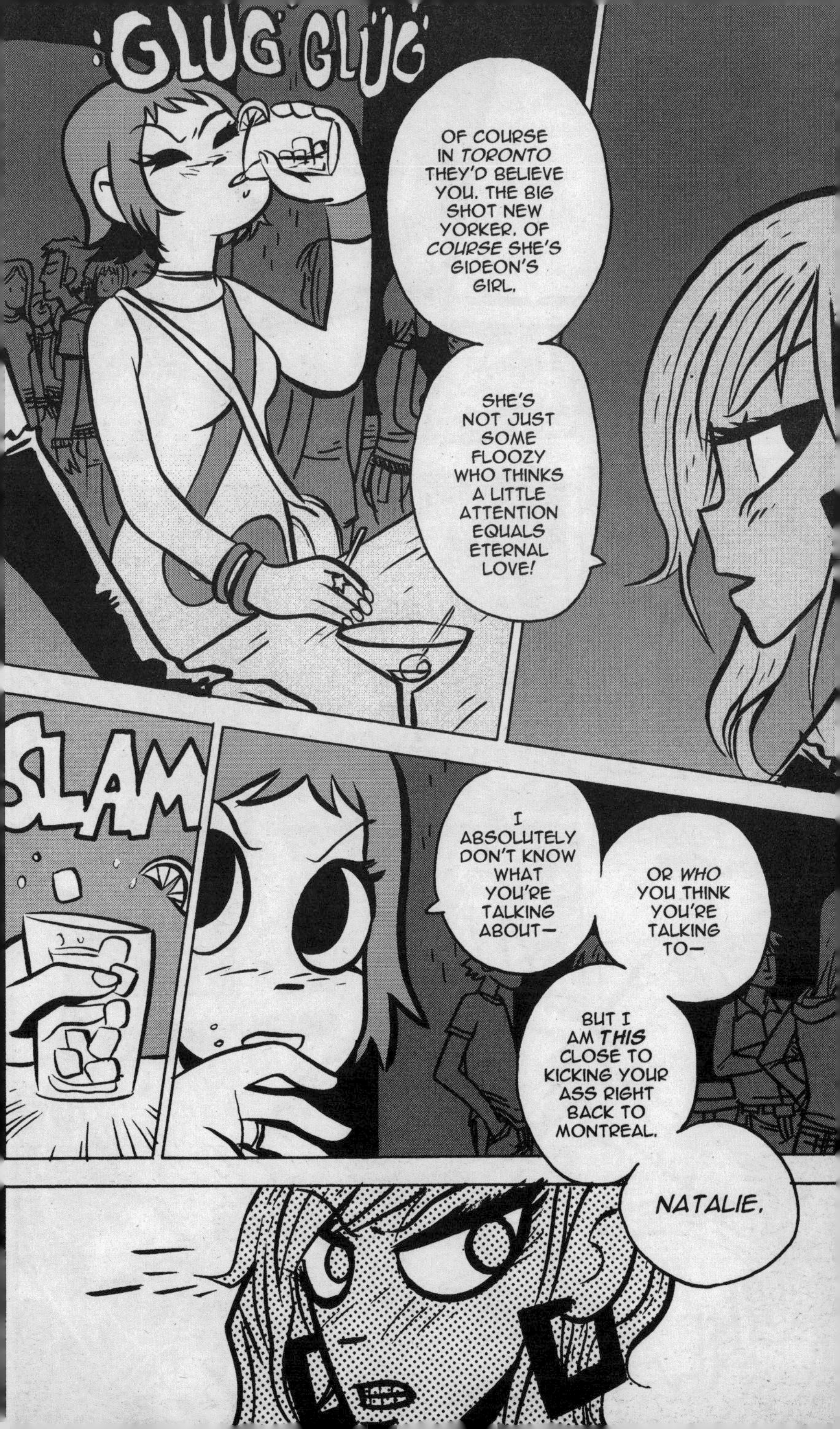
GLUG GLUG
OF COURSE IN *TORONTO* THEY'D BELIEVE YOU. THE BIG SHOT NEW YORKER. OF *COURSE* SHE'S GIDEON'S GIRL.
SHE'S NOT JUST SOME FLOOZY WHO THINKS A LITTLE ATTENTION EQUALS ETERNAL LOVE!
SLAM
I ABSOLUTELY DON'T KNOW WHAT YOU'RE TALKING ABOUT—
OR *WHO* YOU THINK YOU'RE TALKING TO—
BUT I AM ***THIS*** CLOSE TO KICKING YOUR ASS RIGHT BACK TO MONTREAL.
NATALIE.

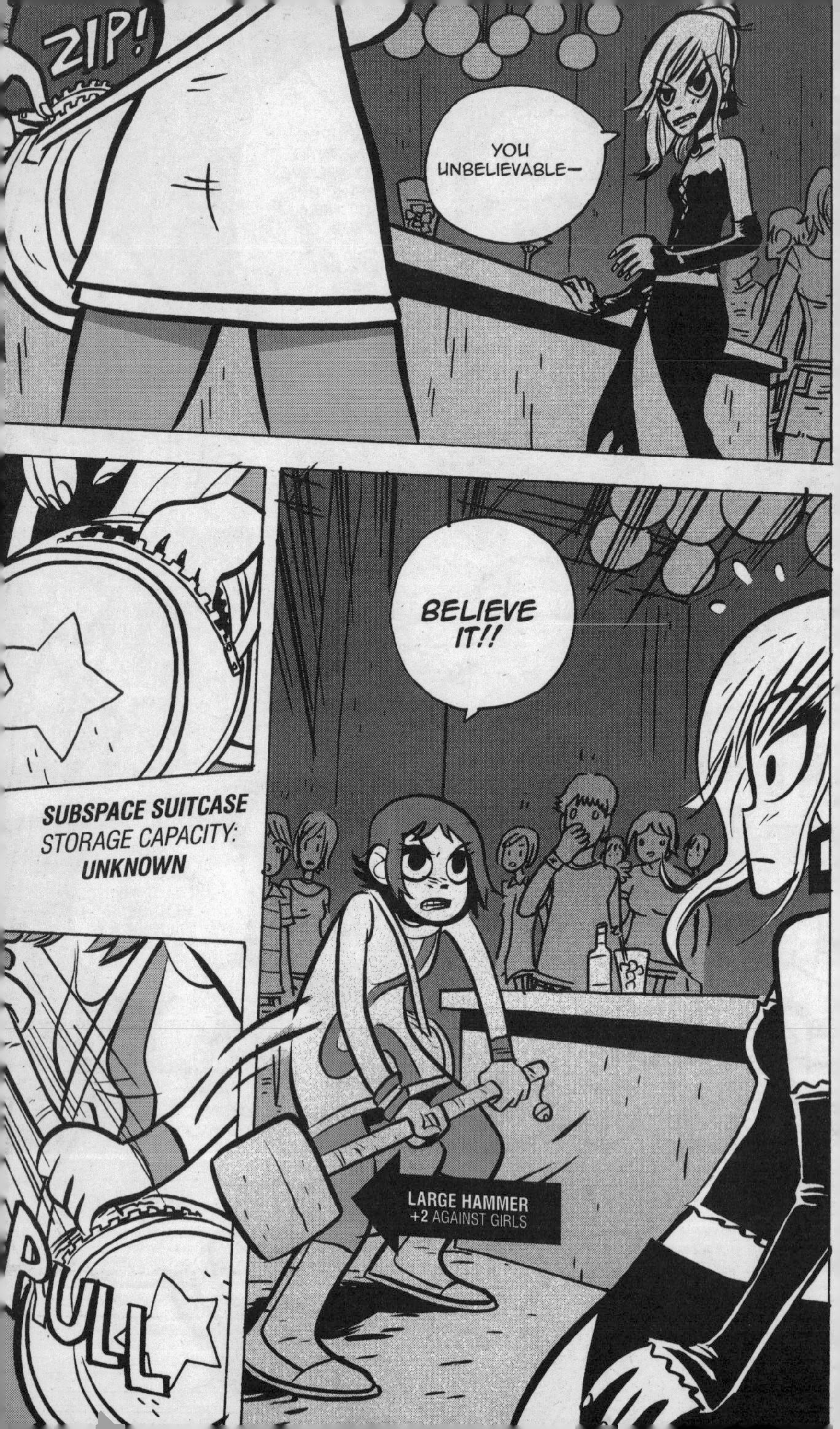

ZIP!
YOU UNBELIEVABLE—
SUBSPACE SUITCASE
STORAGE CAPACITY:
UNKNOWN
PULL
BELIEVE IT!!
LARGE HAMMER
+2 AGAINST GIRLS

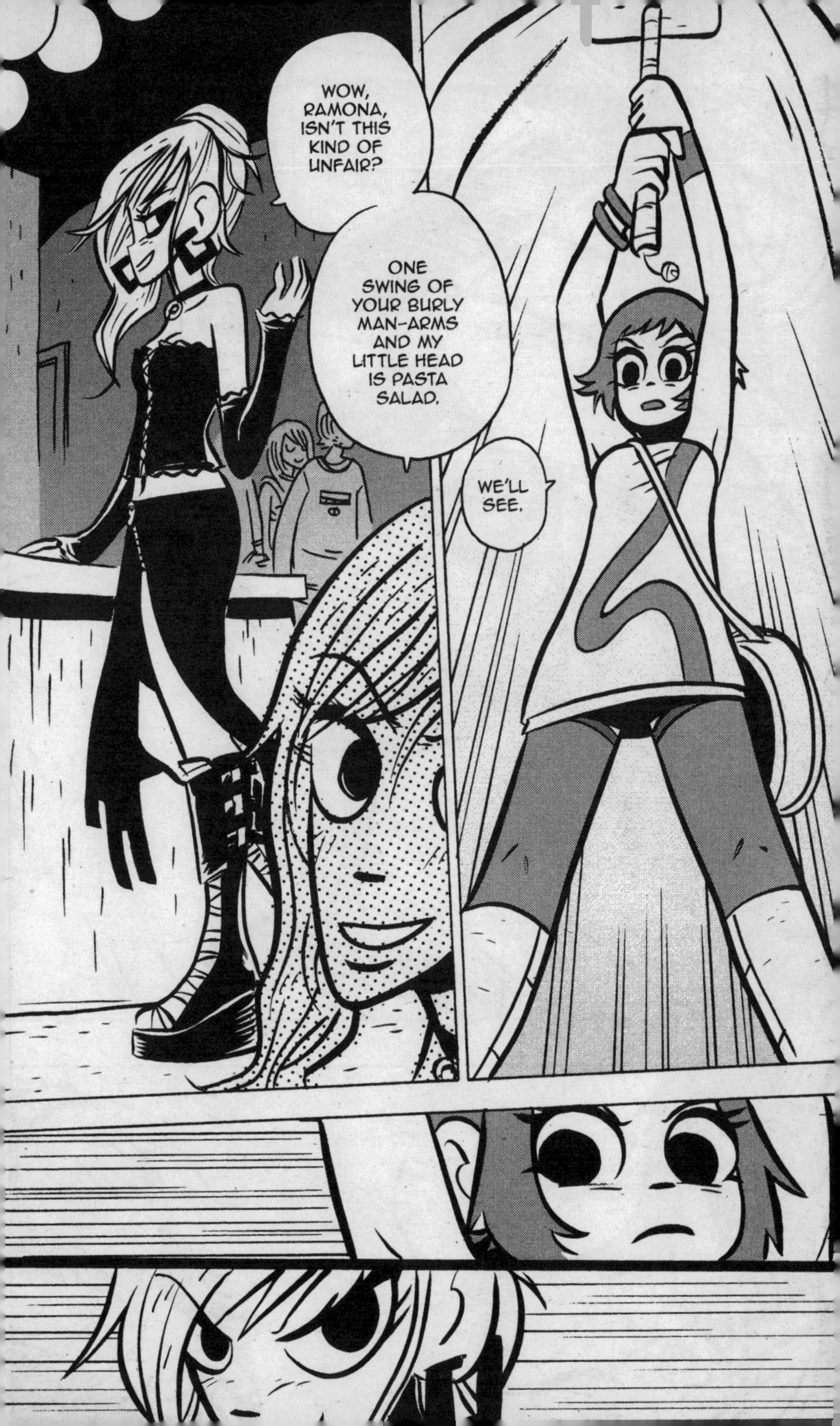
WOW, RAMONA, ISN'T THIS KIND OF UNFAIR?
ONE SWING OF YOUR BURLY MAN-ARMS AND MY LITTLE HEAD IS PASTA SALAD.
WE'LL SEE.

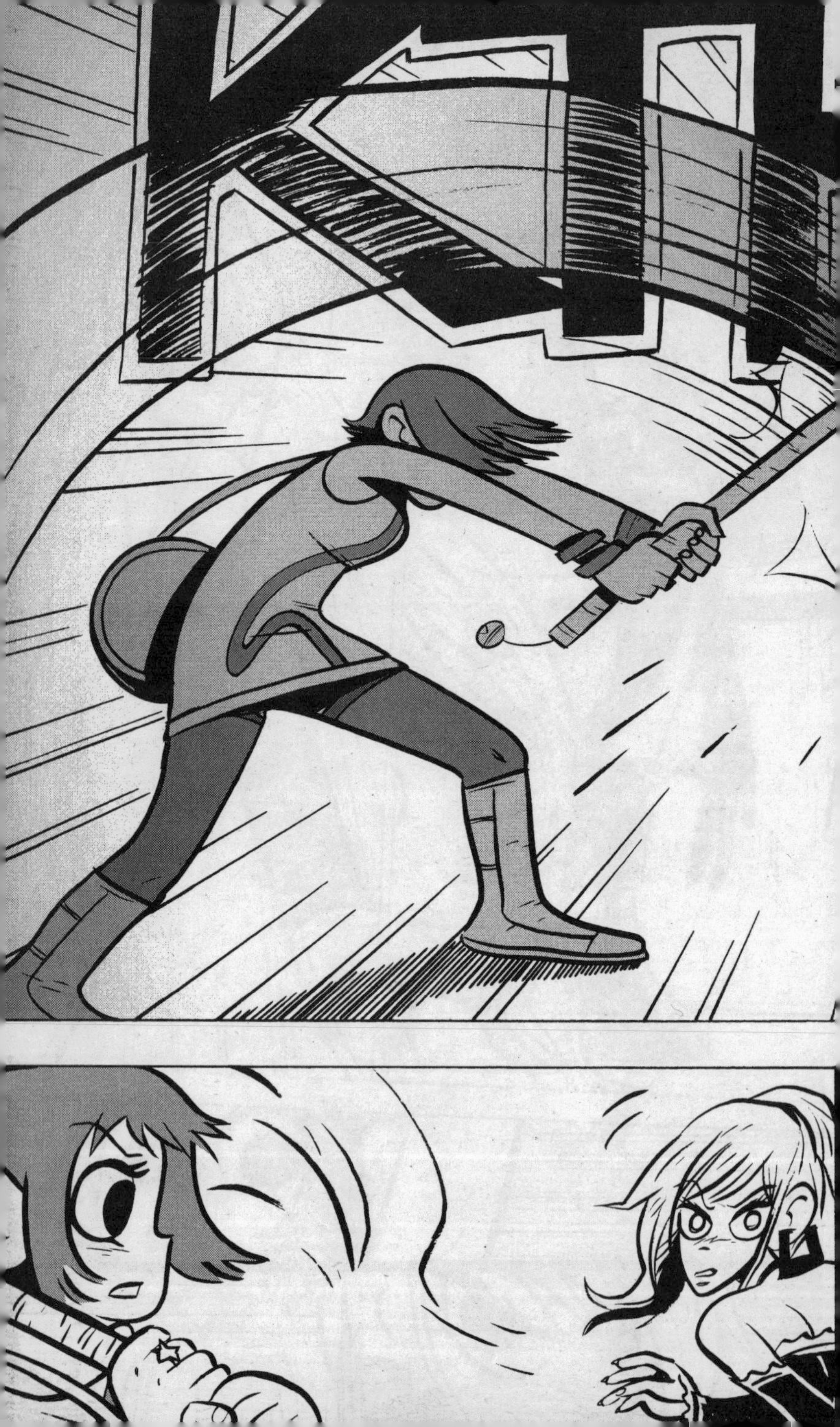

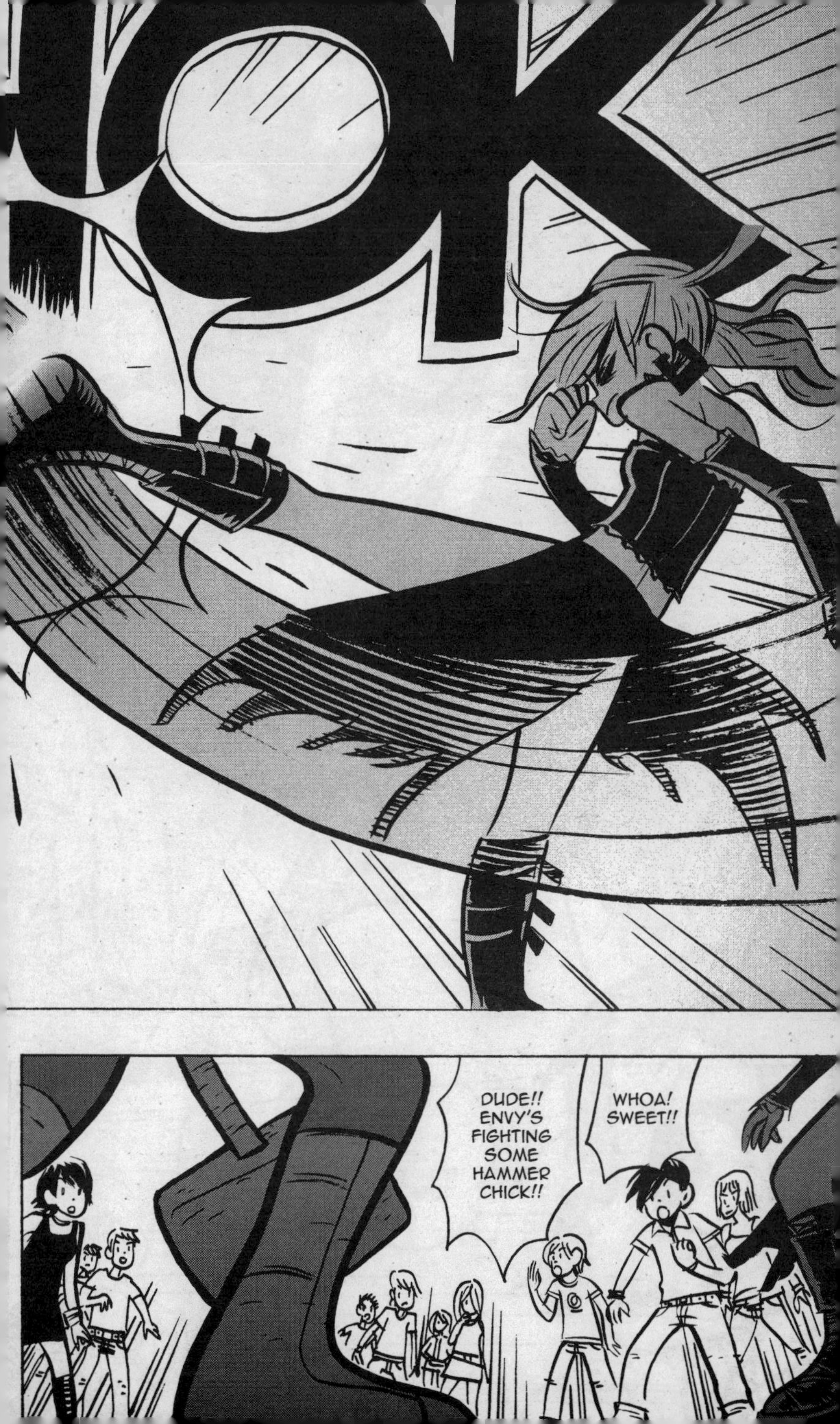
DUDE!! ENVY'S FIGHTING SOME HAMMER CHICK!!
WHOA! SWEET!!

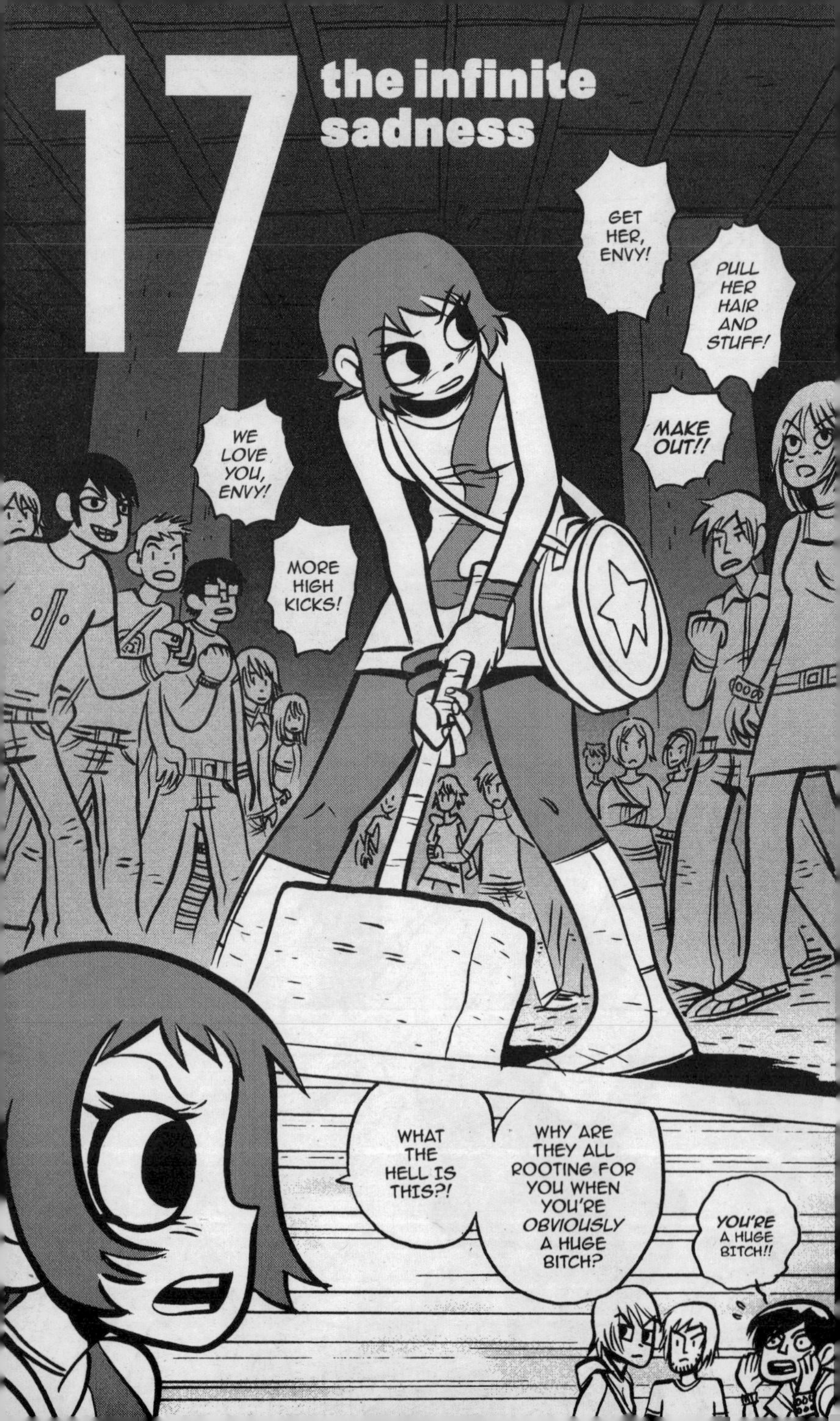
17
the infinite sadness
GET HER, ENVY!
PULL HER HAIR AND STUFF!
WE LOVE YOU, ENVY!
MAKE OUT!!
MORE HIGH KICKS!
WHAT THE HELL IS THIS?!
WHY ARE THEY ALL ROOTING FOR YOU WHEN YOU'RE OBVIOUSLY A HUGE BITCH?
YOU'RE A HUGE BITCH!!

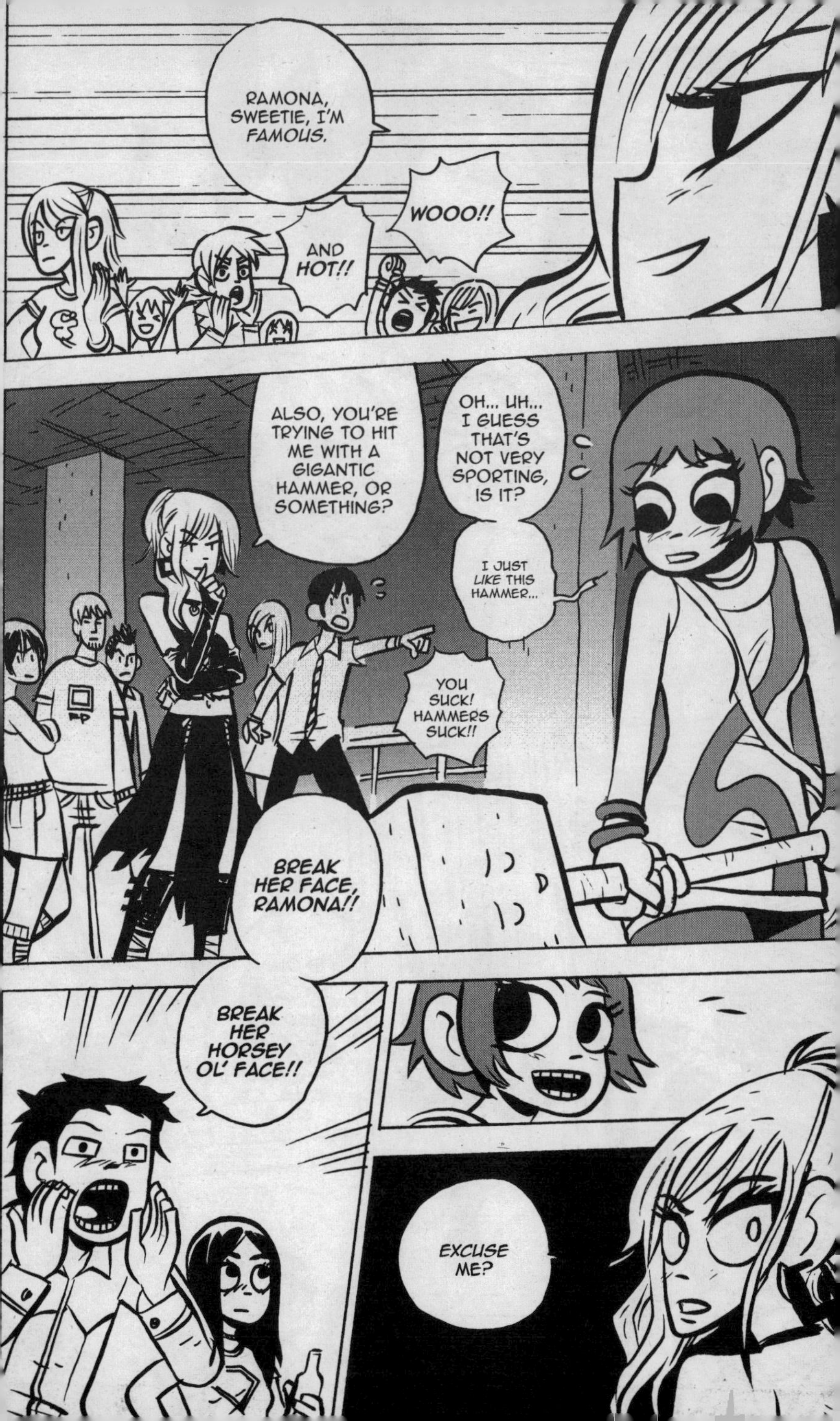
RAMONA, SWEETIE, I'M FAMOUS.
WOOO!!
AND HOT!!
ALSO, YOU'RE TRYING TO HIT ME WITH A GIGANTIC HAMMER, OR SOMETHING?
OH... UH... I GUESS THAT'S NOT VERY SPORTING, IS IT?
I JUST LIKE THIS HAMMER...
YOU SUCK! HAMMERS SUCK!!
BREAK HER FACE, RAMONA!!
BREAK HER HORSEY OL' FACE!!
EXCUSE ME?

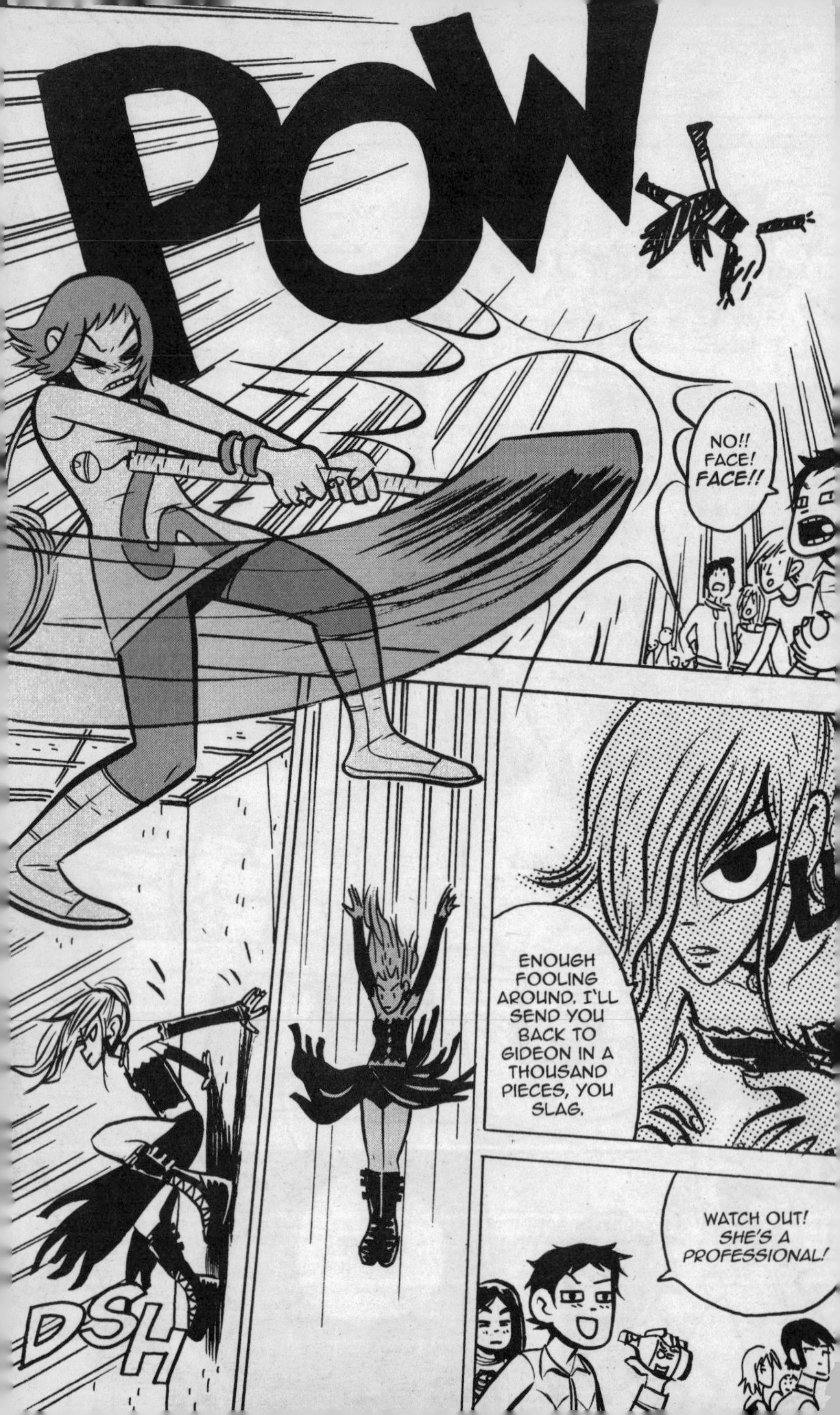
POW
NO!! FACE! FACE!!
ENOUGH FOOLING AROUND. I'LL SEND YOU BACK TO GIDEON IN A THOUSAND PIECES, YOU SLAG.
DSH
WATCH OUT! SHE'S A PROFESSIONAL!

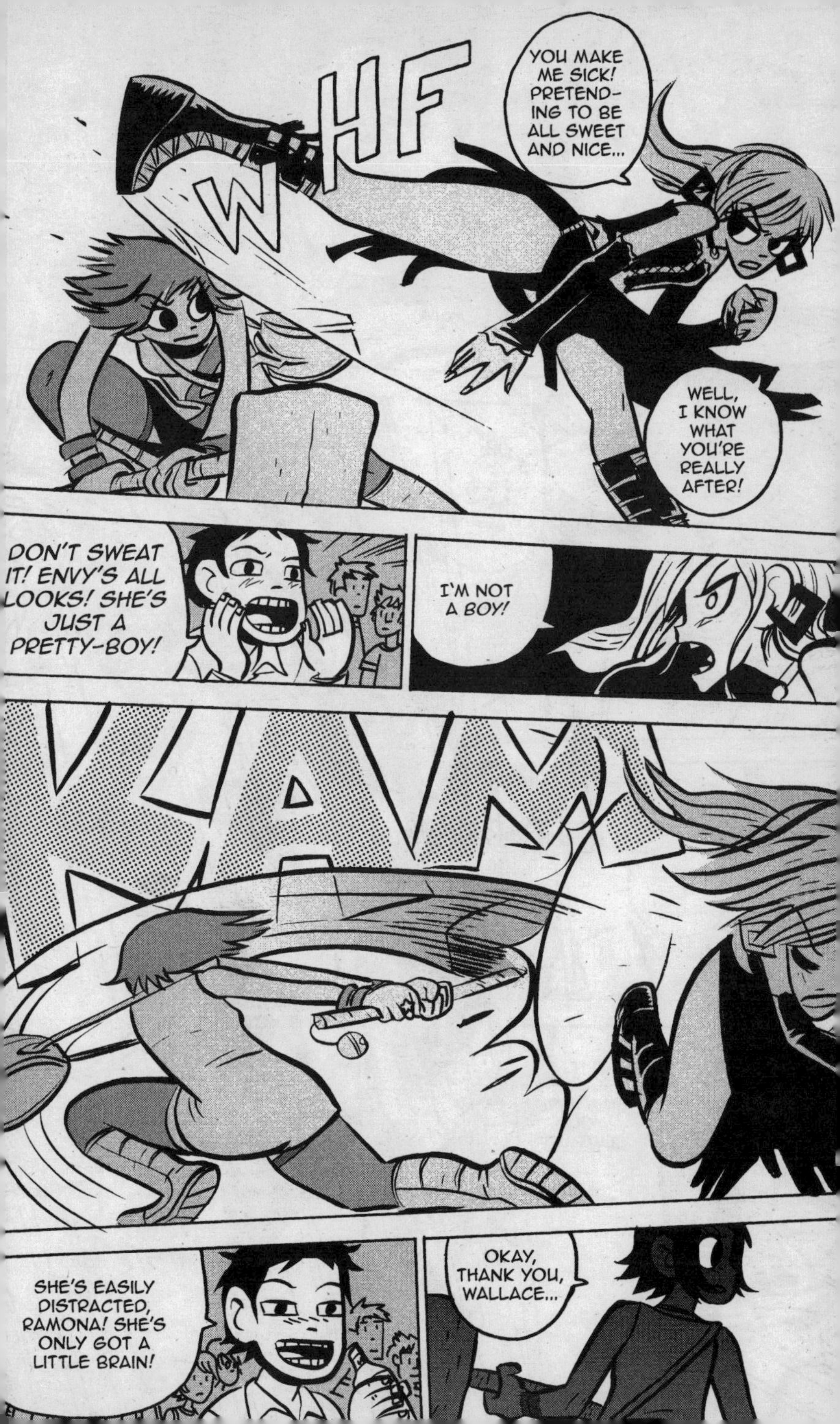
WHF
YOU MAKE ME SICK! PRETENDING TO BE ALL SWEET AND NICE...
WELL, I KNOW WHAT YOU'RE REALLY AFTER!
DON'T SWEAT IT! ENVY'S ALL LOOKS! SHE'S JUST A PRETTY-BOY!
I'M NOT A BOY!
VLAM
SHE'S EASILY DISTRACTED, RAMONA! SHE'S ONLY GOT A LITTLE BRAIN!
OKAY, THANK YOU, WALLACE...

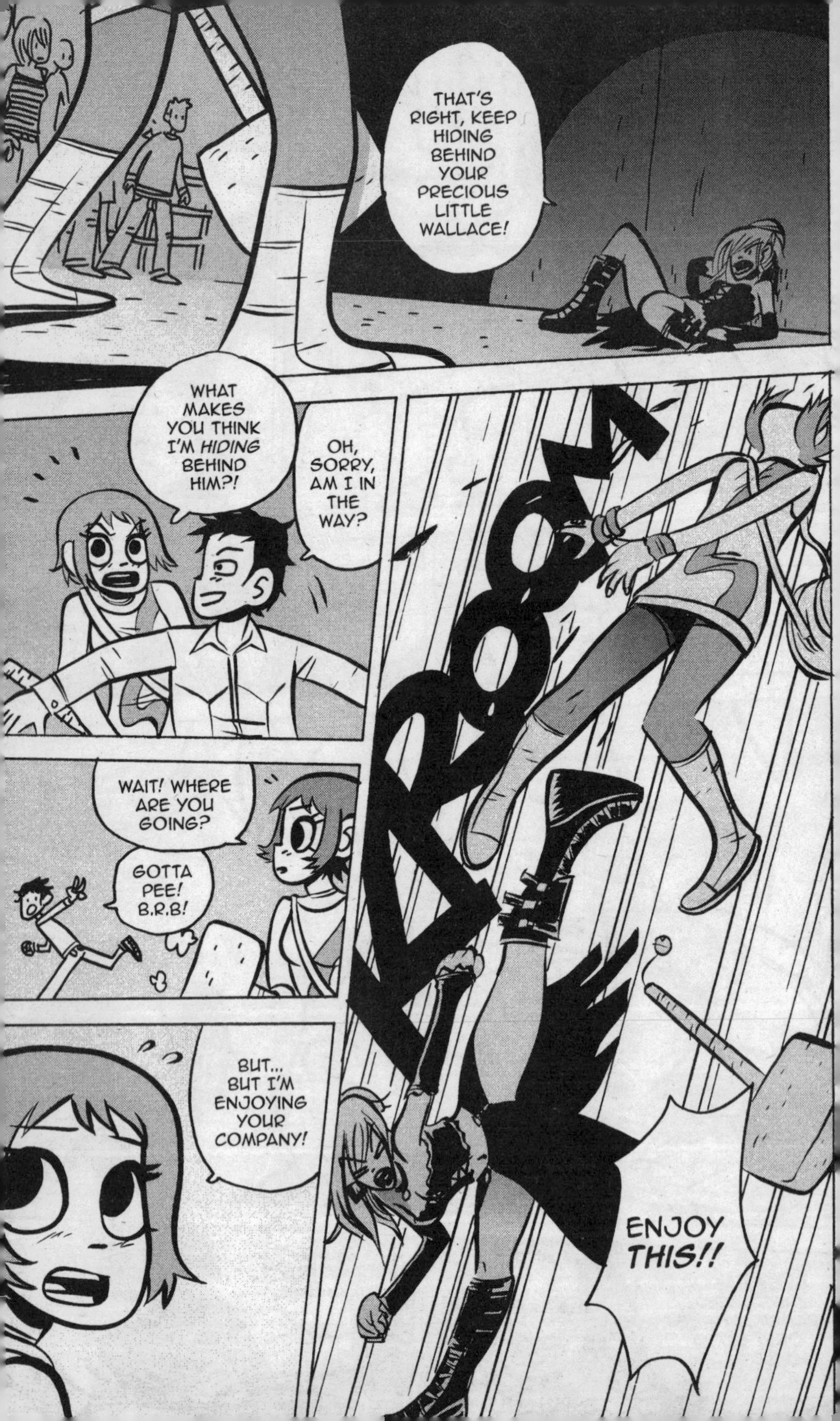
THAT'S RIGHT, KEEP HIDING BEHIND YOUR PRECIOUS LITTLE WALLACE!
WHAT MAKES YOU THINK I'M *HIDING* BEHIND HIM?!
OH, SORRY, AM I IN THE WAY?
WAIT! WHERE ARE YOU GOING?
GOTTA PEE! B.R.B!
BUT... BUT I'M ENJOYING YOUR COMPANY!
KRBOOM
ENJOY **THIS!!**

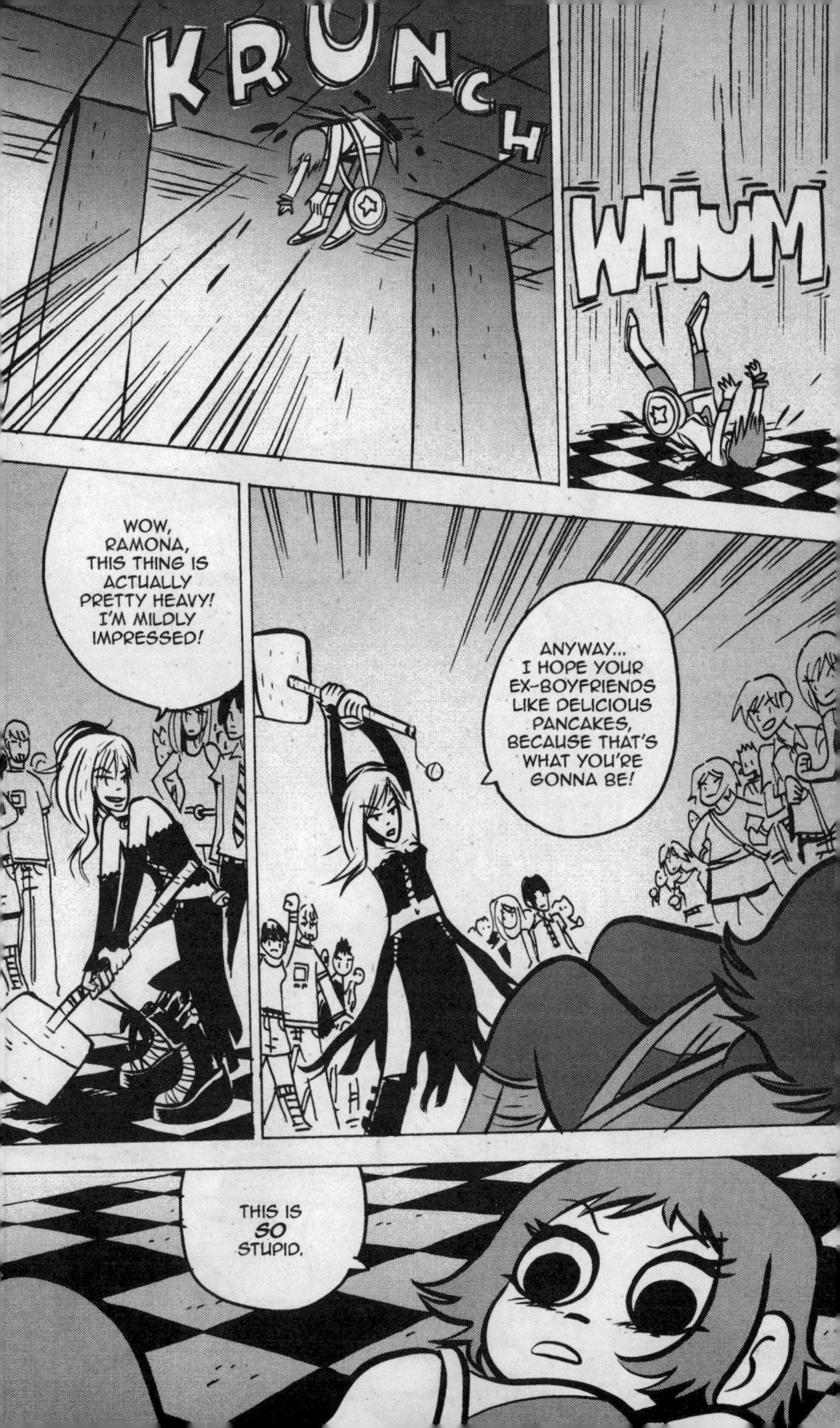
KRUNCH
WHUM
WOW, RAMONA, THIS THING IS ACTUALLY PRETTY HEAVY! I'M MILDLY IMPRESSED!
ANYWAY... I HOPE YOUR EX-BOYFRIENDS LIKE DELICIOUS PANCAKES, BECAUSE THAT'S WHAT YOU'RE GONNA BE!
THIS IS SO STUPID.

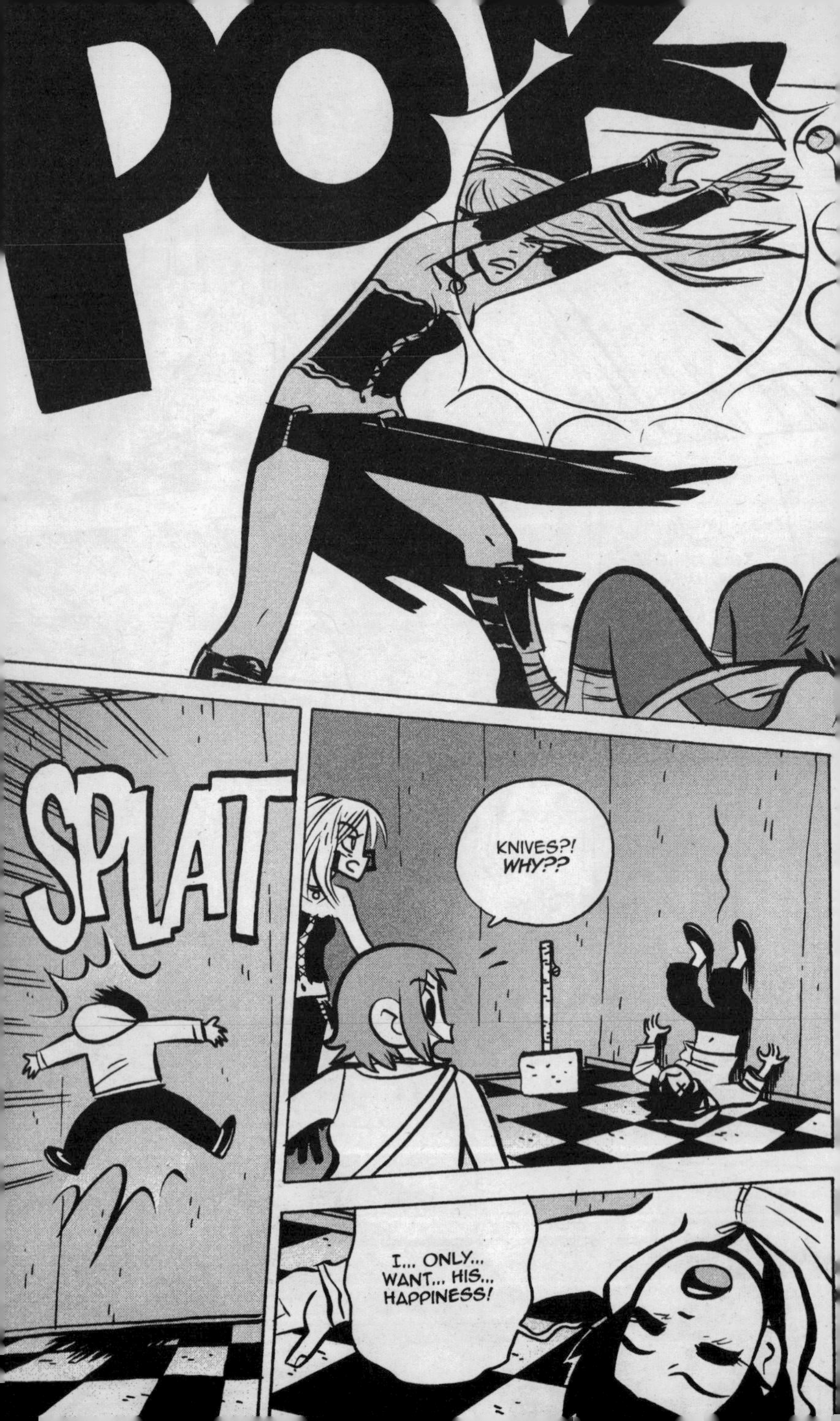
POK
SPLAT
KNIVES?! WHY??
I... ONLY... WANT... HIS... HAPPINESS!

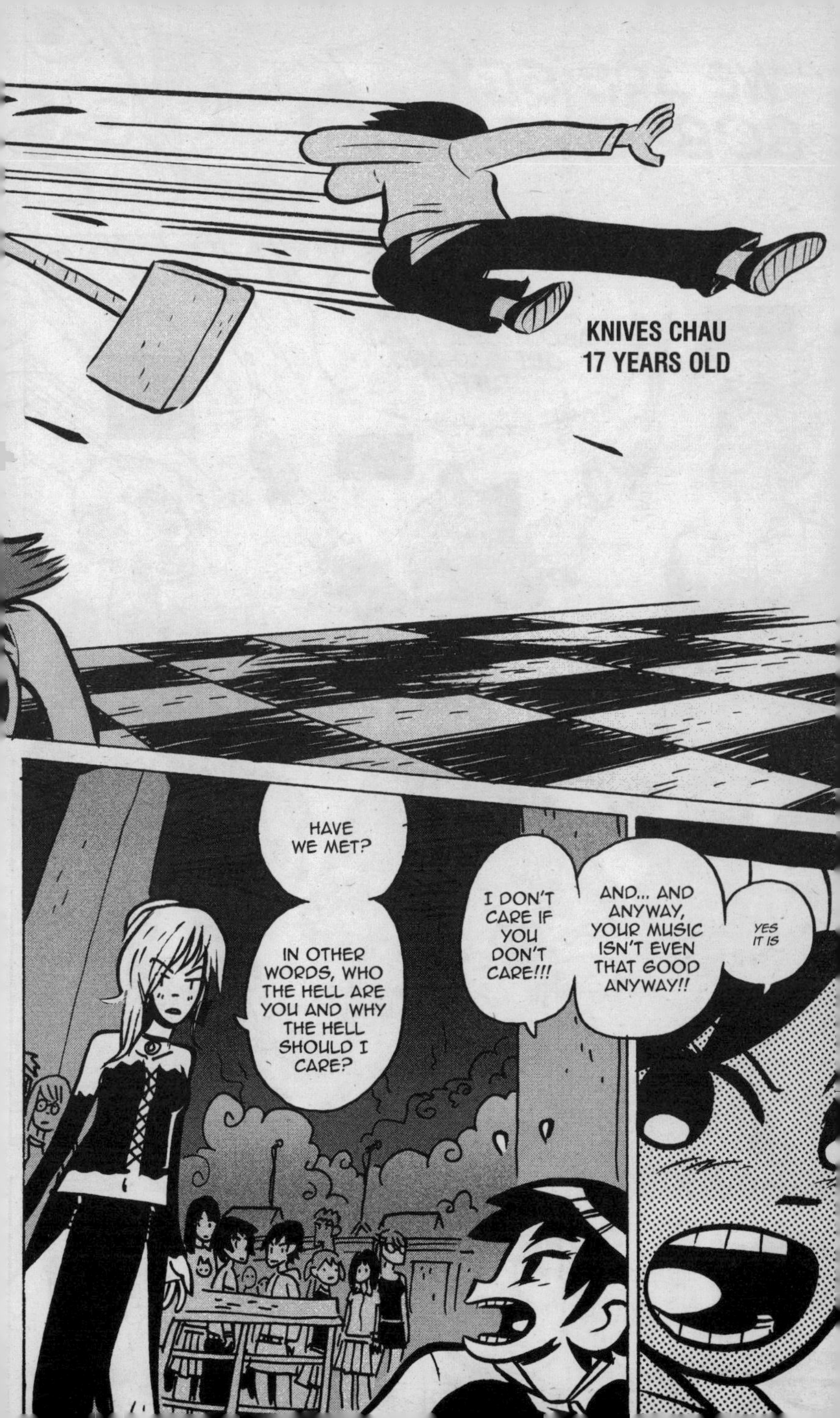
KNIVES CHAU
17 YEARS OLD
HAVE WE MET?
IN OTHER WORDS, WHO THE HELL ARE YOU AND WHY THE HELL SHOULD I CARE?
I DON'T CARE IF YOU DON'T CARE!!!
AND... AND ANYWAY, YOUR MUSIC ISN'T EVEN THAT GOOD ANYWAY!!
YES IT IS

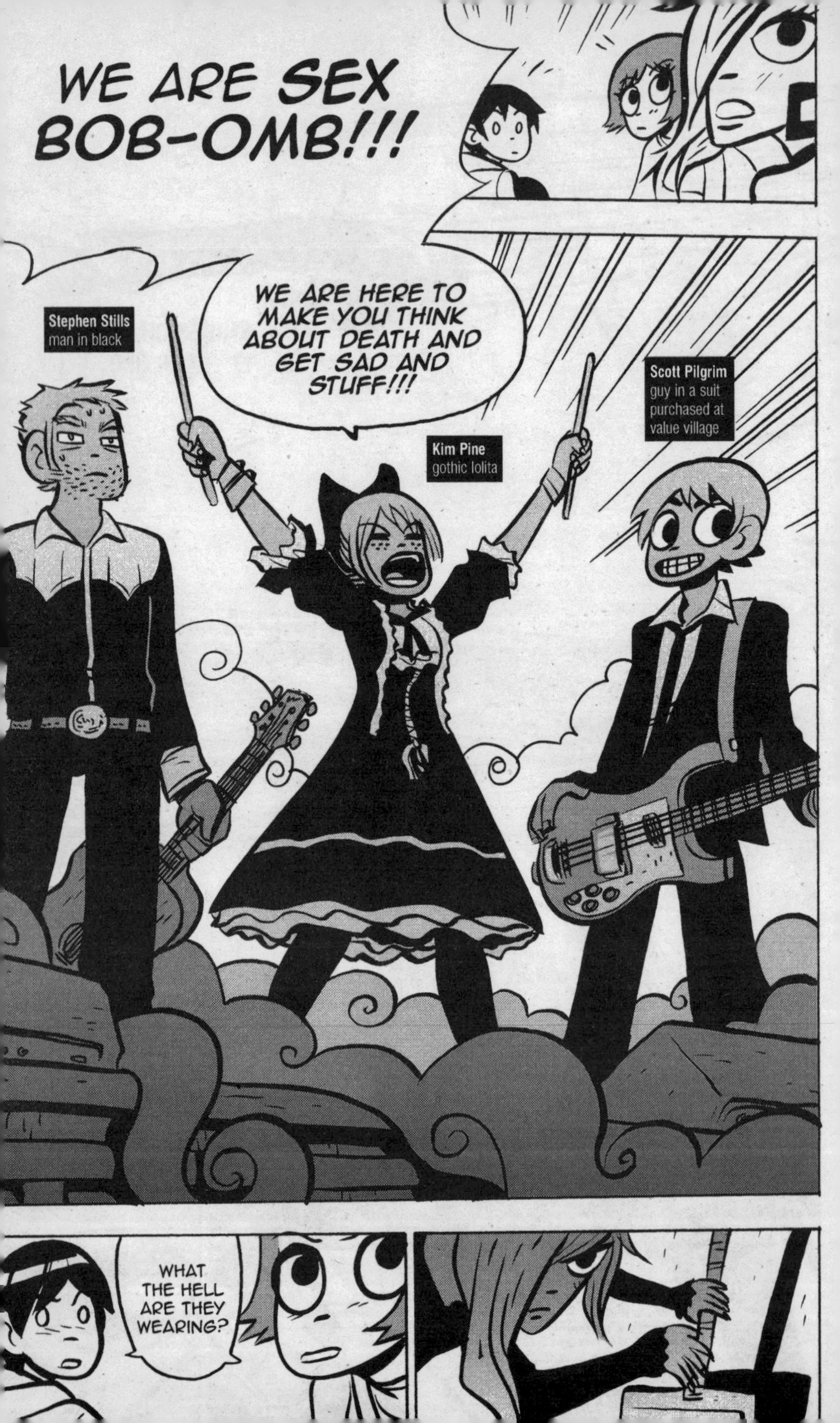

WE ARE SEX BOB-OMB!!!
Stephen Stills
man in black
WE ARE HERE TO MAKE YOU THINK ABOUT DEATH AND GET SAD AND STUFF!!!
Kim Pine
gothic lolita
Scott Pilgrim
guy in a suit purchased at value village
WHAT THE HELL ARE THEY WEARING?

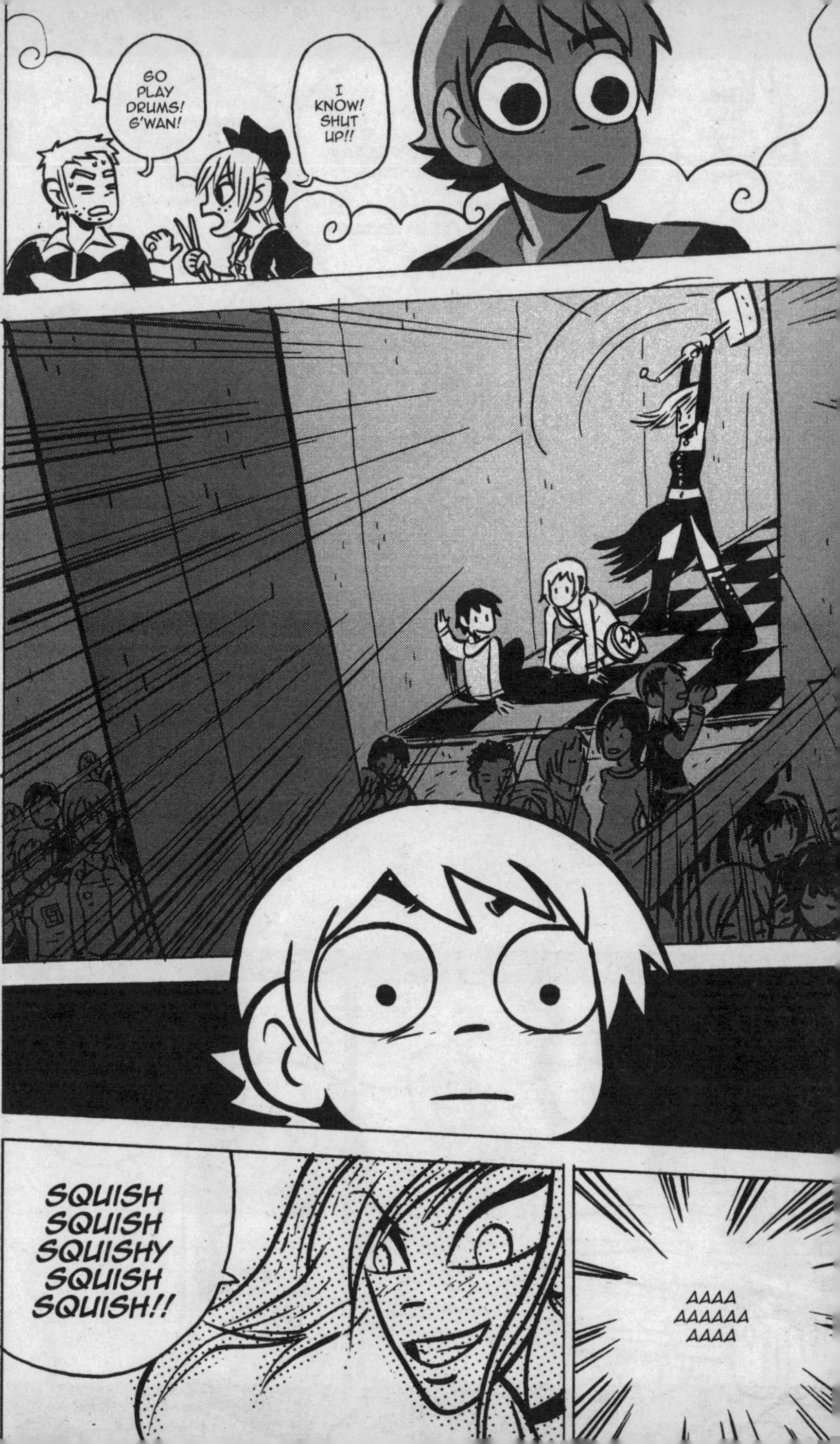
GO PLAY DRUMS! G'WAN!
I KNOW! SHUT UP!!
SQUISH SQUISH SQUISHY SQUISH SQUISH!!
AAAA AAAAAA AAAA

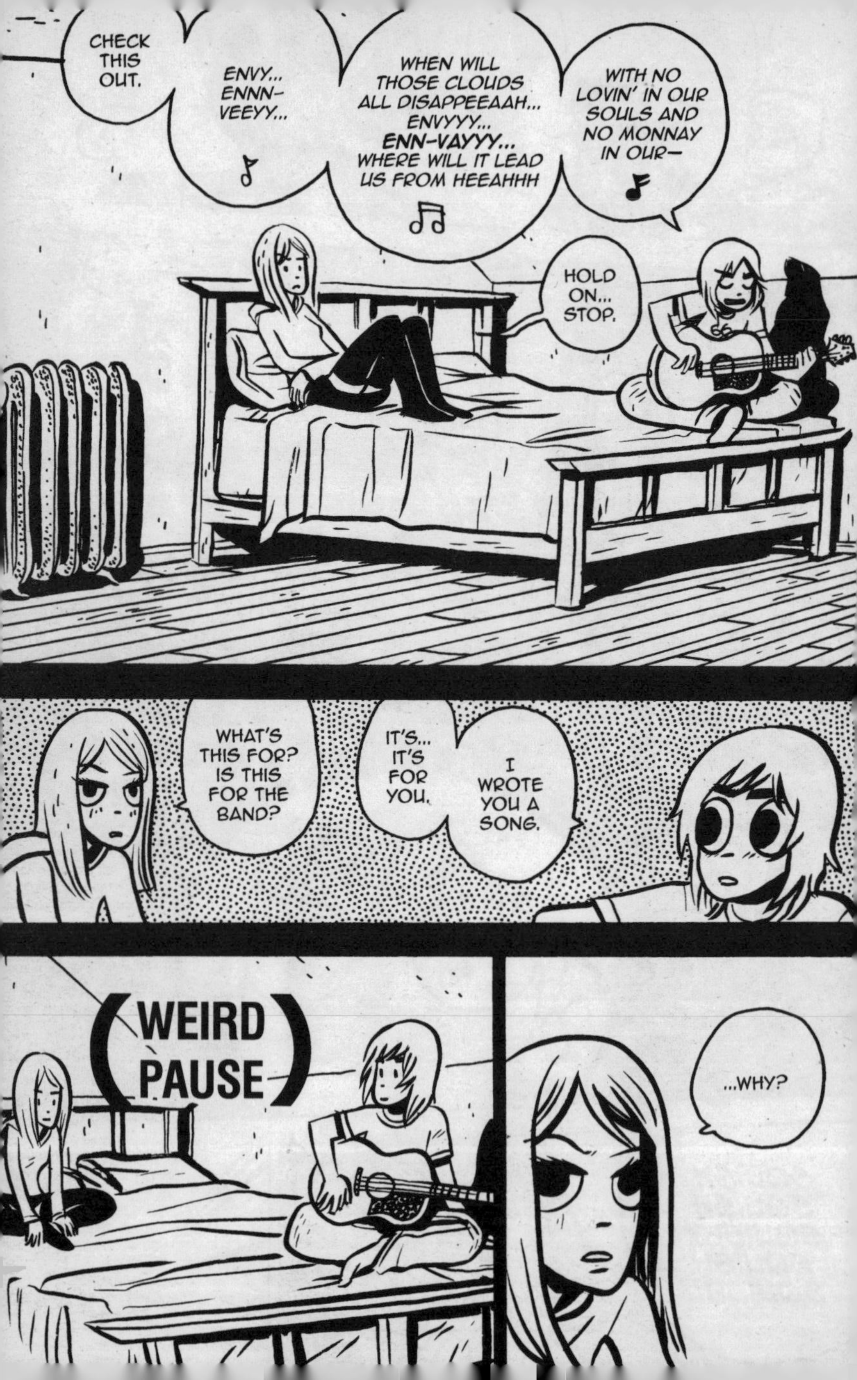
CHECK THIS OUT.
ENVY... ENNN-VEEYY...
WHEN WILL THOSE CLOUDS ALL DISAPPEEAAH... ENVYYY... **ENN-VAYYY...** WHERE WILL IT LEAD US FROM HEEAHHH
WITH NO LOVIN' IN OUR SOULS AND NO MONNAY IN OUR—
HOLD ON... STOP.
WHAT'S THIS FOR? IS THIS FOR THE BAND?
IT'S... IT'S FOR YOU.
I WROTE YOU A SONG.
(WEIRD PAUSE)
...WHY?

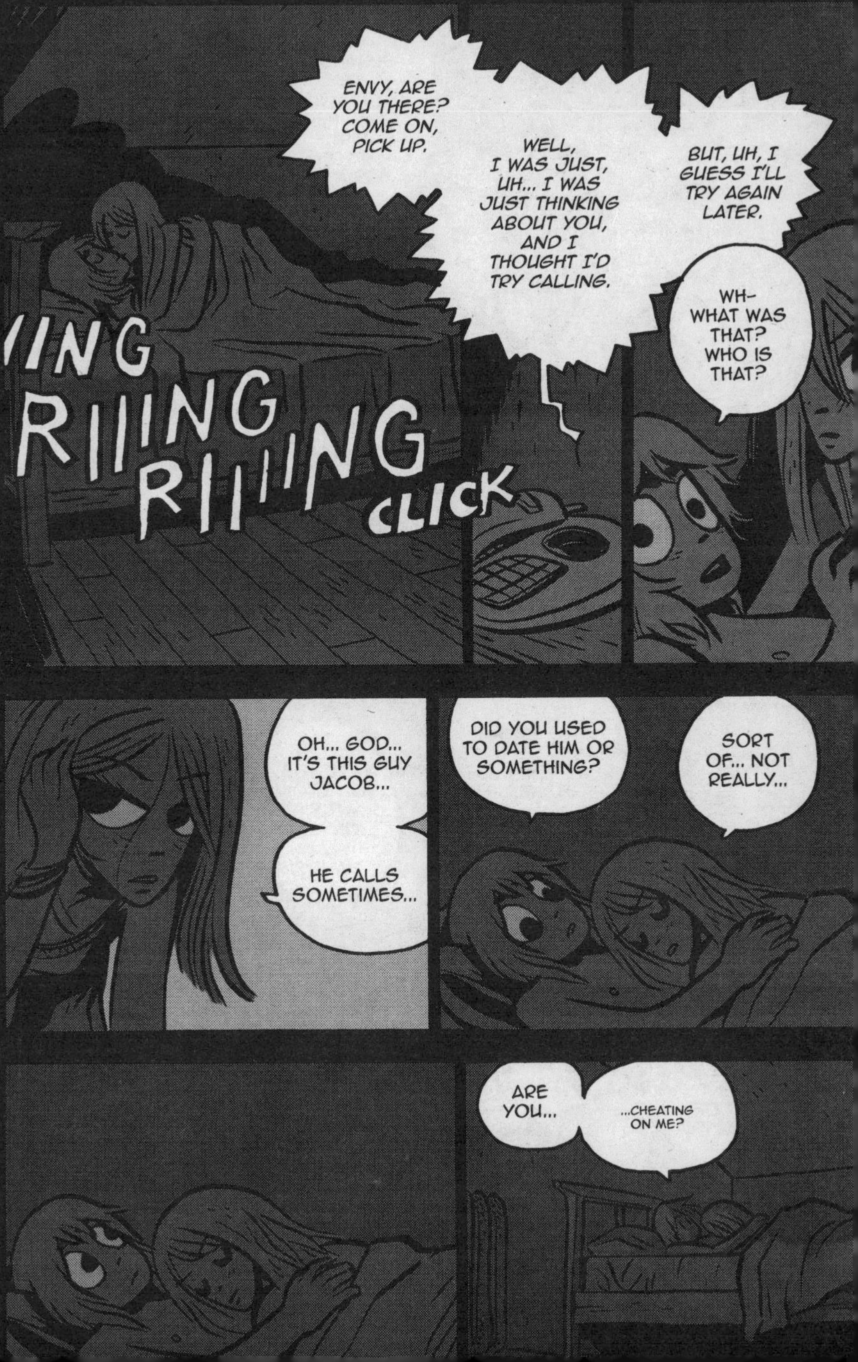
ENVY, ARE YOU THERE? COME ON, PICK UP.
WELL, I WAS JUST, UH... I WAS JUST THINKING ABOUT YOU, AND I THOUGHT I'D TRY CALLING.
BUT, UH, I GUESS I'LL TRY AGAIN LATER.
IING
RIIING
RIIING
CLICK
WH- WHAT WAS THAT? WHO IS THAT?
OH... GOD... IT'S THIS GUY JACOB...
HE CALLS SOMETIMES...
DID YOU USED TO DATE HIM OR SOMETHING?
SORT OF... NOT REALLY...
ARE YOU...
...CHEATING ON ME?

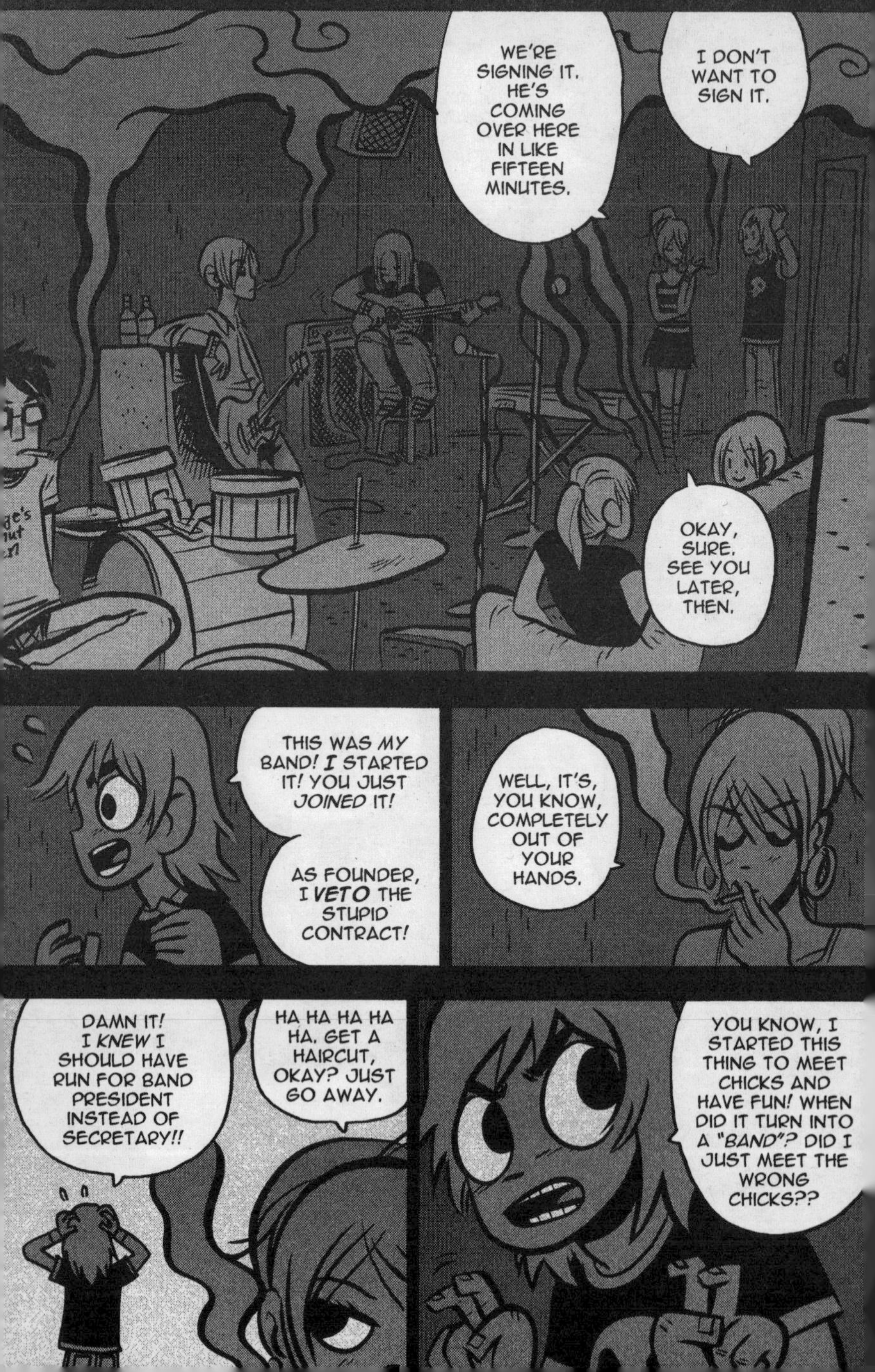
WE'RE SIGNING IT. HE'S COMING OVER HERE IN LIKE FIFTEEN MINUTES.
I DON'T WANT TO SIGN IT.
OKAY, SURE. SEE YOU LATER, THEN.
THIS WAS *MY* BAND! *I* STARTED IT! YOU JUST *JOINED* IT!
AS FOUNDER, I ***VETO*** THE STUPID CONTRACT!
WELL, IT'S, YOU KNOW, COMPLETELY OUT OF YOUR HANDS.
DAMN IT! I *KNEW* I SHOULD HAVE RUN FOR BAND PRESIDENT INSTEAD OF SECRETARY!!
HA HA HA HA HA. GET A HAIRCUT, OKAY? JUST GO AWAY.
YOU KNOW, I STARTED THIS THING TO MEET CHICKS AND HAVE FUN! WHEN DID IT TURN INTO A "*BAND*"? DID I JUST MEET THE WRONG CHICKS??

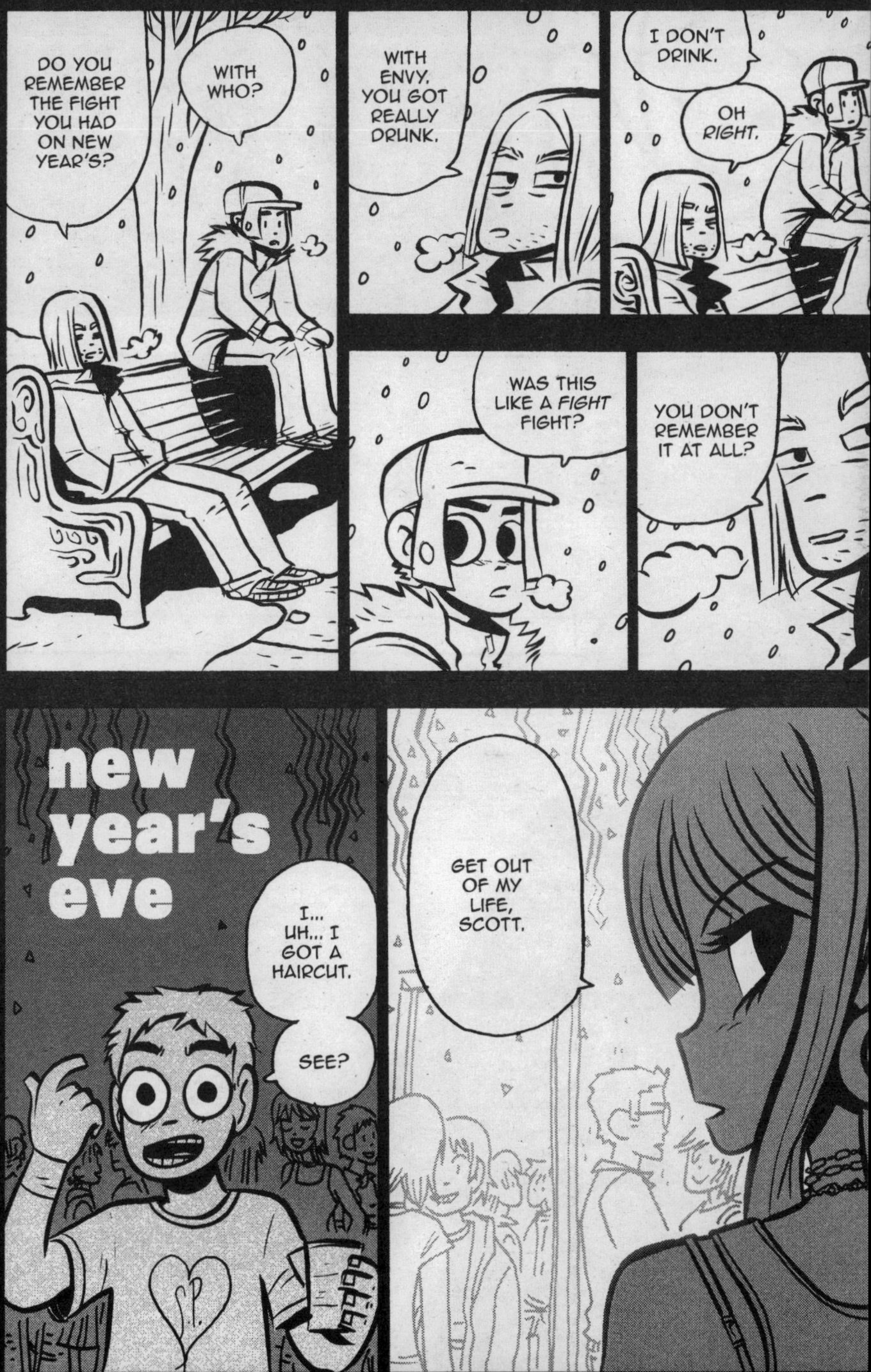
DO YOU REMEMBER THE FIGHT YOU HAD ON NEW YEAR'S?
WITH WHO?
WITH ENVY. YOU GOT REALLY DRUNK.
I DON'T DRINK.
OH RIGHT.
WAS THIS LIKE A FIGHT FIGHT?
YOU DON'T REMEMBER IT AT ALL?
new year's eve
I... UH... I GOT A HAIRCUT.
SEE?
GET OUT OF MY LIFE, SCOTT.

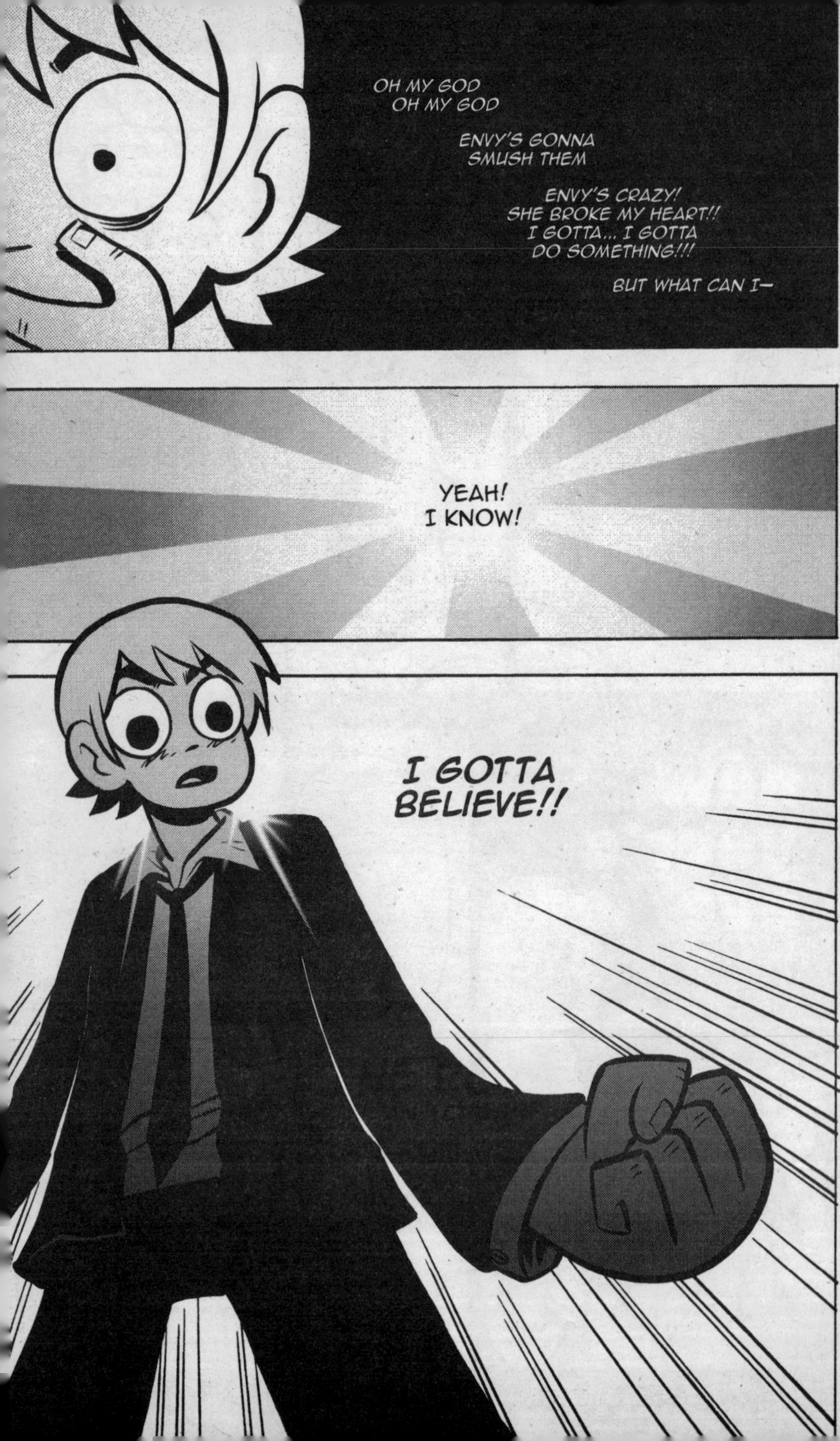
OH MY GOD
OH MY GOD
ENVY'S GONNA SMUSH THEM
ENVY'S CRAZY! SHE BROKE MY HEART!! I GOTTA... I GOTTA DO SOMETHING!!!
BUT WHAT CAN I—
YEAH! I KNOW!
I GOTTA BELIEVE!!

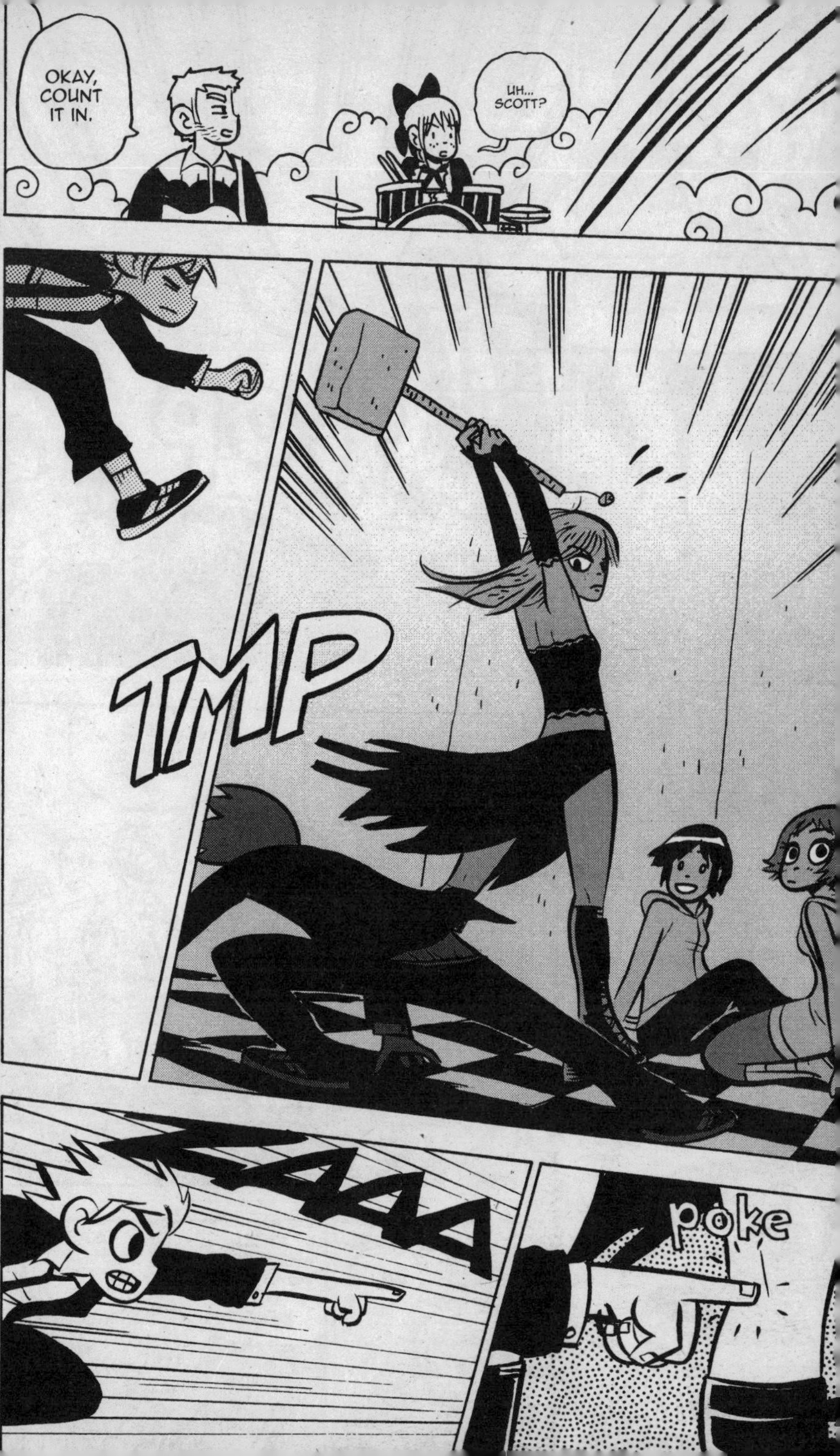
OKAY, COUNT IT IN.
UH... SCOTT?
TMP
ZAAAA
poke

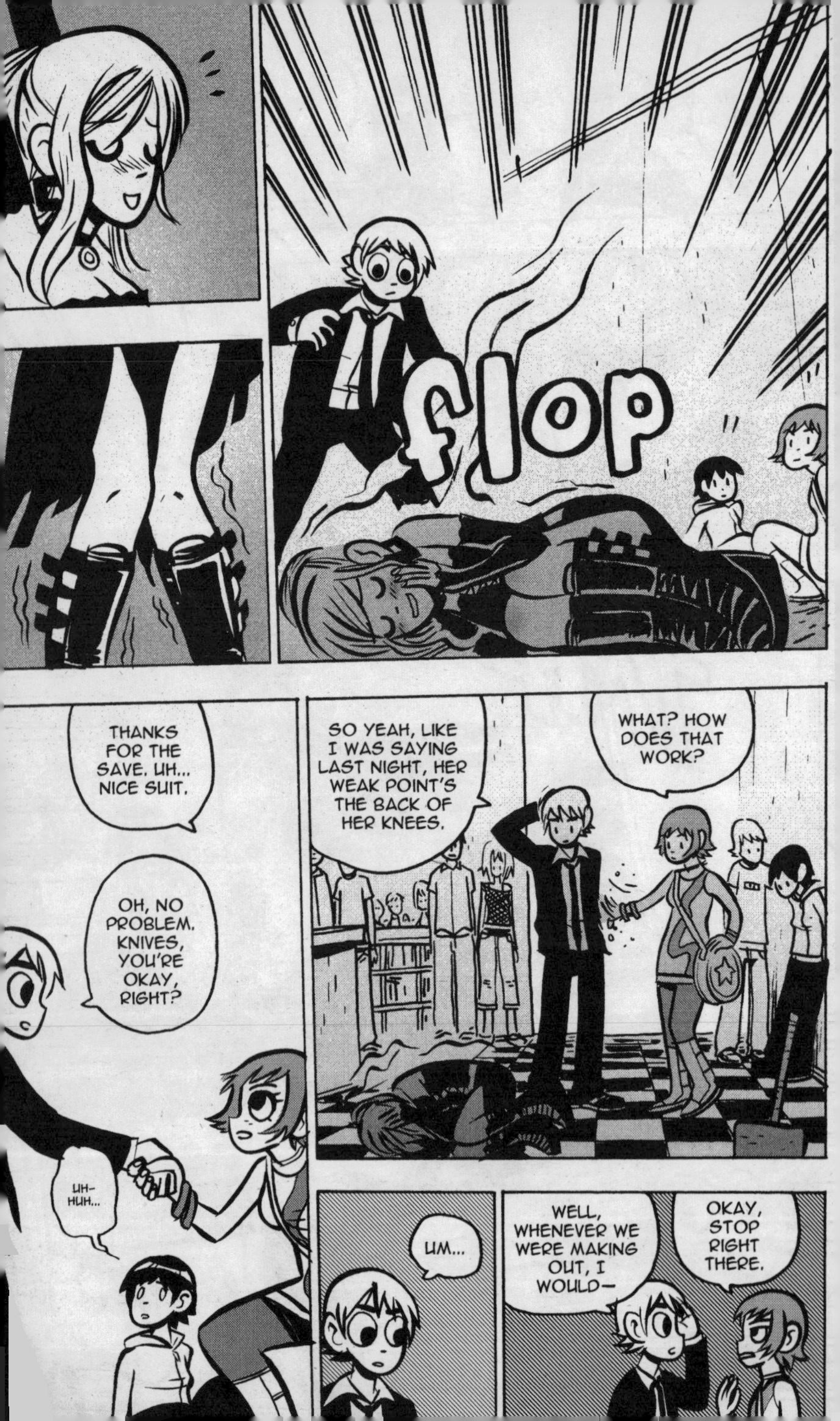
flop
THANKS FOR THE SAVE. UH... NICE SUIT.
OH, NO PROBLEM. KNIVES, YOU'RE OKAY, RIGHT?
UH-HUH...
SO YEAH, LIKE I WAS SAYING LAST NIGHT, HER WEAK POINT'S THE BACK OF HER KNEES.
WHAT? HOW DOES THAT WORK?
UM...
WELL, WHENEVER WE WERE MAKING OUT, I WOULD—
OKAY, STOP RIGHT THERE.

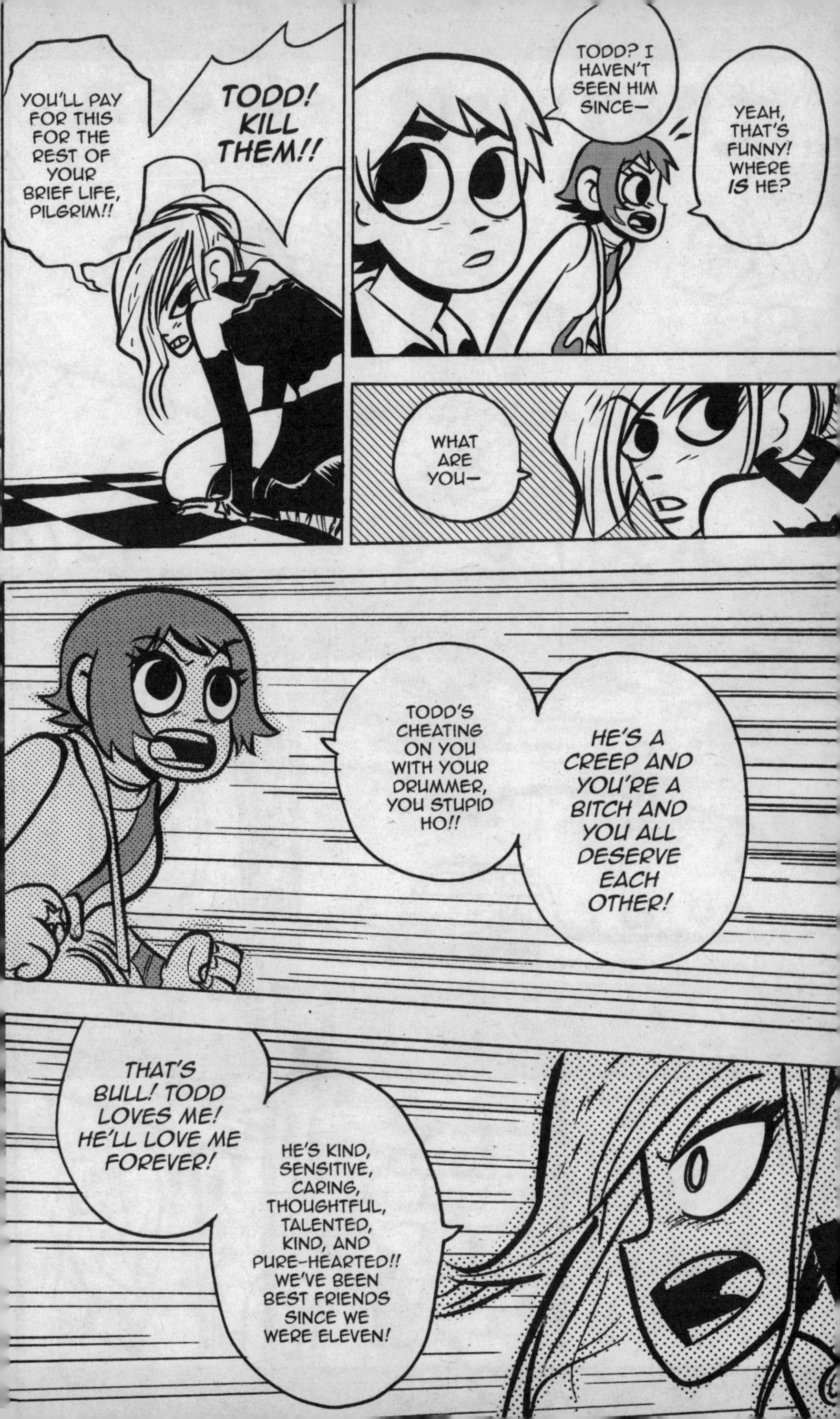
YOU'LL PAY FOR THIS FOR THE REST OF YOUR BRIEF LIFE, PILGRIM!!
TODD! KILL THEM!!
TODD? I HAVEN'T SEEN HIM SINCE—
YEAH, THAT'S FUNNY! WHERE IS HE?
WHAT ARE YOU—
TODD'S CHEATING ON YOU WITH YOUR DRUMMER, YOU STUPID HO!!
HE'S A CREEP AND YOU'RE A BITCH AND YOU ALL DESERVE EACH OTHER!
THAT'S BULL! TODD LOVES ME! HE'LL LOVE ME FOREVER!
HE'S KIND, SENSITIVE, CARING, THOUGHTFUL, TALENTED, KIND, AND PURE-HEARTED!! WE'VE BEEN BEST FRIENDS SINCE WE WERE ELEVEN!

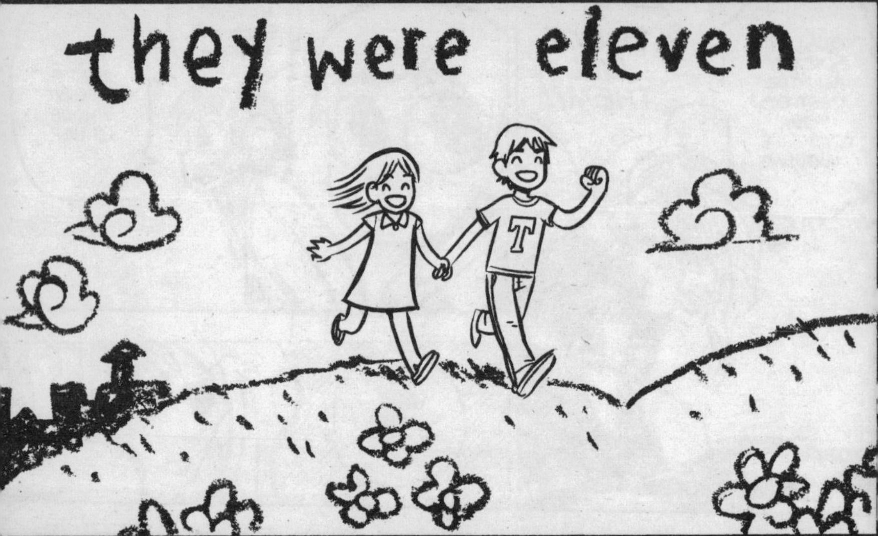
they were eleven

Once upon a time, there was a boy and a girl. They lived as next-door neighbours in a small town called Montreal, and their love was as pure as pure can be.

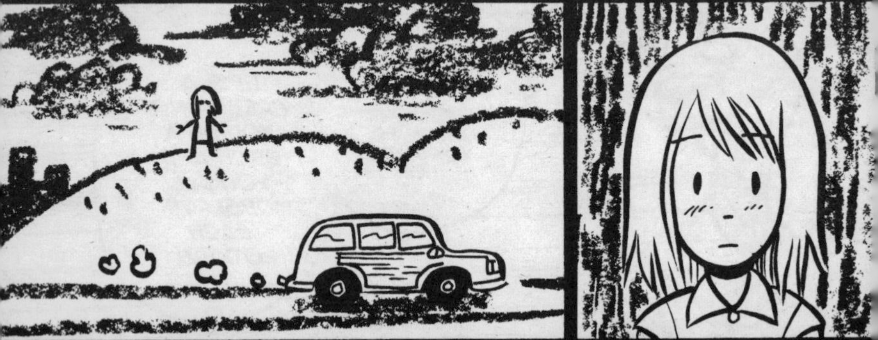

But it was not to last. One day, the boy and his family moved away to a distant land of mountains and dairy cows. The girl grew up alone, and never found another she could truly love, though she tried her hardest.

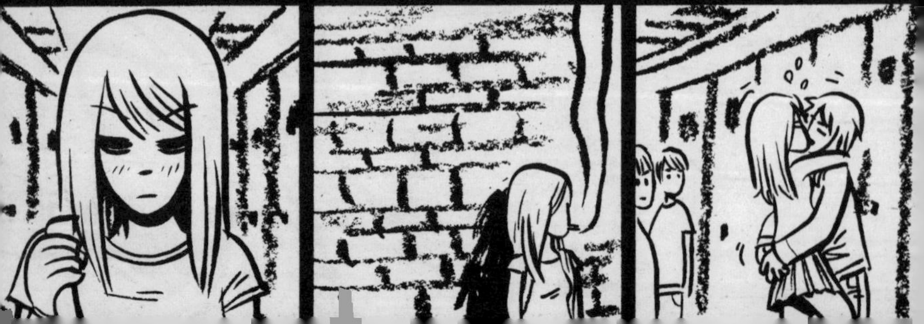

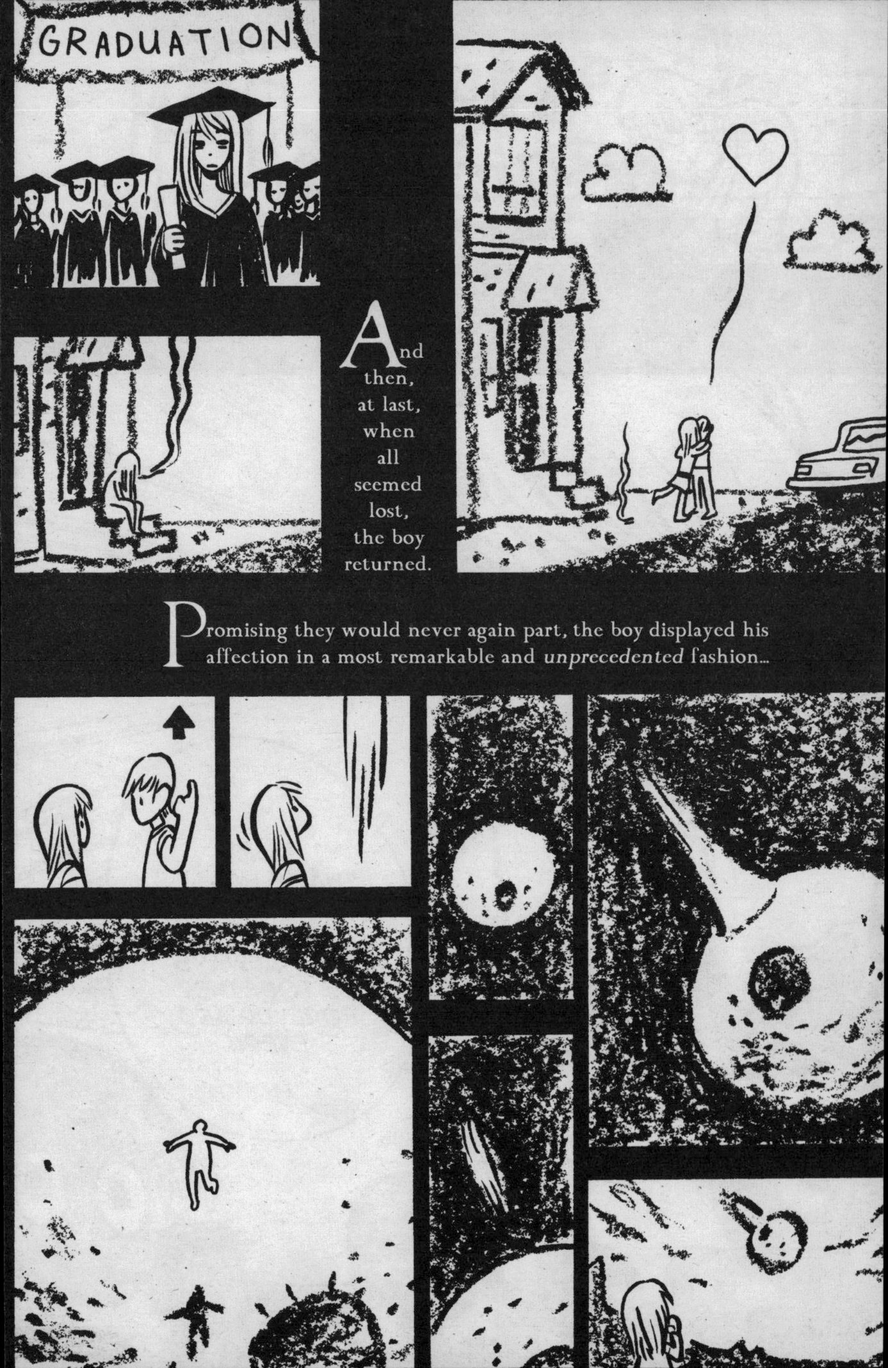
GRADUATION
And then, at last, when all seemed lost, the boy returned.
Promising they would never again part, the boy displayed his affection in a most remarkable and *unprecedented* fashion...

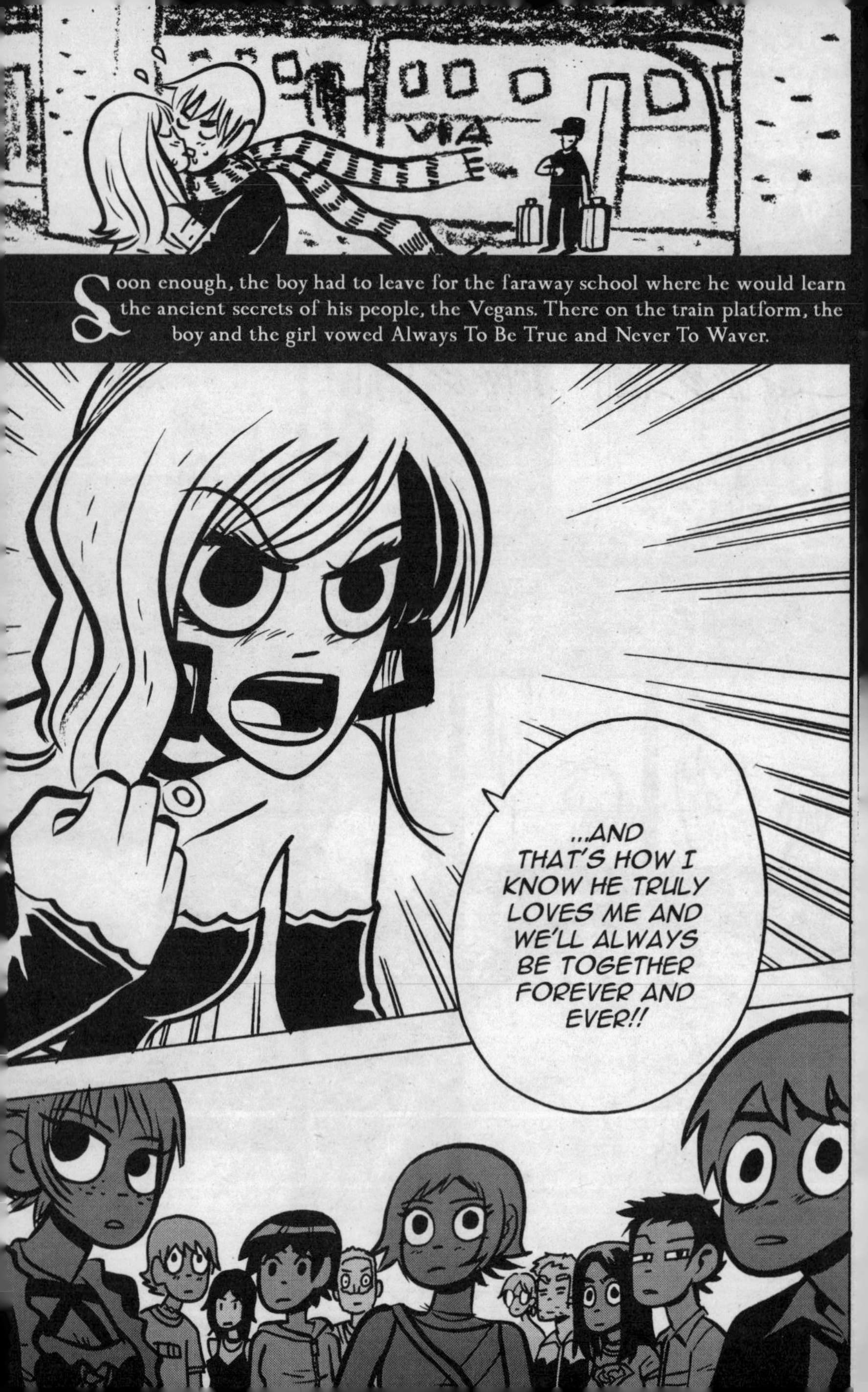
VIA
Soon enough, the boy had to leave for the faraway school where he would learn the ancient secrets of his people, the Vegans. There on the train platform, the boy and the girl vowed Always To Be True and Never To Waver.
...AND THAT'S HOW I KNOW HE TRULY LOVES ME AND WE'LL ALWAYS BE TOGETHER FOREVER AND EVER!!

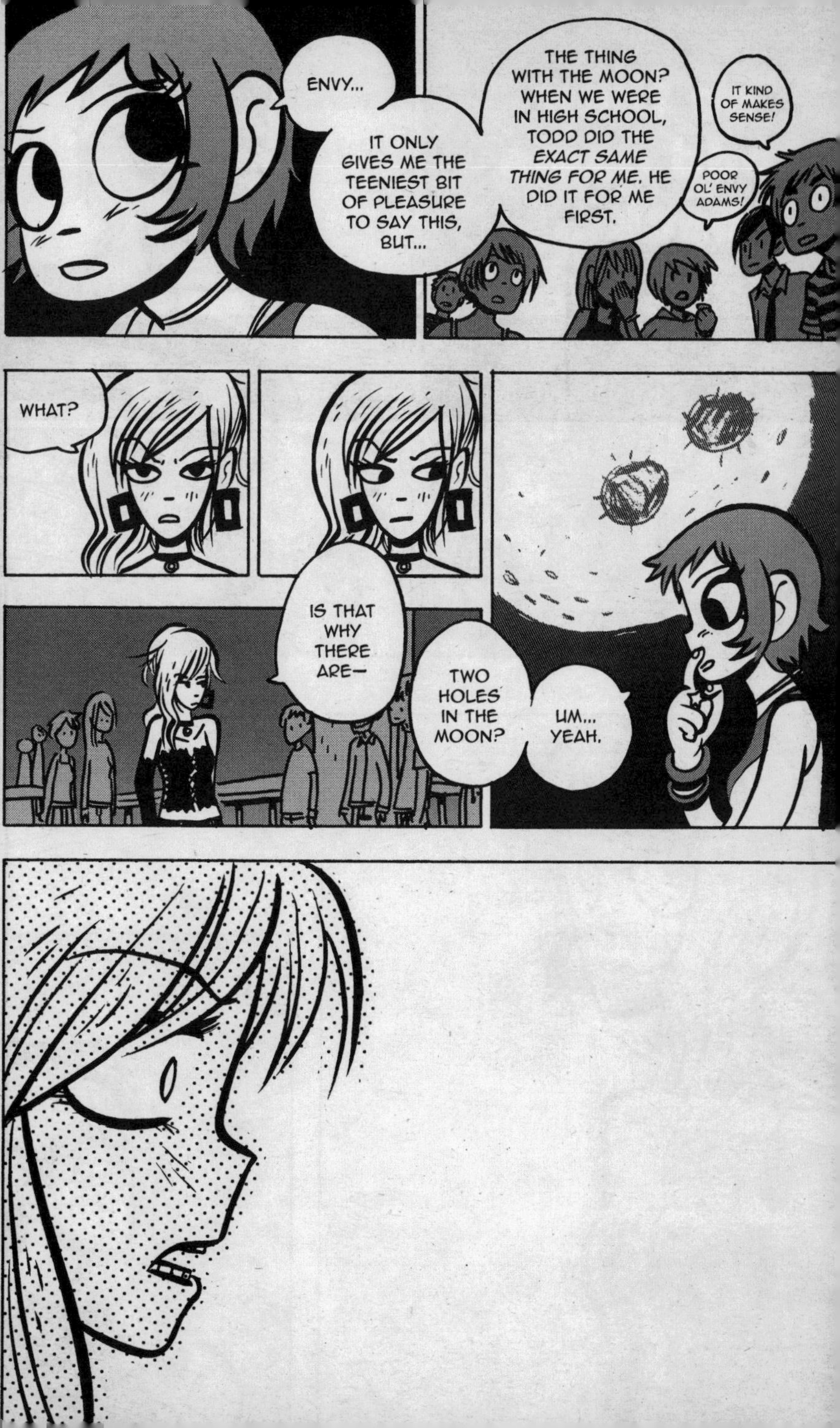
ENVY...
IT ONLY GIVES ME THE TEENIEST BIT OF PLEASURE TO SAY THIS, BUT...
THE THING WITH THE MOON? WHEN WE WERE IN HIGH SCHOOL, TODD DID THE EXACT SAME THING FOR ME. HE DID IT FOR ME FIRST.
IT KIND OF MAKES SENSE!
POOR OL' ENVY ADAMS!
WHAT?
IS THAT WHY THERE ARE—
TWO HOLES IN THE MOON?
UM... YEAH.

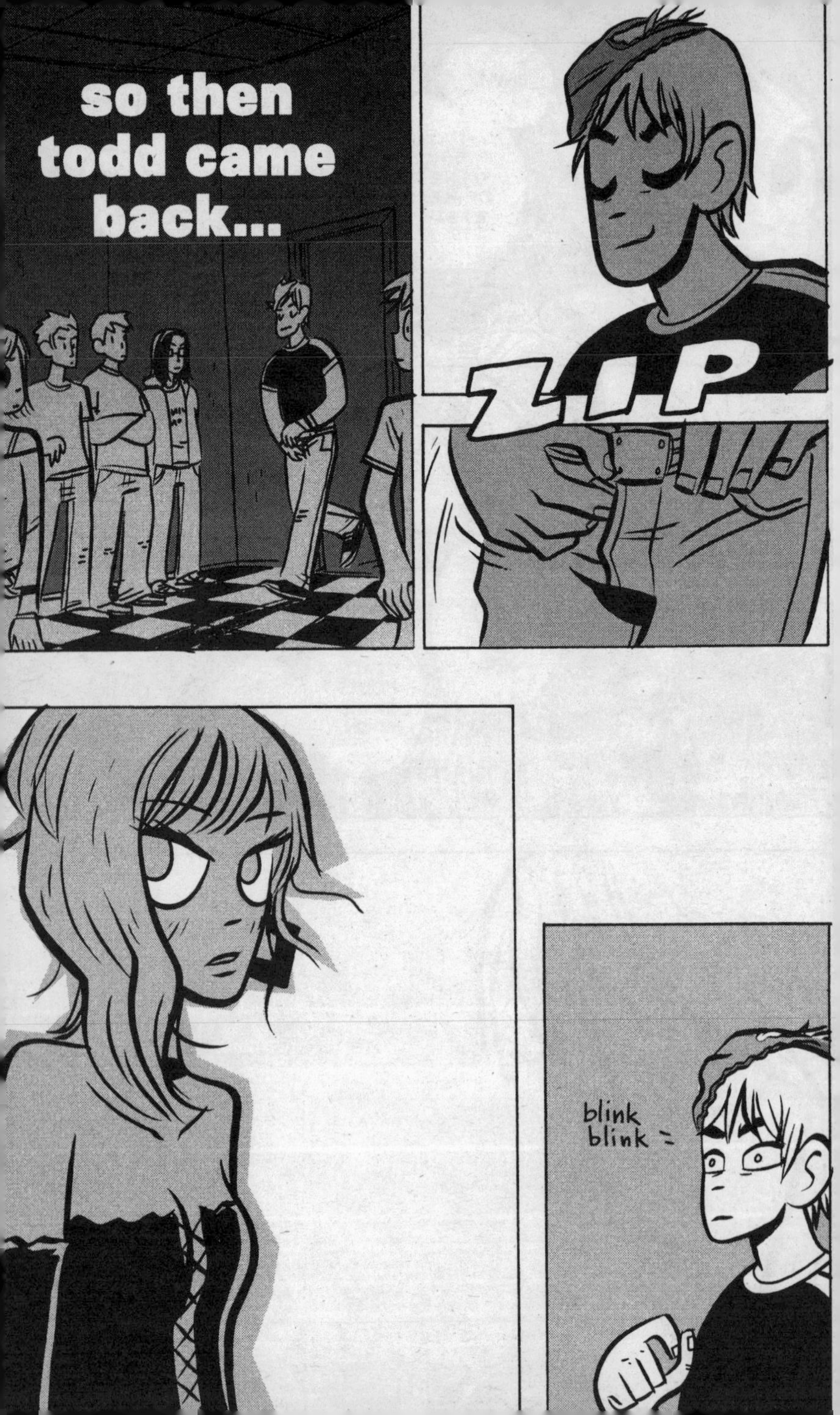
so then todd came back...
ZIP
blink blink

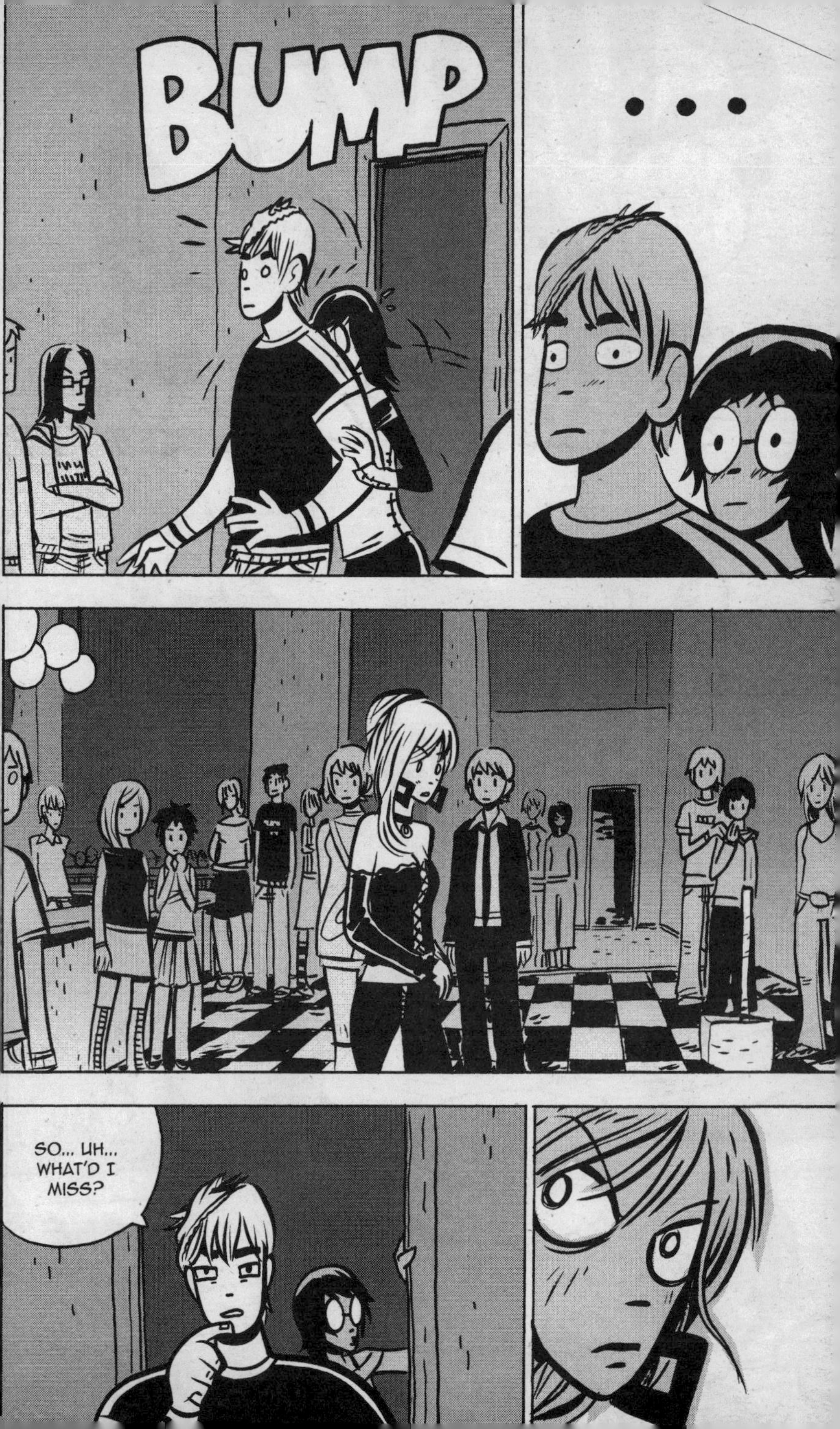
BUMP
...
SO... UH... WHAT'D I MISS?

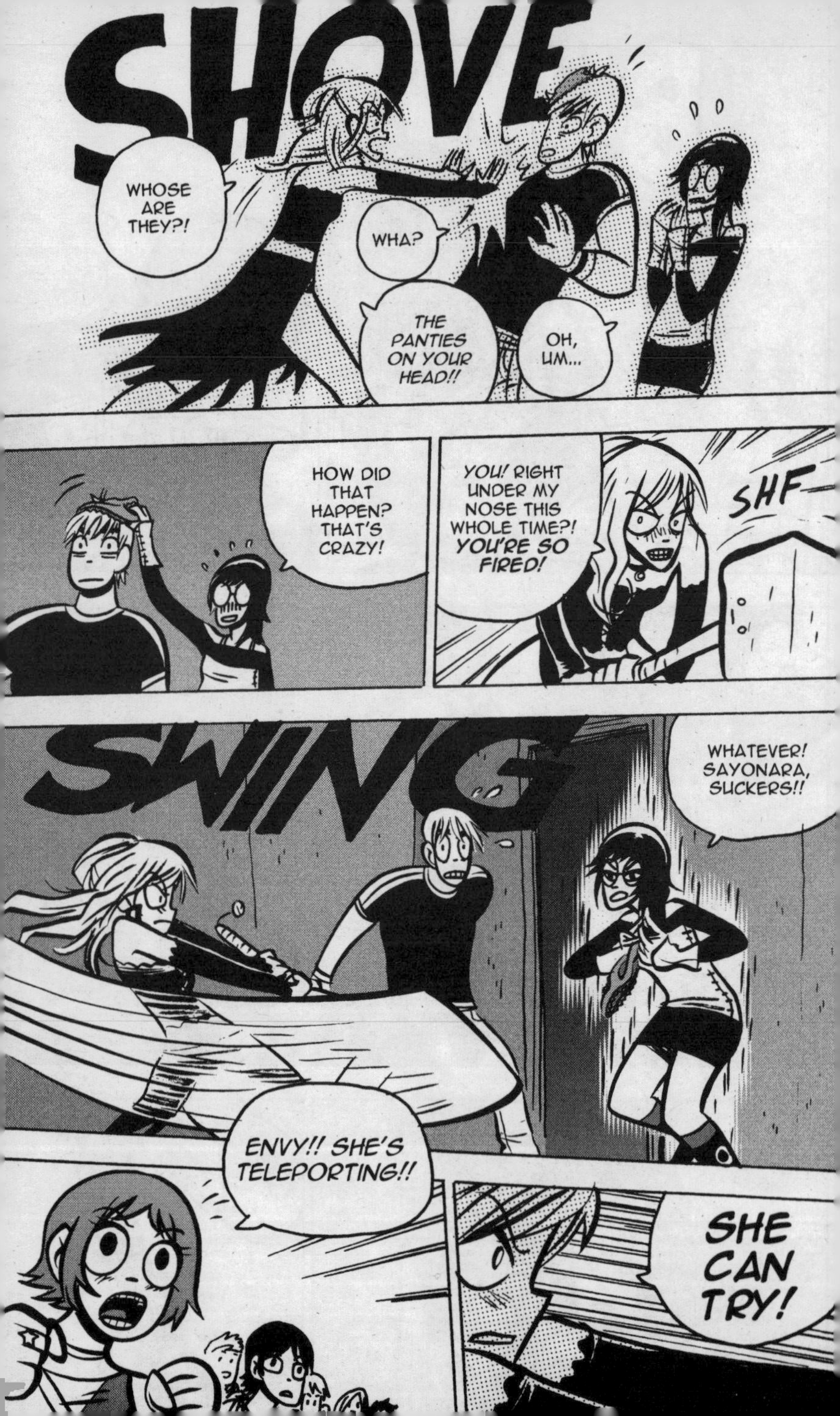
SHOVE
WHOSE ARE THEY?!
WHA?
THE PANTIES ON YOUR HEAD!!
OH, UM...
HOW DID THAT HAPPEN? THAT'S CRAZY!
YOU! RIGHT UNDER MY NOSE THIS WHOLE TIME?! YOU'RE SO FIRED!
SHF
SWING
WHATEVER! SAYONARA, SUCKERS!!
ENVY!! SHE'S TELEPORTING!!
SHE CAN TRY!

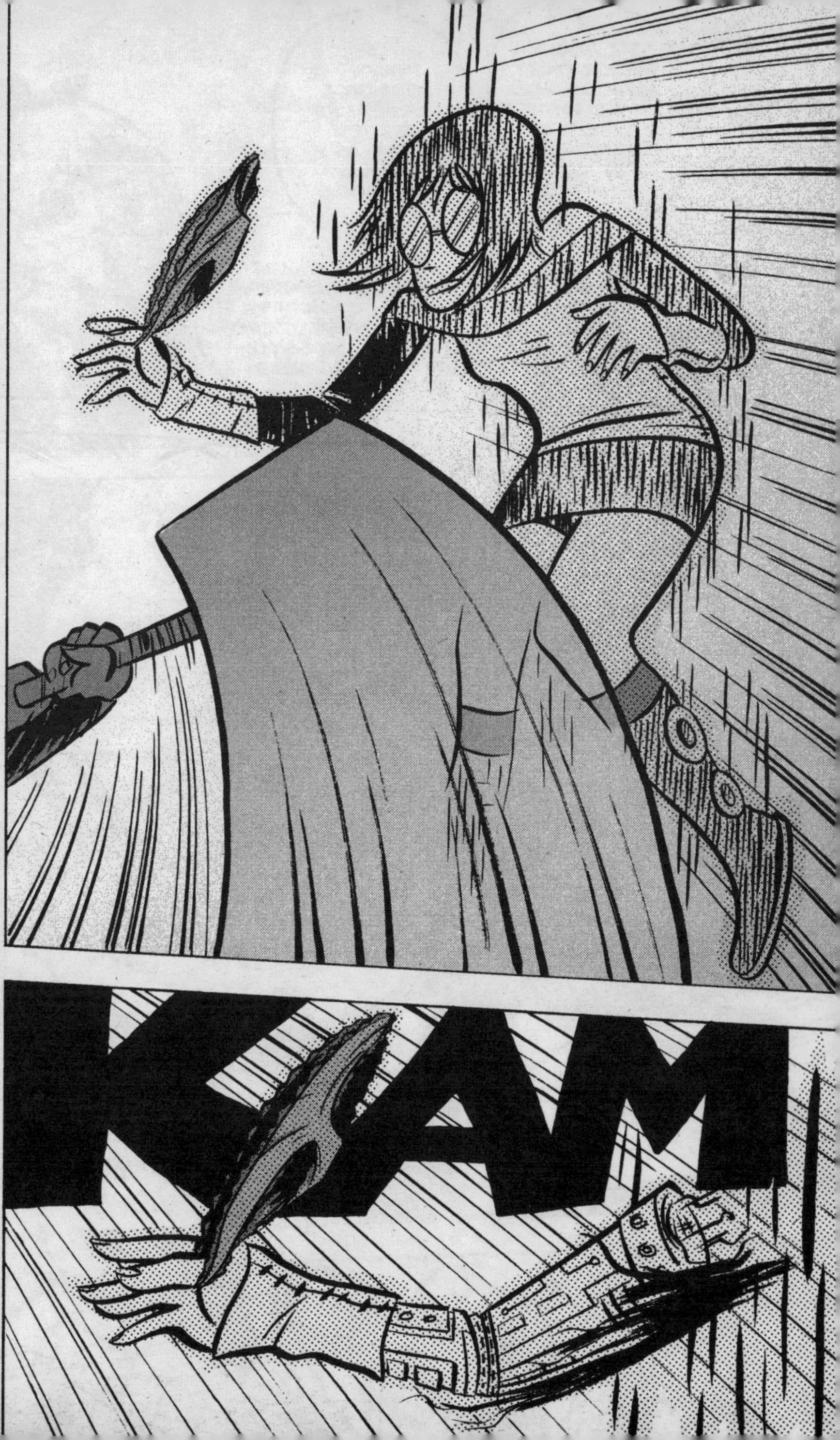
KAM

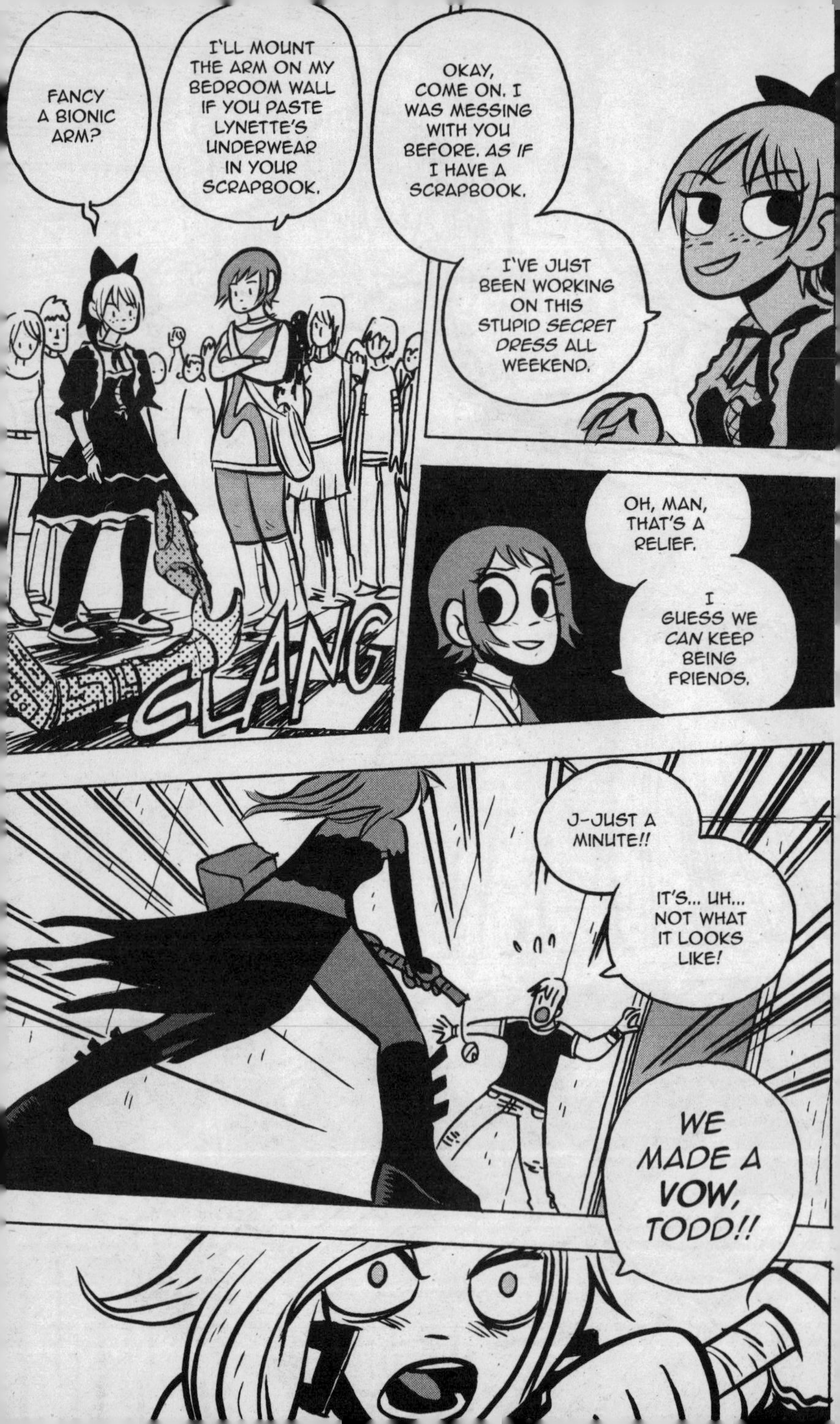
FANCY A BIONIC ARM?
I'LL MOUNT THE ARM ON MY BEDROOM WALL IF YOU PASTE LYNETTE'S UNDERWEAR IN YOUR SCRAPBOOK.
OKAY, COME ON. I WAS MESSING WITH YOU BEFORE. AS IF I HAVE A SCRAPBOOK.
I'VE JUST BEEN WORKING ON THIS STUPID SECRET DRESS ALL WEEKEND.
CLANG
OH, MAN, THAT'S A RELIEF.
I GUESS WE CAN KEEP BEING FRIENDS.
J-JUST A MINUTE!!
IT'S... UH... NOT WHAT IT LOOKS LIKE!
WE MADE A VOW, TODD!!

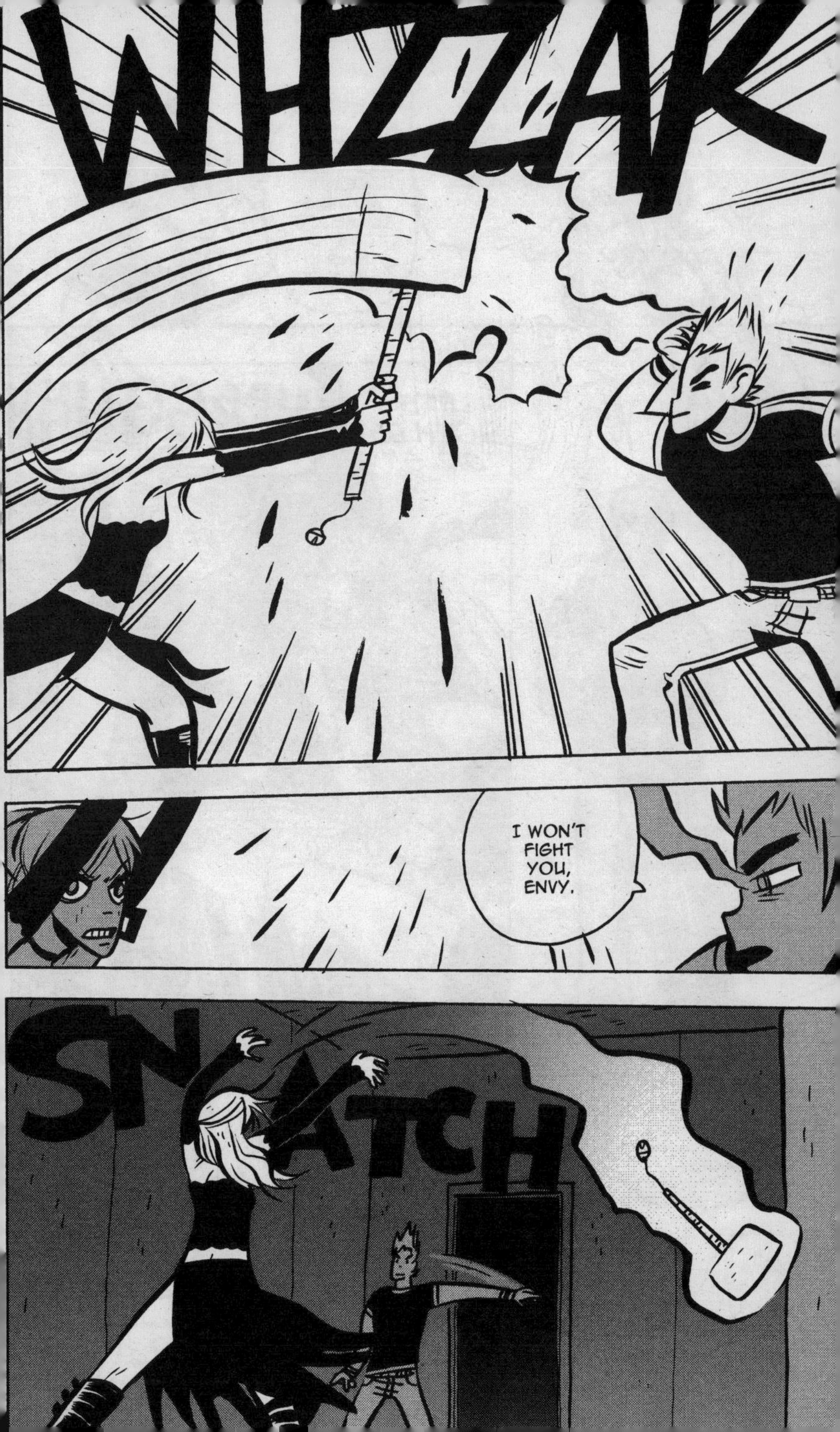
WHZAK
I WON'T FIGHT YOU, ENVY.
SNATCH

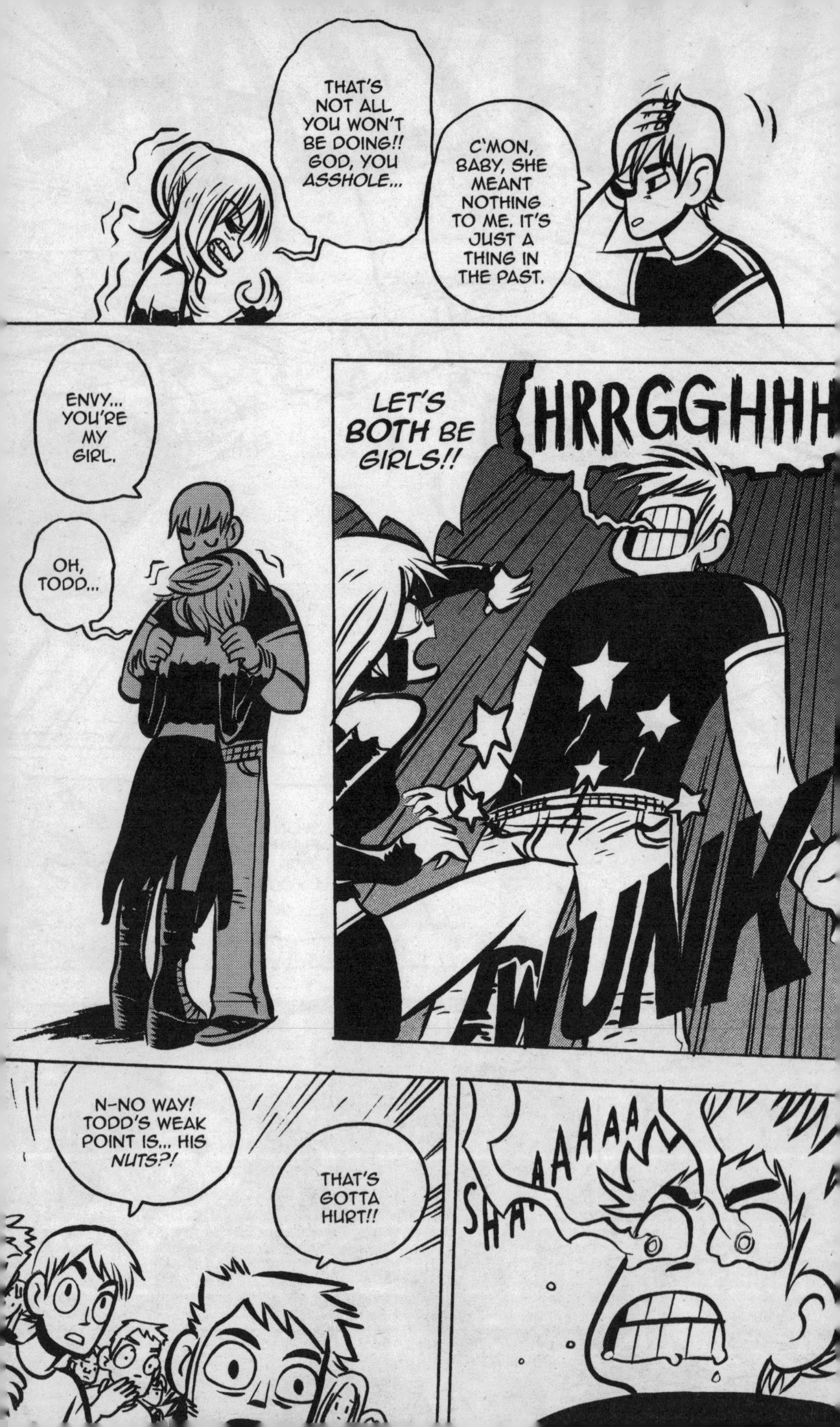
THAT'S NOT ALL YOU WON'T BE DOING!! GOD, YOU ASSHOLE...
C'MON, BABY, SHE MEANT NOTHING TO ME. IT'S JUST A THING IN THE PAST.
ENVY... YOU'RE MY GIRL.
OH, TODD...
LET'S BOTH BE GIRLS!!
HRRGGHHH
WUNK
N-NO WAY! TODD'S WEAK POINT IS... HIS NUTS?!
THAT'S GOTTA HURT!!
SHAAAAAAA

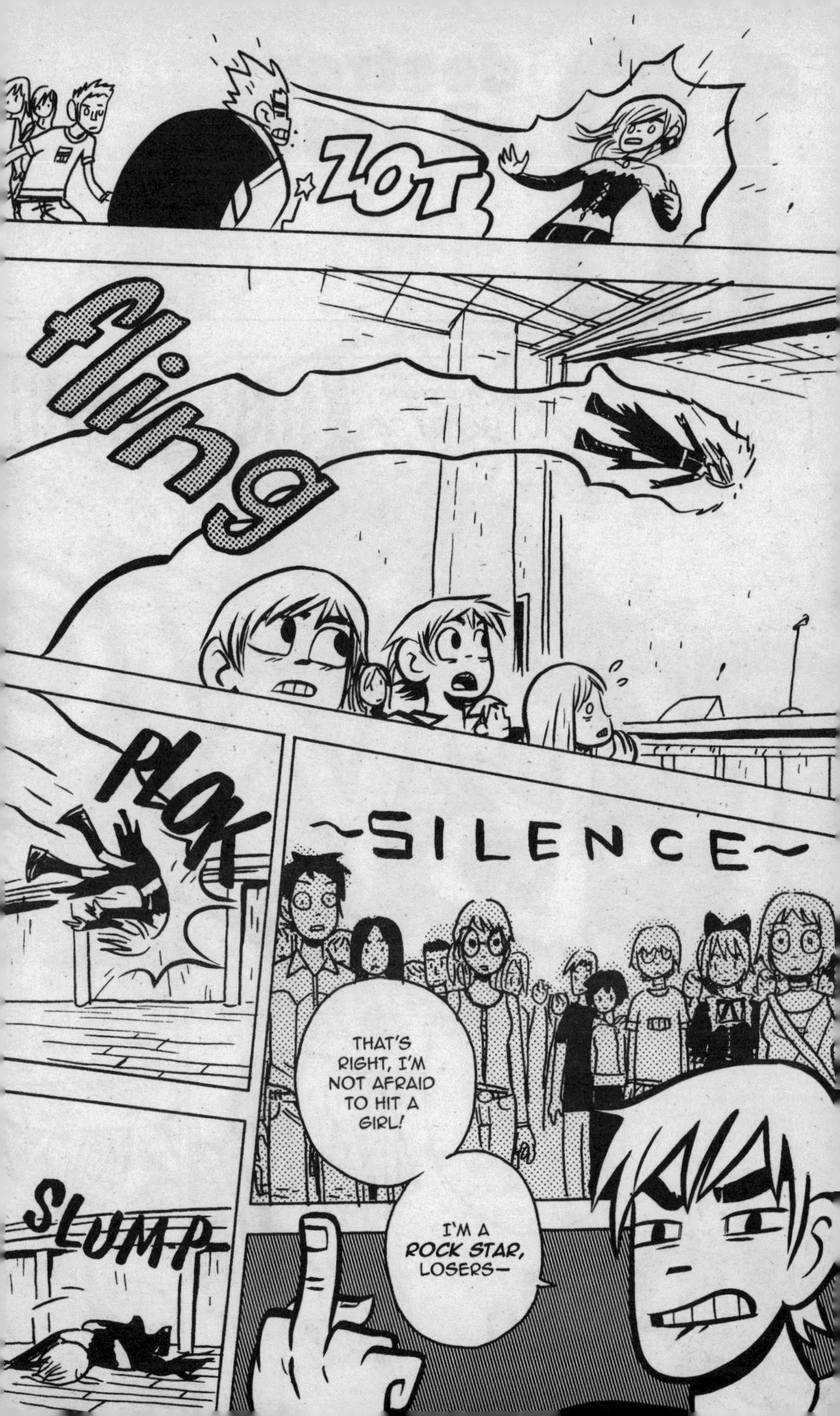
ZOT
fling
PLOCK
SLUMP
~SILENCE~
THAT'S RIGHT, I'M NOT AFRAID TO HIT A GIRL!
I'M A ROCK STAR, LOSERS—

18 destroy all vegans

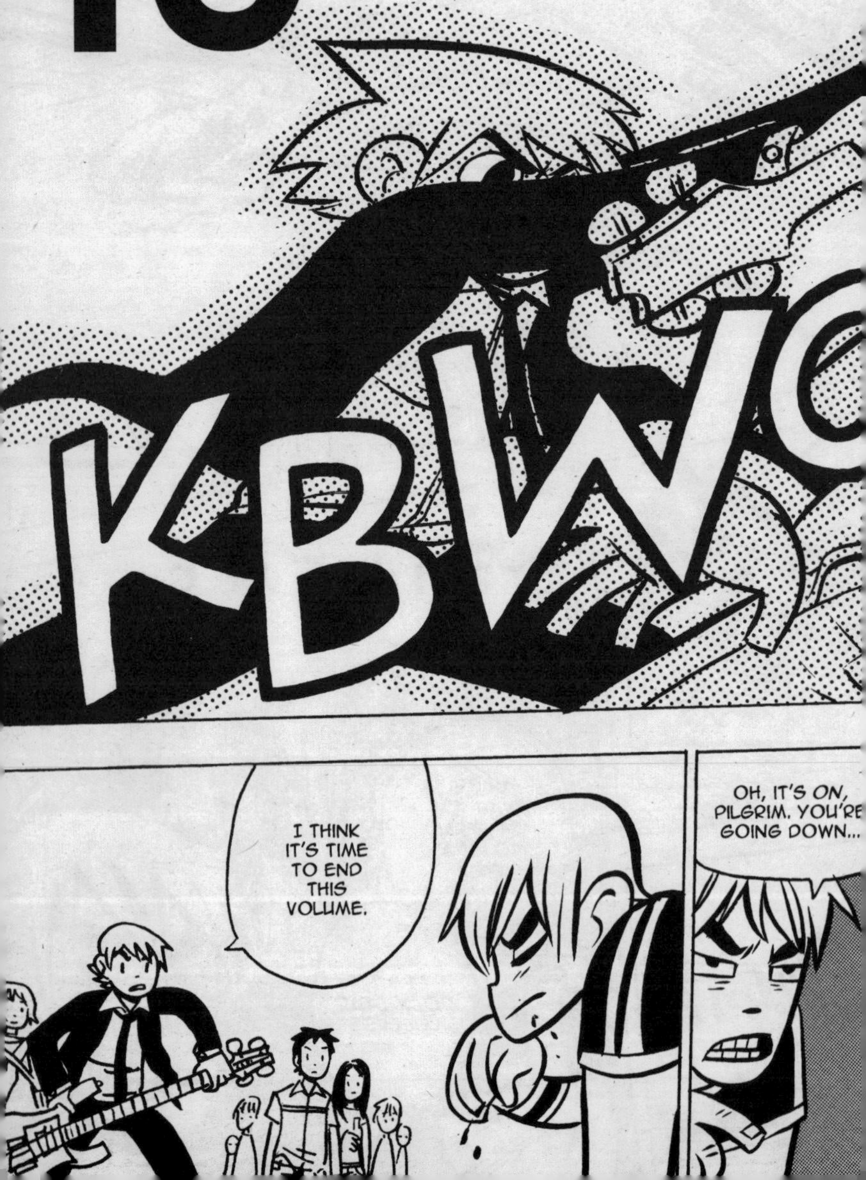
KBW
I THINK IT'S TIME TO END THIS VOLUME.
OH, IT'S ON, PILGRIM. YOU'RE GOING DOWN...

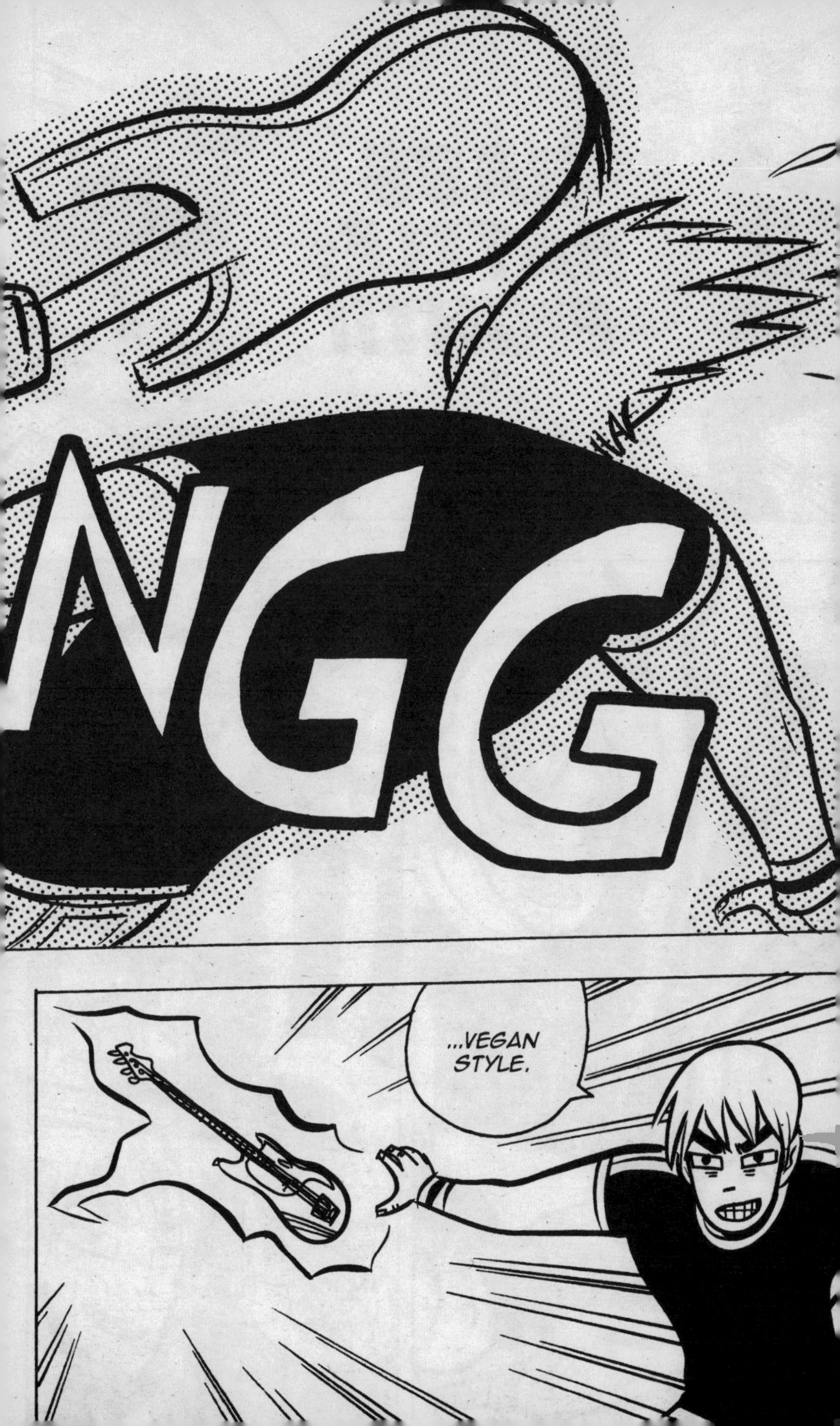
NGG
...VEGAN STYLE.

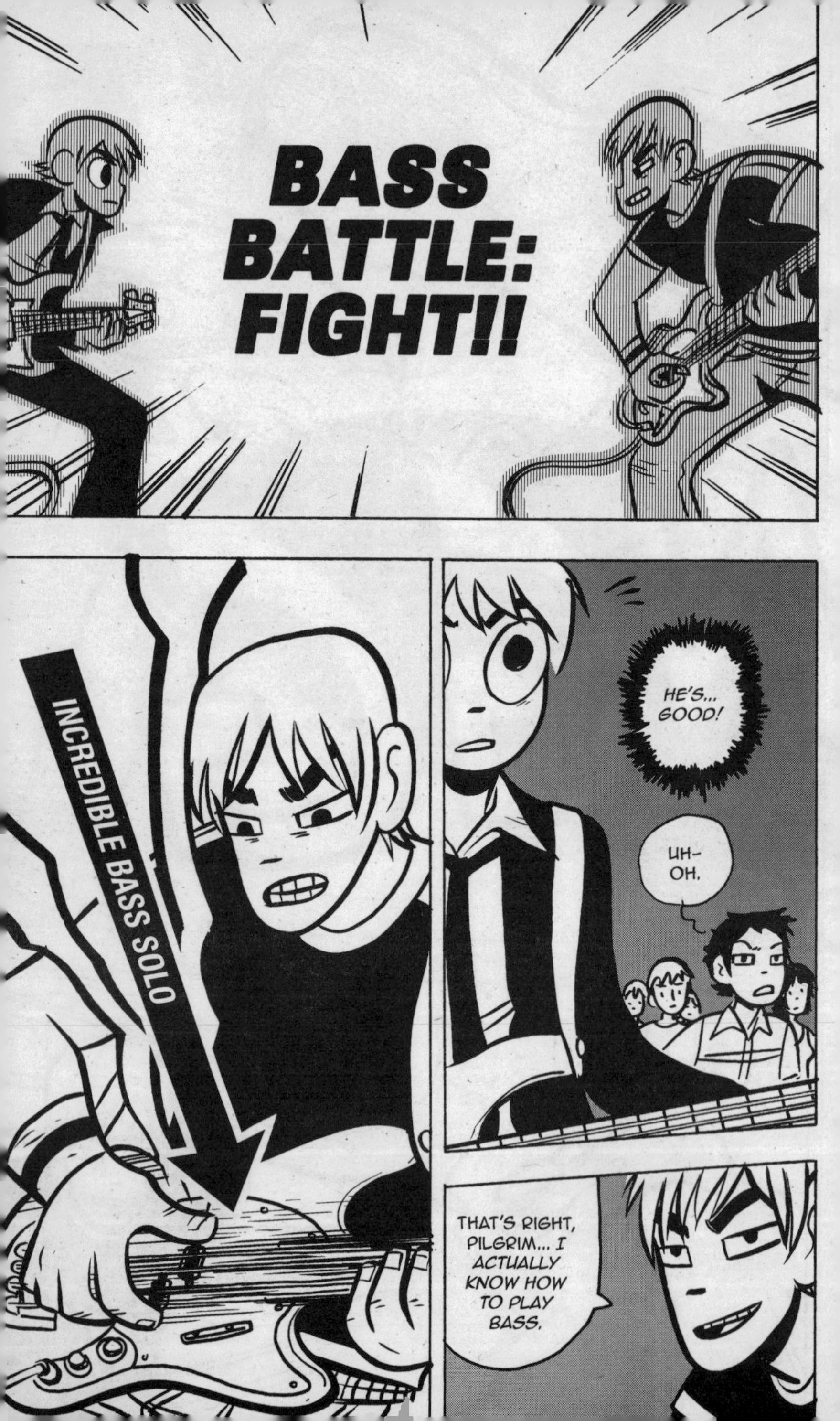
BASS BATTLE: FIGHT!!
INCREDIBLE BASS SOLO
HE'S... GOOD!
UH-OH.
THAT'S RIGHT, PILGRIM... I ACTUALLY KNOW HOW TO PLAY BASS.

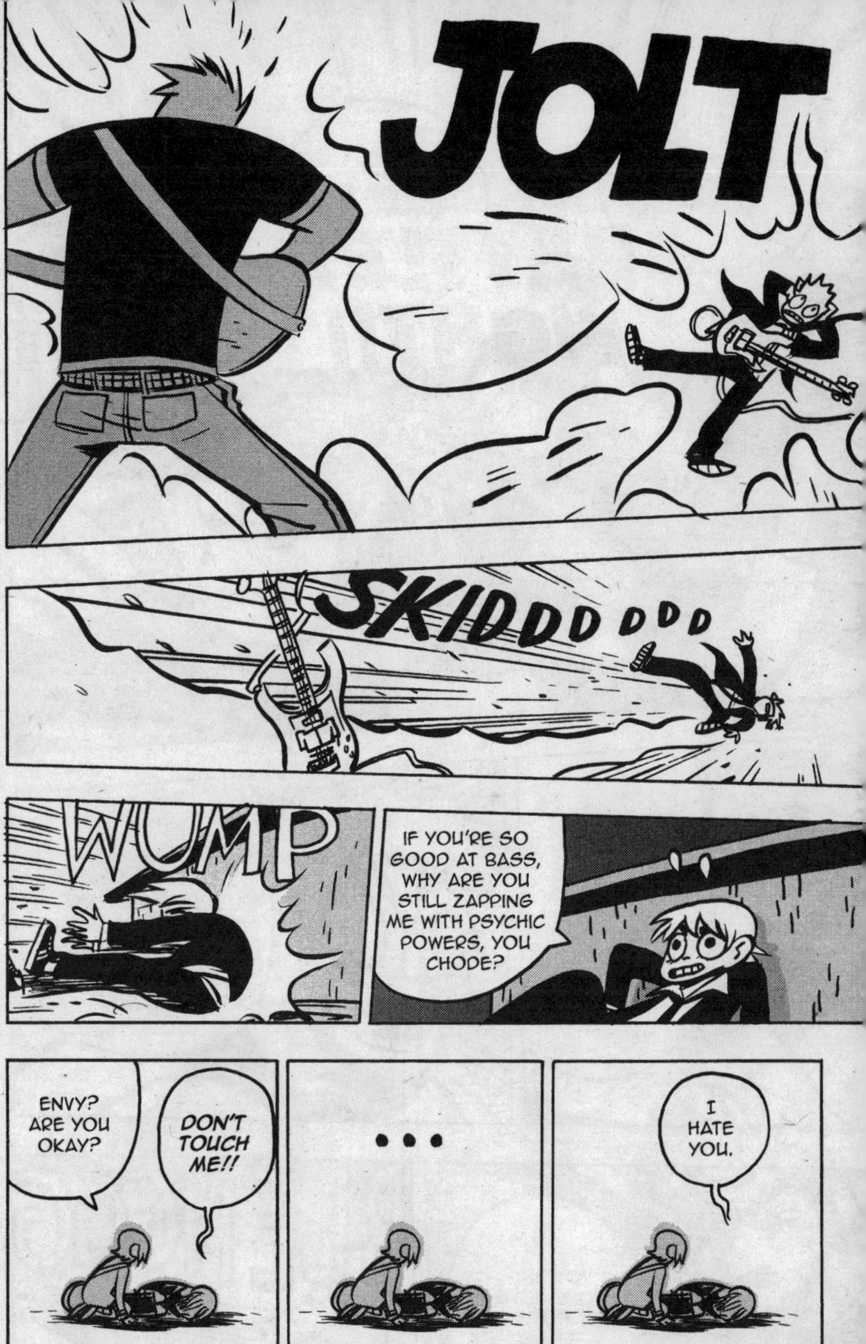
JOLT
SKIDDDDDDD
WUMP
IF YOU'RE SO GOOD AT BASS, WHY ARE YOU STILL ZAPPING ME WITH PSYCHIC POWERS, YOU CHODE?
ENVY? ARE YOU OKAY?
DON'T TOUCH ME!!
...
I HATE YOU.

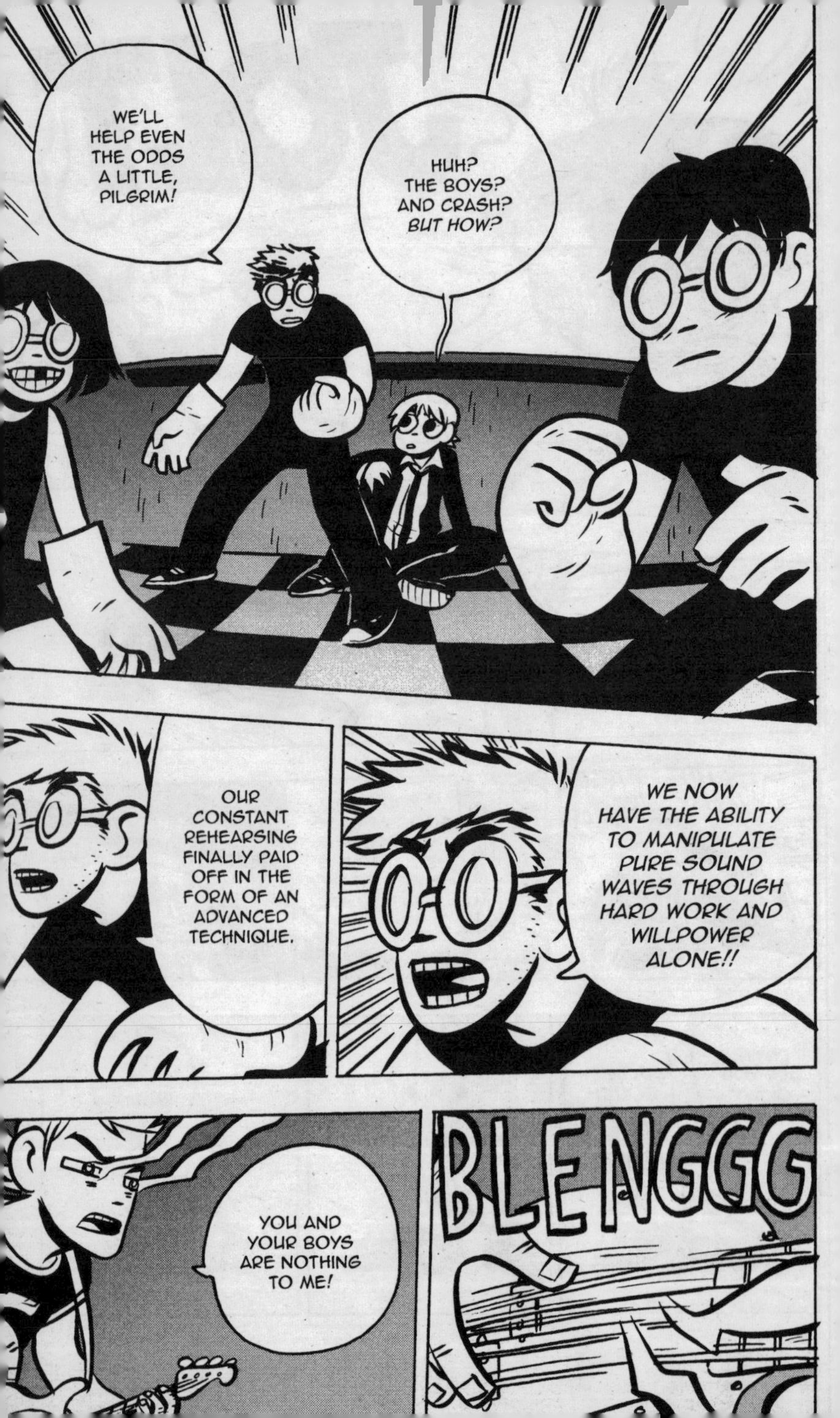
WE'LL HELP EVEN THE ODDS A LITTLE, PILGRIM!
HUH? THE BOYS? AND CRASH? BUT HOW?
OUR CONSTANT REHEARSING FINALLY PAID OFF IN THE FORM OF AN ADVANCED TECHNIQUE.
WE NOW HAVE THE ABILITY TO MANIPULATE PURE SOUND WAVES THROUGH HARD WORK AND WILLPOWER ALONE!!
YOU AND YOUR BOYS ARE NOTHING TO ME!
BLENGGG

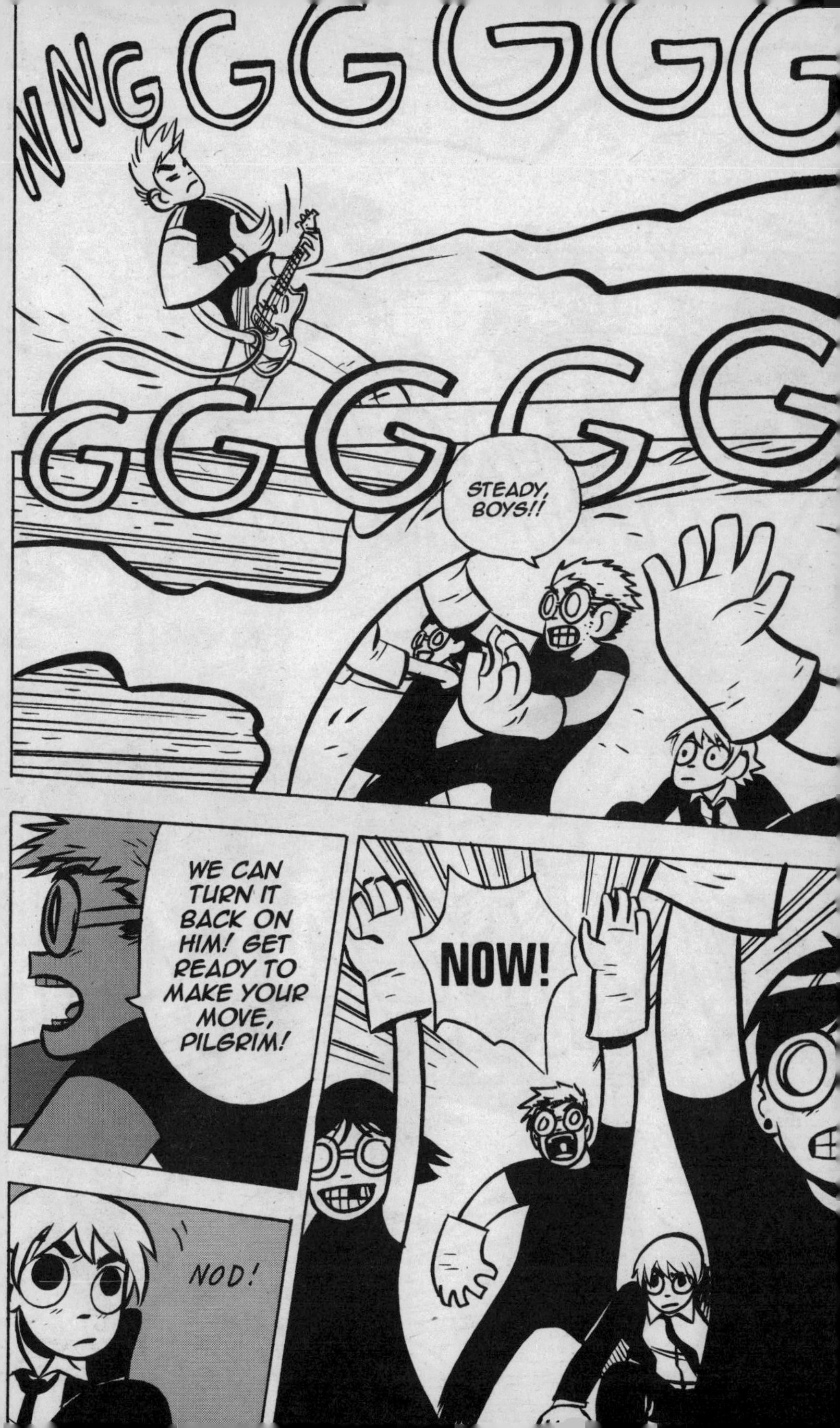
WNGGGGGG
GGGGGG
STEADY, BOYS!!
WE CAN TURN IT BACK ON HIM! GET READY TO MAKE YOUR MOVE, PILGRIM!
NOD!
NOW!

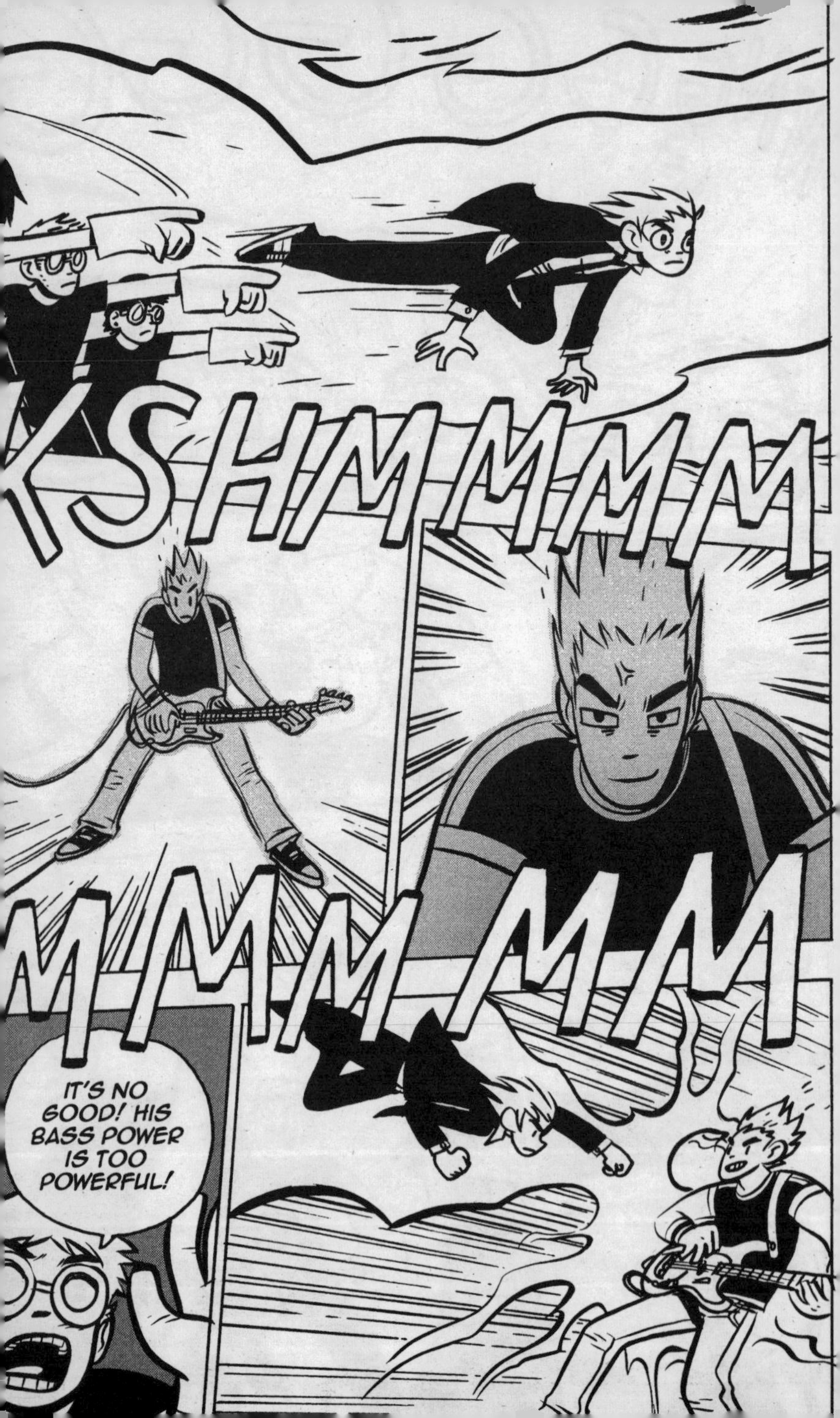
KSHMMMM
MMMMM
IT'S NO GOOD! HIS BASS POWER IS TOO POWERFUL!

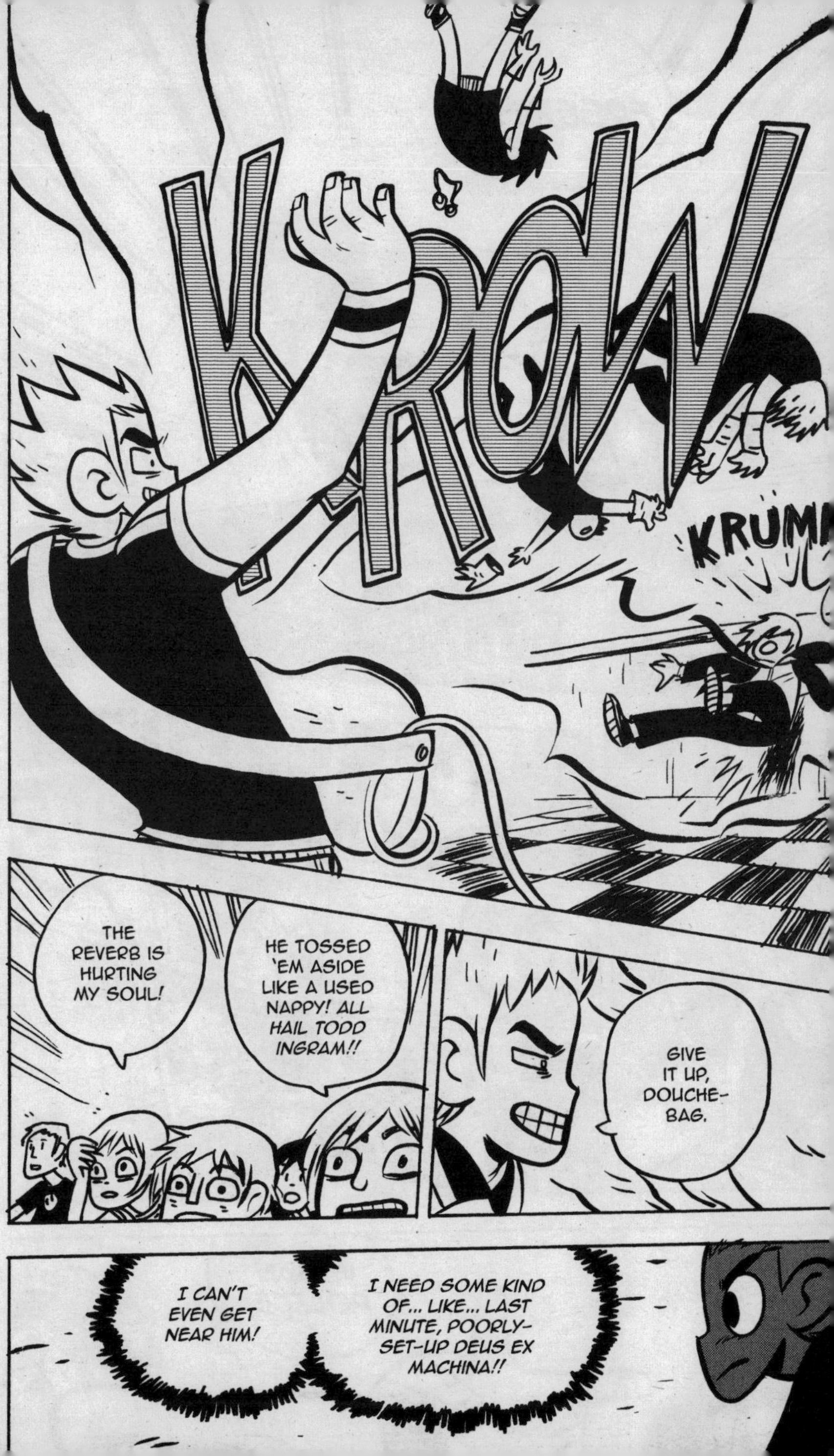
KROW
KRUM
THE REVERB IS HURTING MY SOUL!
HE TOSSED 'EM ASIDE LIKE A USED NAPPY! ALL HAIL TODD INGRAM!!
GIVE IT UP, DOUCHE-BAG.
I CAN'T EVEN GET NEAR HIM!
I NEED SOME KIND OF... LIKE... LAST MINUTE, POORLY-SET-UP DEUS EX MACHINA!!

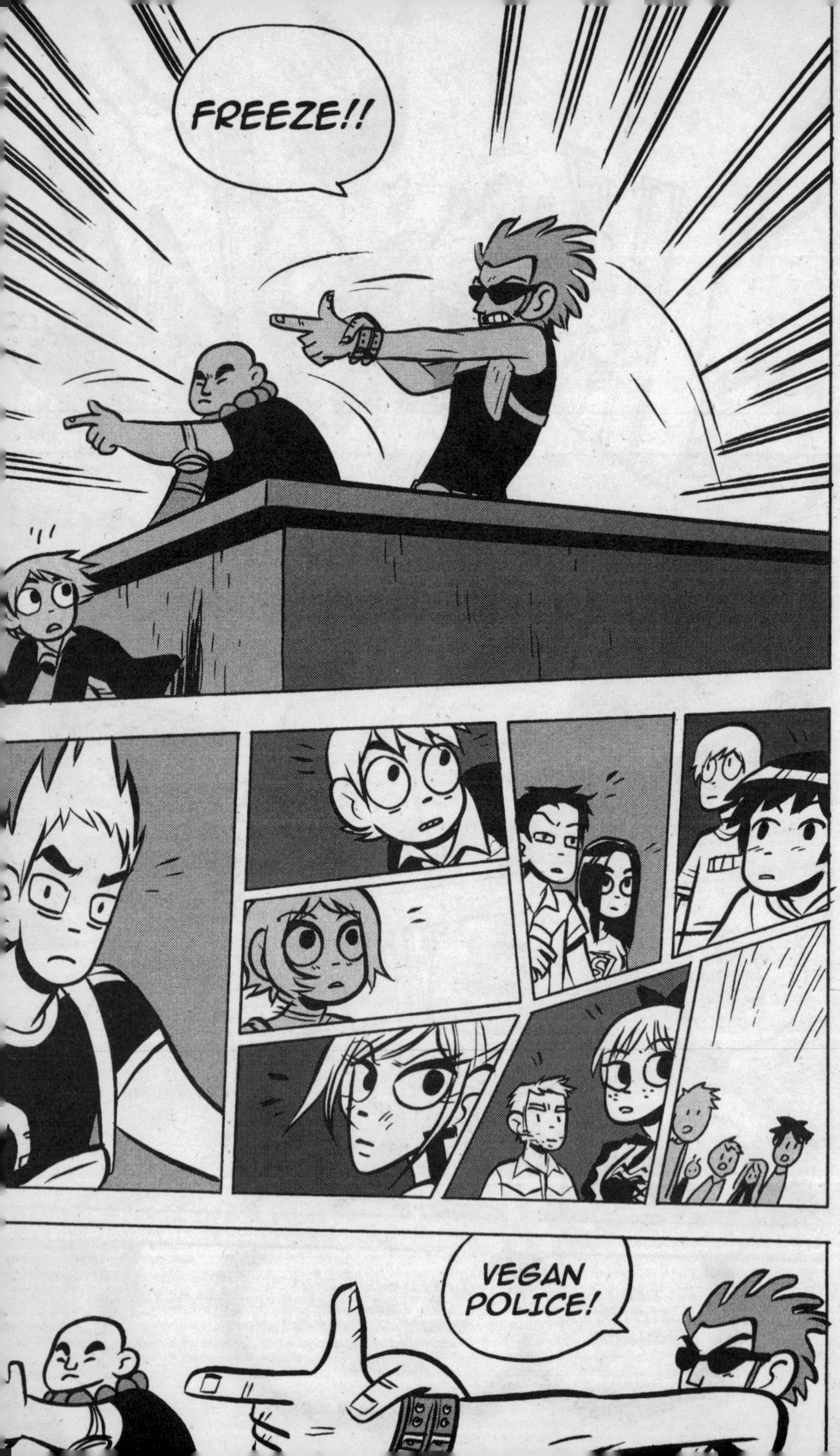
FREEZE!!
VEGAN POLICE!

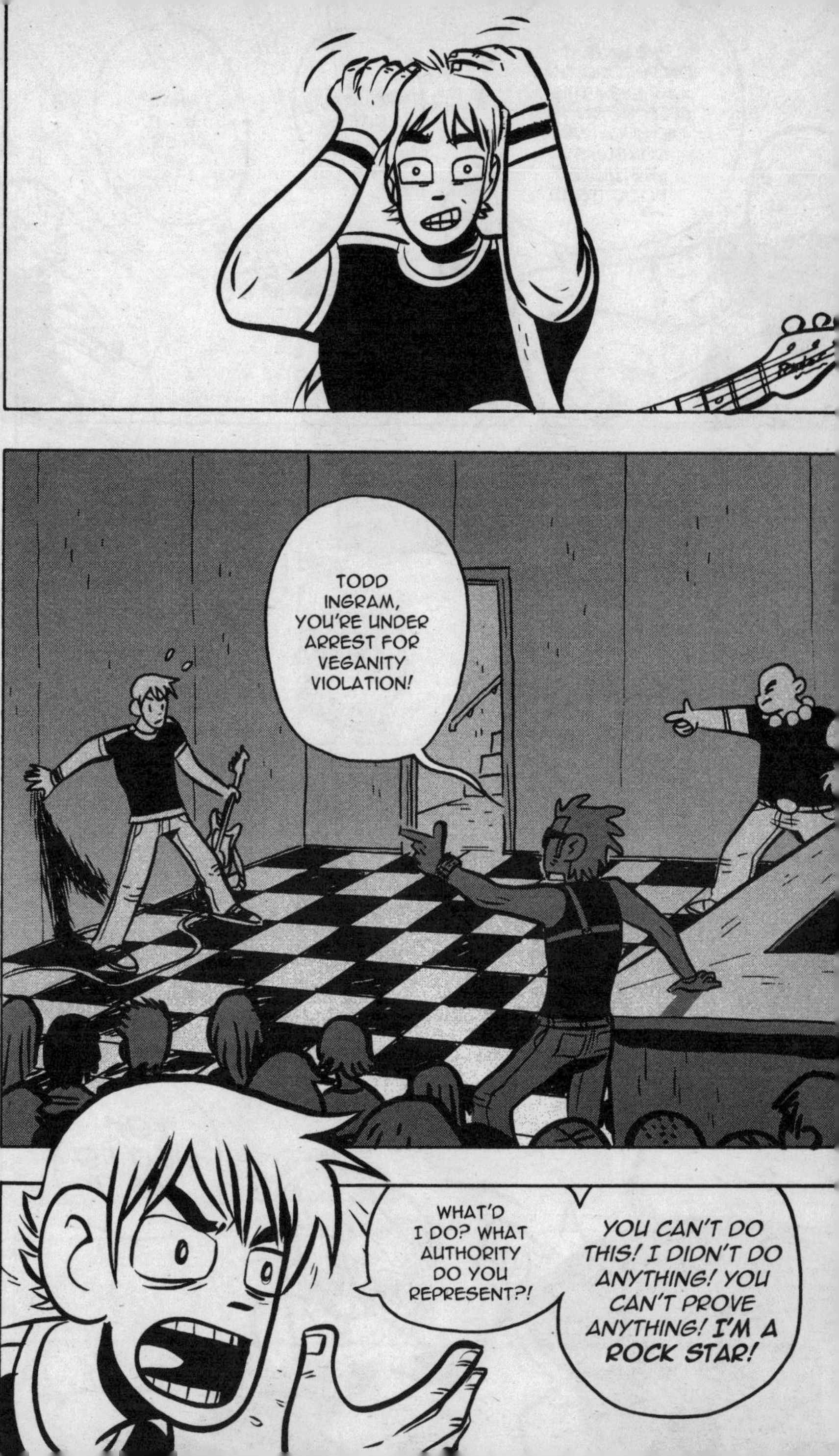
TODD INGRAM, YOU'RE UNDER ARREST FOR VEGANITY VIOLATION!
WHAT'D I DO? WHAT AUTHORITY DO YOU REPRESENT?!
YOU CAN'T DO THIS! I DIDN'T DO ANYTHING! YOU CAN'T PROVE ANYTHING! I'M A ROCK STAR!

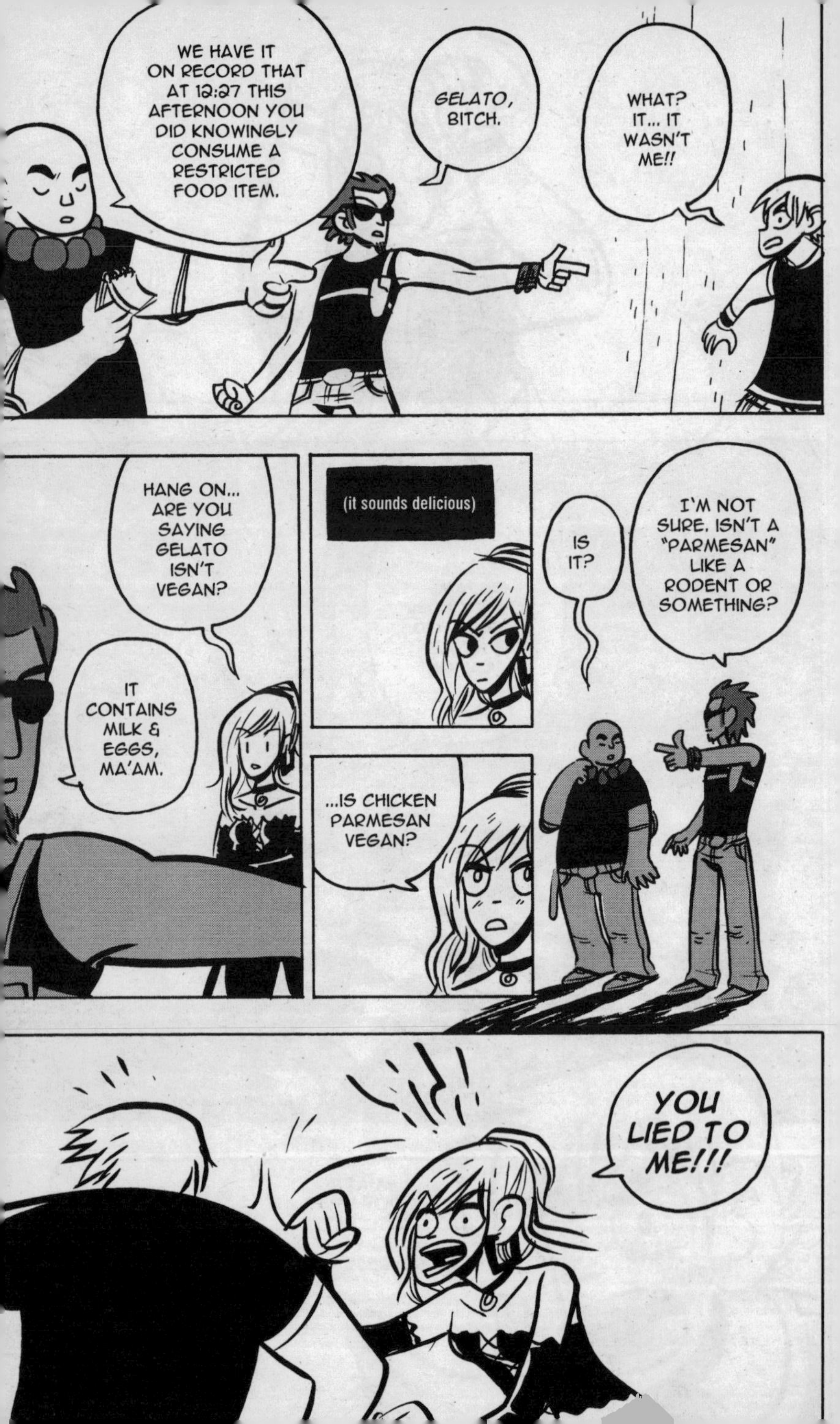
WE HAVE IT ON RECORD THAT AT 12:27 THIS AFTERNOON YOU DID KNOWINGLY CONSUME A RESTRICTED FOOD ITEM.
GELATO, BITCH.
WHAT? IT... IT WASN'T ME!!
HANG ON... ARE YOU SAYING GELATO ISN'T VEGAN?
IT CONTAINS MILK & EGGS, MA'AM.
(it sounds delicious)
...IS CHICKEN PARMESAN VEGAN?
IS IT?
I'M NOT SURE. ISN'T A "PARMESAN" LIKE A RODENT OR SOMETHING?
YOU LIED TO ME!!!

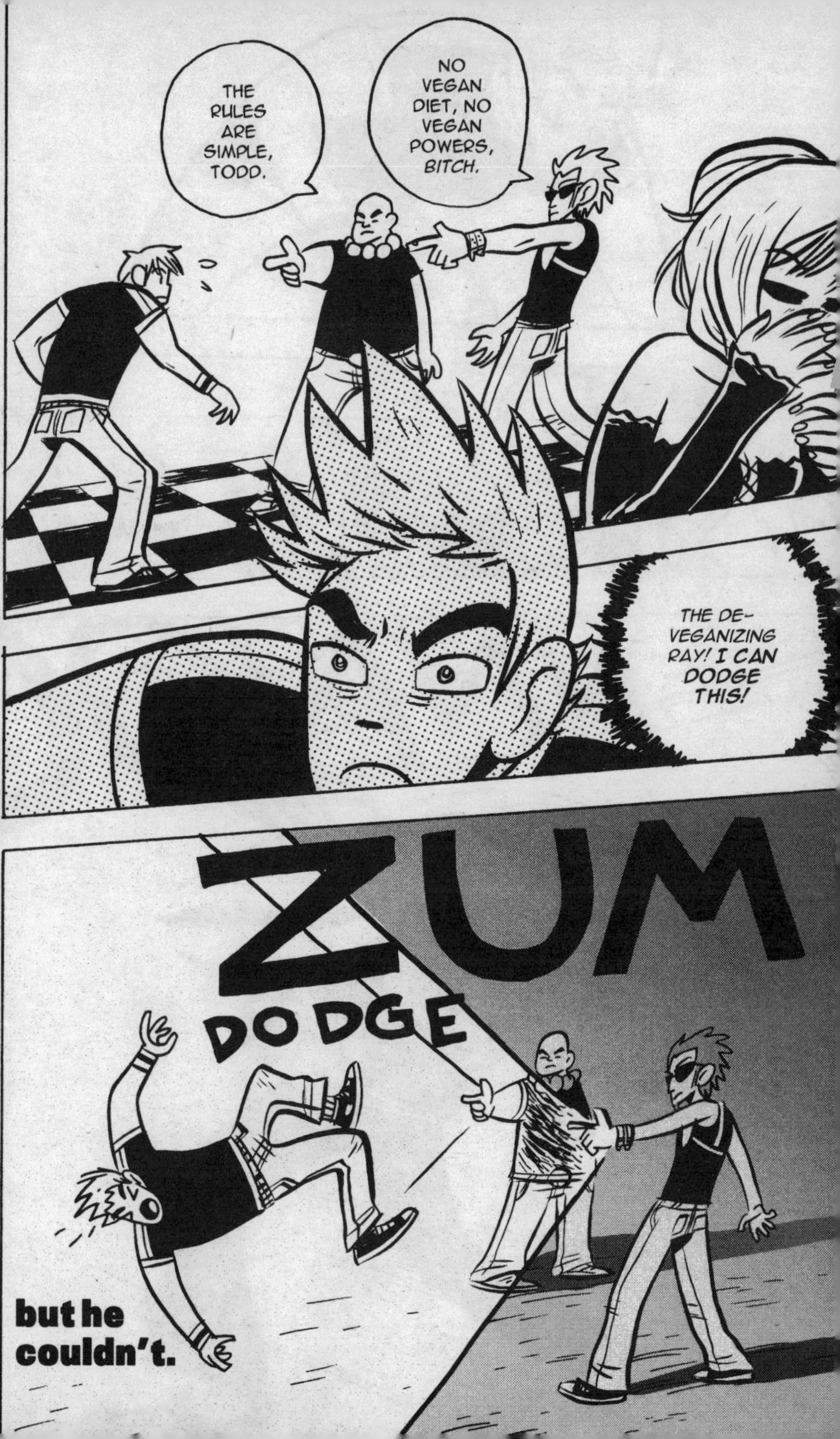
THE RULES ARE SIMPLE, TODD.
NO VEGAN DIET, NO VEGAN POWERS, BITCH.
THE DE-VEGANIZING RAY! I CAN DODGE THIS!
ZUM
DODGE
but he couldn't.

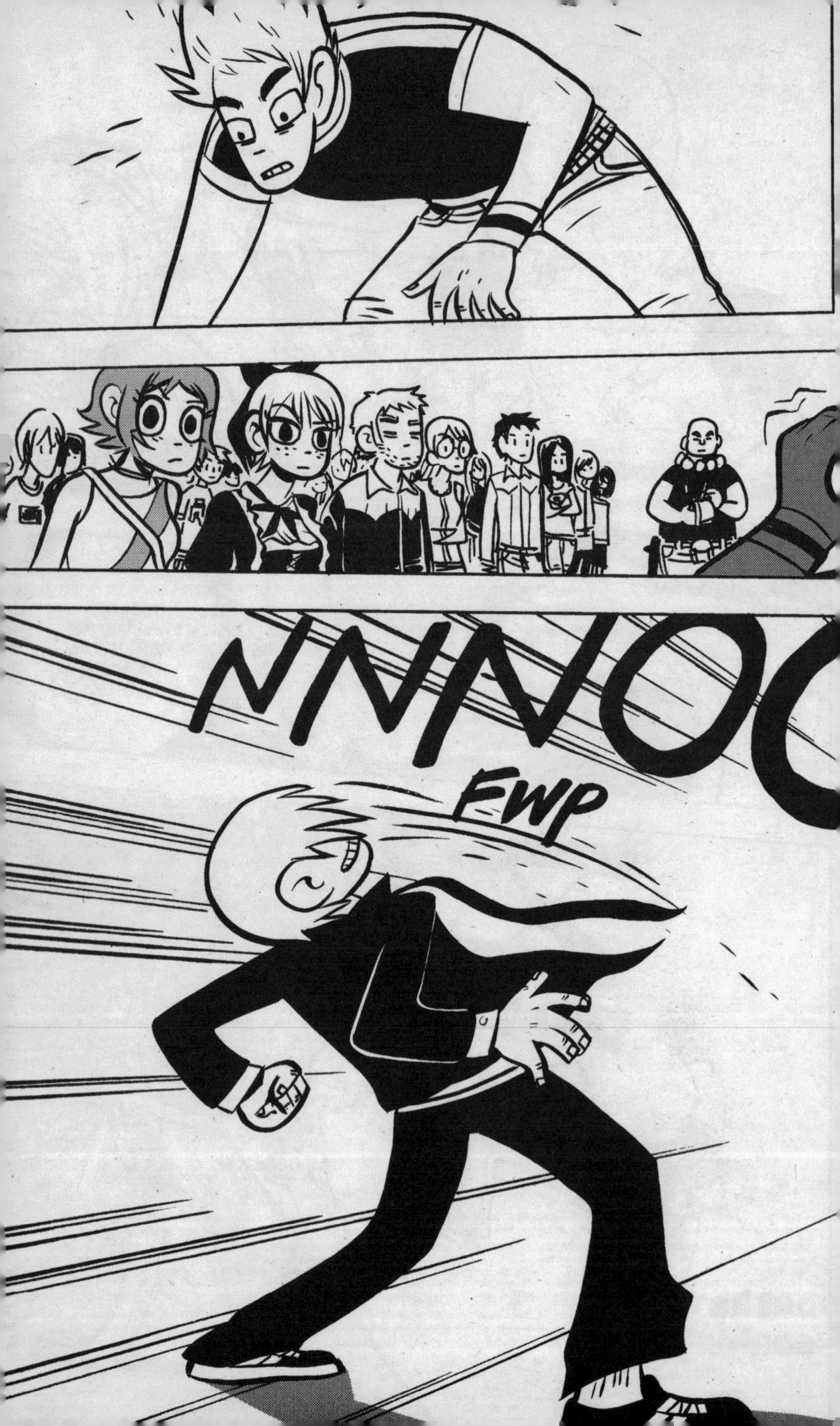
NNNOO
FWP

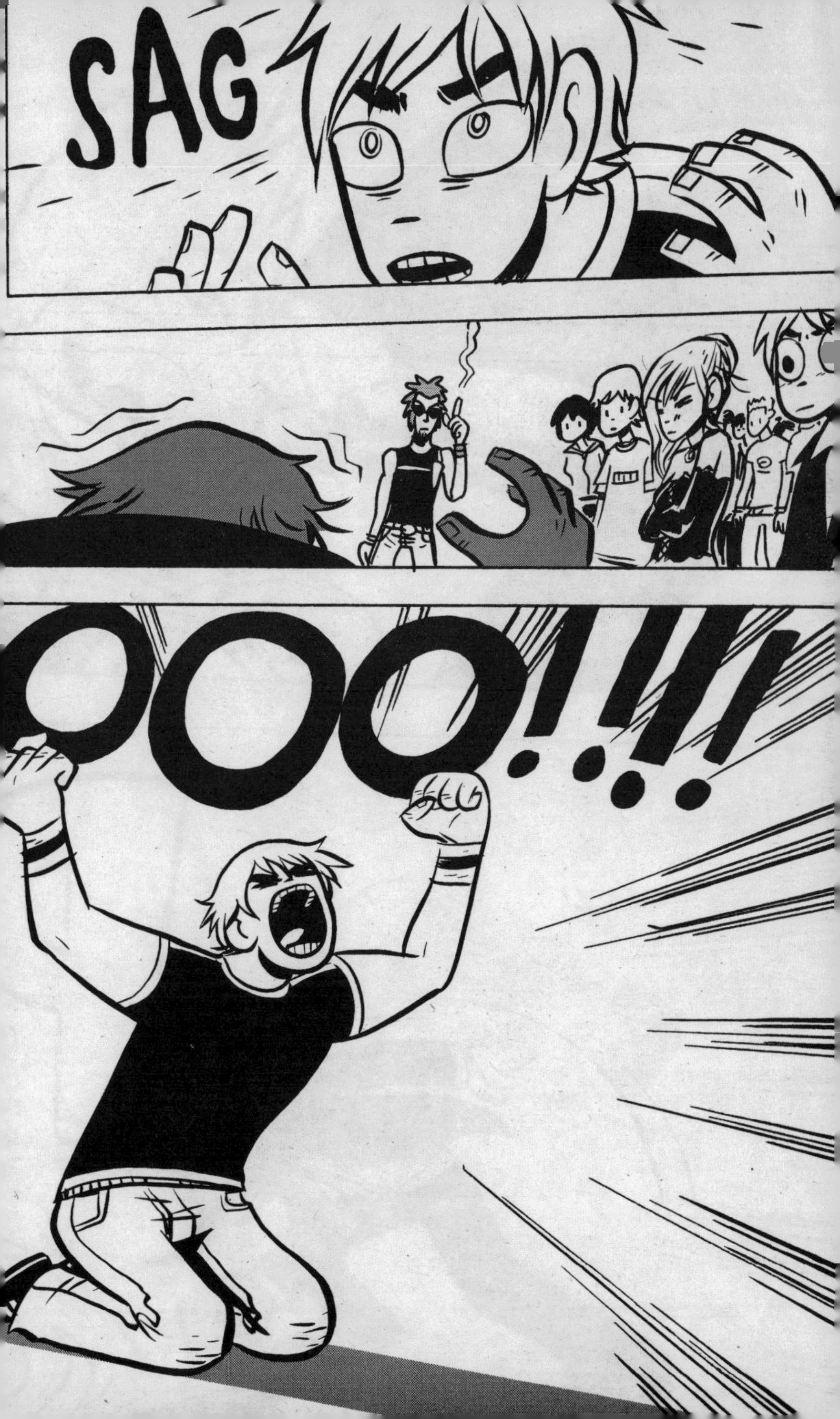
SAG
OOO!!!!

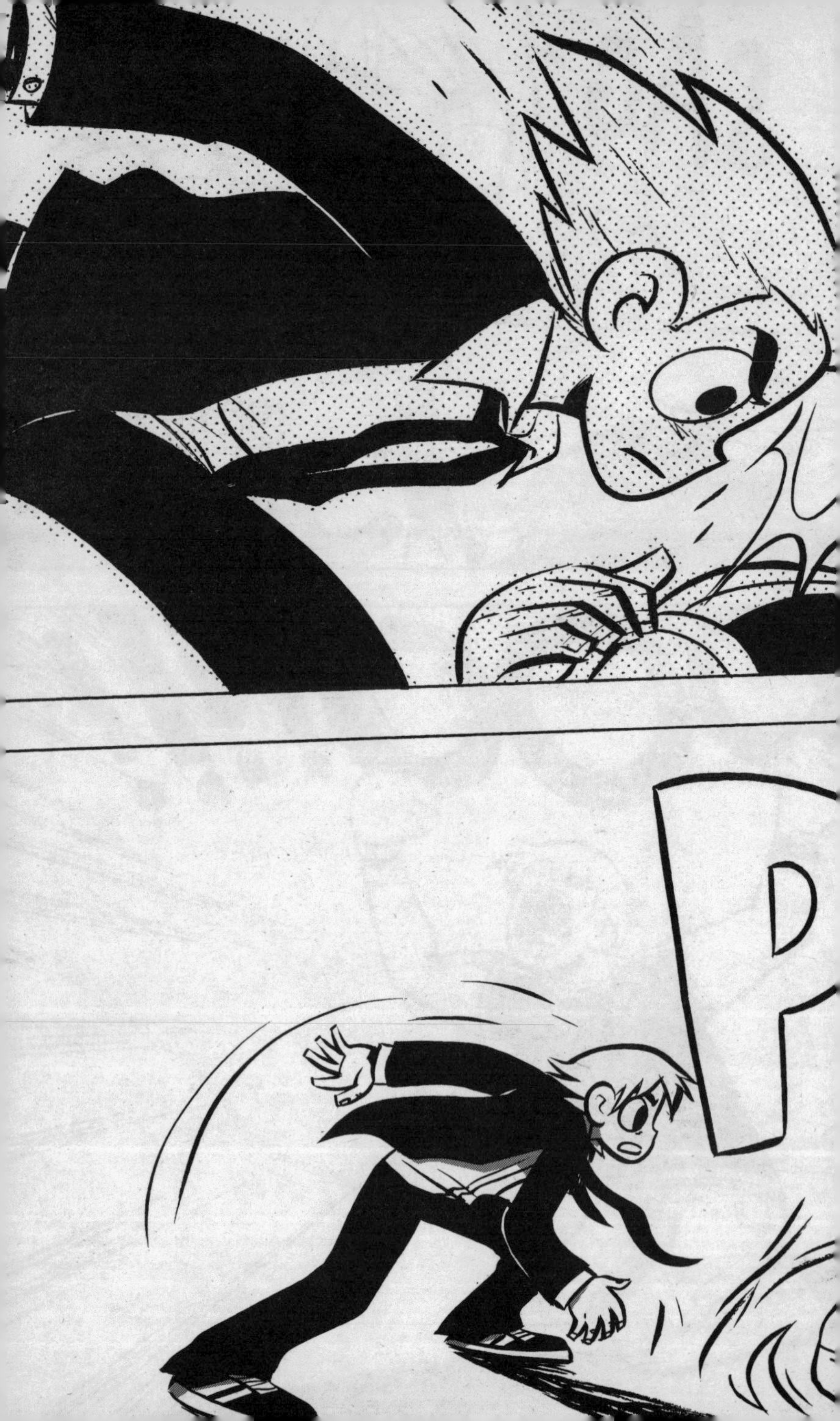
P

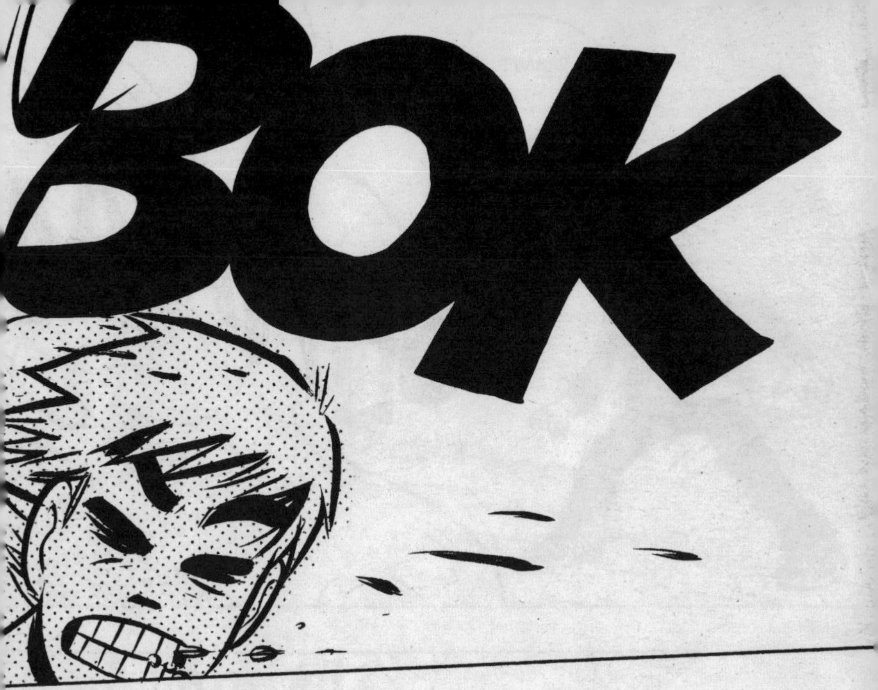
BOK

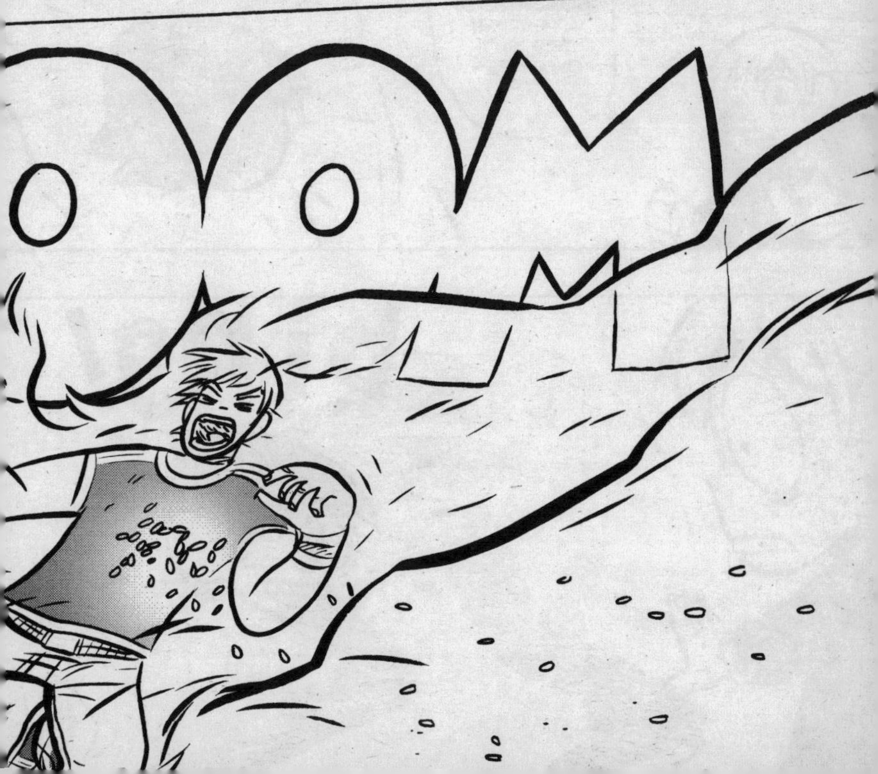
BOOM

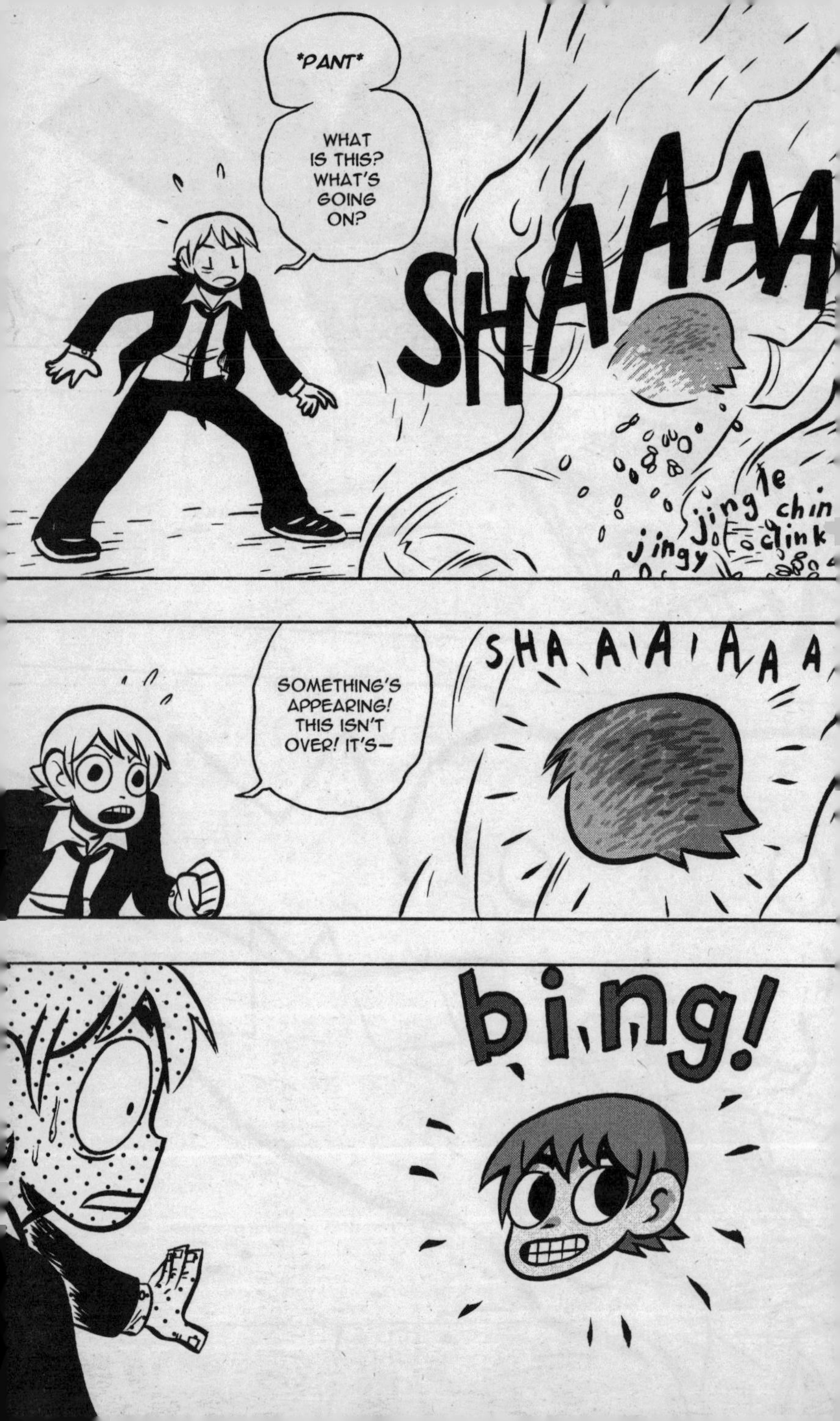

PANT
WHAT IS THIS? WHAT'S GOING ON?
SHAAAAA
jingle
chin
jingy
clink
SOMETHING'S APPEARING! THIS ISN'T OVER! IT'S—
SHAAAAAAA
bing!

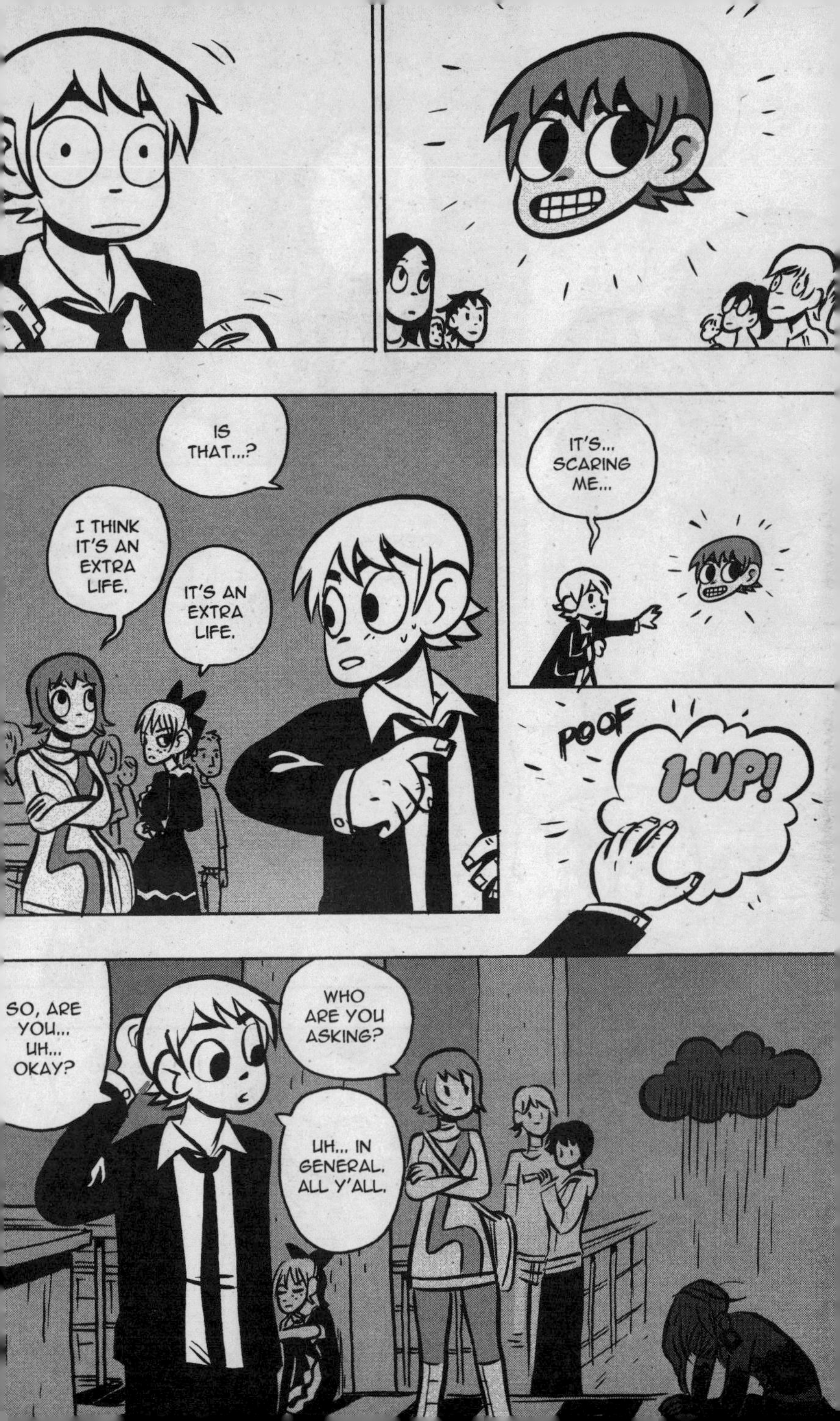
IS THAT...?
I THINK IT'S AN EXTRA LIFE.
IT'S AN EXTRA LIFE.
IT'S... SCARING ME...
POOF
1-UP!
SO, ARE YOU... UH... OKAY?
WHO ARE YOU ASKING?
UH... IN GENERAL. ALL Y'ALL.

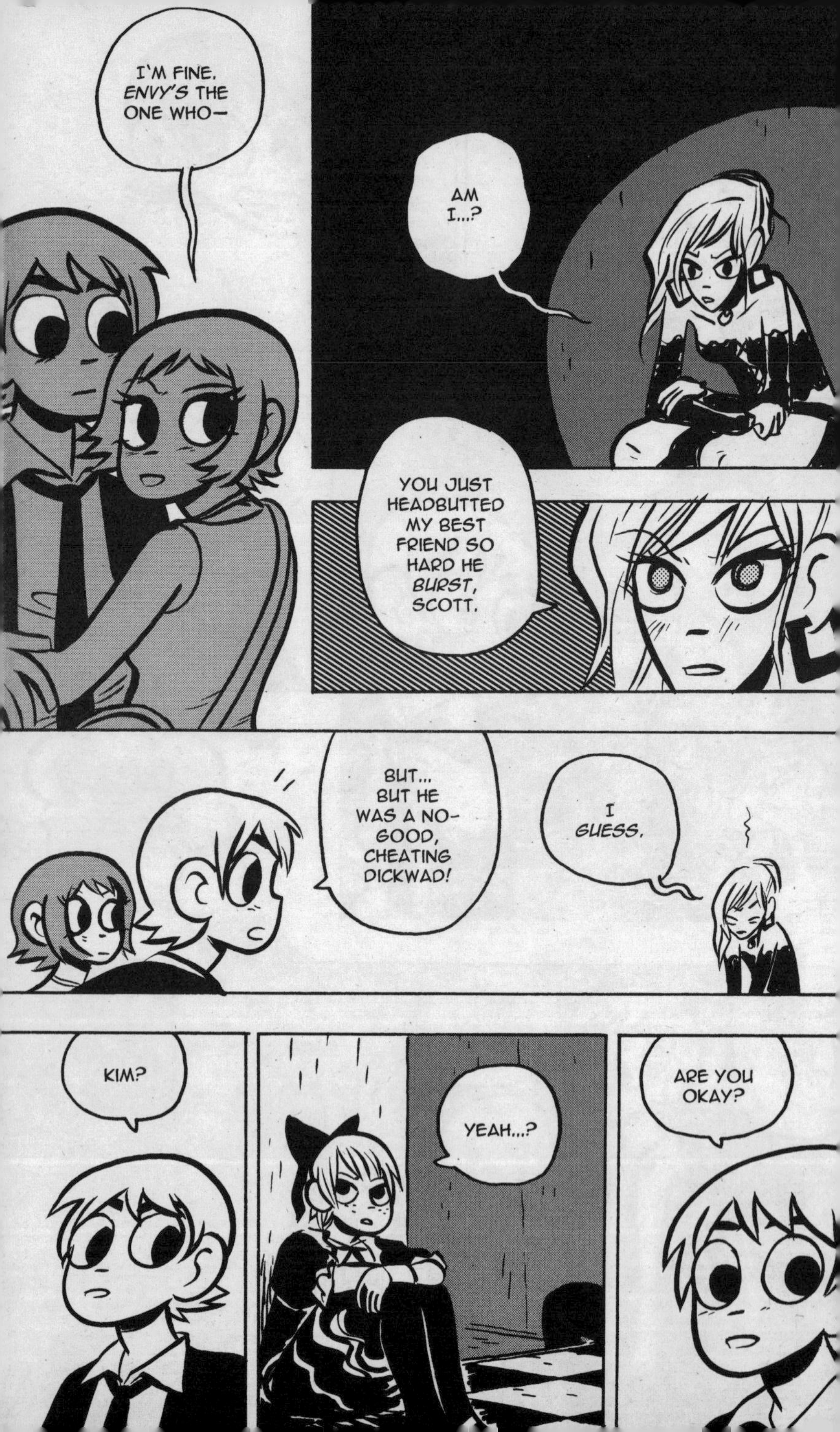
I'M FINE. *ENVY'S* THE ONE WHO—
AM I...?
YOU JUST HEADBUTTED MY BEST FRIEND SO HARD HE *BURST*, SCOTT.
BUT... BUT HE WAS A NO-GOOD, CHEATING DICKWAD!
I GUESS.
KIM?
YEAH...?
ARE YOU OKAY?

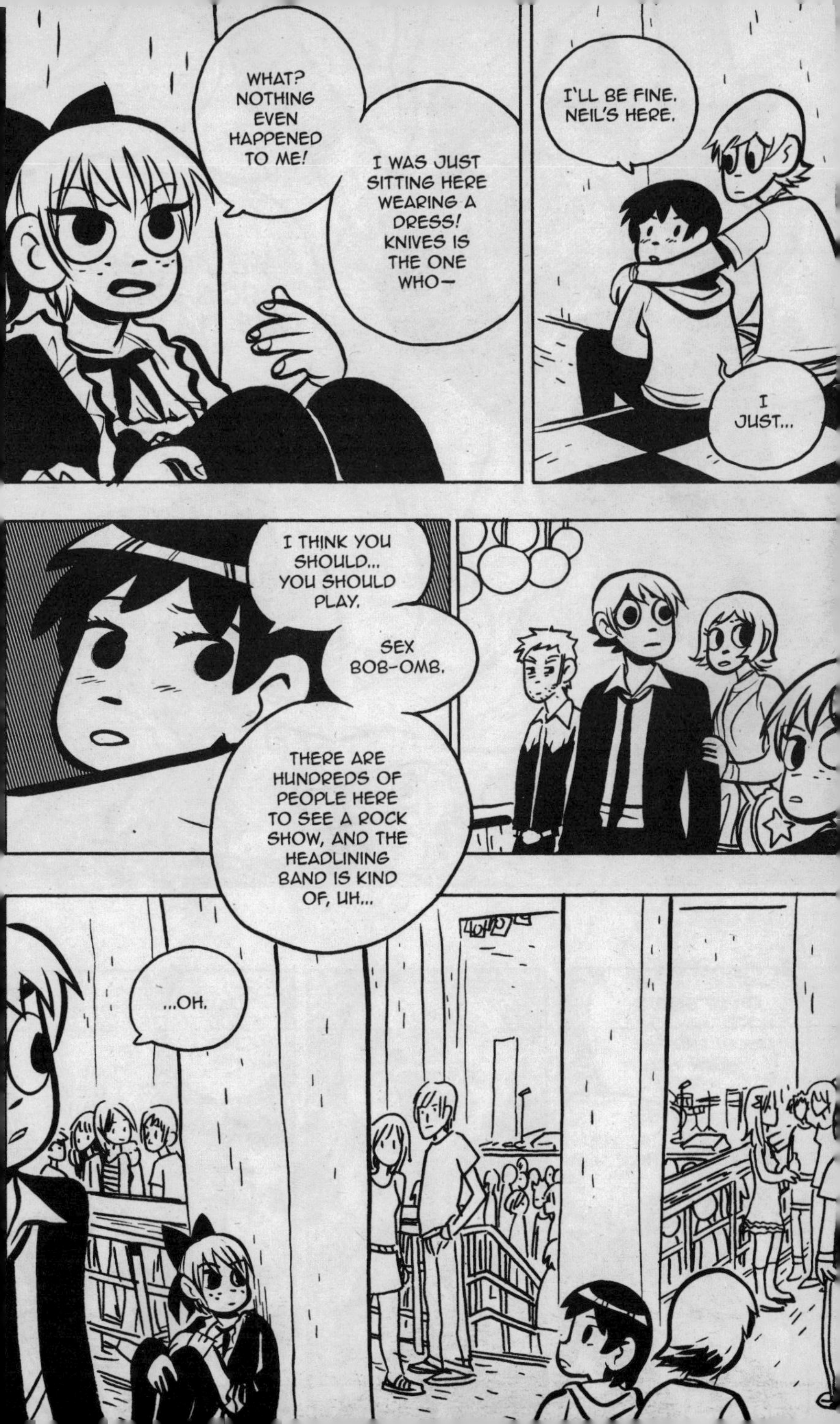
WHAT? NOTHING EVEN HAPPENED TO ME!
I WAS JUST SITTING HERE WEARING A DRESS! KNIVES IS THE ONE WHO—
I'LL BE FINE. NEIL'S HERE.
I JUST...
I THINK YOU SHOULD... YOU SHOULD PLAY.
SEX BOB-OMB.
THERE ARE HUNDREDS OF PEOPLE HERE TO SEE A ROCK SHOW, AND THE HEADLINING BAND IS KIND OF, UH...
...OH.

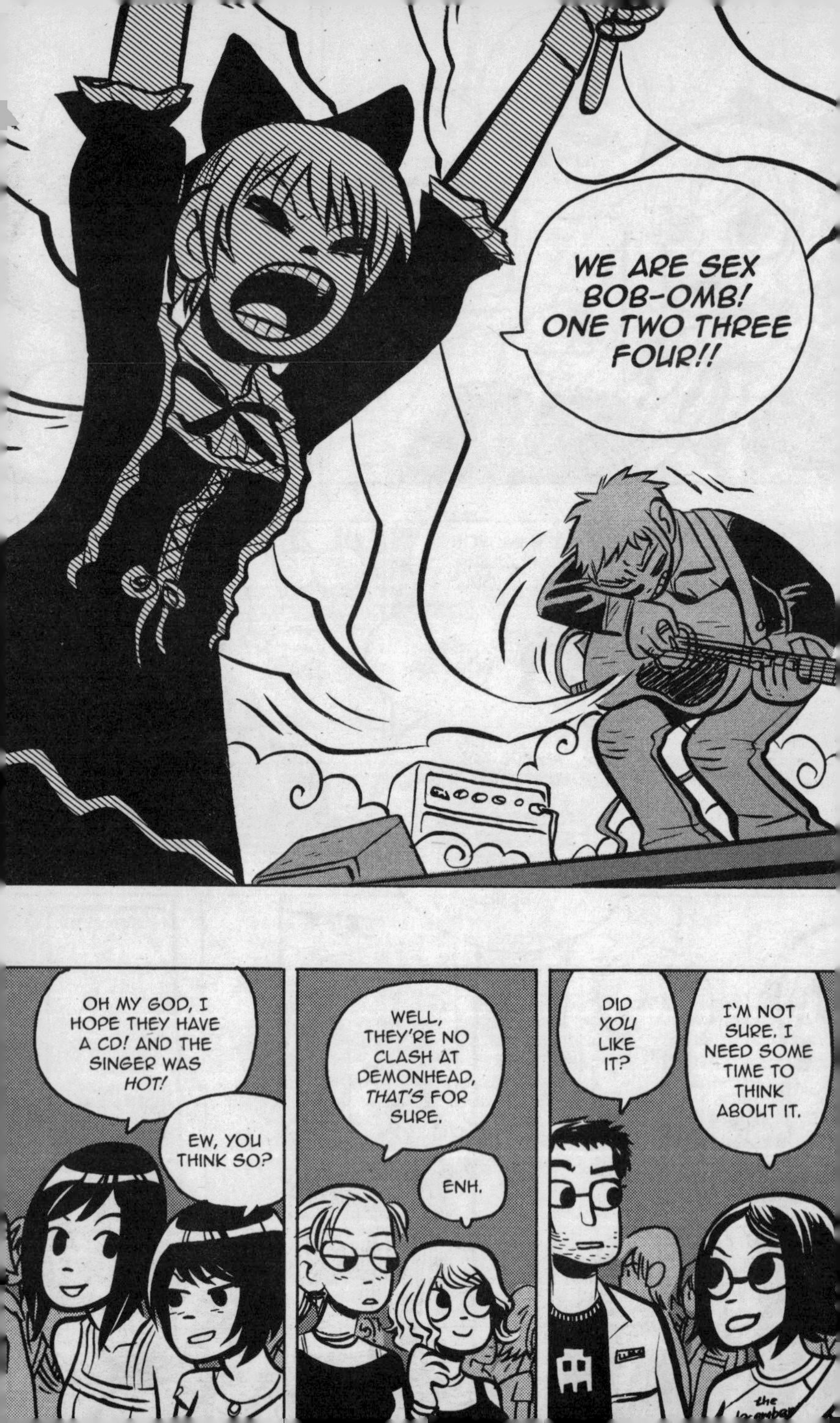
WE ARE SEX BOB-OMB! ONE TWO THREE FOUR!!
OH MY GOD, I HOPE THEY HAVE A CD! AND THE SINGER WAS *HOT!*
EW, YOU THINK SO?
WELL, THEY'RE NO CLASH AT DEMONHEAD, *THAT'S* FOR SURE.
ENH.
DID *YOU* LIKE IT?
I'M NOT SURE. I NEED SOME TIME TO THINK ABOUT IT.

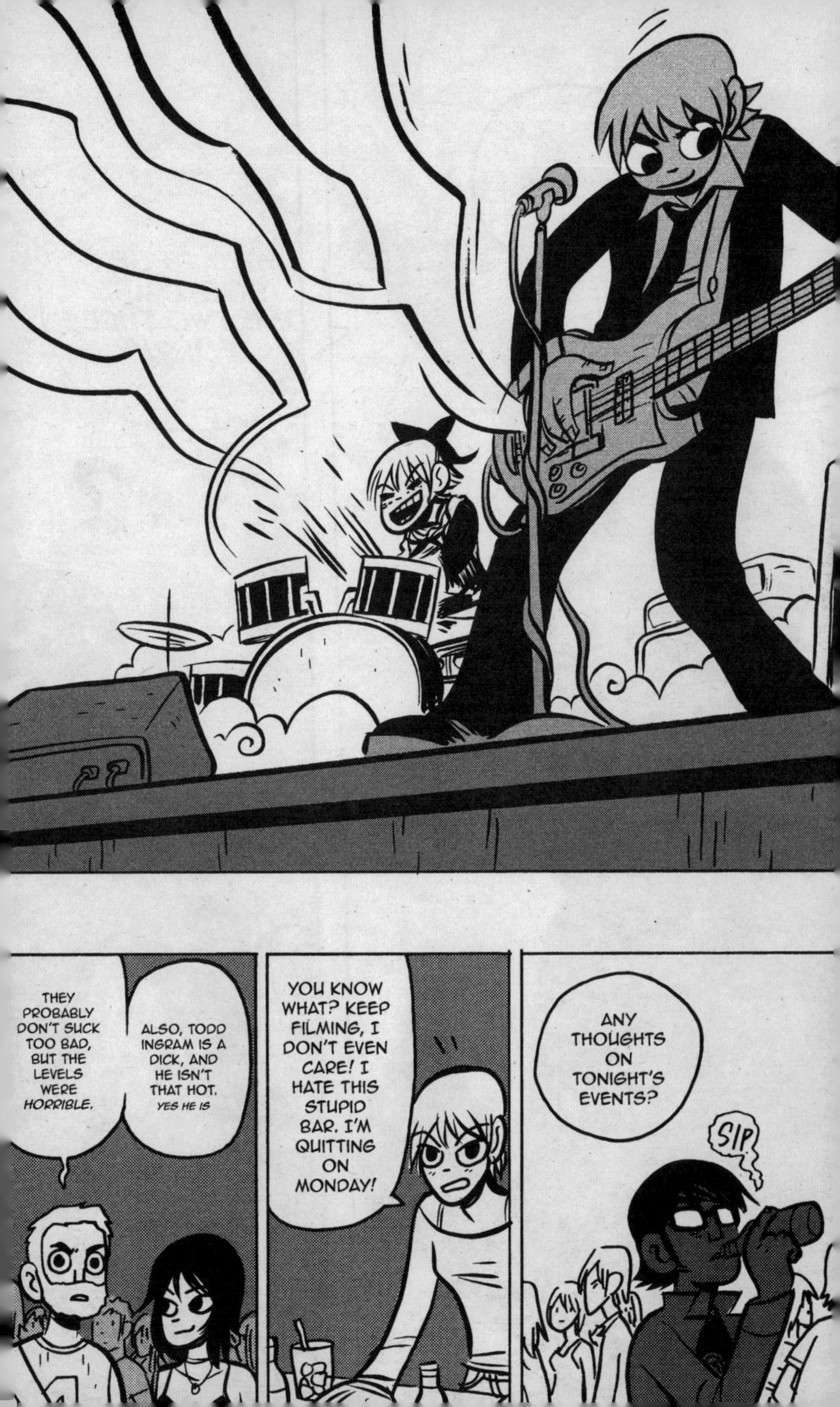
THEY PROBABLY DON'T SUCK TOO BAD, BUT THE LEVELS WERE *HORRIBLE*.
ALSO, TODD INGRAM IS A DICK, AND HE ISN'T THAT HOT.
YES HE IS
YOU KNOW WHAT? KEEP FILMING, I DON'T EVEN CARE! I HATE THIS STUPID BAR. I'M QUITTING ON MONDAY!
ANY THOUGHTS ON TONIGHT'S EVENTS?
SIP

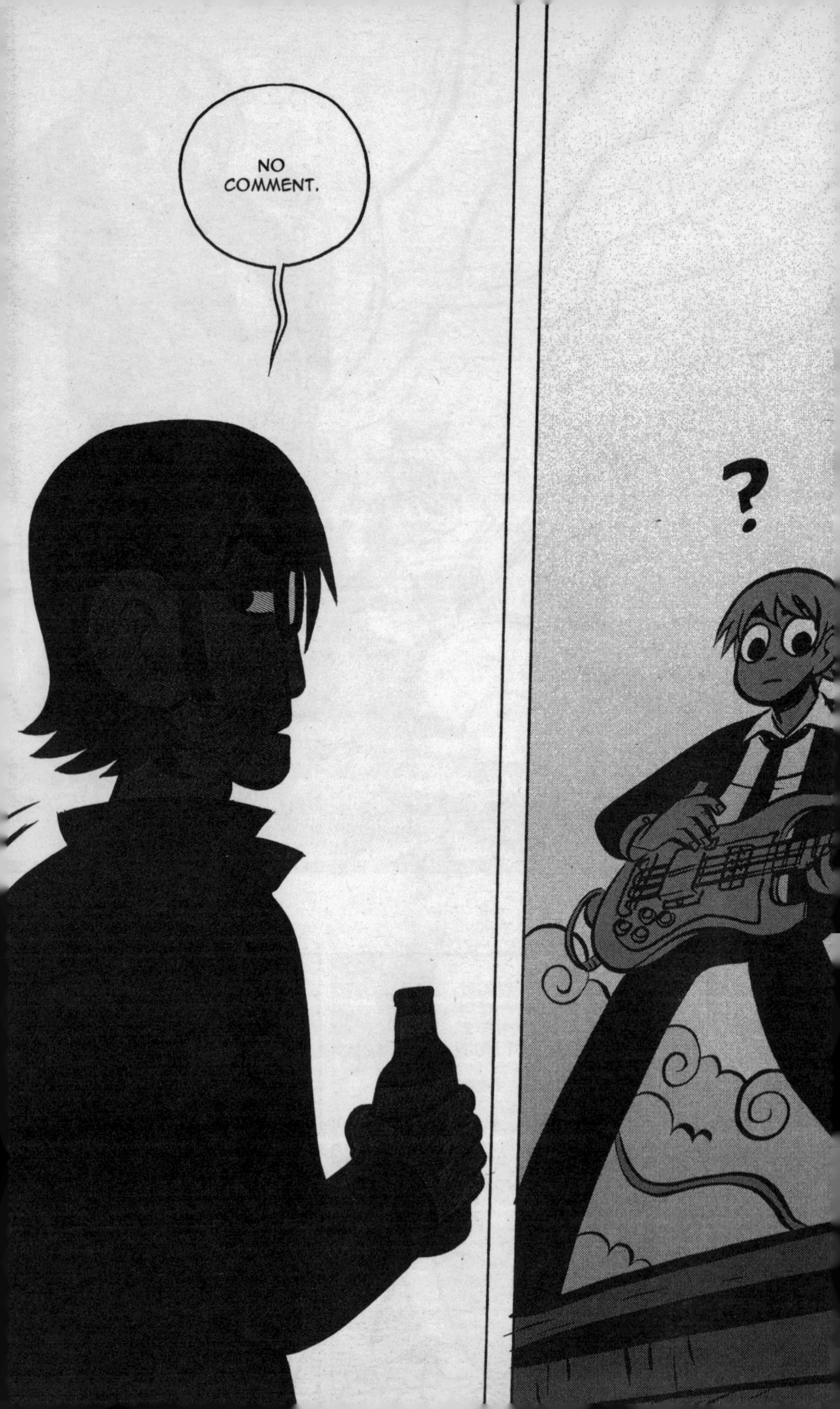
NO COMMENT.
?

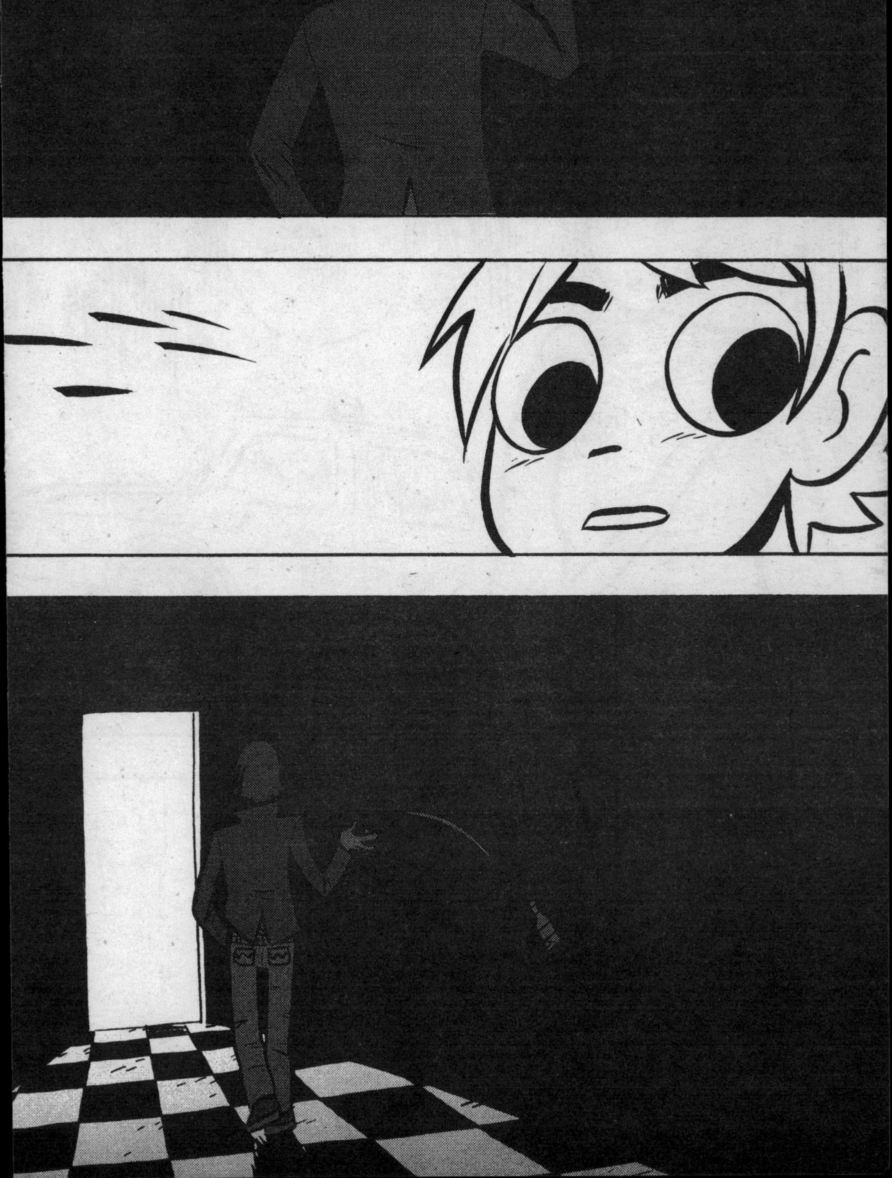

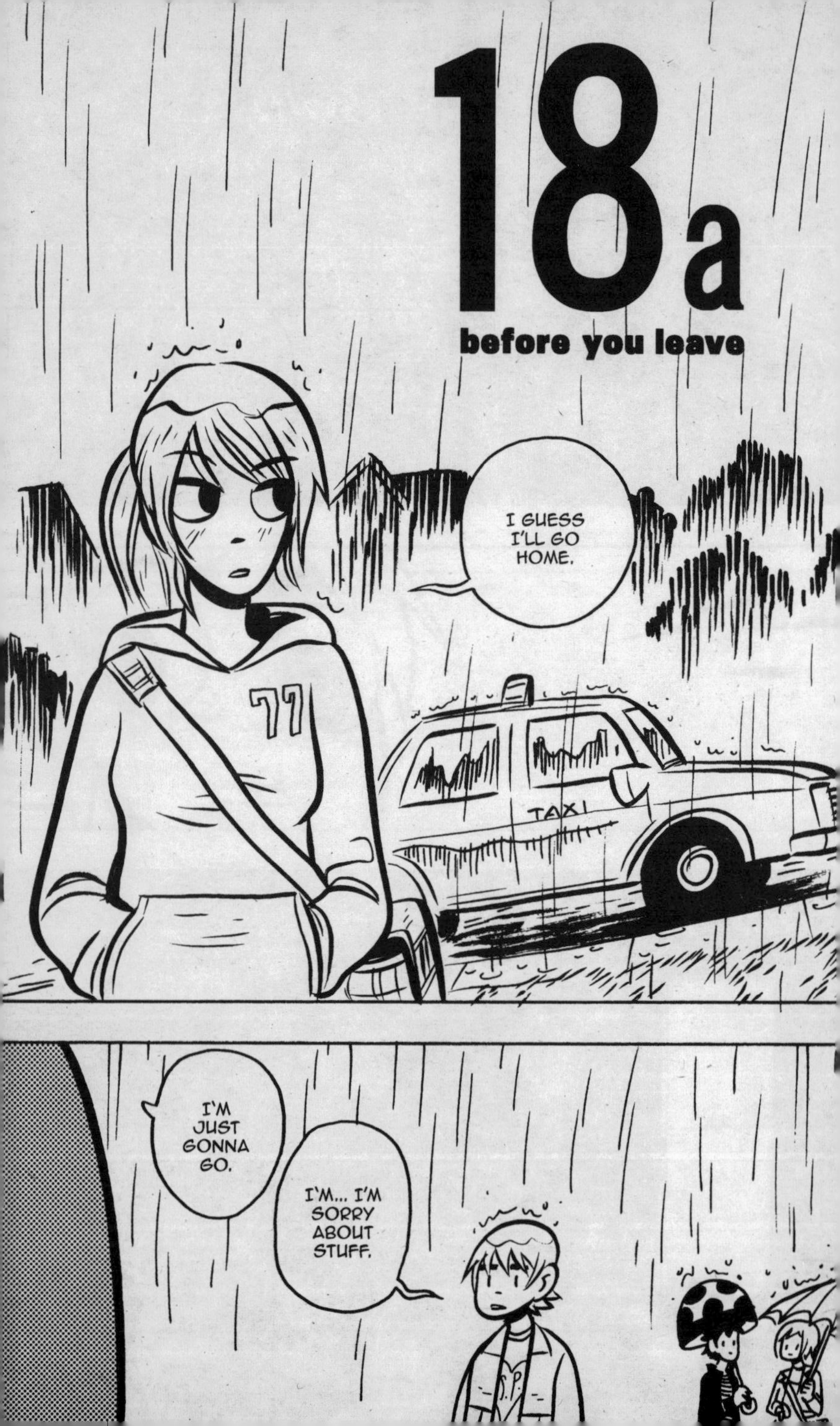
18a
before you leave
I GUESS I'LL GO HOME.
TAXI
I'M JUST GONNA GO.
I'M... I'M SORRY ABOUT STUFF.

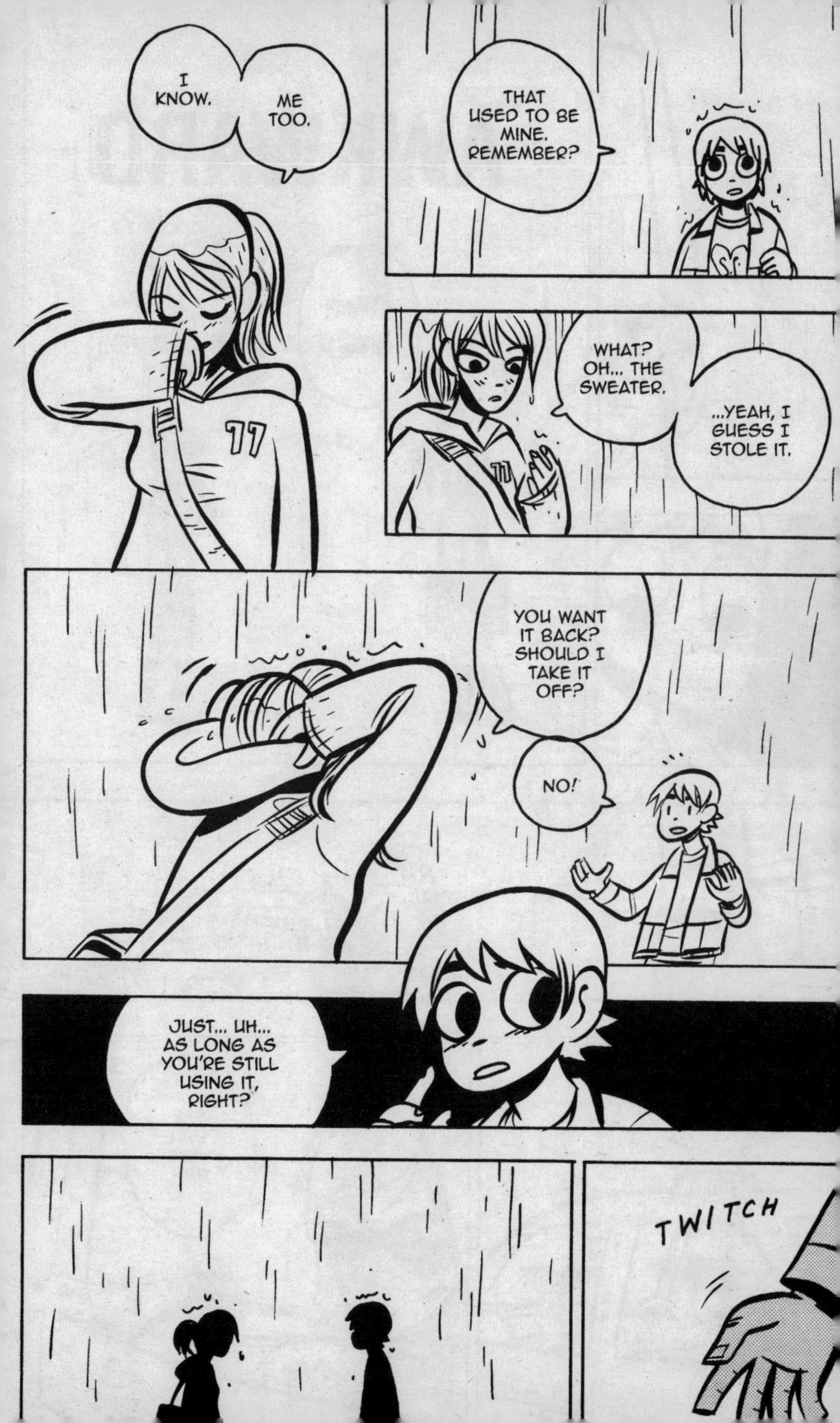
I KNOW.
ME TOO.
THAT USED TO BE MINE. REMEMBER?
WHAT? OH... THE SWEATER.
...YEAH, I GUESS I STOLE IT.
YOU WANT IT BACK? SHOULD I TAKE IT OFF?
NO!
JUST... UH... AS LONG AS YOU'RE STILL USING IT, RIGHT?
TWITCH

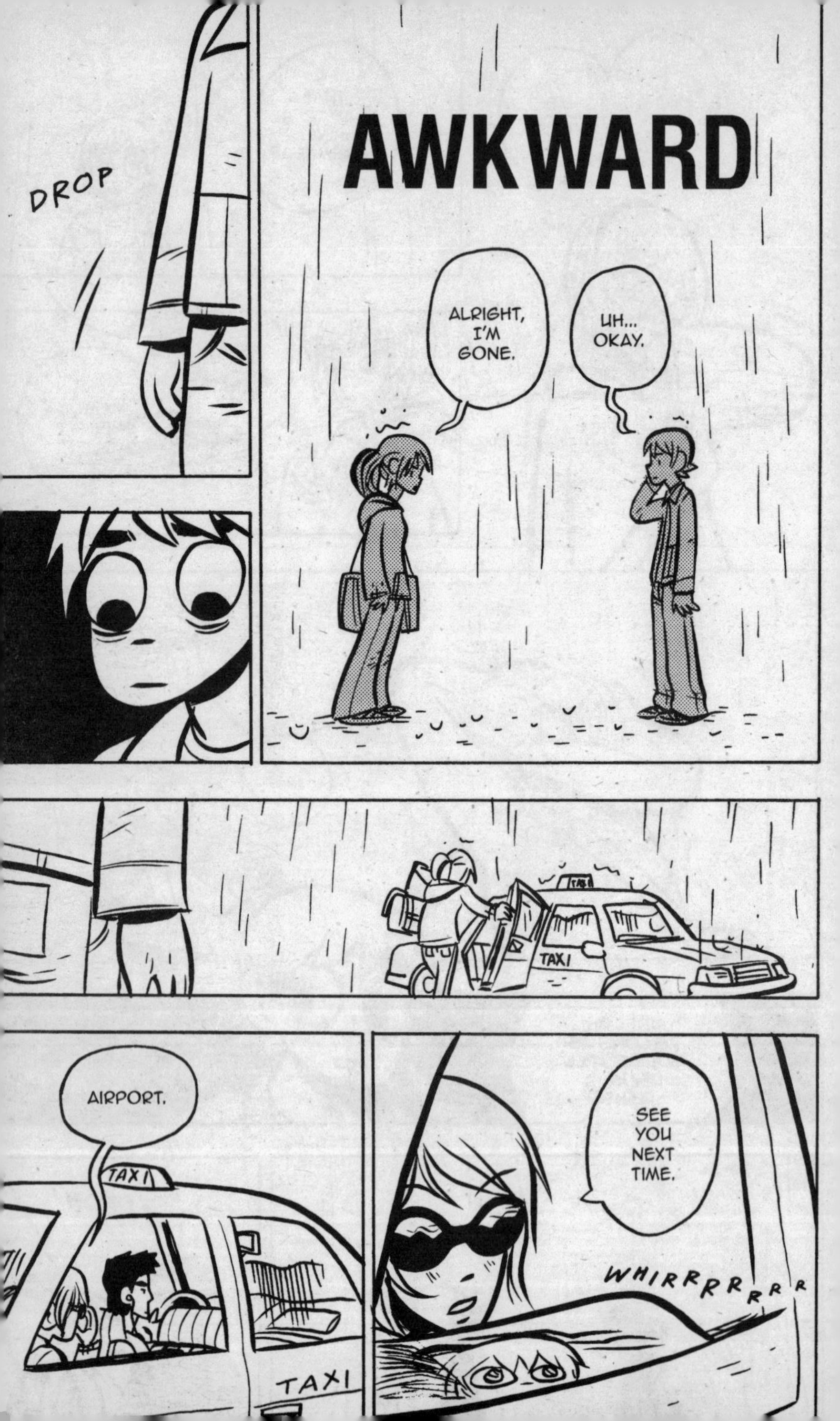
DROP
AWKWARD
ALRIGHT, I'M GONE.
UH... OKAY.
TAXI
TAXI
AIRPORT.
TAXI
TAXI
SEE YOU NEXT TIME.
WHIRRRRRRRR

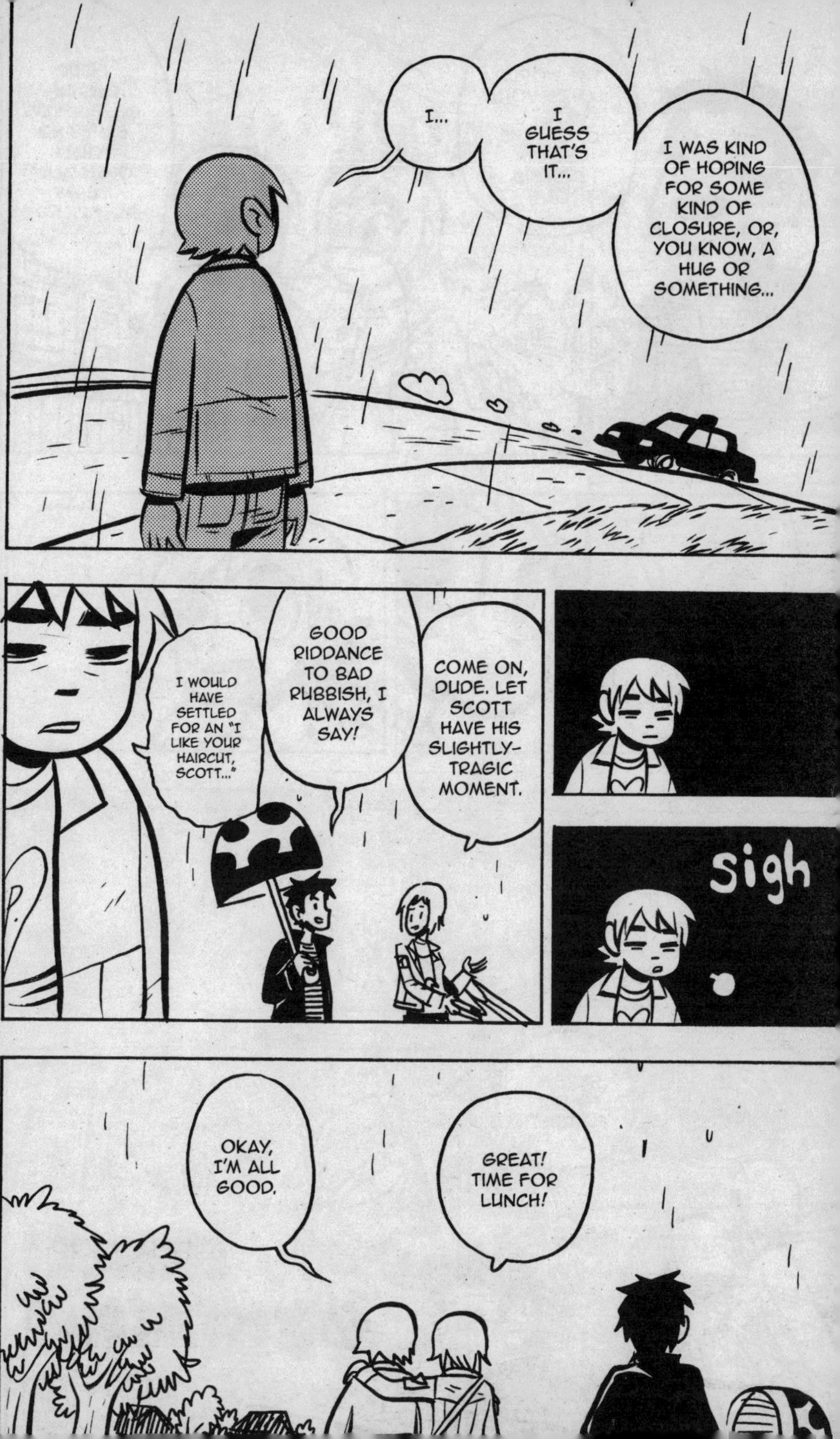
I...
I GUESS THAT'S IT...
I WAS KIND OF HOPING FOR SOME KIND OF CLOSURE, OR, YOU KNOW, A HUG OR SOMETHING...
I WOULD HAVE SETTLED FOR AN "I LIKE YOUR HAIRCUT, SCOTT..."
GOOD RIDDANCE TO BAD RUBBISH, I ALWAYS SAY!
COME ON, DUDE. LET SCOTT HAVE HIS SLIGHTLY-TRAGIC MOMENT.
sigh
OKAY, I'M ALL GOOD.
GREAT! TIME FOR LUNCH!

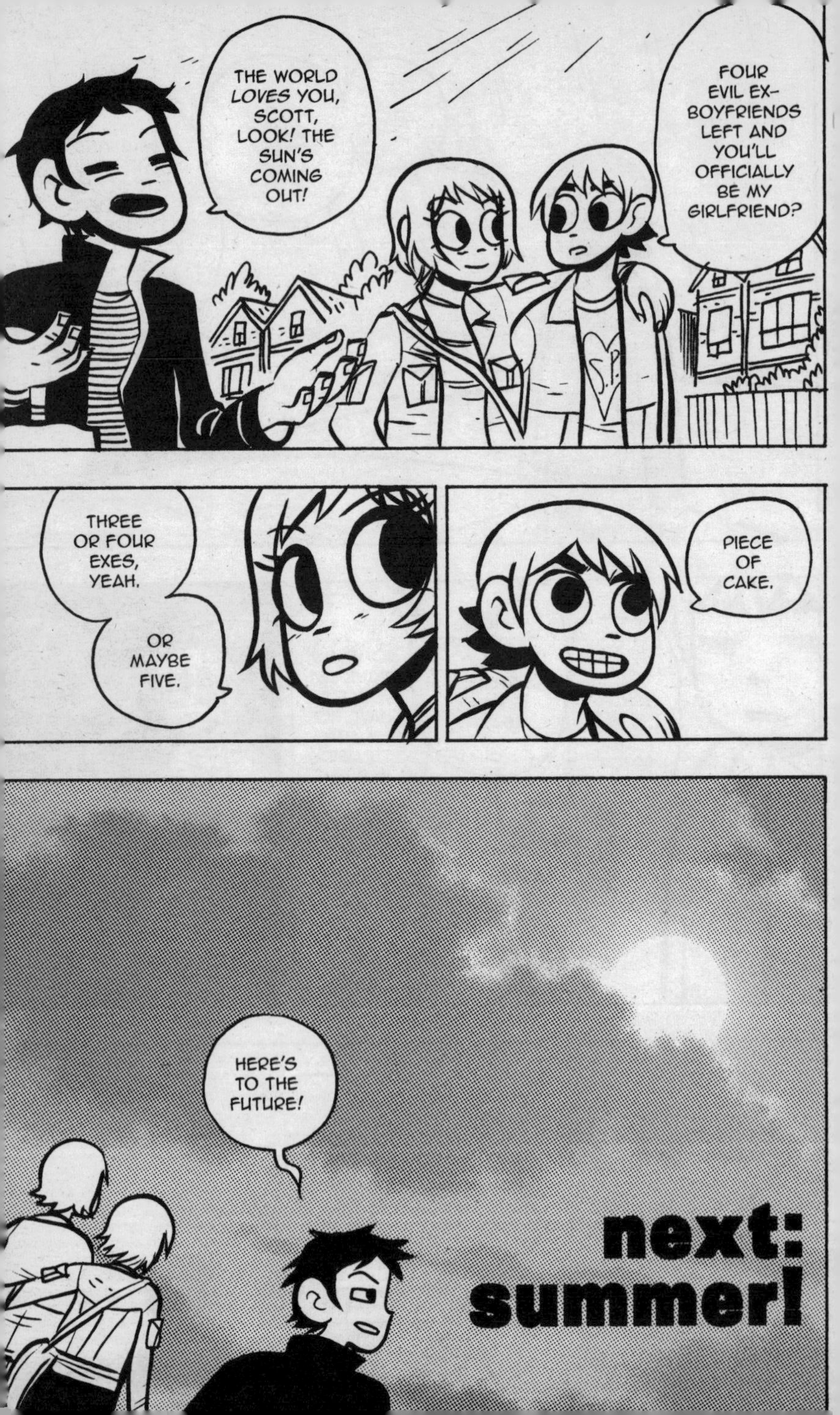
THE WORLD LOVES YOU, SCOTT, LOOK! THE SUN'S COMING OUT!
FOUR EVIL EX-BOYFRIENDS LEFT AND YOU'LL OFFICIALLY BE MY GIRLFRIEND?
THREE OR FOUR EXES, YEAH.
OR MAYBE FIVE.
PIECE OF CAKE.
HERE'S TO THE FUTURE!
next: summer!

I wasn't sure what direction to take with the Vegan Police, so I asked my friend Nathan Avery to help me out. These are his original designs. I chickened out and simplified them a lot, but the spirit is there.

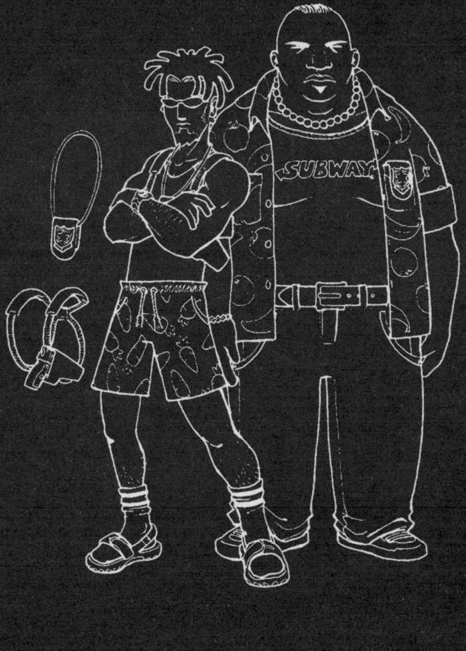
SUBWAY

BONUS SECTION

I THOUGHT IT WOULD BE NICE (OR AT LEAST INTERESTING) TO ASK SOME FRIENDS TO CONTRIBUTE A FEW LITTLE THINGS FOR THE BACK OF THE BOOK, AND HOPEFULLY I CAN GET A FEW MORE THINGS FOR THE NEXT BOOK. THE IDEA IS THAT IT'S FUN FOR THEM (THE CREATORS) AND YOU (THE READERS) AND WE ALL GET TO SEE DIFFERENT INTERPRETATIONS OF THE CHARACTERS OR WHATEVER. ANYWAY, PLEASE ENJOY.

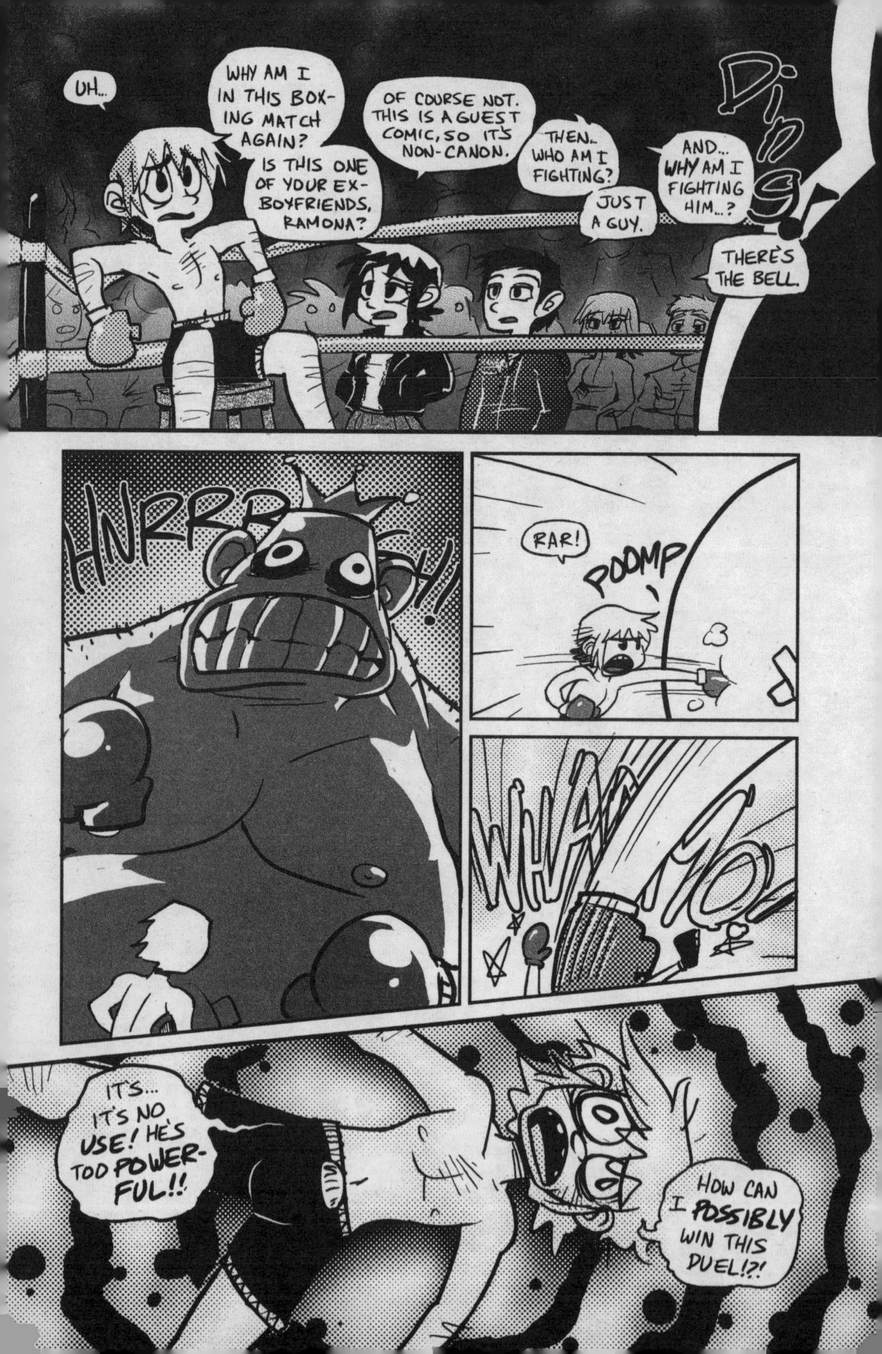
UH...
WHY AM I IN THIS BOXING MATCH AGAIN?
IS THIS ONE OF YOUR EX-BOYFRIENDS, RAMONA?
OF COURSE NOT. THIS IS A GUEST COMIC, SO IT'S NON-CANON.
THEN.. WHO AM I FIGHTING?
JUST A GUY.
AND... WHY AM I FIGHTING HIM...?
Ding!
THERE'S THE BELL.
HNRRRGH!!
RAR!
POOMP
WHAMO!
IT'S... IT'S NO USE! HE'S TOO POWERFUL!!
HOW CAN I POSSIBLY WIN THIS DUEL!?!

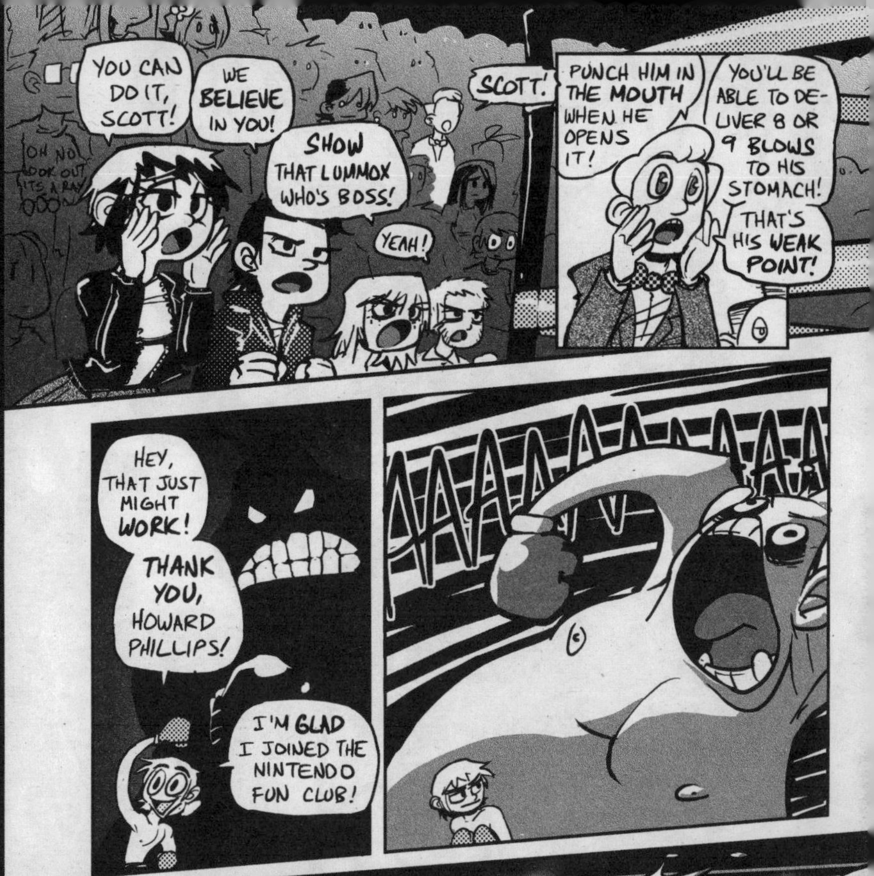
YOU CAN DO IT, SCOTT!
WE BELIEVE IN YOU!
SHOW THAT LUMMOX WHO'S BOSS!
YEAH!
SCOTT!
PUNCH HIM IN THE MOUTH WHEN HE OPENS IT!
YOU'LL BE ABLE TO DELIVER 8 OR 9 BLOWS TO HIS STOMACH!
THAT'S HIS WEAK POINT!
HEY, THAT JUST MIGHT WORK!
THANK YOU, HOWARD PHILLIPS!
I'M GLAD I JOINED THE NINTENDO FUN CLUB!
AAAAAAAAAAAA
"SCOTT PILGRIM VS. KING HIPPO".
by josh l.

JOSH LESNICK draws the webcomic **Girly** ***(www.go-girly.com)*** and I have known him since the first day I went on the internet or something

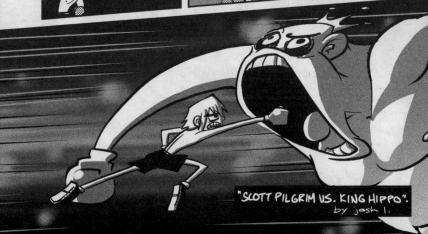

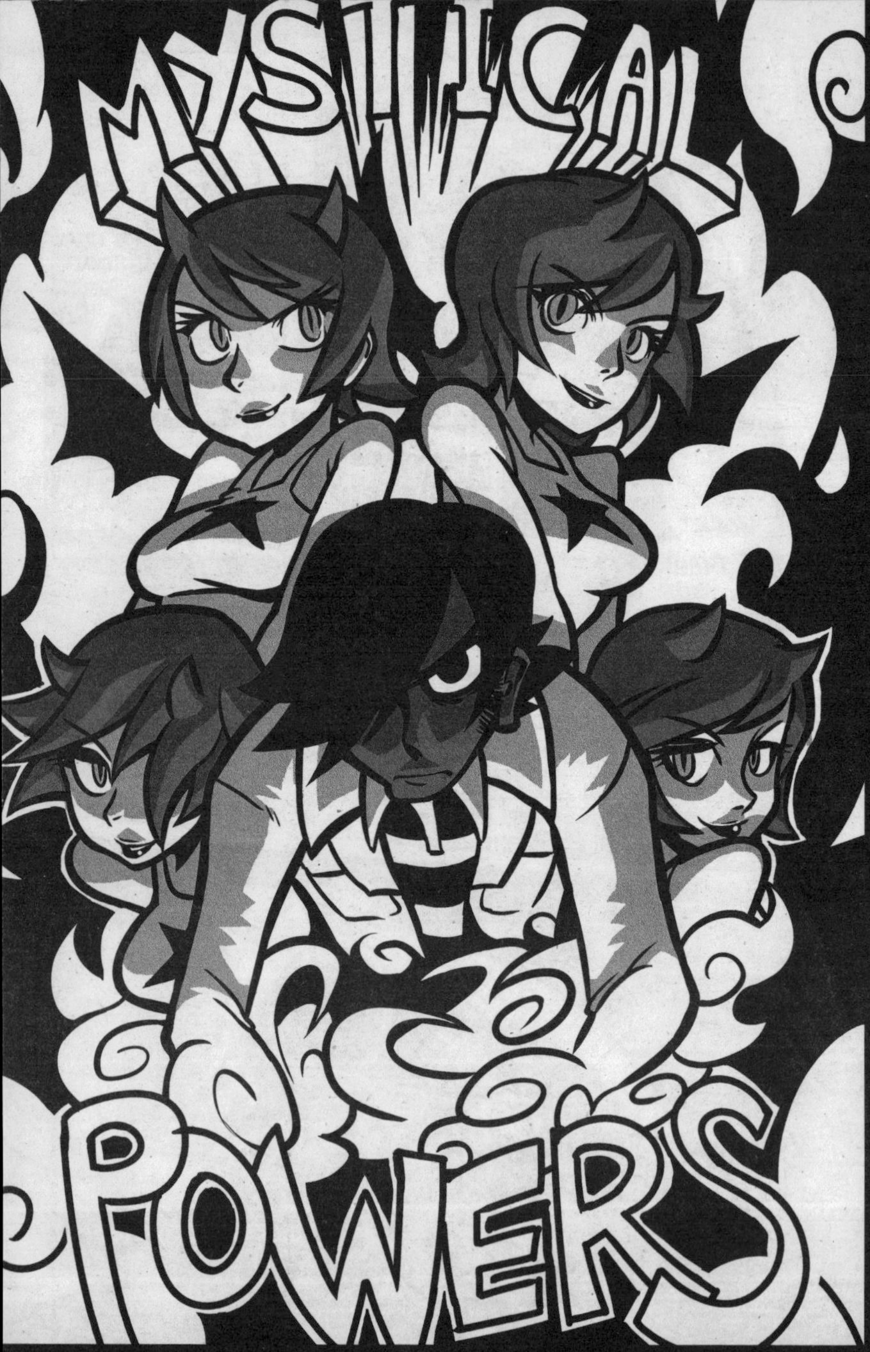
MYSTICAL
POWERS

ALEX AHAD is like the coolest guy ever. I don't think he has any major works under his

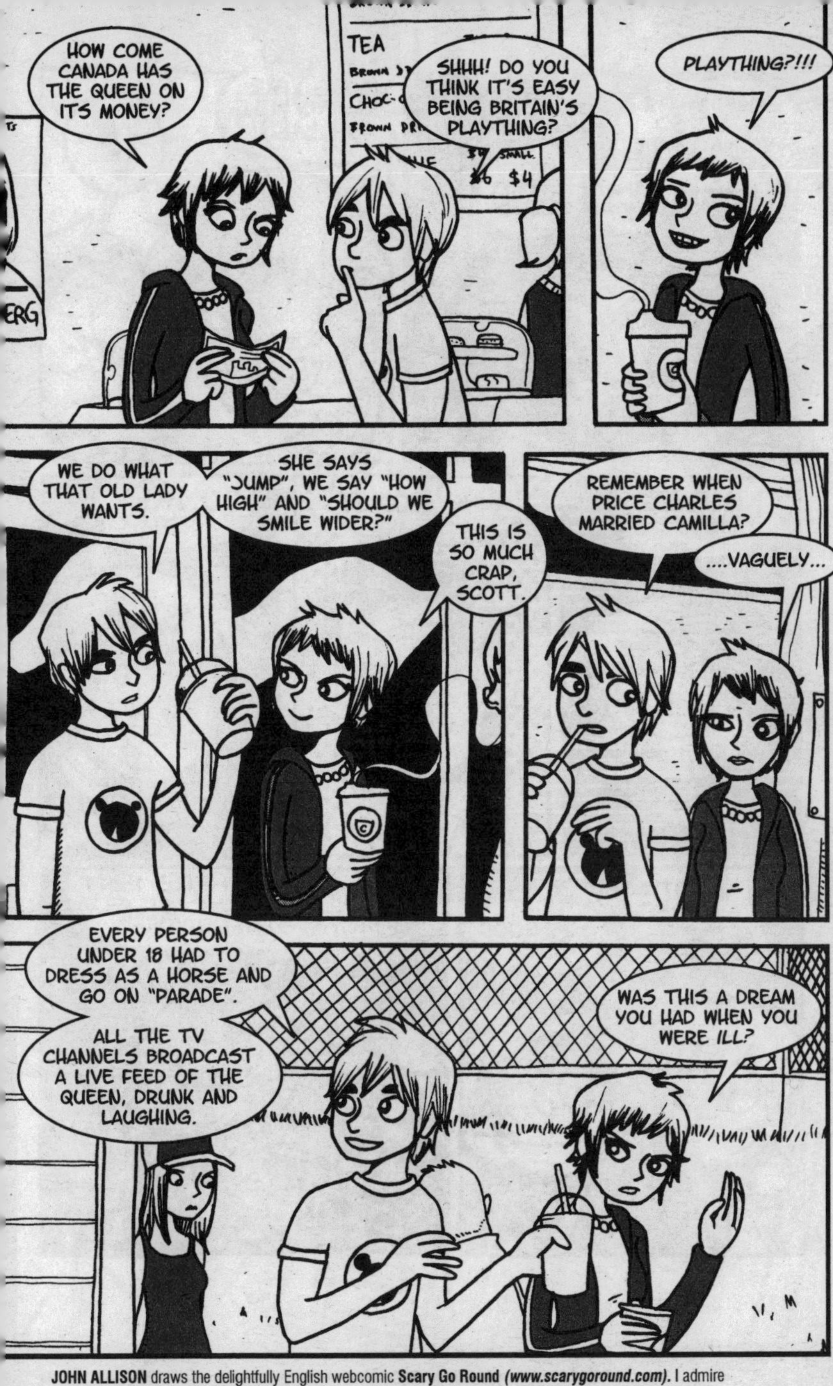
HOW COME CANADA HAS THE QUEEN ON ITS MONEY?
TEA
SHHH! DO YOU THINK IT'S EASY BEING BRITAIN'S PLAYTHING?
$4
PLAYTHING?!!!
WE DO WHAT THAT OLD LADY WANTS.
SHE SAYS "JUMP", WE SAY "HOW HIGH" AND "SHOULD WE SMILE WIDER?"
THIS IS SO MUCH CRAP, SCOTT.
REMEMBER WHEN PRICE CHARLES MARRIED CAMILLA?
....VAGUELY...
EVERY PERSON UNDER 18 HAD TO DRESS AS A HORSE AND GO ON "PARADE".
ALL THE TV CHANNELS BROADCAST A LIVE FEED OF THE QUEEN, DRUNK AND LAUGHING.
WAS THIS A DREAM YOU HAD WHEN YOU WERE ILL?

JOHN ALLISON draws the delightfully English webcomic **Scary Go Round** ***(www.scarygoround.com).*** I admire him for his ability to draw fashion and to change his characters' hairstyles at will, which I strive to emulate.

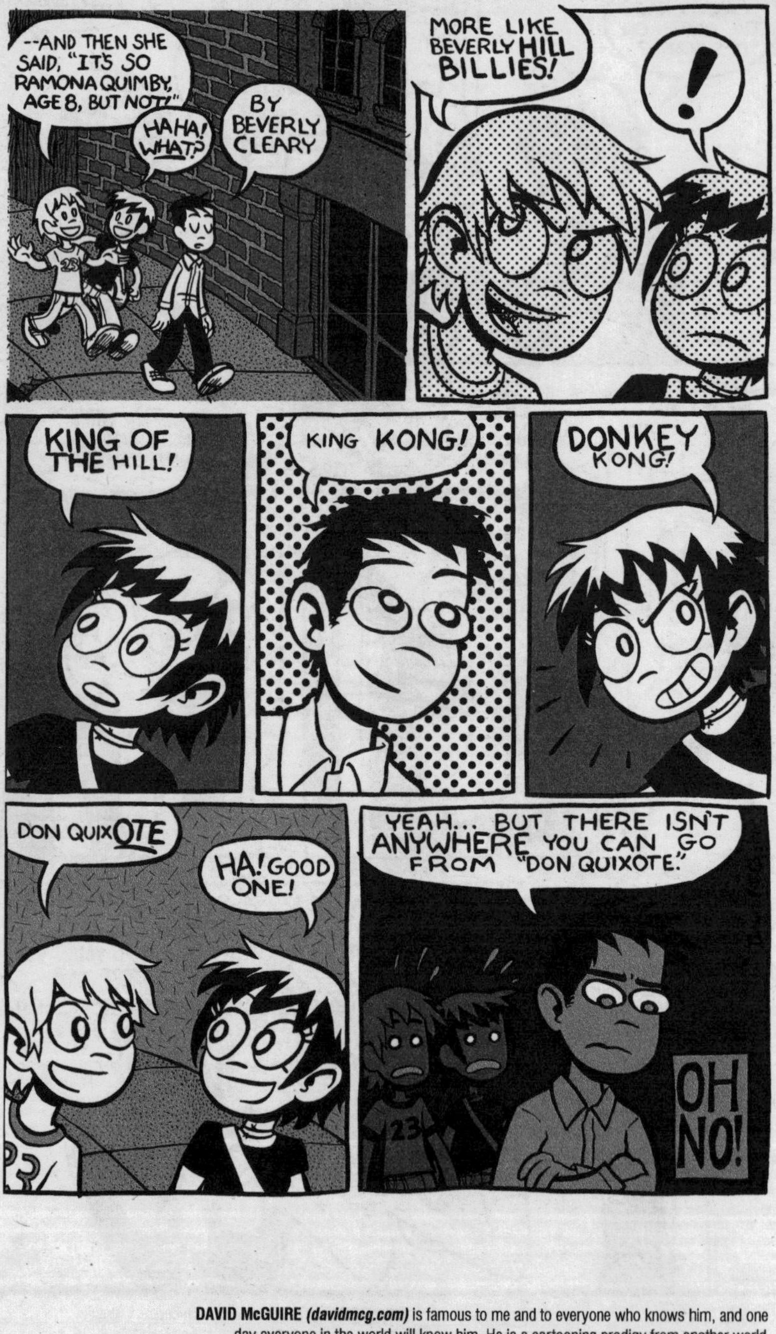
--AND THEN SHE SAID, "IT'S SO RAMONA QUIMBY, AGE 8, BUT NOT!"
HAHA! WHAT?
BY BEVERLY CLEARY
MORE LIKE BEVERLY HILL BILLIES!
!
KING OF THE HILL!
KING KONG!
DONKEY KONG!
DON QUIXOTE
HA! GOOD ONE!
YEAH... BUT THERE ISN'T ANYWHERE YOU CAN GO FROM "DON QUIXOTE."
OH NO!

DAVID McGUIRE ***(davidmcg.com)*** is famous to me and to everyone who knows him, and one day everyone in the world will know him. He is a cartooning prodigy from another world.

author's portrait by Vera Brosgol

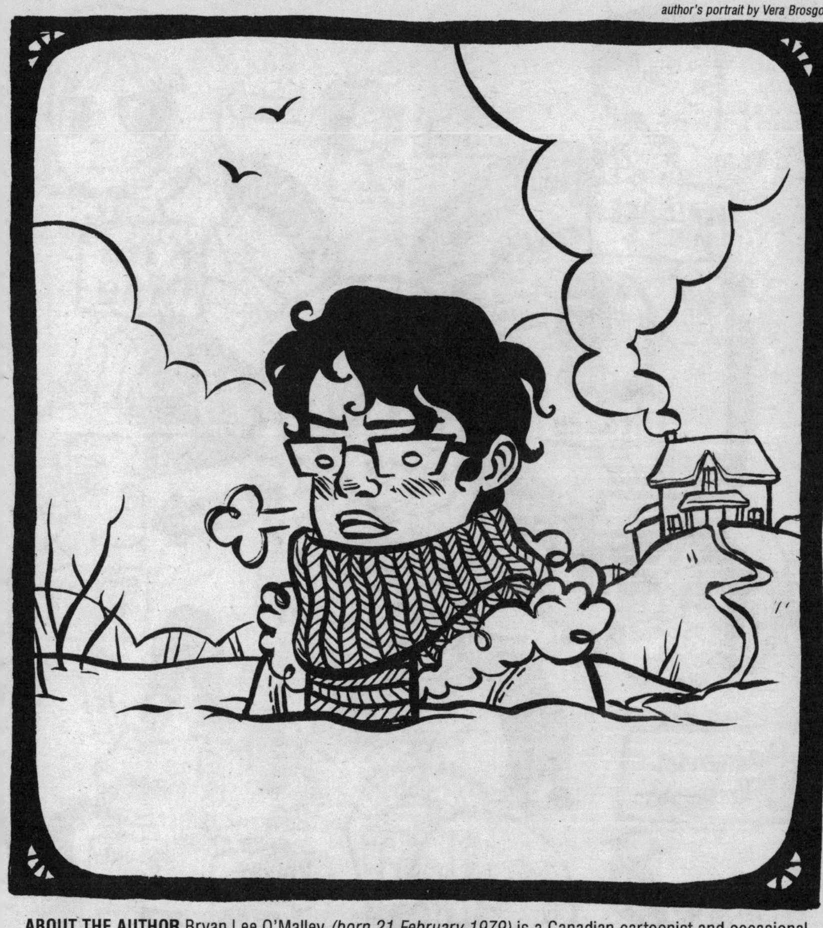

ABOUT THE AUTHOR Bryan Lee O'Malley *(born 21 February 1979)* is a Canadian cartoonist and occasional musician. He lives in the wilderness with Hope Larson (**www.hopelarson.com**) and three cats, and has an extremely great website at **www.radiomaru.com**.

this is kind of like a blog

I got re-obsessed with manga while I was working on this book. Here's some stuff that I can remember reading, in no particular order, that I more or less recommend: **BERSERK** (Kentaro Miura), **GANTZ** (Hiroya Oku), **DEATH NOTE** (Tsugumi Ohba & Takeshi Obata), **AZUMANGA DAIOH** (Kiyohiko Azuma), **LIVING GAME** (Mochiru Hoshisato). There's a lot of good stuff out there if you can get past the fanboy/fangirling...

Some people have been asking about the music I listen to while working on Scott Pilgrim. For each book, I tend to make one mix CD of songs that capture the right mood. I don't have much space here, so I'll just list a few major songs...

PLUMTREE - "Scott Pilgrim" - this is the song that inspired the book in general, by a great Canadian indie girl-rock band from the 90s. Plumtree rocks forever!

JOEL PLASKETT - "When I Have My Vision", "Written All Over Me", etc - he's a guy whose music has had a huge influence on me and Scott Pilgrim. He was also in a great 90s band called Thrush Hermit whose defining album "Clayton Park" is an overlooked classic.

THE FLYING BURRITO BROS - "To Ramona", etc - this legendary band fronted by Gram Parsons in the early 70s is the soundtrack to Scott's mind.

BEACHWOOD SPARKS - "By Your Side" - a swirly cosmic countrified cover of a Sade song. It's the ultimate Scott Pilgrim love song. I secretly love the original, too.

THE REPLACEMENTS - "Left of the Dial", "Can't Hardly Wait", etc - they wrote amazing songs. I always think of them as Ramona's favorite band. They're one of mine.

UNCLE TUPELO - "Grindstone" - the original alt-country band. I equate them with the character Stephen Stills.

NEIL YOUNG - "Borrowed Tune" - and every other Neil Young song. Scott also 'borrowed' a tune from the Rolling Stones in this book, in case you missed it...

SPOON - "Waiting For The Kid To Come Out" - gets me moving every time. This is an old b-side but it screams Scott Pilgrim to me. Rockin' and ramshackle.

OLD 97s - "Let The Idiot Speak", etc - they're a bouncy pop-country-punk-something band from Texas and they've given this comic a lot of juice over the years.

TOM PETTY - "American Girl" - this song plays over the credits of every episode of Scott Pilgrim in my mind. Check out that guitar in the intro! *CLASSIC ROCK!*

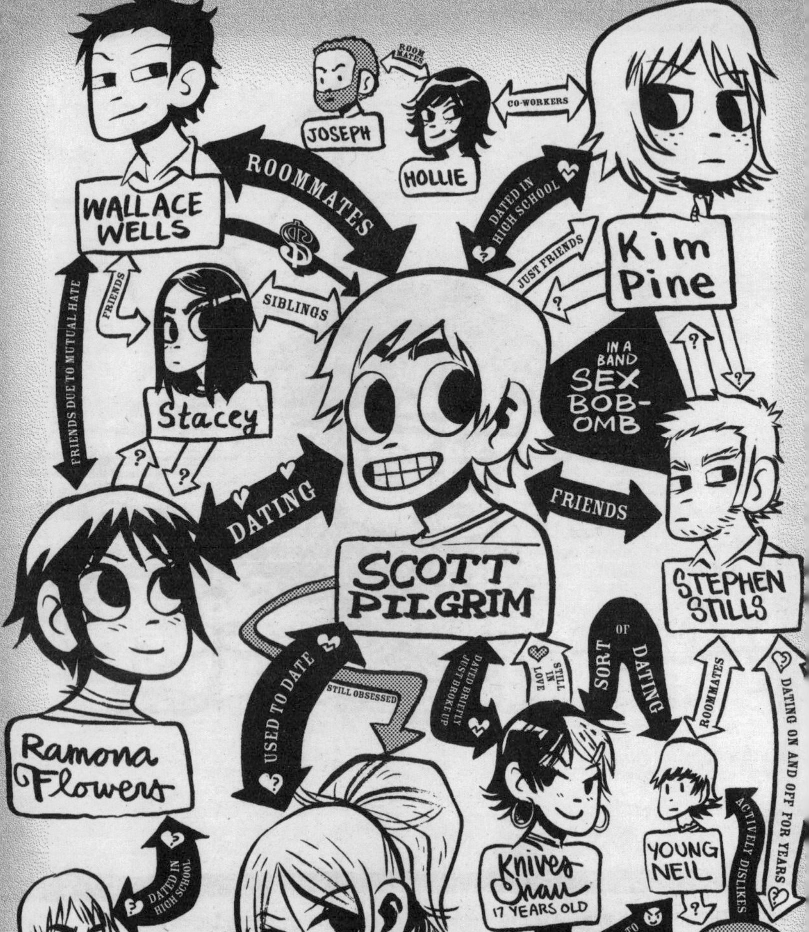
JOSEPH
ROOM MATES
HOLLIE
CO-WORKERS
WALLACE WELLS
ROOMMATES
DATED IN HIGH SCHOOL
Kim Pine
JUST FRIENDS
FRIENDS
SIBLINGS
FRIENDS DUE TO MUTUAL HATE
Stacey
IN A BAND SEX BOB-OMB
DATING
FRIENDS
SCOTT PILGRIM
STEPHEN STILLS
Ramona Flowers
USED TO DATE
STILL OBSESSED
DATED BRIEFLY JUST BROKE UP
STILL IN LOVE
SORT OF DATING
ROOMMATES
DATING ON AND OFF FOR YEARS
DATED IN HIGH SCHOOL
Knives Chau 17 YEARS OLD
YOUNG NEIL
ACTIVELY DISLIKES
ONLY DATING HIM TO MAKE SCOTT JEALOUS
OBSESSED
DATING & FRIENDS SINCE CHILDHOOD
TODD INGRAM
IN A BAND THE CLASH AT DEMON-HEAD
ENVY ADAMS (FAMOUS)
FORMER COLLEGE ROOMMATES
WANTS TO BE BEST FRIENDS (NOW THAT SHE'S FAMOUS)
Julie Powers
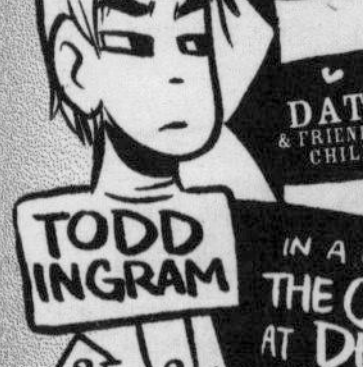
LYNETTE GUYCOTT

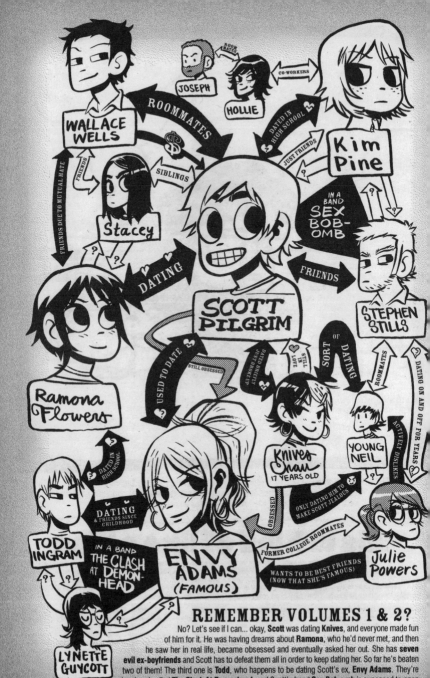

REMEMBER VOLUMES 1 & 2?

No? Let's see if I can... okay, **Scott** was dating **Knives**, and everyone made fun of him for it. He was having dreams about **Ramona**, who he'd never met, and then he saw her in real life, became obsessed and eventually asked her out. She has **seven evil ex-boyfriends** and Scott has to defeat them all in order to keep dating her. So far he's beaten two of them! The third one is **Todd**, who happens to be dating Scott's ex, **Envy Adams**. They're in a band called **The Clash At Demonhead**, and Scott's band **Sex Bob-omb** is supposed to open for them on **Sunday** (that's in two days!). Meanwhile, Knives is suddenly dating **Neil** (presumably to make Scott jealous), **Stephen Stills** is insanely nervous about the show, **Kim** is feeling weird about meeting Envy, and Scott is freaking out too (he isn't over her!). Time's up! Turn to page 1!!!